Praise for

JEMMA FORTE

'An unmissable read'
—Abby Clements

'A witty account of rollercoaster events that will get you
thinking about the "what ifs" in your own life'
—*Heat*

'A must read for all women'
—*Digital Spy*

'An easy-reading story that bristles with warmth and humour'
—*Hello*

'The most imaginative romcom we've read in a while'
—*Now*

'An engrossing and magical read with romance at its core'
—*OK!*

'The perfect mix of funny and emotional'
—*One More Page*

'Addictive, heartwarming yet funny'
—*Chick Lit Uncovered*

'It's clever, it's innovative and I really enjoyed it'
—*Chick Lit Reviews*

Jemma Forte grew up wanting to write for *Cosmopolitan* magazine, be a famous actress or work in a shoe shop (she loved the foot-measuring device in Clarks). Her parents didn't want her to go to stage school because, according to them, she was 'precocious enough already'. However, they actively encouraged her obsession with reading and writing and she wrote her first book, 'Mizzy the Germ', when she was eight. She sent it to a publisher (unwittingly backing up the whole precocious theory) and was dismayed when for some reason they didn't want it.

Years later, due to *The Kids from Fame* (and she blames them entirely), her desire to perform hadn't abated. Hundreds of letters, show-reels and auditions later she finally became a Disney Channel presenter in 1998. After Disney, Jemma went on to present shows for ITV, BBC One, BBC Two and Channel 4 and, when not busy writing, can still be found talking rubbish on telly to this day. *When I Met You* is Jemma's fourth novel. She lives in London with her children, Lily and Freddie.

When I Met You

JEMMA FORTE

HARLEQUIN MIRA®

Published in Great Britain 2015
by Harlequin MIRA, an imprint of Harlequin (UK) Limited,
Eton House, 18-24 Paradise Road,
Richmond, Surrey, TW9 1SR

© 2015 Jemma Forte

ISBN 978-1-848-45364-7

59-0115

Harlequin (UK) Limited's policy is to use papers that are natural, renewable and recyclable products and made from wood grown in sustainable forests. The logging and manufacturing processes conform to the legal environmental regulations of the country of origin.

Printed and bound by
CPI Group (UK) Ltd, Croydon, CR0 4YY

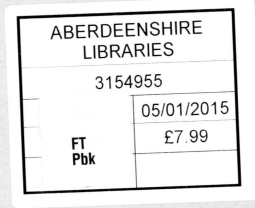

Also by

JEMMA FORTE

IF YOU'RE NOT THE ONE
ME AND MISS M
FROM LONDON WITH LOVE

This one's for you, Dad.

PROLOGUE

I sit up, wondering what time it is, what day it is even. My bedroom's completely dark and the light from the moon is the only thing enabling me to see anything at all. Rubbing my face, I switch on the bedside light and pick up my watch. Three minutes past nine. I only meant to shut my eyes but must have been asleep for ages.

Blurry with sleep, I sit staring blankly into space, wondering vaguely why the rest of the house is so silent until, overcome by both thirst and curiosity, I haul myself up and pad out onto the dark landing to investigate.

Downstairs, there's a note on the dining table from Mum. It reads *'Me and Mar gone to Sheena and Dave's anniversary dins. On mobile. Quiche in fridge. Pete at Josh's for night.'*

Of course, I'd forgotten they were going there. I feel cold and a bit shivery, so as soon as I've glugged back a pint of water, I make a cup of tea, grab some biscuits from mum's stash and head back to my room where I slump onto the bed. The same single bed I slept on throughout my teenage years, which serves as a constant reminder that at the age of thirty-one I haven't come very far. Still, I've wasted enough hours lamenting my embarrassing woman-child status.

It occurs to me then that I should be making the most of the empty house by getting some violin practise in. The one thing I have progressed in over the years. When Mum's around, I only ever get away with playing for about half an hour before the complaints start – apparently classical music makes her feel like a patient in a mental institution – so it'll be nice not to have any interruptions.

I place the sheet music for Bach's solo sonata No. 1 in G minor on my stand. The music's hauntingly beautiful and incredibly hard to do justice to but, once I've practised my scales, arpeggios and a few studies, I feel ready to tackle it. It's not long before I'm completely lost in the music, oblivious to the storm that is brewing outside. The window is ajar, but the sound of the gale howling only adds to the majesty of the sonata. Then, just as I'm in the middle of an exceedingly challenging section, there's a huge rumble of thunder, the skies open and rain starts to pelt down, at which point I place my violin on the bed. I'm just about to pull the window shut when I hear a crashing sound coming from somewhere in our back garden. The security lights at the rear of the house instantly flick on. I jump out of my skin.

Heart thumping, I peer out, trying to see what made the noise. The lights give me a clear view of the patio below, which is undoubtedly the most furnished patio in Essex. You can hardly move on it for swing chairs, heaters, loungers and the like. My stepdad, Martin, makes his living selling garden furniture and equipment. He's bizarrely passionate about it. I swear whenever he visits B&Q or Homebase to check out the competition he goes a bit quivery with anticipation. But I digress.

It doesn't take long to work out what caused the noise. On the right-hand side of the patio, a dustbin lid is lying on the ground and as the wind picks up again, it rolls around, its metal making a terrible din. I guess it must have blown off the bin. Either that or a fox must have disturbed it or something. I yank the window shut. The noise of the storm is instantly muffled but I can still hear the lid clattering around at which point I realise I have no choice but to go outside and put it back on.

Going through the house I switch on every single light. The house is carpeted throughout so as I pad down the stairs into our hallway I don't make a sound. Downstairs it smells in a synthetic, sickly way, of peach, due to the air freshener mum keeps constantly plugged in.

I pass the front room we never use and the downstairs loo, before carrying on straight ahead into our main living area. Usually I don't mind being on my own at night, but the storm's making me twitchy. I chastise myself for being silly.

What am I worried about? I'm not even sure. All I do know is that I'm planning on replacing the lid as quickly as is humanly possible so that I can race inside, upstairs and back to the non-creepy confines of my room.

The keys to the sliding doors, which lead out to the garden, are kept on a hook next to a hatch in the wall that divides the living room and kitchen. Once I've got them I unlock the doors and gingerly slide them open a touch. The wind is fierce. Rain immediately blows into my face but, taking the plunge, I step out into the elements at which point it's quite a struggle to slide the doors shut again. By now the rain's coming down in a torrent so, no matter how quick I plan on being, getting totally soaked is inevitable. Glad of security-conscious Martin's lights, I pick my way across the width of the patio. The wind is almost strong enough to knock me over but with a lot of effort I make it to the offending bin lid, only just as, while I'm bending down to pick it up, an extra strong gust blows it yet further out of my reach. At that point I stop and, with my heart in my mouth, I spin around as a sixth sense heightens the feeling I've been trying to ignore. That I'm not alone.

I must be mistaken though. Fear's playing tricks with my mind because there doesn't appear to be anyone there. Although, having said that, if someone were lurking in the shadows, I probably wouldn't be able to see them from here anyway. Not if they didn't want me to. They could easily hide themselves away down the alley that spans the side of our house.

'Who's there?' I yell, feebly and somewhat pointlessly. My voice was never going to carry very far against the noise of the storm. By now I'm soaked to the skin and shivering with cold. I pull myself together. My imagination is running away with me. I just need to get the blasted lid back on the bin, get back inside and into a hot shower. Heart thumping, I make a dash down the lawn for the lid again. Got it. I grab it, then turn and run towards the passage that runs down the side of the house where the bins are kept. Rain pummels my head and face and, gasping for breath, I slam the lid on, making sure it's secure. As soon as it is, with adrenaline coursing round my body, I make for the house. Turns out, however, I wasn't being paranoid. All my instincts had kicked in for good reason, for just as I'm about to reach for the door, I hear heavy, terrifying footsteps behind me. At this point, I scream so loudly I almost don't recognise my own voice. It's a guttural sound, a scream of survival, because I honestly believe I'm about to be killed, raped, or both. Just as my fingertips make contact with the door handle, a strong arm makes a grab for me and in that instance I don't think I'll ever be able to describe the depth of pure terror that I feel.

I'm terrified, rendered totally incapable of rational thought. My body shuts down completely. My legs go to jelly. I want to scream again but as I try to, a black-gloved hand clamps my mouth shut. The man's gripping on to me so tightly now I can feel his breath on my face. Then, the most eerie thing of all happens. In a rasping, deep, terrifying voice, my assailant says, right into my ear, 'Don't scream, Marianne.'

Well, that does it. The fact he knows my name makes the whole experience beyond sinister and I honestly think

I'm going to pass out on the spot. This person has singled me out. He must have been watching the house. He knows everyone's out and now he's going to do something to me. I'm on the brink of collapse when the attacker says something else I'm not expecting. Though at first I think it's some kind of sick joke.

'Don't be scared. It's me. It's your dad.'

And in that second my whole life implodes.

CHAPTER ONE

ONE DAY EARLIER

'So, are we decided then? Warm Caramel for the over-all colour with a few Heavenly Honey highlights taken through the front,' I said, flicking shut the colour chart.

'Fine,' agreed Mrs Jenkins.

It was Saturday morning and I was at work at Roberto's hairdressers on Chigwell High Road, certain then that this was precisely the kind of dull day that would pass without event or revelation, only to end up wiped from my memory. It often bothers me how an entire twenty-four hours can pass and all I will have done is function, chat on the phone, sit on the bus, watch TV, breathe, get through. It scares me. Too many instantly forgettable days and before you know it, life will have passed by completely. I think this is why I love travelling. When I'm away from home, in some exotic place, the quota of memorable days definitely increases.

After my A levels, much to the disappointment of my music teacher, Mrs Demetrius, who was desperate for me to apply to music college, I took a course in hairdressing,

got a job at Roberto's, saved up, then went backpacking
round the world instead. It's not that I hadn't wanted to
play music professionally, I can think of nothing better,
but I'm not deluded. You don't see many adverts for violin
players down the job centre, do you? College would have
been very expensive, and besides, I'd always wanted to
see places other than Essex. Earth is a big planet after all.

I'm thirty-one now though and it has occurred to me that
unless I want to become a middle-aged crusty with friends
dotted around the globe, but barely any on her own doorstep, who still lives with her parents, I probably need to
start figuring out what to do with my life. Though in truth
I'm not that bothered. Most of the time I'm happy existing
in my perpetual cycle of working, saving and travelling.
It's other people who assume I should be panicking about
not being engaged/pregnant/a homeowner. Not me.

I admit, living with Mum and Martin has its moments.
In an ideal world of course I'd love my own space. But on
my wage I can't see it happening. I've looked into getting
a mortgage a few times – every time mum and I have a
row – but because I'm on my own I'd need a gargantuan
deposit, so it's pointless. With rents so extortionate too,
there's just never a good enough reason to leave home.
I pay mum far less each month to live in her nice house
than I would to live in a depressingly small flat, plus this
way I can afford to save up to go away. My last trip was
to Vietnam, Cambodia and Thailand. Next on the list is
South America. It really helps that Roberto always has

me back in between, knowing he's getting a reliable cutter who hardly ever asks for a pay rise.

As soon as Mrs Jenkins was settled at the sink I headed to the tiny staff room at the back of the salon. On the way, I grinned at my reflection in one of the many mirrors. I was still getting used to my new, short, choppy bob, which is dyed a rich, burgundy plum colour. I like it. I think it suits me. In the staff room – which is where all the good magazines disappear to in case you're wondering – I flicked on the kettle and, while it boiled, went to fetch my mobile from my jacket pocket. I wished I hadn't when it rang immediately and stupidly I answered without checking caller ID first, only to find my sister, Hayley, on the other end.

Hayley loves me deep down – I mean really deep down. Imagine an oil rig drilling into the sea bed and you get the picture – but she has a strange way of showing it.

'So, make sure you're not late tomorrow. Gary's parents are coming at three and I don't want you turning up after they've got there. I need you to make an effort Marianne,' she'd managed to say before the phone had even reached my ear. 'And wear your black trousers or something that flatters you. Wendy's very classy so I don't want to be shown up like the time you wore those awful cut-offs and don't…'

I held the phone away from my ear and zoned out, as I often do when my sister's mid-way through one of her rants. Life's too short, as was my break, so rather than commit an offence punishable by death, that is to say, rather than interrupt Hayley, I put the phone on the side so she could drone on to herself while I made a cup of tea.

Just then Jason poked his head round the door. 'Got a minute Marianne?'

Jason's dad owns Roberto's. Jason's dad *is* Roberto and the salon is very much a family-run business. His mum sits on reception and his two older brothers are cutters, as is their cousin Mark. Jase has become a good friend since I started working here. He's reliable, sweet and you've got to love him because unlike the rest of the male population he finds Hayley as irritating as I do.

I stirred my tea and pointed with my other hand towards my discarded phone from which a horribly familiar nagging sound was still being omitted.

'Hayley?' he mouthed.

I nodded wearily, before reluctantly picking up again. She was still going.

'…and don't refer to Mum as anything except Alison. Alli sounds so naff for a woman her age and Gary's parents hate nicknames.'

That at least *was* useful to know. I made a mental note never to mention my nicknames for her in-laws in their presence. Hyacinth Bucket for Wendy – she's a massive snob – and Cyclops for Derek – on account of his roving eye. 'Anything else?' I interjected 'Because I really should be getting back to work.'

Hayley tutted and put the phone down. Her own special way of signing off on phone calls, designed to make you wonder, just for a second, if she might have been involved in a car crash, a mugging, or been kidnapped.

'How does Gary cope?' asked Jason, shaking his head, though deep down he knew the answer to that one. Hayley's stunning and, when she was at school, boys were always trying to come round ours for tea, just so they could catch a glimpse of her. Dwayne Richardson even told me once that Hayley was number one in year ten's 'wank bank'. You can imagine how charmed I was by that piece of information.

Hayley's thirty-three now and her rather glacial brand of beauty turns heads more than ever. Gary first clapped eyes on her six years ago, giving out pamphlets at a car show in Earls Court, wearing a pair of hot-pants and a small halter-neck top – Mum had told everyone she had a modelling gig. The minute he saw her he was smitten and when Hayley found out he owned his own car dealership in Ilford, so was she.

'Coming out tonight Marianne?' asked Jason casually.

'Saving.' My reply was automatic.

'You don't say,' he said with a hint of frustration. 'Look, it's Lindsey's birthday, everyone's coming and you haven't been out in ages. Besides, you should let your hair down before tomorrow.'

Gary's family were coming round en masse tomorrow, hence Hayley's nagging. To say I was dreading it would be an understatement.

'And by the way, Mrs Jenkins is ready, waiting for her transformation,' he winked.

'Thanks,' I said, slugging back the last of my tea. 'And I *might* come.'

Jason rewarded me with a big grin.

'I do have a job to get through tomorrow morning, but I suppose you could be right. A hangover might be the only way to cope with Hayley after that.'

'Yes!' he said, punching the air. 'Miss Haversham is actually coming out. I can't believe it. We'll have to brush the cobwebs off you first.'

CHAPTER TWO

Once I was out I was pleased I'd come. It was so long since I'd got ready for anything other than work and I'd saved more than I'd hoped this month, largely due to my second job – which we'll get to later. It was mid-April and my plan was to have enough saved by the summer in order to buy a ticket to go away in the autumn, my cunning plan being to escape the winter… and my family… and having to sort my life out…

Still, that was all a long way off so Jason was right. It was time I had a bit of fun.

I was just coming off the dance floor where I'd been flinging myself about with the other girls from the salon when Jason sidled up to me. 'All right?' he asked, head nodding in time to the beat.

I smiled at him. He scrubbed up well. In fact I would go as far as to say he looked quite cute. Jason and his brothers are all a version of each other but he's the best looking of the three. At thirty he's the youngest and the tallest and, unlike his brothers, Ruben and Jake, isn't yet showing signs of balding. All the brothers have strong noses, though

Jason's face is the only one that really gets away with it. His long, slightly broken nose gives him a kind of Roman look and in fact, thinking about it now, if you were casting Cleopatra, Jason would make a perfect Mark Antony.

Now he winked at me and I was on the verge of winking back when someone tapped me on the shoulder. I spun round.

'Teresa!' I exclaimed, surprised and delighted to see my old best friend standing there. I hadn't seen her for years, which was sad because at one stage we'd practically been joined at the hip.

'All right,' she said now, almost shyly.

We stood grinning at one another dopily for a second or two and Jason nodded at me before slipping off, leaving us to it.

'So, how's it going?' I asked.

'Not bad, you know,' she said, shrugging in a way that told me things were fine but nothing special. 'Still working for *The Land of Nod*.'

'Great,' I said, despite the fact my heart had just twanged with both sympathy and empathy. Teresa had started working at the bed shop on the High Street after college, but had vowed it would never become permanent. It's fair to say neither of us have exactly fulfilled our potential.

'I've just been promoted from branch manager to regional manager,' she went on to say, her tone slightly defensive.

'Well, that's brilliant. Good for you,' I said sincerely. 'It's so nice to see you by the way, you look great.'

I wasn't lying. Teresa had always been a curvy girl and though her curves were erring on the side of slightly overweight, she carried herself well, with just the right amount of swagger. She had frizzy black hair, olive skin and a confidence that had always stood her in great stead. Tonight she was wearing her usual big, gold hoop earrings. Throughout our teens I'd always been quite envious of how comfortable she was in her own skin. She seemed to bypass that gawky stage where your limbs have a life of their own and all you want to do is pull your sleeves over your hands and gaze at the floor. She may not have been the most beautiful girl at school or have had the absolute best figure but it didn't matter. Her confidence was so appealing.

'Ah thanks, I was just about to say the same. Love the hair.'

I grinned, pleased she liked it.

'So anyway, what about you?' she asked. 'I know you were away for a while but what are you up to now? Doing anything with your music yet?'

I shook my head. 'No. Still hairdressing. Still at Roberto's, which is great though because it means I get to go travelling loads. I just got back from Asia recently, which was amazing actually.'

To my chagrin Teresa looked neither impressed or interested, just surprised. 'Oh really? That's a shame. I would have sworn you'd be in some orchestra or something by now.'

'Not going to happen,' I said bluntly. 'I still play for pleasure, always will, but anything else just isn't realistic.'

She'd touched a nerve. I knew she only looked so disappointed because she cared, but it was frustrating. If it was that easy to become a professional violinist I would have done it.

Teresa looked mildly put out.

'It would be a lovely dream but it's never going to happen. Too expensive, too tricky, too competitive, too late. Anyway, what else is up with you? Have you got a boyfriend?' I asked, quickly changing the subject.

By way of reply she stuck out her left hand. On her ring finger sparkled a tiny diamond.

'Oh my god. I don't believe it. Who are you engaged to? Not Darren?'

'Yeah,' she said. 'Been engaged six months now. We're going to get married next year, if we can afford it. I've been meaning to ring and tell you for ages actually but…'

'Oh honestly don't worry,' I said, helping her out. We were equally guilty of not keeping in touch. 'And congratulations. I'm really happy for you. God, so many people from our year are getting hitched now or having babies. I can't believe I didn't even know. I'm sorry I've been so… you know.'

'I know. We've both been busy haven't we?' she said, taking her turn to help me out now. 'So come on then, have you got a fella?'

'Kind of,' I say. 'I met someone travelling recently. But no one serious.'

For the second time Teresa looked distinctly sorry for me. 'Don't worry babe, it'll happen,' she said. 'You remember my cousin, Sharon? I'm actually here for her hen night tonight and at one point, no one thought she'd ever meet Mr Right.'

I just smiled. It was easier and probably more polite than trying to explain that her sympathy was wasted on me. I wasn't hankering after settling down like so many people my age seemed to be. Personally I prefer to dip my toe into relationship waters without taking the plunge. Keeps things simple, prevents getting hurt. That might sound cynical, but in my experience most men are only after one thing or end up letting you down. The 'Martins' of this world are few and far between so, until I meet that rare thing, a man I can truly rely on, I'm happy as I am thank you very much. Only, whenever I say that, people tend not to believe me.

'How's Hayley?' asked Teresa suddenly, a cheeky grin on her face.

'Same as usual,' I said, rolling my eyes. In the past Teresa and I had spent many an hour discussing Hayley and what a cow she could be. 'And Mum's mad as ever. She's decided Hayley's destined to win *Sing For Britain*.'

Teresa's stunned face said it all.

'Oh yeah,' I nodded. 'Hayley's actually considering going to the auditions this summer.'

'Shit,' said Teresa, her face creasing into an incredulous grin. 'Still, I reckon Julian Hayes would well fancy her.'

'True,' I agreed. Julian Hayes is the head judge and a multi-millionaire Svengali whose production company make the show. 'Trouble is he's not deaf though.'

Teresa laughed. 'Look, I've got to go. I'm going to sneak off soon and meet Darren, but I'd love to meet up some time.'

'Definitely.' I really meant it. Teresa was one of the best things about my life for a long time and it was sad that we'd let our friendship drift. For my part I think I've been waiting for something to change, something to happen, so that I had something to say. But there's no point putting life on hold. I needed to make more effort. As I watched her walk away I vowed to do something about it.

*

A while later, after a particularly vigorous dancing session with the, by now very rowdy, gang from the salon, I suddenly noticed a really good-looking guy. I'm talking stand out from the crowd attractive, with green eyes and a lazy grin, which inhabited a face that all fell into place beautifully. What was even more unusual than spotting somebody so nice looking and seemingly age appropriate in this particular 'nitespot' was the fact that he appeared to be looking at me. Though I was only sure of this once I'd taken the precaution of looking over my shoulder, half-expecting to find a supermodel standing behind me, waving daintily at the man of my dreams.

*

The next thing I knew he seemed to be heading in my direction. Of course there was still a chance this handsome stranger was only on his way over to ask whether I had a pen he could borrow, or to tell me that my hair was on fire, so I stared at the barman, trying to get his attention, so it didn't look like I was just hovering, waiting to be chatted up, which obviously I was.

'Let me buy you a drink.'

Pretending to be terribly surprised, I turned around only to be met by the wonderful sight of him in close up. He was absolutely gorgeous. I felt like clapping my hands.

*

Forty minutes later and I was letting myself be seduced by a real pro. His name was Simon and, as I may have already mentioned, he was very good looking. It crossed my mind that Simon must never, ever meet my sister, for if he did he would realise that she was the sort of girl who was in the same league as him, that is to say the premiership, whereas I'll do but am probably more second division.

Simon's eyes searched my face as I spoke, which was very distracting and made it hard to concentrate on anything I was saying. He was charming, funny and complimentary to the point where I was beginning to feel like a bit of a sexpot. The only thing that was weird was that he hadn't been snapped up already. There was no ring on his finger. I checked. He clearly wasn't gay, so what was wrong with him?

I decided not to stress about it and instead enjoyed hearing him tell amusing stories, which he peppered with questions and compliments. At one point he commented on my hair. He said that only someone with great cheekbones could get away with such a strong look. I knew they were only words, but hearing them made me swell with pleasure.

Anyway, things with Simon – how grown up is that name? I can't imagine anyone calling a baby or a toddler Simon – were going swimmingly, when out of the blue he suddenly said, 'So listen, do you fancy leaving here? I'd like to go somewhere where I don't have to shout at you over the music. Your place?' As he said this he looked me up and down in a way that made my belly flip and my nerve endings tingle, for it conveyed perfectly what he had in mind.

Mind racing I tried to work out what to do. Not having built up to the question or bothered with any cheesy coffee euphemisms, he'd rather ambushed me, but the intention was implicit. Did I want him to come back to mine so that we could have sex? The short answer was, yes please. The long answer was more complicated.

The first thing preventing me from diving in with both legs open was the fact that I could predict that if something happened tonight, Simon would probably write it off as a one night stand and I'd never see him again. Whereas I would undoubtedly be left feeling bereft and desolate, having managed to fall in love with him somewhere between now and him leaving. He really was that gorgeous. I've probably already alluded to the rather complex issues I have when it comes to men. Growing up, knowing that my dad *chose* to leave has been hard, and my subsequent, fairly predictable trust issues have resulted in me acquiring a reputation as one of Essex's most chaste girls, although Hayley's thoughtfully made up for the two of us on that front. Pre-Gary there weren't many people round here she didn't sleep with – another subject I suspect might be taboo in front of Gary and his parents.

The second and most significant reason I wasn't entirely sure what to do about Simon, is called Andy. I met Andy in Thailand. He's Australian, loves travelling like me and when we got chatting one day, as we lay lazily alongside each other on hammocks, we instantly hit it off. We ended up sharing two unforgettable, beautiful months together, which only came to an end because I'd run out of money and had to head home. Meanwhile Andy, who's a registered scuba-diving instructor, was heading to Koh Tao where he knew he'd pick up some work. So our blissful existence came to a natural end, though Andy did promise that once he'd had his fill of Thailand he'd head for Europe.

Now we email all the time and Andy has indeed made it to Europe. He promises England is on his list of places to come but three months on I'm starting to wonder whether he really means it. Being completely honest, I'm a little frustrated with the whole situation. I mean, if he really wanted to see me that badly, Andy could have come here weeks ago. As it is, he seems to be ambling round Europe, determined to see every single continental inch of it before coming here, which won't give us a great deal of time together before his ticket runs out and it's time for him to head back to the other side of the world.

And now I found myself faced with the temptation of Simon, and I was starting to think that maybe for once I should put everything out of my head and just sate my desire to have drunk, wonderful sex with this handsome Jude Law lookalike when yet another problem popped into my head. And this one was the real passion killer because for a second I'd forgotten that, age thirty-one, I live with my parents and have a single bed. Fuck. My. Life.

'We could go to yours?'

'Not tonight. I've got people staying so it would be a bit awkward,' said Simon.

'Hmm, well, I'd love you to come back,' I replied truthfully. 'But I've got work in the morning, so I should probably get home and get some sleep.'

'What job can be so important on a Sunday morning that you can't be tired for it?' he said, looking so intensely into my eyes I had to look away for a second as I was hit with a wave of leg-buckling desire. Distracted by lust, I nearly made the mistake of telling him exactly what I was going to be doing in less than twelve hours, but in the nick of time it hit me that I definitely shouldn't. Not at this stage anyway because, apart from being a chiropodist – or having a single bed – the truth was about the least sexy thing in the entire world. So I lied.

'I've got an acting job,' I said, wanting to cling on to the feeling that I was someone sexy and dazzling for a short while longer. Someone like my sister – yes, I know I'm obsessed, but you try being related to a Claudia Schiffer lookalike and see how undamaged you remain.

Simon raised his eyebrows at this, clearly impressed. 'I should have guessed someone quirky like you would do something interesting.'

'Well, you know,' I simpered, shrugging, not one hundred percent liking his use of the word quirky.

'What are you acting in?'

'Oh… um… an advert,' I improvised desperately.

'Great, I'll look out for it.'

At that point I realised I hadn't thought this lie through properly at all. 'Oh it's only going out in America,' I added hastily. 'It's for… an airline.'

'A sexy air hostess eh? I love it,' said Simon, his eyes darkening as all sorts of inappropriate visions popped into his head, which made me giggle a bit because frankly, whenever I see air hostesses doling out synthetic meals and asking you to do up your seatbelt they never look that sexy to me. Just tired, smothered in foundation, mildly bored, resentful of passengers who are getting on their nerves, and like they're desperate to take their court shoes off.

'I can already see you in your uniform, like in those Virgin ads. Gorgeous.'

Not long after this I said my goodbyes. I'd drunk far too many vodkas by now to be coping with all the lies I was having to think of, and I'd also reminded myself that of course I *did* have work in the morning – that bit was real – so suddenly I was anxious to get some sleep. I wrote my number on a paper napkin and thrust it into his hand. 'Call me,' I said, trying not to sound like I was giving him an order.

'Oh I will,' he promised before giving me a long, lingering kiss on the lips.

CHAPTER THREE

This morning I woke up with bison breath and the dim recollection that I'd had a good night.

My head felt too heavy for my body, I was in pain and would have swapped my worldly goods for an aspirin. My bones ached and I had no idea how on earth I was going to get through the day. In short, I had a hangover. Still, if I heard from the wondrous Simon, it would have been worth it. So, I clambered out of bed and lurched towards the bathroom, comforting myself with the thought that this morning I'd be earning two hundred pounds for three hours' work. Enough to buy me an entire week of travelling in South America, an incentive that propelled me into my clown costume.

Yes, clown costume. For when I'm not working at Roberto's, despite the fact most of my peers are *having* children, I, Marianne Baker can be found on many a weekend dressed as Custard the Clown, entertaining them, complete with oversize shoes, red nose and curly blue wig. I also wear a stripy shirt, huge brown trousers held up with comedy braces and a green tailcoat, which has a big plastic gerbera in the buttonhole that can squirt water. Once I'm in full costume and have made up my face I'd love to tell you I start to embrace my role but, in all honesty, I never feel smaller or more stupid than I do when I'm in that ridiculous bloody outfit. I literally have to think of the money the entire time I'm in it.

Of course, when I made the decision to peddle myself as a children's entertainer I could have taken the more attractive option of investing in a fairy or princess costume, but after a lot of research I realised this would limit my earning potential. Fairies are two a penny and no self-respecting boy would ever want a fairy anywhere near his party. So, investing in a unisex clown costume had seemed like the best option. Not taking into consideration my own ego.

Fully clowned up I sneaked through the house as quietly as I could in my silly shoes. They're so big it's like trying to walk in flippers. Mum and Martin had already warned me that they needed a lie in this morning as they were going out for Sheena and Dave's wedding anniversary that night, so I knew they'd be annoyed if I woke them up.

Four-year-old Jack's party was being held at his parents' house – funnily enough he didn't have his own pad yet – in posh Buckhurst Hill. It was due to start at eleven, so I was aiming to arrive at ten-fifteen for setting-up purposes. Thankfully, parents of small children always stipulate the time these parties have to end, which in today's case was one o'clock. No one, it seems, is capable of dealing with armies of small children for more than a few hours at a time…

This last thought caused me to suffer a huge relapse during which I had to steady myself on the banister. 'Armies of small children' isn't a prospect anyone should have to consider when suffering from a hangover. In that moment I decided the only way to cope with the day was to take each minute as it came. Bedtime was simply too far away.

As I tiptoed along the landing my brother, Pete, emerged stealthily from his bedroom.

My nerves were frayed from lack of sleep – and vodka – so I gasped loudly with a dramatic inhalation of breath, in the same heart-stopping way Mum does when I'm driving and she thinks I'm too close to another car. Only I never am.

'You gave me a shock,' I accused, when in fact the hysterical noise I'd made was far more shocking than anything.

Pete didn't bat an eyelid. I don't think his pulse works in the same way as other peoples. Neither did he react to the way I was dressed, which to be fair he's seen many times before. Instead he merely skulked through to the bathroom, still in his pyjamas.

I haven't really told you about Pete yet, have I? He's my brother, well, my half-brother. My mum's 'precious prince'. I don't mind Pete. He's pretty easy company, made even more so by the fact that he hardly ever comes out of his room. He's obsessed in a pretty unhealthy way with Elvis and spends the majority of his time listening to The King's albums on full volume while playing Xbox. Pete's a funny boy really. He lives in a world of his own. He's nineteen and if I'm honest I don't really know him very well at all.

After a life-saving cup of tea, piece of toast, couple of headache pills, pint of water and a Berocca I left the house. Fresh air was good and as I started piling bags of clowning equipment into mum's Rover – or 'Tina' as she likes to call it, Mum has a habit of naming inanimate objects – I decided I might be OK today after all.

As I slammed the boot shut my phone beeped telling me I had a text. I had butterflies as I went to check it. Ridiculously I was hoping it might be from Simon, despite the fact it was far too early to expect to hear from him. Dating etiquette dictated that it would be at least a couple of days before I did. However, it *was* from him wishing me good luck with the shoot… He'd signed off with *hope to see you soon sexy.*

As I pulled away I grinned at myself in the mirror. A white face, black eyes and red nose beamed back at me. Thank Christ he couldn't see me now.

The party was the usual version of hell on earth once it got going. I get paid a lot for being a clown, but I earn every penny of that money, let me tell you. Little Jack, who was actually exceedingly cute, was trembling with the excitement of it all when I arrived. He was four today and he and his merry band of twenty friends wanted to celebrate hard. It was down to me to show them how. Understandably, when a parent's forked out so much money for an entertainer, they want their money's worth. They want to be able to stand back, mainline white wine and let the person they're paying deal with the hysteria.

Before the party began, while I was setting up in their conservatory style kitchen, Jack's mum was busy cutting crusts off sandwiches so Jack's dad took the opportunity to take lots of photographs of the birthday boy. At a certain point Jack grew bored of posing and his dad suddenly swung his excited son around in the air before giving him a giant bear hug. It was a touching scene and I experienced, not for the first time, a pang for the childhood I didn't have. It wasn't the party and fuss I yearned for when I felt like this. My mum certainly couldn't have afforded to do big parties like this. Our treat was always to take a friend to McDonald's for tea, which we loved. It was witnessing such a close family unit that made me sad, because for a few short years I know it's what I had. I wish I could remember what it felt like to feel so complete. Growing up I missed my dad so much on special occasions, particularly on birthdays. I longed for him to be there. Always. And every year when I blew out my candles I wished he'd come back. I'd close my eyes and imagine him turning up, full of joy to see us and with an explanation that would make me understand why he'd left.

Still, it wasn't to be, and gradually over the years I'd started to accept that I'd never know and that he obviously didn't care.

Jack was a lucky boy.

Once the celebrations got going the noise was incredible. It always is. It's like an inverse equation. The smaller the person, the more noise they create. My hangover was only made bearable by the fact that as I went through my clowning motions I kept remembering how gorgeous Simon was, and how into me he'd seemed. I couldn't believe he'd already been in touch too. It was the boost I needed, so summoning up the energy from the bottom of my size fourteen clown shoes I supervised games, performed tricks and made lots of jokes about bottoms. This does the trick every time. Jack wet himself laughing. I mean *actually* wet himself laughing. Still, after a change of trousers, for Jack not me, just as I was beginning to run out of steam, the kids were sat down for twenty minutes on the floor, around a Spiderman plastic tablecloth where paper plates of sandwiches, sausages and carrot sticks were displayed. These were all largely ignored but, when the biscuits and cakes came out, it was like vultures descending as the children scrambled to consume their body weight in sugar. Once the white stuff had penetrated their veins, and they were one Haribo away from full-blown diabetes, the kids went crazy. With lunch over I knew I was on the home straight but that still didn't stop me from praying hard for it all to be over soon. After they've eaten is always the point when the kids feel familiar enough with me to start climbing on me, kicking me and punching me in the face, all in the name of fun of course, while demanding complicated balloon puppets and more lavatorial humour. Today was no different.

Fortunately, the majority of kids at this particular party were pretty sweet and a couple even made me yearn to breed. A handful of others, however, had the opposite effect and made me want to perform an immediate hysterectomy on myself with no anaesthetic. The worst offender was a girl called Maisie. Maisie was, frankly, a little cow. This sounds strong I know, but I do not buy into the view that all children are delightful beings. They're not. Some are, but others are most definitely hideous and will undoubtedly grow into mean-minded, horrid adults.

Anyway, the party was drawing to a close so I started to hand out treats and to squirt them with my plastic flower. Hilarious… But Maisie, the little charmer, kept wriggling round me so that she could delve into my bag herself and grab more sweets than she was really entitled to.

'Can you put those back please, angel?' I asked nicely between gritted teeth for about the twelfth time. By now I was really hanging in rags, my headache had returned and I was desperate to get into something more comfortable. This wouldn't be hard. I was wearing a hot, heavy, itchy clown suit for goodness sake. I could have slipped into an eighteenth-century crinoline and it would have felt like leisure wear.

'No,' Maisie answered defiantly, looking deep into the bowels of my soul in the way that only the most brattish of children are capable of doing.

'Please Maisie, otherwise there won't be enough for all the other boys and girls.'

Unblinking, Maisie put her hand back into the bag and extracted yet another handful.

'But I haven't had any sweets yet,' said another little girl, who'd been waiting patiently for ages and who was watching the scene in horror. This little girl was of the cherubic variety. She was small, cute and very polite.

'I know. You've been waiting very nicely,' I said. 'So listen Maisie, you need to give some of those sweets to Georgia here, because she hasn't had any and you've had loads.'

'No,' said Maisie.

'Yes,' I replied. My tone was icy. My patience was wearing thin and I was so weary that at this point I just needed her to *do as I'd asked*.

'Please Maisie,' begged Georgia rather pitifully, her blue eyes brimming with tears at the sheer injustice of the situation. At this rate I'd be crying with her soon. 'Just let me have one.'

I looked at Maisie and nodded hard, indicating that she should do the right thing – though admittedly it's hard to be taken seriously when dressed as a clown, unless someone suffers from a phobia of them, which a surprising amount of people do, then it's easy – but Maisie ignored me and simply shoved nearly every single one of the stolen sweeties into her precocious gob. 'Can't have them now,' she lisped meanly, syrupy dribble pouring out of the sides of her engorged cheeks.

At this point two things happened. Firstly Georgia burst into tears, and secondly I decided that I'd had enough. I was not going to let a four-year-old dictate to me, and I wasn't going to let Georgia go home unhappy. So I tried to grapple the few sweets that were left in Maisie's sticky mitts away from her, at which point she threw her head back and screamed so piercingly I honestly thought the conservatory-style kitchen we were standing in would shatter and that shards of glass would kill us all.

'Blinking heck,' said Jack's mum, bounding over, looking all concerned. 'Is she OK?'

'Oh, she's fine,' I replied airily, but probably not that convincingly given that Maisie had turned a startling shade of purple and was punching me hard with her fists.

I tried to shake her off.

'She can be a bit of a madam that one,' admitted Jack's mum. 'Still, someone should be here to collect her soon. You're doing a great job.'

'Fantastic,' I said, trying to sound jolly, which was difficult. Maisie's punches were surprisingly painful. Lots of parents were starting to trickle in by this point though so the hostess left me to it and went to start helping match children up with their shoes, coats and parents.

'You're not a nice clown,' spat Maisie. 'You're an evil clown.'

Looking around to make sure no one was in earshot I bent down so that I was at eye level with Maisie and said in as menacing a tone as I could summon up, in order to really exude a 'clown gone psycho' sort of vibe, 'And you're a horrid, mean little girl, aren't you?'

Immature I know, but worth it to see the stunned look on her face before she burst into tears. This time the tears were genuine.

With mums and dads arriving the timing wasn't great. When it comes to bookings I pretty much depend on word of mouth so a child standing next to me wailing in distress isn't exactly the best advertisement for my skills in entertaining. Then things suddenly took a dramatic turn for the worse, at which point Maisie's histrionics became the least of my worries. For headed my way was someone who looked scarily identical to Simon.

What the hell?

The world seemed to tip on its head as my scrambled brain searched desperately for an explanation of any kind that might explain his presence. Maybe he had a twin? Or a clone? Maybe I was so dehydrated I was hallucinating? Swiftly however, I came to the horrific realisation that none of these things were true at all and that, of course, it was definitely him. Shortly after this revelation it also dawned upon me that I was dressed as a clown, and that I'd told him I was working on a glamorous advert today. Him seeing me dressed as Custard the freaking Clown was never the plan and what the hell was he even doing here? Panic started bubbling upwards.

Mortification flooded through my system and if I'd been capable of running in my comedy shoes I would have seriously considered fleeing the building. As it was I was trapped, fenced in by a ring of small people, so I turned around, hoping to blend into the background as much as possible. Not easy in a tailcoat and blue curly wig. Plus Maisie was still bleating on, hell-bent on creating a scene, so in desperation I bent down and buried my red nose into my bag of tricks, hoping to look like a busy clown. One who was too busy to say goodbye to any of the children. A clown who just didn't give a shit.

Then, confirming my worst fear, I heard someone who sounded identical to the Simon I'd been flirting with last night. 'Maisie darling, what's wrong sweetie?'

And she said back. 'That clown said I was a nasty little girl.'

Mind racing, I wished sincerely that the ground would open up, or that a shovel would appear so I could at least start digging and give it a helping hand. Was Simon her uncle? Of all the flipping brats he could be related to.

'That clown there?' he said and at this point I felt a sort of calm, defeated acceptance of the situation. I also thought his question was stupid. How many other bloody clowns could he see?

'Yes Daddy.'

Daddy?

Suddenly I was filled with a new, quite horrid, sense of enlightenment that superseded any of the embarrassment I was suffering from. That one word had changed everything. Slowly, I turned around and without making

eye contact demanded to know, 'Is she your daughter?'
As I asked, I surreptitiously pulled my wig down a bit to
obscure my face. My red nose had started to pinch a while
back, but now I was grateful for it.

'Yes,' replied an aggrieved-looking Simon, clutching
the revolting Maisie to him protectively. Knowing that
'Daddy' couldn't see, she stuck her tongue out at me. 'And
I think you owe her an apology,' Simon continued, totally
unaware that I was me. 'She said you upset her.'

I was just about to make up some bullshit excuse before
making my escape when my gaze was drawn to something
else. Simon was wearing a gold band on his left hand,
which he certainly hadn't been wearing in the club. And
that did it. Prior to seeing that ring I had still been grappling
with explanations for everything. Simon was divorced
but remained devoted to his hideous daughter. Simon had
adopted Maisie as a single father because her natural parents had rejected her for being so vile – let's face it, this
was a possibility. And yet that band of gold told me that
this was all utter rubbish and that I had been well and truly
bullshitted. What was it with these men?

I was furious and simultaneously found myself actually
wanting to be recognised, at which point I slowly slipped
off my wig, pulled off my nose, stared hard and waited
patiently for his pea brain to compute. Seconds later it
started to happen. His face was a picture of horror as slowly
the penny dropped.

'… Marianne?' he eventually stuttered, his face growing almost as pale as my white one.

'Yes,' I answered defiantly, painted face held high.

'What are you… doing here?'

'What does it look like I'm…' I swallowed down the 'f' word. 'What does it look like I'm *doing* here? Entertaining your daughter and her friends is what I'm doing here,' I hissed, my voice livid.

'Right, well nice to see you again,' he lied, looking longingly towards the exit.

'You utter pig,' I muttered.

'Come on Maisie,' Simon pleaded. 'We're going darling, now.'

'Where's Mummy?'

'Waiting in the car,' he whispered urgently, as if whispering would cancel out the reference to the cuckolded mother of his child. 'Go and get your party bag from Jack's mum.'

'So, Mummy's in the car is she?' I blustered, once Maisie had charged off in search of more treats she didn't deserve. 'Maybe I should come outside and introduce myself to Mummy?'

Simon looked terrified.

'What, you don't like the idea of that? Why's that then?'

'Just stay away from my family,' he sneered icily, his face contorted in rage.

'Maybe I'd be doing her a favour?' I added, enjoying watching him squirm, though admittedly my enjoyment would have been even greater had I been wearing something more standard.

'Look, you crazy bitch, just keep away all right?' was his charming riposte, after which he gulped, looked around and then pegged it.

It was awful, and as I stood there trying not to cry, feeling hurt and stung, not only by Simon's actions but by his venomous tone of voice, I felt truly gutted and absolutely humiliated.

Half an hour later and it was a rather pathetic clown that left that party, worn out, upset and mortified. As soon as I'd been paid, I left almost as hastily as Simon and Maisie had, and only once back in the safe environs of Tina did I let the true extent of my horror catch up with me. The shame of it all. Then I caught a glimpse of my clown face in the rear view mirror and despite everything had to swallow back a laugh that was in grave danger of turning into a sob.

It wasn't meant to be like this.

CHAPTER FOUR

As I put the key in the lock, I felt fed up and dejected. My mood wasn't improved when Mum's voice immediately hollered through from the kitchen. 'That you Marianne?'

'Yes.'

'Well hurry up and have your shower because I could do with a hand in here.'

The day was feeling more like an endurance test by the minute. I felt dreadful and the last thing I felt like doing was helping Mum get ready for a state visit from Hayley, Gary and his bloody family. Especially since I could hear that Pete was upstairs, blasting Elvis as usual. I know he's younger. I know I should have a place of my own. I know I need to pull my weight but I also know Mum will never expect anything of Pete simply because he's male. She's raising a Neanderthal. My mum's a sexist.

I heaved myself upstairs and locked myself in the bathroom, where I began the process of changing from a clown back into a normal person. As I stood under the shower, the pan-stick make-up dripped off my face and disappeared down the plughole, along with any hopes I might have been harbouring about Simon. What a bastard. Thank god nothing had happened. At least now I could still tell Andy I'd waited for him. The thought of Andy made me instantly nostalgic – and guilty – and as the water pounded my head, I wished more than anything I was miles away from here, on a beautiful beach with him. Preferably lying in a hammock eating a banana pancake at my favourite time of day, five o'clock. Although that's only my favourite time of day when I'm on the beach, not when I'm at home. That is to say I don't like it when everybody's pouring out of work after a gruelling day, battling home in heavy traffic, or on the bus without a seat, head squashed into someone's armpit. But five o'clock on the beach is another story altogether. It's when the sun's starting to dip and its rays are losing their intensity, but it's still so beautifully warm that you can feel yourself drifting off into a peaceful, dreamy slumber.

'These vol-au-vents aren't going to stuff themselves!' Mum shrieked up the stairs, putting paid to any more of that whimsy.

Ten minutes later I'd shoved on some black leggings and was just about to pull an oversized sweater over them when suddenly I pictured Hayley's look of outraged disapproval. Off they slid again and I selected instead a dress and belt that I didn't think even she could take umbrage with. I dragged a brush quickly through my hair, another reason to love having short hair, along with the fact I no longer feel like a poor man's Hayley. We both used to have long, straight, blonde hair, only hers was that bit blonder and straighter. Since going for the chop, I feel more like I have my own identity and less like people are constantly comparing us when we're together.

I hoped my outfit would keep her happy today. Not because I gave a shit whether she approved or not, but because I couldn't be bothered with any more scenes. Still rattled by my confrontation with Simon, I slapped on a bit of mascara and some blusher and then went downstairs to help stuff Mum's ruddy vol-au-vents.

'You need to give your eyebrows a rub,' said Mum, who was in full flap mode. 'You've still got black make-up on them. Other than that though, you look nice.'

I was surprised. I don't usually get many compliments from Mum – they're usually all reserved for Hayley or Pete and, on occasion, Martin – and when I had my hair cut short she acted as if I'd mutilated myself. Today Mum was wearing too tight white capri pants with perspex wedges and a v-neck fuchsia sweater that matched her lipstick. Her ash blonde hair was looking bouncy. She'd obviously tonged it to within an inch of its life and her eyes and cheeks were plastered with shimmery make-up. She's good looking my mum, attractive for her fifty-one years, though her sweet tooth contributes towards what she calls her muffin top. Last year, Martin bought her an exercise bike, which she keeps in the bedroom and goes on religiously every day. She likes to watch *Loose Women* while she's on it and has been known to devour an entire packet of biscuits as she pedals.

As I rubbed my eyebrows viciously with a bit of kitchen towel she rushed around the kitchen, making sure it looked pristine. 'When Wendy and Derek get here, I want to fill them in about *Sing For Britain*,' she said. 'You know how much your sister looks up to Wendy, so if we can just get her on side.'

I sighed.

'The forms have come through, so now I've got all the dates for the London auditions. You will back me up about what a good idea it is, won't you?'

'I'm not backing you up Mum,' I said wearily. Having heard about nothing else for months the subject was starting to wear rather thin, especially since she wouldn't listen to reason. Going on the show would spell disaster for my sister. Sad but true I'm afraid. I flicked the kettle on for a much-needed cup of tea. 'I've told you already Mum, I don't think Hayley should audition. The judges will crucify her. She can't sing.'

Mum narrowed her eyes at me, outraged. 'Marianne Baker, how can you say such a thing? Don't be jealous, it's not attractive. Just because you have no idea what you're doing with your life.'

I despaired. Ultimately it was pointless trying to say anything because the fact that I don't have my own life particularly well sorted out – thanks for pointing that out Mum – means she wrongly assumes I'm jealous. This really upsets me because I certainly am not and am only saying anything because I've got Hayley's best interests at heart. It's hurtful that she thinks I'm so selfish. She won't listen to reason though and it's just such a shame her enthusiasm is so misguided.

Mum is the living definition of a pushy stage mum, or at least she is when it comes to Hayley. In fact, if you were to look up pushy stage mum in the dictionary you might find a picture of her with a frenzied look in her eye, which is the look she gets whenever Hayley opens her mouth to strangle a tune. Ideally it would be an animated picture so you could also see her mouthing the lyrics without realising she's doing so.

Mum and Martin sent Hayley to stage school when she was eleven. At the time they did ask nine-year-old me if I wanted to go too, but fairly half-heartedly and I can still remember the relief on their faces when I declined. They simply couldn't have afforded two sets of fees and that was fine. I'd never been interested in singing or dancing, only violin, so it probably wouldn't have been the place for me anyway, although I did sometimes wonder why they never encouraged my passion as much. Maybe if they had, I would have got further with it? Who knows?

Now Hayley's 'career' is pretty much Mum's reason for being, which is a shame for a few reasons. Firstly, because I strongly suspect Hayley only goes along with Mum's obsession because she's never been allowed to consider for a moment what it is she might actually like to do herself, and secondly because even if she did want to be a star I can't see how it would ever happen because she's simply not that good. She's already thirty-three and all her showbiz 'career' amounts to so far is one fleeting appearance in an advert for a cruise company, a few shit modelling jobs, panto, and wearing hot-pants at events where she gives out leaflets. It doesn't help that other people egg Mum on because Hayley's so beautiful. Though just because someone's beautiful doesn't mean they have what it takes to become the next Elaine Paige. Singing in tune helps for a start. Still, this small detail has never bothered Mum or Hayley, or at least it hadn't until a few years ago when Hayley grew utterly sick of never having Christmas off because of panto. She'd had enough. She was starting to get too old to play one of the villagers anyway and was sick of failing every audition she went to. By now she was settled and married to Gary, so shifted her focus from becoming a star, to bearing his children, which personally I think is wonderful. When she told me she wanted to try for a baby it was the first time I'd ever seen Hayley speak truly passionately about anything. Her entire face lit up in a way it never does when talking about performing. I could see then how caring for someone else could be the making of her. Plus, becoming a parent would take the pressure off as Mum would surely, finally, have to back off.

'Guess who I bumped into last night?' I said now, determined to avoid a row, so deciding to change the subject.

'Who?' she asked, still looking huffy.

'Teresa.'

'Oh did you?' she exclaimed. 'How is she?'

'All right,' I replied. 'It was really nice to see her actually.'

'Well of course it was,' said Mum. 'You two were such good friends.' She looked at me with a knowing expression. 'Didn't I tell you something significant would be happening now that Mercury's in retrograde?'

'Er, I don't know, did you?'

'Yes,' she insisted. 'I did. It's also the reason you're being so bloody bolshy. Still, don't worry, Venus will be rising soon and things will start going your way. Now, get the bowls out for the crisps and nuts will you? Then, when you've filled them up, take them through to the lounge.'

Being treated like a child makes you feel like a child. I wished I could go to bed and fester there for the remainder of the day but got up wearily to do her bidding.

'How was work today anyway? Nice little kiddies were they?'

'All right,' I muttered, not wanting to talk about it.

'Ah there you are,' said Mum through the hatch as Martin walked into the lounge, laden with bags from the off-licence. 'I was starting to think you'd run off and left me.'

On the left of our lounge is an enormous leather suite that rests against a wall, which acts as a partition between the lounge and the kitchen. This wall has a hatch in it, meaning if someone's busy cooking in the kitchen, by opening it they can still keep an eye on the telly. Quite often I'll be fully engrossed in a programme when suddenly I'll glance up only to find Mum's head hanging out of the hatch directly above me. This can be quite disconcerting.

'As if,' said Martin, rounding the partition to enter the kitchen and sidling up behind Mum as she re-wiped the surfaces for the thousandth time.

Mum met Martin when I was ten and Hayley was twelve. Their eyes had met across the big McDonald's in Romford. I remember it clearly because we'd gone there for my birthday treat and they'd got chatting in the queue. It was a chat that had descended pretty quickly into saucy innuendo about whoppers, which were easy even for a child to decipher. Still, I hadn't minded too much because I remember it was the first time in ages I'd seen Mum smiling. When we'd left, Martin had taken Mum's number, and Mum had continued to be in a perky mood for the rest of that evening. Seeing her spirits lift that day was the best birthday present she could have given me.

Dad had left six years previously, which was when we'd had to move out of our house in Hackney and into a damp council flat in Romford. My memories of that time are grim. Mum was depressed and totally unmotivated to find work, as a job would have meant losing her benefits. It was weird though. We were so poor, yet she still owned fur coats and jewellery, left over from her old life with Dad. When she wore them they used to look quite grotesque against the backdrop of our life of penury.

As awful and heart breaking as this period was, looking

back, I think it was the last time Hayley and I were really close. Our grief united us for a while I suppose. And I don't think grief is too strong a word. To have your father in your life one day, a man who adored us and who was, as far as I can remember, a safe, big bear of a figure, our protector, to have him just up and leave was beyond devastating. All I know is that he was a pilot and one day he simply flew to Australia and never returned, abandoning his family without so much as leaving a note. The pain is less raw but I don't think it will ever truly go away. Then Martin came along, Martin who was as working class as us, but who had done well for himself and had his own business. The only thing missing in his life at that time was someone to share it all with.

Mum and Martin had only been seeing each other for a few months when he asked us all to move into his house in posh Chigwell, the one he had before buying this place, and I don't think Mum needed long to make up her mind. I believe he saved her in many ways, and Hayley and me for that matter. We're very different but he's very kind and the closest thing I've had to a dad since mine left. In fact, often I've wished he'd made more of his role as 'stepdad' but his nature means he prefers to stay in the background and not to interfere, so my mum's always been in charge of the important stuff. Still, I'm not knocking him, any man who takes on a woman who comes complete with two young daughters has got to be not only reasonably kind but brave, too.

He still gets on my nerves sometimes though.

I watched now as he grabbed Mum's love handles and gave them a good squeeze.

'Oi you, don't grab my extra bits, makes me feel fat,' she squealed.

'You are not fat my angel,' said Martin predictably. 'You're built as a woman should be and besides, it just gives me more to love.'

I tried not to shudder and, as Mum untangled herself from Martin's grip, concentrated on putting crisps into bowls. My hangover was so bad my hands were shaking, so half of them ended up on the floor. Mum frowned at me on her way to the fridge where she got out a bowl of tuna mix, which she handed to me along with a tray of pastry cases.

'What time are they coming?' I asked, removing the cellophane and getting to work spooning the gunky mixture into them. I was starting to feel quite nauseous and realised then I desperately needed some food to restore my blood sugar levels. I bent down to pick the dropped crisps up from the floor and shoved them in my mouth along with a bit of fluff from the carpet.

'Three o'clock,' Mum replied, the soles of her feet padding against her wedge heels as she bustled around.

'Why are they coming again?' enquired Martin, putting bottles away.

'Good question,' I remarked, stealing a spoon of tuna mix for myself and cramming that in my mouth, too.

'Do they need a reason? They are family,' replied Mum. 'Although I must admit, Hayley was so adamant we were all here I have got my suspicions.'

'What?' I asked, wondering if they matched my own. Personally I was hoping Hayley might finally be pregnant. She and Gary had been trying for two years now and the stress of being disappointed every month had only heightened her already neurotic behaviour. But maybe this get together meant it had finally happened? Gosh I hoped so. It would just be lovely, but Mum had other ideas.

'Well,' she said now, her eyes wide with excitement. 'The other day I told her about an open audition that I saw in *The Stage*. What's the betting she went and got it?'

Not for the first time I felt the urge to query her psychic powers but resisted. The irony of the fact she never knew anything in advance was always lost on Mum and Martin.

Martin wandered next door into the lounge, where the TV was blaring. 'Oof,' he said, collapsing heavily and gratefully into his favourite armchair before putting his feet up on the leather pouffe. 'What was the audition for?'

'*Les Mis*,' stated Mum. At this point they were conversing through the hatch in the wall.

'Mum if you wipe those surfaces any more you're going to make a hole in them,' I said a bit impatiently, though what I was really thinking was; *Do you honestly think your daughter, who has no real rhythm and sings sharp, is going to make the chorus of one of the most famous West End shows? Are you out of your mind?*

'You're right love,' laughed Mum. 'Look at me getting myself into such a lather. They can take us as they find us can't they? Martin, why don't you switch off the telly and stick on a bit of music instead? Help me to relax.'

'Sure,' said Martin, who'd just that second picked up the newspaper but happily bounded into action, ready to please as ever. 'What do you fancy?'

'Ooh, bit of Mariah?'

Mariah Carey has always been Mum's ultimate hero.

As *Hero* came on, Mum abandoned her cleaning and started dancing round the kitchen, using a tube of Primula cheese spread as a microphone. As she sang tunelessly and gyrated her hips Martin came over and stood watching through the hatch, nodding his head and clapping, with a delighted look on his face, as if he were being treated to a private audience with the world's greatest performer. Thankfully, this ridiculous scene was interrupted by the doorbell and the arrival of Wendy, Derek, Hayley and Gary.

'They're here,' Mum clucked, signalling to Martin to switch off the music before rushing to open the door, which he did before turning the TV back on.

I followed Mum and Martin into the hallway and while everybody noisily greeted each other, I hung back, feeling tired and grumpy. Eventually Hayley broke away and we walked back through to the lounge together.

She was looking particularly gorgeous today. Hayley's hair is naturally white blonde and hangs in a perfect sheet down her back. She has fair skin, with a pinkish tone to it so she never looks pasty, just delicate, and her features are neat and even, giving way to a full mouth – possibly due to all the exercise it gets. Like me she has a flat stomach, longish legs and a small waist, but unlike me she also has big breasts. You know how there are different versions of Barbie? Surfing Barbie, caravan Barbie, disco Barbie etc. Well, she's 'wannabe footballer's wife' Barbie, only paler. Today she was wearing skinny jeans, Ugg boots and a leather jacket with a tight t-shirt underneath. She looked immaculate, but then she always does and puts hours into getting ready even if it's just to pop to the shops.

'All right,' she said, her eyes flicking me up and down in a blatant attempt to check that what I was wearing was acceptable. I must have passed the test because she didn't say anything.

'All right,' I replied. 'How are you doing?'

'Good,' she said, popping a crisp in her mouth. 'What have you been up to? Still washing people's greasy heads at Roberto's?'

'Yeah. Jake was asking after you the other day,' I said slyly.

Hayley glared at me, a warning sign not to say anything else. Jake is one of her past conquests. One of the many she left broken hearted, wondering what had just happened to him.

'Saved up enough for South America yet?' she said,

swiftly changing the subject as her husband Gary came lumbering in.

'Another couple of months I reckon.'

'Cool,' said Hayley and then she smiled, a genuinely warm smile, and that was when I knew she *must* be pregnant.

I smiled back at her broadly and raised my eyebrows questioningly. She immediately scowled back. 'What? Don't look at me like that. You look like a retard,' she added charmingly.

She didn't say this with quite as much conviction as she usually would though, and I was on the verge of asking her whether she had anything to tell me, but then Gary piped up.

'All right sis,' he said, in his weird voice. The tone of his voice is really strange. It's slightly high pitched and seems to emanate from the back of his throat, or his nose possibly. He always sounds like he's got a cold. I guess he's what you'd describe as adenoidal.

He patted me on the arm and I shuddered. I find Gary pretty revolting if I'm honest. He goes to the gym every day and his honed body is so muscle-bound he can barely walk. His thighs are huge and his jeans, which tend to be pale blue Levi's 501s, permanently look like they're straining against them. He always wears the same kind of t-shirts too. White but embellished with glittery stuff, sequins, logos or jewels, which tend to plunge into a deep V neck, which gives what I bet he thinks is a tantalising view of his pecs, but is in fact an off-putting glimpse of his muscular man boobs. He wears a lot of chunky, silver jewellery and his hair is styled into unimaginative spikes. He has tattoos on his biceps and Hayley thinks he's gorgeous. I'm sure she's not alone, but I think he's horribly beefy and the thought of having sex with him leaves me repulsed.

Not of course that I would ever want to have sex with my sister's husband, but you know what I mean. Just to be crystal clear, I've only even considered it in the first place because he's such an overtly sexual person. Gary leaves a trail of pheromones and testosterone in his wake wherever he goes and is always pawing Hayley in public. Sometimes when doing so his breath quickens and, even in a room full of people, you can tell he's a bit aroused and that he'd like to get Hayley on her own. I know… it's foul. Also, he looks at other women, including me, a bit inappropriately sometimes. I know he doesn't fancy me or anything but he definitely checks me out and I don't like it.

'Marianne,' said Wendy, Hayley's mother-in-law. Today she looked a bit like the Queen, only minus the pearls. Her hair was set and she was wearing a lilac skirt suit with a navy handbag. 'How are you? Still no boyfriend?'

'Er no,' I replied, wondering why this was always her first line of enquiry but reluctant to tell her about Andy. Why should I?

'Let me get you a drink,' interrupted Martin, leading Wendy away by the elbow back towards the kitchen and giving me a little wink. I flashed him a grateful smile in return.

Half an hour later and things weren't going quite as badly as I'd thought they might. I'd noticed that Hayley had declined a glass of wine and was on the orange juice and it was all I could do not to start nudging people. The men were on beer and Mum and Wendy were tucking into a bottle of white. Still feeling wrecked from the night before I had a cup of tea and ate my body weight in crisps and vol-au-vents.

'So anyway,' Mum was saying, her face slightly flushed. The wine had gone straight to her head. 'You said you had something to tell us Hayley and I don't think I can take the suspense any more. So what is it? Are you going to be treading the boards you clever girl? Or have you landed some amazing modelling contract somewhere?'

'No Mum,' said Hayley, rolling her eyes ever so slightly but still smiling. 'No, the reason Gary and I wanted you all here today... actually hang on a second, where's Pete?'

'Oh that bloody boy. Has he buggered off upstairs again? Go and get him would you Mar?'

Martin leapt up to do her bidding and we could hear him in the hall, hollering up the stairs at his son.

As Pete thudded back down the stairs Mum smiled politely at Wendy and Derek before saying, 'S'cuse my French.'

'Not at all,' said Derek, a self-important, ruddy-faced

man who I sometimes think fancies Mum. Like father like
son with their creepy roving eyes.

Looking thoroughly underwhelmed – his default
disposition in life – Pete re-entered the room, only this
time he was dressed as a teddy boy, which is how he likes
to dress when he goes out with his friends. Or rather, friend.
He only has one friend, Josh, that any of us know of anyway.

'Hello Pete,' said Wendy, looking disdainfully at him as
her eyes swept up and down the length of him, taking in his
drainpipe jeans, creeper shoes, long coat jacket and quiff.

Pete grunted. He's a man of few words.

'Isn't he handsome?' said Mum, girlishly. 'You can see
where he gets his looks from though can't you,' she said
before striking a pose that she obviously thought made her
look like a model.

Martin laughed uproariously. 'You certainly can, my
love.'

I sighed. My family are so weird. From the outside looking in, they probably appear deeply ordinary, an average
suburban family, but sometimes I honestly wonder whether
I'm adopted. It would explain so very much. And yes, I
know everyone goes through phases where they feel like
their family isn't on their wavelength, but I often have
moments like this when I feel like mine are a completely
different species.

*

'So anyway,' said Hayley, frowning in Mum's direction.

She was perched on Gary's meaty thigh, looking dainty as anything, and turned back to look at him so tenderly that I think that was the precise second I knew for sure what their news was. I was instantly filled with happy emotion, plus that feeling again that this could be the making of her. Hayley needed someone to love who adored her back and not just because she was pretty.

'We're pregnant,' she announced to the room, unable to conceal the news a second longer.

I knew it.

Wendy instantly leapt from her seat, clearly delighted. All her usual frostiness and affectation vanished as she let the good news infuse her with grandmotherly excitement. I too squealed and raced over to give Hayley a hug. Derek's reaction was more unusual.

'What do you mean *we're* pregnant? You're not pregnant are you son?' he demanded to know, looking utterly thunderstruck in Gary's direction.

Still, once he'd been reassured that this was a physical impossibility, he too was pleased as punch and there was much backslapping between himself, Gary and Martin. Even Pete managed to mumble something about how having a child had been the single most important thing Elvis had felt he'd done, which coming from him was practically a speech.

'I'm going to be an aunty,' I shrieked as I hugged Hayley again and, for the first time in years, I felt her usually tense shoulders relax a little as she hugged me back.

'I'll be asking you to babysit all the time,' she said, her odd manner making this sound more like a threat than she probably meant it to.

'Any time,' I said as we pulled apart.

After that there was a sort of happy pause and briefly I wondered what we were all waiting for, and then I realised. We were waiting for Mum. So far she hadn't said anything and her silence had become conspicuous.

We all ended up staring at her and, finally sensing that something was required of her, she clapped her hands together and widened the rather fixed grin she was wearing even further. 'Well, well done both of you,' she said eventually. 'I'm really pleased. Though don't think I'm going to let it call me Granny. I'm far too young to be a granny aren't I Mar? So it'll be Nana Alli all the way. And when are you due my darling?'

'Well,' said Hayley, 'Strictly speaking I shouldn't really have told you yet because I'm only eleven weeks so I haven't had my scan yet, but all being well it's going to be a November baby, so he or she will be here for Christmas.'

'Oh,' came the collective soppy gasp from all of us, apart from Mum who looked vaguely distracted. By this point her luke-warm reaction was starting to annoy me. Apart from anything else I could see Hayley was starting to get wound up by it. I didn't blame her.

'Oh, well that's great,' she said, looking faintly doubtful. 'But just thinking aloud then Hayls, you'll be all right for the first lot of auditions but we might have to work out what to do about the live shows, all being well and you get through of course.'

'Mum!' exclaimed Hayley. She looked genuinely shocked. 'Are you actually thinking about *Sing for Britain*? Tell me that's not the first thing that's entered your head? I know it's a shame I can't do it now, but I promise you I'm much, much happier that this is happening.'

I don't usually feel sorry for Hayley but at that moment I really did. My sister had my future niece or nephew in her belly, Mum's first grandchild, but all she could think about was her own pipe dream.

'Course it isn't love,' she added hastily. 'But someone's got to think about these things don't they? I mean Beyoncé didn't just sit back and let her pregnancy ruin everything, did she?'

Hayley looked dumbfounded, but for a second I thought she was going to let Mum's insanity go, mainly because she usually likes to appear terribly demure around Wendy and Derek. However, perhaps it was all the hormones or something because in the next moment she let rip.

'Ruin everything? Is that what you really think? That my baby would be ruining things? Ruining what anyway? I'm thirty-three for Christ's sake and totally sick of going to crap auditions, which I never get. And besides, there's always next year anyway. This year, however, we're having a baby Mum. A baby that has taken us two years to make, so which stupidly, I thought you might be pleased about. Especially given I don't have a fucking career to worry about because I'm not frigging Beyoncé.'

'Hayley,' boomed Derek. His ruddy face had taken on a purple hue, so horrified was he by such a display of emotion in public, especially from a female. Little did he know that when not in their presence Hayley likes to swear like a sailor.

'I'm not sure you should be addressing your mother like that, young lady.'

'Sorry,' muttered my sister, instantly horrified to have lost control in front of the in-laws.

Mum looked mildly rebuked but typically wasn't wise enough to know when to keep her mouth shut. 'Don't be silly Hayls,' she insisted. 'Having a baby doesn't have to mean giving up your dreams this year. You don't want to leave these things too late.'

'Maybe you should leave it love,' suggested Martin quietly, which was the most I think he'd ever stood up to her in all the years they'd been together.

'All right Mar,' replied Mum stonily, unused to anything that even remotely resembled criticism from him. I noticed she had a creeping patch of redness developing on her chest.

'Well, we're all delighted for you Hayley anyway,' interrupted Wendy, and for once I was firmly on her side. 'I for one cannot wait to be a granny. It's unbelievably exciting and I can't believe you've kept it secret this long Gary. Ooh, imagine a little Gary running around at Christmas.'

We all tried, but it was hard. For starters the baby would only just have been born so it being able to run around was unlikely, wasn't it? Secondly, the thought of a muscular, dwarf baby version of Gary was disturbing. I hoped who-ever was in there looked like Hayley.

Later, when they finally all left, it was a relief. Pete skulked out the front door, seconds after their departure. I planned on escaping too, albeit only to my bedroom, but needed a word with Mum first.

'What did you have to go on about *Sing for Britain* for?' I said.

'Don't you lecture me,' she snapped.

'I'm not lecturing, I'm just saying.'

'Well don't. Honestly, I don't know where I've gone wrong with the pair of you. You living at home, single, wasting your life away and now Hayley, throwing away her chance of success.'

I recoiled, stung by her words. 'That's out of order,' I said. 'And believe you me, being here isn't ideal for me either.'

'Er, that's enough. I've had enough shittiness today off Martin, Wendy and Hayley thank you very much,' said Mum stroppily, hands on hips.

'I'm sorry if I came on a bit strong love,' said Martin.

I checked to see whether he was joking. He wasn't. 'But Mum,' I said frustratedly. 'She's pregnant. It's amazing and you should be so excited about it. This is all she's ever wanted.'

'And I am happy for her,' she insisted, not looking it at all. 'It's just I want Hayley to have something to fall back on in life. She's such a talent and it seems criminal that that should go to waste.' Her bottom lip wobbled slightly.

I gave up. Frankly I was too bloody hung-over. I felt like total shit by now so I went to my room where I got into bed and promptly fell asleep, despite the fact it was only five-thirty in the afternoon. And despite the fact the wind was howling and an almighty storm was brewing outside.

CHAPTER FIVE

FIVE HOURS LATER

When I woke up, groggy from my unscheduled nap, I could never have imagined what lay ahead. Yet here I am, standing outside, in the middle of a huge thunderstorm, trying to compute that my dad is back. My dad is back? It can't be true. Apart from anything else, if he's my dad, why is he gripping on to me so hard? It's too surreal. Just at that point, he finally removes his gloved hand from my mouth at which point, because I don't fully believe anything he's telling me, rather unimaginatively, I scream my head off again.

'Fuck's sake Marianne,' the man claiming to be my long-lost father yells, though another crash of thunder ensures I can only just about hear what he's saying. 'Stop that flaming screaming will ya? It's me, your dad. I'm not going to hurt you.'

At this point he lets go of me and spins me around to face him and there, in the blustering gale and rain, I get the first glimpse of him in twenty-seven years.

Immediately I know it's definitely him. Without any photos – Mum has systematically destroyed all the ones that ever existed of him, even going so far as to cut him out of any group shots – it's been impossible to preserve much memory of what he looked like, given that I haven't seen him for so long. And yet I must have retained a handful of residual images, because something deep in the recesses of my mind makes a match with this tall, slightly menacing looking hard man who's standing before me, dressed top to toe in black, rain pouring down his face. He's got dark brown, almost black hair, that's very short at the sides, slicked back on top and receding at the brow. He has green eyes, like me, sharp cheekbones, a nose that looks like it's been in a few fights in its time and a crooked mouth. It's my dad, and now that he's standing before me, bathed in a shaft of harsh, overhead, patio lighting I realise I can't have forgotten him like I always thought I had, because he looks so familiar. The same, only older, every line on his face visual evidence of the time he's chosen not to spend with us.

I'm pretty sure at this point that he means me no physical harm but I'm still astonished by what's happening and wary of what his next move might be. I also can't stop staring. Probably because, when you've wondered about somebody all your life, when finally faced with them in the flesh you need to drink in every detail of them. It's him and I can't believe it.

I must be having some out-of-body experience because

when someone yells, 'What the hell are you doing here?' it takes a few seconds to register that it was me who said it, and that I'm crying. Really crying. In fact, I'm positively sobbing my heart out, probably due to a mixture of shock, anger and fear. Not that I can feel the tears. By this stage it's raining so hard the two of us couldn't be any more wet through if we jumped in a lake.

'Let's go inside. You'll catch your death standing out here,' he orders, his rough Essex accent a voice from a previous lifetime.

'Not sure Mum would be so keen on that idea,' I manage to stammer. I've never been as cold as I am right now. I'm numb.

'Get in,' he insists gruffly.

In the end it's pointless to resist and, besides, what am I going to do? Send him back into the ether, possibly never to see him again? I have far too many questions to let that happen so I nod and go to slide the door across with numb fingers.

Once we're both inside he pulls the door shut, which immediately dulls the sound of the driving rain. We both stand there, staring at one another, dripping wet, making a huge puddle on the carpet. All I can think is what now? I have no clue how to proceed, or what to say or do in this strange situation. My head's swirling, my teeth are chattering. To be fair, I think I'm in shock.

'Why don't you get some towels or summink?' says the

man who has had the audacity to announce himself as my dad. Like he has the right.

On autopilot I do as I'm told. I go upstairs, strip my wet clothes off, dry myself and stick on a tracksuit and my slippers, all the while trying to digest the fact that downstairs is my missing parent. It's a lot to take in and as I make my way back downstairs again I'm half-expecting him to have disappeared.

However, there's nothing about tonight that correlates with any of my expectations.

Now, as I proceed with caution into the lounge, to my surprise, I find my father has gone into the kitchen and is stirring a pan of milk on the hob. He's peeled off his soaking wet, leather coat and has dried his face off with a tea towel. I can tell because it's sitting impertinently on the side, screwed up and discarded, a bit like we have been. He's taken off his trainers and is in his socks. White sports socks. Now that the initial shock is wearing off, lots of rather more violent emotions start to encroach on my dumb state and the oddly domestic sight of him stirring a pan of milk suddenly enrages me. How dare he do something so ordinary in such an extreme situation? How dare he help himself to our milk, from our fridge? There isn't anything normal about him coming back like this, so doing something as domestic as making hot beverages shows a blatant lack of respect for the drama he's inflicting upon me. I feel insulted on Mum's behalf. Thinking of her only increases the magnitude of what's happening.

'See you've made yourself at home then,' I say frostily.

'Get that down your neck,' he says, before pouring the hot milk into two mugs and handing one to me. The mug he's using is Martin's favourite. Mum gave it to him on Valentine's Day. It says *Hot Stuff* on it.

Staring into my own mug I notice my hand is shaking like a leaf. Hot chocolate. How twee. 'What the hell do you think you were doing?' I say coldly. 'Why were you creeping round the house like that? I could have had a heart attack. I thought you were a burglar. Have you got a problem with doorbells or something?'

'I didn't mean to scare you. I went round the back 'cos I wanted to see you on your own, so I waited till your mum and her fella had gone out. Then, I did try the bell as it goes, but there was no answer, so I came round the back again.'

'But you grabbed me.'

''Cos when I reached out you screamed like a banshee.'

As I open my mouth to protest he says, as gently as his gruff voice will permit, 'Drink your drink.'

Chilled to the bone, slowly I take a sip, only to find that it's the perfect drink for the situation, hot, sweet and good for my strange state. I let the warm liquid defrost me from the inside but then, not wanting to pussyfoot around any longer, ask in a small voice I hardly recognise, the question I've wanted answering since I was a child, 'Why did you leave us?'

And Ray, that's his name, and I'm certainly not about

to start calling him Dad, turns to me and says, 'You know, I've dreamed of this day, Marianne.'

'Whatever,' I retort, hot rage boiling underneath the surface. This man has caused me so much pain my entire life simply by choosing to not be there, so hearing anything he has to say was always going to be hard. Such triteness is inexcusable though. Nothing he can say to me now will ever excuse his absence. As for turning up here unannounced, it's unacceptable, inappropriate and above all, not bloody fair.

'What's your mum told you?' he says, leaning back against the breakfast bar.

'Just the basics,' I fume. 'That you were a pilot and that you pissed off to Australia because you couldn't handle family life. Made for a lovely bedtime story I can tell you.'

Ray just stands there staring sadly into his cocoa. Then, to my absolute annoyance, a grin slowly spreads across his big brutish mug and he chuckles. He throws back his massive ugly head and actually laughs.

'What?' I say, and at this point I'm beyond seething.

'Sorry,' he says. 'It's just I can't believe she said I was a pilot.'

The world tips on its axis and I become keenly aware of the fact that I can't take much more tonight. She *said* he was a pilot.

'Well, what's so funny about that?'

'I was never a pilot,' he says, his face grave once more.

'Marianne, I don't know how to tell you this, so I'm just going to come out and say it. I was in prison.'

I don't believe this is happening. I put my mug down on the side and go to take a seat at the dining table, the one nearest the radiator. Needing time to fully absorb what he's just said I use warming my hands as a delaying tactic. My head's spinning and it's also occurred to me that Mum could be back at any time. I glance back at Ray to see whether he's joking but he looks deadly serious.

'Prison?' I manage eventually, not sure I want to hear anything else he's got to say. Not convinced I don't want him to just leave, so I can pretend that none of this ever happened. So that life can continue as… well… not quite normal, but as good as.

'Yeah. I'm not proud of it, but at least I've served my time, though I can honestly say that living with the regret of what I did and what I put you, your sister and your mother through hasn't been easy. You look so like her by the way. Not the colouring, but around the eyes and that.'

'Right,' I say faintly, not trusting myself to say much more apart, that is, from the question from which there's no escaping. 'So… what did you do? Why were you in prison?'

Ray inhales and looks up at the ceiling as if deliberating whether or not to tell me.

'If you don't tell me, I'll find out somehow,' I say, steeling myself to hear what heinous crime my long-lost dad committed all those years ago.

'All right,' he says quietly, his huge bulk making our kitchen look smaller than usual. 'I was arrested for murder.'

'You murdered someone?' I sob. It couldn't get any worse. It all feels so surreal and part of me hopes I'll wake up in a minute. I know if the floodgates open I won't be able to close them again so fight to keep calm.

'Well yeah, but not on purpose. It's a long story,' he says sadly. 'In the end I got done for manslaughter… and arson.'

I can't look at him. It's as if the walls are closing in on me, and it dawns upon me that I know virtually nothing about this man who's standing in my kitchen. This man, who's taken the liberty of helping himself to milk from our fridge. This monster, who's telling me now, calmly, that he's killed someone. What was I even thinking when I let him in the house? I have to get him out, preferably before Mum and Martin get back.

'Well, now you've got out, it's nice you thought to look us up,' I say, sarcastically, yet with a hint of caution. I'm a bit worried for my own safety. I don't want to rile him. He's just told me he murdered someone. My dad's a murderer. As thoughts pop relentlessly into my confused head, they're more like newsflashes.

'I got out eight years ago,' he says abruptly.

'Oh,' I say, taken aback.

Another shocker I wasn't expecting. In fact, if this evening takes any more curve balls I'm going to get the bends. Strangely, the fact he's been out of prison for eight years but has only just got round to looking us up pisses me off even more than finding out he's killed someone. I know that probably displays an awful lack of perspective but it's more personal I suppose. Plus I'm probably not really thinking straight.

'So, why didn't you come looking for us eight bloody years ago then?' I demand to know, feeling such a surge of white fury it almost overpowers me. How dare he? How can he say he's dreamed of this day when he could have had it any time he liked over the last eight years. I'm so angry I feel like screaming.

'I promised your mum I wouldn't, but things have changed.'

'Oh yeah? Great, well what's happened then? Have you murdered someone else?' I cried. 'Or did it just occur to you what a shitty job you'd made of being a dad. Or maybe it's not something you've ever taken particularly seriously so you just thought you'd do it on a whim. Is that it, or what?'

'I've got cancer, Marianne. They've given me six months to live.'

And these words change the direction of everything once again. I stare at his face, willing him to be lying but can tell immediately he isn't. Instead, I see a man who looks strangely resigned to the news he's just imparted and even though I barely know him the anger dissipates and is joined by crippling sadness at the injustice of the whole shitty, crappy situation.

'Cancer of what?' Even though I'm already sitting down,

my legs feel decidedly wobbly. I wipe my face as tears fall silently down it.

'Of bloody everywhere at this stage, but it started in my colon. Cancer of the bumhole basically. Not the most glamorous,' he jokes, though it's so far from being funny, it's tragic. His face is stricken.

'Right,' I manage. 'Well… I'm sorry.'

'Me too Marianne, me too,' he says, rolling his green eyes heavenward in order to quell and stave off whatever it is he's feeling, which can't be good.

'Are you scared?' I ask, curious to know. Was it fear that had made him come back? Was he so selfish that he was only seeking us out because suddenly he needed us? I'm so confused right now I don't know what to think.

'No,' he says simply. 'I ain't scared of dying. What does scare me though is not explaining anything to you and your sister. I've always left you alone for good reason but lately I've realised that might not have been the best plan after all. I'm so sorry I frightened you earlier.'

I think he can tell my brain is completely overloaded because the next thing he says is, 'Look, it's a lot for you to take in. I should go now anyway, in case your mum and her bloke get back, but I'm gonna give you my number and if you could just give me a call, maybe tomorrow, I'd appreciate it.'

I must have nodded because he picks a biro up and looks around for something to write on, settling eventually on an old receipt.

'There,' he says.

I take it from him and he crosses the room, clearly planning on making his exit the same way he arrived.

'Why tonight?' I ask, a swell of emotion suddenly surging through me as I desperately try to figure out so many things. I don't want to cry while he's here.

He shakes his head and smiles ruefully. 'Didn't have a plan really. I've just been watching the house a bit, you know, trying to figure out the best time to approach you.'

'Right,' I say, not knowing quite what to make of that either. I'm pretty sure what he's just described amounts to stalking, not that it seems to matter very much somehow.

He slides the glass doors open a fraction and as he does the rain howls in again. As I watch him pull on his still wet coat, it occurs to me that I hope he has somewhere warm to go to. And that confuses me even further because a big part of me hates him, and yet this instinct contradicts that. He's just about to disappear into the stormy night when he stops, turns and says one final thing, and of all the things I hadn't expected about tonight, including seeing my dad for the first time in decades, finding out he went to prison, discovering he killed someone and is dying of cancer, the thing he says to me as he vanishes back into the storm is the thing that surprises me the most.

'By the way, I heard you playing earlier Marianne. Through the window. You play beautiful. Bach wasn't it?'

'Um… yes,' I whisper, wondering how on earth my dad, the murderer, could possibly know that.

*

I wander back to my room in a trance, mind racing as it desperately tries to compute everything it's found out. My violin's still lying on the bed where I left it, so I put it and the bow back in its case before sliding it underneath my bed. Then, utterly drained and emotionally spent, I collapse onto the bed and stare at the rain as it smashes against the window-pane, letting the tears slide quietly down my face and onto my pillow.

Seconds later I hear a key in the front door downstairs. Mum and Martin are back. Quickly I switch off my bed-side light, plunging my room into total darkness. I can't face Mum. If she sees me she'll instantly know some-thing's up and I'm nowhere near ready to discuss what's just happened.

I can hear her and Martin giggling and shushing one another, clearly pissed after an unusual Sunday night out to celebrate Sheena and Dave's wedding anniversary. I'm hoping they'll go straight to bed, but Martin spends what feels like hours making sure the house is locked up, while Mum crashes and blunders her way around the kitchen, burning toast by the smell of it – it's always the same when she goes out with Sheena. In front of her she pretends she has the appetite of a sparrow, but then makes up for it when she gets home by eating her body weight in carbs.

What feels like hours later they eventually start making their way up the stairs, though their progress is painfully slow and agonising to listen to.

Mum seems determined to stop on every stair, wheezing with laughter, while saying things sporadically like, 'Stop it Martin' and, 'Don't, I'll pee my pants Martin.'

Five long minutes later, they're finally ensconced in their room, presumably passed out because the house falls silent once again, at which point I succumb to a proper sob. Perhaps a good cry is what I need? It's been a hell of a weekend. And with that final thought I drift off into restless sleep, wishing I'd appreciated the relative simplicity of life before today.

CHAPTER SIX

The next morning I wake up feeling drained. My very first thought is that I can't handle work today so I phone Jason and pretend to be ill.

Once I've got him off the phone I find the tatty receipt my father wrote his number on and stare at it, trying to absorb what it means. My heart aches in my chest. I've spent my entire adult life missing having a dad, wondering why he didn't love us enough to stay in touch. I've coped by repressing as much of these emotions as possible while pretending to the world that I'd have no interest in seeing him again. But him showing up has exposed this lie for what it is. Now he's come back I am forced to admit it's all I've ever really wanted. Only not like this. As I stare at the unfamiliar handwriting, I find myself thinking how little I know about the person it belongs to. Is my dad evil? He did kill someone after all, and yet if that's the case, why do I feel so desolate about the fact he's going to die? It's all so overwhelming and gut-wrenchingly disappointing. Over the years, in my mind I've built him up into a romantic sort of Heathcliff-type figure. A good-looking, charismatic cad. It's hard to admit, but I've often wondered whether Mum was to blame for him leaving. I thought she might have driven him away. One psychic prediction too many, perhaps?

I've invented everything though, convincing myself along the way that I've based these notions on more than just my own pathetic daydreams. As it turns out, Ray's more roguish looking than handsome and now that he's really here it's obvious that the truth is far more unpalatable and complicated than I could ever have guessed. I'm going to have to reappraise everything I've ever thought. Do I even want to get involved? If he's telling the truth, he's only going to end up dying on us anyway.

As this incredibly bitter thought enters my head I feel ashamed. God it was all such a mess. What the hell was Hayley going to say when she found out? Should I even tell her given that she's pregnant? I don't want to stress her out. I decide then just to sit on it for a while. My head is too scrambled to make any decisions.

Downstairs the usual morning chaos is in full swing. Martin's leaving for work and Mum's nagging Pete to eat more than just a piece of toast for breakfast.

'My little soldier can't survive on toast alone. Do you want me to make you a quick bacon sarnie my lovely? Or how about a bit of scrambled?'

Pete grunts by way of reply and looks annoyed when she ruffles his hair, which he's clearly spent hours doing. Moments later he gets down from the breakfast bar, picks up his rucksack of books and drags himself off to college, giving me a cursory glimmer of a smile in passing, oblivious to Mum's incessant commentary and fussing. As ever Mum seems to feel it's necessary to see him right out, so that she can yell her goodbyes from the drive.

Once this daily ritual of over-the-top mothering is over, she makes her way back into the kitchen and sighs contentedly before asking brightly, 'So, how are you this morning?'

Today Mum's dressed in a bright turquoise tracksuit, which she's accessorised with beads and her favourite silver and Perspex wedges. She simply doesn't do flat shoes and only takes her beloved wedges off if she's about to get into bed, the bath or a swimming pool. Sometimes she even wears them on her exercise bike. 'Not working today, Marianne? I thought your day off was Wednesday.'

'No,' I mumble, as I fix myself a bowl of cereal while wondering how on earth to broach the subject that her ex-husband is out of prison and has reappeared, in our back garden. 'Are you a bit happier about Hayley's news now you've had a chance to think about it?' I enquire disapprovingly, buying myself time more than anything.

Mum tuts and rolls her eyes despairingly at the mention of my sister. 'Course I'm happy Marianne, I'm ecstatic,' she says, sounding anything but. 'And if that didn't come across, well then I'm sorry. I just don't want Hayley to wake up one day and realise she's missed the boat. She's so talented but if I'm totally honest, sometimes I wonder whether she's got the right attitude for showbiz, you know?'

'If she hasn't got the right attitude for showbiz,' I say, spooning Shreddies into my mouth, head still whirring, 'She's probably not cut out for it, is she?'

Mum's face looks tired underneath all the make-up. I can tell she's hung-over from last night. 'Look,' she says as she flaps around, tidying up. 'Is it wrong that I want you girls to do something exciting? Something glamorous, obviously. I haven't turned into one of those feminists with hairy armpits or anything, but I want you to be fulfilled. I want you to do something worthwhile, like beauty therapy or ideally, in Hayley's case anyway, performing. As it is I've got two daughters in their thirties, one with bags of talent but no ambition and another who wants to be some sort of hippy. Frankly Marianne I'm praying you're going to get inspired at some point and start taking hairdressing more seriously. If you did, you could have your own salon one day.'

I roll my eyes, not in the mood for a lecture.

'All I'm saying is that when your dad upped and left, I realised I'd wasted my life being a girlfriend and wife to him. I was so young, still am really, but life has passed me by and I've never had anything to fall back on. I don't want that for my girls.'

The fact she's even referred to her past life with Ray is very unusual. I seize the opportunity to turn the conversation back round to him.

'So, when my dad left, did you ever wonder whether there was more to it than him just wanting to… get away?' I ask tentatively, searching Mum's face for clues. Knowing she lied to us all these years is a hard pill to swallow and not something I've had the chance to even consider until this very second.

She looks away and busies herself with heaving the vacuum cleaner out of the cupboard and plugging it in. This all gives her time to think. I see that now and find myself wondering how I could have been so dense all these years not to have noticed her rubbish attempts to conceal the truth. Angry suddenly, and determined to get an answer, I get up and pull the plug out of the wall just as she's started vacuuming.

'Hey,' says Mum, looking annoyed. 'You know I don't like talking about that time, so let's drop it shall we? Plug me back in.'

I shake my head. I can't do it. I can't pretend and don't see why I should have to any more. 'I know he went to prison,' I say steadily.

Mum freezes and even though her back is to me at this point, her shoulders go rigid, so I know she's heard what I just said.

'Who told you?' she asks, her voice little more than a whisper. When she turns to face me, her skin has gone a rather strange colour. The colour of a mushroom. Not the black bit, the grey bit obviously.

'I found it on the internet,' I say, not sure I should deliver all the facts just yet.

'Right,' she says, swallowing. She looks momentarily confused because of course the information isn't online or I would have found it long ago, but then she seems to accept that it must be.

'Why didn't you tell us? Why have you lied to us all these years?' To my horror my eyes start filling up. 'You had no right.'

Abandoning the vacuum cleaner, Mum sinks down onto one of the stools at the breakfast bar and for a second seems close to tears herself. Taking a deep breath she runs her immaculate peach fingernails through her hair.

'How could I tell two young girls their dad was a criminal? You were four Marianne, are you telling me you would have understood that? That you would have liked to have known he was a villain?'

I consider this for a while. 'OK, I understand why you didn't tell us when we were little. But later, when we were older, didn't we deserve to know the truth then?'

'And how would you have felt? You believed what I'd told you. What day would have been the right day to break my daughters' hearts?'

I swallow. 'I don't know. Look, I get that it was hard for you Mum. I really do. Being left to deal with everything must have been awful, but surely it would have been better at some point to tell us the truth? At least we would have known he didn't leave us out of choice. As it is I've spent my entire life staring at pilots in the airport, scanning their faces for family resemblances. I haven't even been to Australia because I thought it had too many unpleasant associations.' I wail, as these side effects of the whole situation occur to me.

'I'm sorry, all right,' says Mum, sounding more angry than sorry. 'But I was ashamed too you know. My husband was a low-life criminal and I put up with it, and turned a blind eye for years. I was still so young when he went down, far younger than you are now,' she adds pointedly. 'And I was heartbroken if you must know. I lost my husband that day, just as you lost a father. He let me down,' she shouts and her voice becomes quite shrill.

'I know,' I reply quietly.

Mum pauses as she tries to find the right words to express what she wants to say. 'Look, the one right thing I did was have you girls, and the day he went, I realised you deserved better than the start you'd had. I wanted better for you. So I started afresh. We were better off without him anyway.'

'Were we?' I stammer. 'Surely that wasn't your decision to make alone? Like it or lump it that man is our dad and if we'd known he was in prison then maybe we could have decided for ourselves whether we wanted him in our lives or not. Don't you think we had a right to that choice?'

'No, I don't actually,' says Mum plainly. 'I had to do what I thought was right, for all of us, and it wasn't flaming well easy I can tell you.'

'Why wasn't it?' I sob. 'I want to know, all of it. I need you to tell me what happened. You owe me that at least.'

Mum looks at me for a while and it's as if the day she's been dreading for so many years has finally arrived. Maybe it's even a relief for her because she doesn't put up any more of a fight. Instead she just tells me everything. And for once, I can tell it's the truth.

'When I met Ray, your dad, at school, he was the lad everyone looked up to. He was… what's the word? He was… charismatic. All the girls fancied him,' she says, looking vaguely glassy eyed. 'And when he picked me, when he could have gone out with anybody, I couldn't believe it. But he was a troublemaker Marianne and by the time we'd left school he was already up to no good. Not that I knew quite what a bad crowd he was in with. All I did know was that by seventeen he was one of the only lads who had their own car and that he always had money to take me out. He dressed really nice too, looked after himself. Anyway, I'd got myself a job working for my mate Tracy's mum in her shop, only Ray didn't like me working. He said it was up to him to look after me and I suppose I liked his old-fashioned values in a way. I mean, I liked my job too, but I liked being looked after better. I was probably a bit lazy to tell you the truth.'

She gets up from the breakfast bar at this point and comes to sit down at the table next to me. She swallows hard and I can see it's difficult for her to talk about this time in her life. Or rather how unused to it she is. I remain silent, not wanting to put her off her stride. I'm still so full of mixed emotions but need to hear what she has to say.

'Then I got pregnant. Your dad had just turned eighteen by this point but I was still only seventeen. Anyway, a week after I told him I was expecting he asked me to marry him, at your Nan's house, in his room, and I said yes. It doesn't sound very romantic but actually, at that stage, we were really in love…'

Mum pauses for a second and sniffs before staring into the middle distance.

'You all right?' I ask flatly.

'Yeah, it's just funny talking about it. Seems like a lifetime ago now. Stick the kettle on will you Marianne? I'll have a milky coffee, but use my sweeteners.'

'So what happened then?' I ask, getting up to make her coffee.

'Well my mum, your Nana, was furious that I'd got myself preggy, so I moved into Ray's mum's and it was only really then that I properly realised what sort of people he was mixed up with. He was forever popping out on some business or other but it was obvious he was up to no good. Not that I did anything about it. I knew we'd soon have a mouth to feed, so it was easier to accept the money without asking how he'd got it I suppose.'

'How had he got it?'

'Extortion, burglaries, credit card scams. You name it, he did it. Though he was never involved with drugs. Ever,' she says adamantly, like that made everything else perfectly OK.

I give her her coffee.

'Thanks, lovey,' she says dolefully. 'Anyway, we were all right for a while, happy really. Then, when Hayley was tiny and you were on the way we eventually got our own house off the council. You know, the one in Hackney, and at that point Ray became less discreet about his business than he was when we were living at his mum's. People were always coming round ours at funny times, often in the middle of the night. It used to drive me mad. I'd see cash changing hands but all business conversations used to take place behind closed doors. Ray used to say he'd tell me things on a strictly need to know basis, though I obviously didn't need to know very much because I was permanently in the bleeding dark.' She laughs at this and rolls her eyes with mock frustration as if she were talking about something really silly and trivial as opposed to turning a blind eye to her husband's criminal activity.

She gets up to fetch her biscuit tin and frowns for a second as, upon opening it, she discovers how depleted her supplies are. Still, she must be equally as engrossed in what she's saying because she just takes a biscuit without saying anything.

'Of course, I'd know when he had a *really* big job on because before he'd leave he'd tell me where I could find cash if I needed it. Give me the name of someone I could go to if I needed help and that. I used to hate it when he got like that though. I wouldn't sleep a wink, wondering whether he was ever coming back, but he always did, and he'd always have a nice present for me and something for you girls.'

I must give her a disapproving look because she suddenly looks quite shame-faced. 'I know I know, but like I said, I was young and by this point I was bringing up *two* little girls and besides, he was my man Marianne. It wasn't my place to question. I mean, I should have done, I know that now, but at the time it just wasn't the way people like us operated. Anyway, when you were four and Hayley must have been six, there came a night when things didn't go to plan. Your dad had something big on. I knew it was big because he was all jittery for weeks and I couldn't say anything right. I remember that night so clearly. Before he left I told him I had a bad feeling but he wouldn't talk to me or tell me anything. You know how I'm a bit psychic don't you?'

I frown. I don't. She's not.

'Anyway, this time your dad didn't come home for a week. Longest week of my life that was and when he did come back he was a changed man. He told me he was wanted by the police and that things had gone seriously wrong.'

Mum looks away, as if the end of the story is going to tell itself.

'Go on,' I say frustratedly.

She stares mournfully into her coffee. 'He'd been paid to arson a warehouse by someone so that they could claim on the insurance. Though normally he wouldn't have done a job like that himself, or at least that's what he told me after, but he owed a bloke a favour you see and he was the sort of bloke you didn't muck about, so… Anyway, it all went wrong. Ray thought the security guard had left the building to patrol the grounds, but he hadn't. He'd gone back in, though to this day no one knows why. Maybe he'd heard the phone ringing? Or needed the loo? Or fancied taking his thermos flask with him? Something like that.'

I experience a wave of sympathy for Mum. I can tell she's been wondering these things for years.

'That poor, poor man died in the blaze,' she says sadly. 'So suddenly your dad was on the run for murder. But they got him in the end of course.'

'He's back.'

'What do you mean?' she says, looking up sharply and I feel bad for blurting it out but know it's the only way I'm ever going to get the words out.

'He's back,' I repeat.

'Back where?'

This could go on.

'I saw him, Mum.'

'Where? Where did you see him? In the street?'

I hesitate. Judging by her appalled face it might be better to lie at this juncture. 'Yeah… in the street.'

'Did he see you?'

'Er… yeah.'

'What did he say? You didn't tell him where you lived did you?'

'Um no. He er… he got out… years ago.'

'I know,' says Mum, still looking deeply agitated about the fact I've seen him.

'He's ill Mum.'

'Good,' she says.

'That's not very nice,' I retort. 'He hasn't got a cold you know. He's really ill.'

'I said good!' she shouts, and her voice wobbles dangerously. 'As far as I'm concerned he's dead to me and I don't want you having anything to do with him Marianne, do you hear me?'

I hear her all right but I can't believe what she's saying. She can't tell me how to deal with this. I need to work out for myself what I'm going to do. As a grown woman. I can understand *her* not wanting to see him, but she can't decide what's right for me any more. In fact her reaction now is merely pushing me towards seeing him again. First though, Hayley needs to know what's going on. I know that now. It will stress her out more if she finds out at a later date that I've seen him and didn't tell her. It should be up to her to decide whether she wants to talk to him, even if it's just to have a go at him or to ask him things she wants to know. After all, she's carrying his grandchild and there's a chance Ray might still be around when it's born. I get to my feet.

'Where are you going?' Mum asks nervously.

'Nowhere, just out for a bit.'

'But we need to talk. I need to know you're not going to do anything stupid, Marianne. If your dad bumped into you that wouldn't have been a coincidence. You need to be careful and you have to promise me you won't see him. I don't want Martin worrying about this.'

'I can't promise I won't see him Mum, but you don't need to worry about Martin. I won't say anything,' I say, picking up the car keys from the hook where we keep them.

'Tell me where you're going. Why are you taking Tina?'

'I'm popping to the shops,' I lie.

This seems to appease her. 'Right, well I'll see you later then. Are you here for your tea?'

I nod.

'Great, we'll all eat it together,' she says slightly manically, as if our previous conversation never even happened. She stands up, brushing crumbs from her biscuit off her and taking her mug to the sink. 'Chicken Kievs I'm doing with jacket spuds. Then we can talk about what song Hayley should do for *Sing for Britain*. I know she blew up the other day but once she's had a chance to cool off I'm sure she'll come round. Besides, doing the show preggy would make a really interesting story for the viewer. It would be different anyway, wouldn't it?'

I do a double take. Is she serious? I think she is. Do you see what I mean now? Actually insane.

CHAPTER SEVEN

Hayley and Gary live at the end of a cul-de-sac, a few miles from us in Chingford. The entire house is decorated in various shades of white and when we were all invited round after it was finished Hayley got really cross with us for not being able to tell the difference between the apple white she'd painted the hall and the hessian white she'd painted the lounge. It just all looks white but, according to her, the difference should be as obvious as if she'd painted one room blue and one orange. Her carpet is also an off-white and her curtains are a pale shade of something anaemic too. As a result it's one of the least comfortable houses to be in because you're terrified to touch anything in case you sully it somehow. Even her sofa, a new purchase as of the Boxing Day sales, is white. Martin's terribly jealous of her white leather suite because he hadn't spotted it for himself. His obsession with boring shops is seasonal, you see. During the summer months it's all about Homebase, but come winter and the Boxing Day sales, the second DFS and Land of Leather have flung open their doors, he's there. In fact, this moment is probably the most meaningful and spiritual part of Christmas for Martin. Consequently, as a family, we're always first in the queue at one or other of these places, no matter what the weather. No one except me ever questioning the fact we're standing there shivering, when we could be at home eating leftovers and watching telly. Is it any wonder I like travelling so much?

Partially due to the lightness of their carpets, Hayley and Gary are obsessed with people taking their shoes off when they enter their domain too, which is fair enough. Like most people I appreciate that the thought of dirt from the street being trampled into your carpet isn't that nice, but they are ridiculously anal about it. To the point where I honestly think if there was a fire in the house and Hayley was stuck inside, she'd insist on the firemen taking their boots off before coming in to save her.

Gary's just as OCD as she is though. His clothes are always immaculately ironed and their bed never looks as though anyone's slept in it. I love the thought of a child coming along to shake things up in Evans Towers, though I'll have to take it on special outings to dirty places in order to build up its immune system. I'll scout out really grubby church halls and play areas, then set the child free to eat stuff off the floor and chew on grimy toys, like babies are supposed to.

I ring the bell, my mind back on the task in hand. When the door opens Gary's standing there looking as Neanderthal as ever.

'All right sexy, to what do I owe this pleasure?' he says, eyeing me up and down. His voice too high pitched for one so muscular.

'Is Hayley in?'

'No, she's getting her nails done. You're lucky you caught me. I just came home to pick up some paperwork to take back to the garage. Come in and wait if you like.'

I hesitate. Did I really want to sit and make small talk with Gary? Then again, what I had to tell Hayley couldn't exactly wait.

I shrug and my foot's only halfway over the threshold when Gary says 'Your…'

'Shoes, I know, don't worry,' I finish for him.

My heart sinks. Damn, I'm wearing my knee-length black boots, which don't have a zip. Getting them on is relatively easy, you just sort of pull them on and heave them into position, like adjusting a pair of support tights. Getting them off is another matter though. In the end I have no choice but to sit spread-eagled on the floor and prise them off with the other foot, going red-faced from exertion. This isn't an approach I feel particularly comfortable taking while Gary's standing over me, but finally they're off. As I pull myself back to standing, I feel like I've had a workout.

I notice that Gary's own feet are bare, tanned and pedicured. He obviously has regular sun beds. He pads back towards the front room. 'Can I get you a drink while you wait. Squash, Coke Zero, Fanta?'

'No thanks,' I say, settling myself down on the couch, picking a copy of *Grazia* off the coffee table. 'So, congratulations on the baby.'

'Yeah, thanks,' says Gary, looking genuinely chuffed. 'Better be a boy though,' he adds, which ruins any vague sense of warmth I'd just been momentarily feeling towards him.

'Er, why? Have you suddenly turned into a nineteenth-century estate owner who needs a son and heir?'

Gary doesn't answer. He probably doesn't understand what I've said.

'Be nice to have a chip off the old block,' he says 'Though I don't care really.'

'That's good of you.'

'Tell you what I will be pleased about, is getting some action again. Hayley won't let me go near her at the moment. Says she's worried about "hurting the baby".'

'Right,' I mutter, not convinced this is any of my business.

'Still, when you're as well equipped in that department as I am I suppose it could be a problem.'

Stunned, I look up from the fashion pages and stare at him aghast. Did he just say what I think he did? To my horror I realise he probably did because he's staring in the general direction of his horrid crotch, which he's kind of thrusting. Disgusting.

'Gary, please don't be gross. I'll be sick.'

'Don't knock it till you've tried it babes,' he says, at which point I decide it's time to go. Hayley will just have to wait a bit longer to find out about our dad having returned. I simply cannot cope with Gary and his revolting ways while I've got so much on my mind.

'I'm off,' I say, making a swift exit, which is hindered by the laborious process of getting my stupid boots back on, while Gary stands and watches again, smirking at my obvious discomfort. I'm totally against adult Crocs, unless you're a nurse or medic of any kind, but find myself considering investing in a pair I could use when coming round here, to facilitate swift exits.

'Tell Hayley I called round,' I instruct Gary, who has seriously crossed the line today as far as I'm concerned. Honestly, just because he's gone without for a few weeks. I shudder with revulsion.

'I'll tell her babe,' he says, cretinous face leering at me.

Back in the car I wonder what to do. I feel anchorless. I can't think of anything but what's happened and the thought of going into work tomorrow and acting like everything's normal – which I'm going to have to do – fills me with dread.

Right, there's probably only one thing to do and there's no point delaying it further, given that I've been waiting my whole life for it. I scrabble around in the pocket of my skirt and produce from it the, by now, very crumpled receipt.

After a few more moments of agonising, I take a deep

breath and force Gary and his inappropriate comments
out of my head, knowing that what I'm about to do will
alter the course of my life for ever. It's time. Time to take
control of things, time to make my own decisions. I dial
the number.

CHAPTER EIGHT

Just off Romford High Street, on a narrow side road, there's a small café called 'Ron's' where cab drivers tend to congregate, waiting for jobs to be radioed in. This is the designated spot where I am to meet my dad.

When I got back from Hayley's, Mum was deeply suspicious when I said I was going out again and interrogated me for ages, so in order to get her off my back, I told her I was off out to meet Jason. I know I'll have to come clean about what's going on eventually but, today, I just wanted to leave the house with as little fuss as possible.

I've made a bit of an effort with my appearance. I'm wearing a floral tea dress and a little jacket. I've also plastered on the make-up. In many ways I hate Ray for everything he's done and yet I still want his approval and for him to see me looking nice. This is too confusing to analyse at any great length, plus if I stop to think about everything for too long, my head's probably in danger of exploding.

As I sit on the bus – Mum needs Tina tonight – I try to read a newspaper that someone's left on the seat next to me but can't concentrate on the words. I'm nervous, really nervous, about seeing Ray, but also strangely excited. It's weird. Despite what he's put us through, I don't think I could contemplate not trying to get to know him. Of course, the fact he's so ill has acted as a pretty strong catalyst for me, in terms of making my mind up. It's not like I have the choice of making him sweat for a few months before agreeing to see him. Though, with regard to that, I'm starting to wonder whether maybe he's exaggerated his illness a bit, in order to get my sympathy. It would be rather a sick thing to do but given that I'm on my way to meet him now, effective too. My doubts stem from the fact that he looks like such a big strong man. Not one who'll be going anywhere any time soon.

After a fifteen-minute bus journey and a short walk along the high road, I shove open the door to the café, which was his suggestion for our designated meeting spot. It's very full.

I'm the first to arrive and manage to nab the only free table left. I feel a bit like a rose among thorns. Grizzled cabbies surround me chatting away, drinking their tea and eating fried food. Still, it's as good a place as any for our meeting, plus nobody I know is in any danger of popping in. I sit for ten minutes, but don't mind. I'm early and on the dot of quarter to eight, which is the time we'd arranged to meet, Ray appears.

I smile nervously and half get out of my seat, hovering

as I wave in his direction. Once he's spotted me I sit back down again, awkward and clunky, unsure of how to be.

'Hi,' I say shyly as he approaches.

'All right,' he says, looking relieved to see me and just as nervous. 'Do you want a cup of coffee or something?'

I nod even though I don't really want a coffee. I hate coffee.

The café's lighting is stark to say the least. It's perfect for this situation though because I'm fully intent on sussing Ray out as much as possible. As he places two cups of coffee on the table I scrutinise his face.

'You trying to see whether I'm really ill?' he asks gently.

I'm startled. Had I been that obvious?

'It's all right, I do it myself,' he says. 'But just so you know, I am. That ill I mean, and shit as it may be, that ain't gonna change.'

'Right,' I say weakly, desperate for more information but not wanting to ask, in case he can't face talking about it. However, Ray seems to pick up on my need to know more about his illness because although at first he looks reluctant about doing so, he starts to tell me.

'Three years ago I was feeling really knackered all the time and then I noticed a bit of blood when I… well, when I went to the toilet and that.'

I nod in order to demonstrate that I know what he's getting at.

'Anyway, long story short, they found out I had cancer of the colon, so I had an operation to remove half of it. After that they blasted me with chemo and radiotherapy and for a long time I was good as gold. Until a couple of weeks ago when during one of my check-ups they discovered it was back, only this time it's spread,' he says plainly, conveying the facts precisely as they are, so there can be no confusion on my part. 'It's on my liver and in my lymph and there ain't much they can do about it. There are things they can do to help but they can't cure it no more,' he says, needing me to get it, needing me to be very clear on the subject. He was going to die.

It's so horrendous and I wish more than anything that he'd got in touch years ago. Not at this stage, when death's hanging over everything. So much wasted time, and sad that it took something this drastic to galvanise him into action.

'You've still got your hair,' I remark cautiously.

'Well, chemo was a while ago now but also not all types of chemo make your hair fall out anyway. It depends on the drugs they give you, which are all tailored to the individual. I got lucky,' he adds wryly.

'I'm sorry, I suppose it's just that you seem… all right,' I whisper apologetically, because as much as I know he needs me to accept what he's just told me, I'm having real trouble digesting it as fact.

'I am all right,' he says, nodding in agreement. 'I really am at the moment. In fact, ever since I got my head round the fact that there weren't no more they could do, I've felt positively good. I get a bit tired and that, sometimes have trouble sleeping, but you know…' he trailed off.

I can't bear it. It must be so frightening knowing what pain lies in wait. I can feel terror advancing on me like an army just thinking about it. The certainty of the end is something surely we're not really programmed to deal with.

'What about America? They probably have more advanced medicine over there don't they?' I say, clutching at straws.

'A bit,' he agrees, smiling ruefully. 'But they don't perform miracles, which is what I'd need.'

We both concentrate on our coffees for a while until he says gruffly, 'Nice that you seem to care a bit though.'

I shrug, not sure what I feel really. I mean, if anyone told me they were dying I'd feel sad. It is sad. Tragic in fact. The fact he's my father makes it even more poignant than if he were some stranger of course, and yet that's still kind of what he is to me. What do I really know about him after all?

I decide to swerve this potentially thorny subject and instead ask something I'm curious about more than anything. 'So, while you've been going through all of this, who've you been with? Are you married? Do you have kids?' My tone is deliberately light but I can't look at him as I ask this. It's something I've been fretting about all day, knowing that the answer could change my life all over again.

'No. I never re-married. I was in prison such a long

time and I guess… I don't know really. I guess it wasn't something I went looking for again.'

'What about friends?' I ask, allowing myself to breathe. I'm relieved there aren't lots of relatives in the background if I'm honest. But at the same time don't like the idea that he's been through all of this on his own. It seems too horrific.

'Yeah, I've got "friends",' he says, seemingly mildly amused by my line of questioning. 'I've got some good old mates and the people at the hospital have been amazing too. I've had a lot of support and of course there's my key worker who's been there every step of the way.'

I must look non-plussed because he goes on to explain.

'You get assigned a key worker when you find out you've got cancer. They're basically a nurse who makes sure you're dealing with everything all right, keeps an eye on you. Mine's called Matt. He's a top bloke as it goes.'

I don't know why I'm surprised his key worker's a man. I'm pleased he's got someone looking out for him though. Equally I feel saddened and angry because if only he'd thought to find us years ago maybe some of that support could have come from me, his own flesh and blood.

'Anyway, I didn't come here to talk about all of that,' says Ray, determinedly upbeat all of a sudden. 'I want to know about you Marianne. Tell me everything. What you like, what you don't like. Have you got a boyfriend?'

I shake my head and stare fixedly into my coffee, which I still haven't touched.

'I'm surprised, you're a pretty girl.'

I blush flame red at this.

'You should see Hayley. She's the pretty one out of the two of us,' I mutter.

Ray suddenly looks a bit sheepish and I guess then that he probably has seen her. I don't ask. It's all quite unnerving.

'So how come you're still living with your mother then? I would have thought you'd have wanted your own place by now. What are you now? Thirty-one?'

I nod. 'Let's just say it's not really out of choice.'

'Oh. Right.'

There's a long silence, which I'm probably expected to fill, but don't. Eventually he says, 'So, you're single, living with your mum, anything else? What do you do? What makes you, you?'

I shrug. I know I'm being very wooden but in reality I don't know whether I'm ready to have such a personal chat yet. I'm here for answers, not for a heart to heart.

'Are you gonna help me out a bit here or what?' jokes Ray nervously.

'Sorry,' I say. 'It's not that I don't want to tell you about myself, it's just… there's not really a huge amount to say.' I sigh heavily before eventually giving in. 'I'm a hairdresser, I live at home because I can't afford to move out and I'm sort of seeing someone but it's extremely early days. That's about it really,' I mumble, uncomfortable in this odd, interview-like scenario. Doubts over my ability to cope with the situation are creeping in. There's just so much to absorb and it's all so… strange.

'So you are seeing someone then?' says Ray, leaping on this titbit of information, eager to engage in more of a two-way conversation and displaying over-the-top levels of interest as a result.

'Well, sort of. I met an Australian guy in Thailand and hopefully he's coming to London soon.'

'An Aussie, eh,' he says in a tone that irritates me. It's ever so slightly mocking. 'And Thailand, when did you go there then?'

'Last year. That's kind of what I do. I travel. Then, when I've run out of money, I come home, work again… at the salon, then I save up until I have enough to go off again.'

'Right,' says Ray, still nodding, only I can't help but notice, he looks a bit bemused.

'What?' I say, feeling defensive.

'No nothing. It's just… you know, I've never really heard of anyone describing "going on holiday" as what they do.'

There's so much I could say back to this. I have to sort of wrinkle my entire face in an effort not to reply back too forcibly, though what I say still packs a bit of a punch. 'Well, it's probably more worthwhile than spending half your life in prison.'

'Fair point,' Ray agrees, fists planted squarely on the table. He's wearing the same black leather coat he was wearing the other day and his shoulders are so broad in it, he's practically the same width as the table. He's slim though. Despite his big build he certainly couldn't be described as a fat bloke. He's just very tall. He's wearing a gold cygnet ring on the little finger of his right hand and everything about his presence is big, in a way that could be reassuring or menacing, depending on how you viewed him I suppose.

Another silence follows, one that definitely couldn't be described as comfortable. Feeling deflated I start fiddling with the packets of sugar that are on the table in an aluminium pot. I realise in that moment that I want so much from this man, want him to *be* so much, the reality can't possibly measure up. Then he says, 'You like your music then?'

I nod, feeling immediately defensive and inexplicably like I might be about to cry. This is so much harder than I thought it would be. I swallow hard and stare at the table.

'You play beautiful. When I was outside your house that night and I heard you playing, I couldn't believe it. That's why I was surprised when you said what you did. With that talent I thought you must be a music teacher or something. In fact I don't know why you don't use it. You must be professional orchestra standard.'

Still feeling borderline tearful, I give him a watery smile and reply quietly, 'Nowhere near.'

'Blimey,' he says, in a way that suggests he doesn't get how much better I could be.

'What would you know anyway?' I ask lightly, determined not to let my emotions get the better of me. 'I don't remember you and Mum exactly being into classical music. In fact the only thing I can vaguely remember is you and her singing that Lionel Richie tune all the time. Was it *Dancing on The Ceiling*?'

'You remember that?'

'Sort of. Dunno. Maybe Hayley told me. But whatever. It reminds me of you when I hear it.'

He laughs and the atmosphere lightens. 'Wow, I can't believe you remember that. And you're right, your Mum was obsessed with that song. Funny,' he says looking wistful. 'I'd forgotten about that. Anyway I get what you're saying Marianne, not that there's anything wrong with that tune mind, gotta love a bit of Lionel, but I learnt about a few things in prison as it goes. Educated myself a bit. You've got to make the time pass somehow.'

'Was it awful?'

'It weren't no picnic,' he says frankly. 'There are some nasty characters in there and if you want to survive you have to keep your head down, making sure at the same time that people know not to mess with you. That's something you have to make very clear from the very beginning, or you're stuffed.'

I'm not going to ask how he achieved this but clearly he did.

'Anyway, I figured I might as well try and learn a bit while I was in there, you know? I'd never taken much notice of anything they taught me at school and that didn't get me very far so I figured seeing as I was going to be there so long I might as well not waste the time completely. So I read books about things and looked at things, like religion and that.'

I'm impressed. And surprised.

'I also got quite into that sort of music, if you must know. I don't think I'd ever really heard classical music before I went to prison but I love it as it goes. I'm a Bach man myself. I mean him and Mozart obviously but then who don't like Mozart?'

I shrug, hardly able to believe what I'm hearing. It's quite moving. This is the first time anyone I'm related to has professed even the slightest bit of interest in the thing I love more than anything in the world. In ten minutes of knowing him, I already feel like I might have more in common with him than my mum. This thought is so disloyal it almost hurts to think it, but it's true. My dad likes classical music. Furthermore, he's someone who seems open to discovering and discussing more than just the same old things, the same old routine stuff. I look at Ray and there's so much I want to say to him in that instance but can't even begin to find the words.

'So what level you at then?' he asks. 'With the violin?'

'Well I passed grade ten when I was sixteen and have continued studying it ever since. I also took Music at A level and got an A. I play the piano a bit, too.'

He nods, looking genuinely impressed. 'Good for you girl. That's… you know… that's really special.'

'Thanks,' I say, not used to discussing my music or in

anyone showing any interest. The whole paternal pride thing's a bit of a novelty too. I know he means well but it feels a bit unnatural. Makes me feel self-conscious more than anything else really. I'm just not sure he has the right.

'So give me an example. I mean do you reckon you could play something like Mozart's Concerto No. 5?'

'Oh yeah,' I answer confidently.

'Blimey,' he says, looking quite in awe of this and shaking his head. His gaze is drawn to my hands, which are still fiddling with a packet of sugar.

'May I?' he asks, gesturing that he wants to have a look.

'Er, sure,' I say doubtfully, feeling strangely nervous as he reaches for my hand and turns it over.

'Well, look at that,' he says, commenting on the calloused fingertips of my left hand.

'You think that's bad, look at the thumb on my bow hand,' I say, proffering it for him to examine.

'Does it hurt?'

'No, not at all, they've been toughened up. I won't ever be asked to do any hand modelling but…' I shrug, pulling my hands away again. Reality has suddenly crept in again. The minute he crosses a certain line and is too friendly I remember what he's done and how much pain he's caused me.

'I told Mum you were out of prison by the way.' I say this knowing full well it will break the spell. He can't think he can just appear out of the blue and that everything will be normal straight away. It can't be. It isn't.

'Oh right,' he says, his face clouding over. 'What did she have to say, then?'

'She doesn't want me seeing you.'

'Well, that figures,' he says, his expression darkening, at which point I can see how frightening he might appear if he was angry.

'The minute I went inside it was like I was dead to her. Do you know she only visited once, and that was to tell me to stay away.'

In that moment, hearing that, I experience a pang of intense anger towards my mother. I know she had her reasons and I'm not saying that what Ray did was right. I mean, obviously it wasn't. It was horrendous and had unspeakably tragic consequences but to have cut herself off from him in the way she did seems so clinical and cold. She knew full well what he was like and what he was up to when she was living with him, so why abandon him altogether?

'So what did Hayley say?' he says, interrupting my dark thoughts. 'Did she say when I can see her?'

'Um yeah but she's just not sure when,' I reply quickly, reluctant to tell him that if my instinct's correct it won't be a case of when, but if. Still, I'll be doing my damn best to try and make it happen. Ray's our dad and I'm starting to care less and less about what he's done, and more and more about the fact that he's here now, albeit a bit late, but here nonetheless. Just not for long.

CHAPTER NINE

A few days later, for the second time this week, I find myself sitting outside Hayley's house. Only this time I called first to make sure she was going to be in. I sit listening to Capital Radio for a bit, summoning up the courage required for the task ahead. I'm tired. I made it into work today but it felt like the longest day ever. Jason was in a right strop with me. I've got so much on my mind that I forgot that, as far as he was concerned, I'd been ill. As a result, when he enquired after my health I looked totally vague at which point he guessed that I'd been lying. He then proceeded to pester me all day about what I'd really been doing, only I didn't feel like explaining things to him just yet. In the salon with everybody ear-wigging didn't feel like the right time or place, but he took my refusal to answer very personally and it had him questioning our friendship and whether or not I trusted him. Frankly it was the last thing I needed. I've got enough on my plate without putting up with his moods, too. It was a relief to escape.

Right, it's time. I can't put it off any longer. Hayley has

a right to know what's going on and I just hope she doesn't shoot the messenger.

I ring the bell and start taking off my ballet flats – purposefully selected for the occasion – as she answers the door.

'All right,' says Hayley, who's wearing a candy pink tracksuit. Her stomach still looks completely flat I notice, but her boobs are huge.

'Your boobs have grown.'

'I know, they're massive aren't they.'

'Shame she won't let me play with them,' shouts a familiar voice through from the lounge. 'What's the point of having tits like that if I'm not allowed to go anywhere near them?'

My heart sinks.

'Don't mind me,' he leers, strolling into the hall looking coiffed and sporting his spangliest t-shirt yet. 'I'm off out with the boys. Don't wait up babes,' he says to Hayley, before kissing her on the cheek and patting her playfully on the bum.

'I won't. Have fun but don't get too pissed. I can't stand the smell of booze at the moment.'

Gary catches my eye and mimics her nagging to me. It's not done with any affection though, so I ignore him. As he swaggers out I notice Hayley retch slightly. I don't blame her. Gary has left a literal cloud of aftershave behind him. I feel like retching myself.

'What do you want then?' says Hayley once Gary's

gone and we've heard the souped-up engine of his BMW 3 Series revving down the cul-de-sac, doing its best to announce to the world what an idiot he is.

'Because if Mum's sent you here on a mission to nag me about *Sing for Britain*, you can cock off.'

'She hasn't,' I say, wishing Hayley didn't have to be so aggressive all the time. 'I've come because I need to tell you something.'

'What?' says Hayley, padding through to the lounge and sinking into the squeaky, white settee. She tucks her feet prettily underneath her.

'Well, this might come as a bit of a shock,' I say, trying to cushion the blow. I don't want my alarming news to affect the baby in any way. 'Our dad, our real dad, isn't in Australia.'

Hayley looks me straight in the eye. 'You don't say,' she says drily.

'No, he really isn't,' I insist, assuming she doesn't believe me. 'I know it sounds like a wind-up but he's here.'

'Right,' she says, not looking even mildly interested.

'You don't look surprised,' I say, wondering why the hell she doesn't.

'Oh Marianne, you didn't believe all that shit about him being a pilot did you?'

I nod dumbly. Why would I not have?

'You didn't then I take it?' I ask hesitantly, feeling betrayed yet again. Wasn't anyone around here ever straight with me about anything?

Hayley shrugs. 'So where's the scumbag been all this time then?'

'He was in prison.'

'Figures,' she says, pretending to examine one of her acrylic nails though I can tell this piece of news has had an impact.

'Yeah, but he's out. In fact he got out eight years ago,' I say, almost wincing as I say it.

'Eight years ago,' she exclaims looking just as outraged as I had when I found out, which is quite comforting somehow. It feels incredibly important that Hayley and I are on the same page about all of this to at least some extent.

'Yeah I know,' I say. 'That's how I felt when I heard.'

'I half-expected him to be in prison, or something like that,' says Hayley angrily. 'Whenever Mum mentioned him and told people all that crap about him fucking off to Australia, I could tell it was bullshit. I could tell something had happened that she was too ashamed to tell the neighbours about. But why didn't the bastard come and see us as soon as he got out? And anyway, how do you know all this?'

'Because I saw him.'

At last Hayley looks satisfyingly flummoxed. 'When?'

'Last Sunday. Don't tell Mum, but he came to the house.'

'Cheeky bastard,' says Hayley rolling her eyes, which are suddenly looking a bit tearful, heavenward. She looks like she's struggling to keep her emotions intact so I reach over to take her hand. However, the minute my hand makes contact with hers, she pulls hers away. 'This family,' she snaps. 'Always a bloody drama. Anyway, I need something to drink. Do you want a Coke?' she says, stomping off to the kitchen.

'No thanks,' I call after her. It seems so sad that Hayley feels unable, or just *is* unable, to display any emotion in front of me whatsoever. Like it's a sign of weakness.

Minutes later she returns looking completely composed, though tellingly there's no sign of any drink.

'Are you free next Wednesday?' she says as she sits back down.

'Oh, er... yeah,' I say, not wanting her to change the subject that still needs so much discussion as far as I'm concerned. 'Wednesday's my day off. Why?'

'I've got my scan and Gary has to work so I need some-one to come with me.'

There was never going to be any 'I would like you to come with me' or 'please would you' but the fact that Hayley is even asking me to go with her is amazing. I feel unbelievably chuffed, and excited actually, about seeing the baby. I also feel disconcerted by her attempt to ignore the fact that our dad has reappeared in our lives, but with Hayley you have to take the nice moments when you can.

'Oh my god. That would be amazing. I'd love to come. Thanks Hayley.'

For three whole seconds Hayley indulges herself and allows her face to express a bit of excitement.

'Have you thought of any names?'

'Well, if it's a girl, I like Sarah,' she offers, immediately looking at me anxiously as if worried what I might think of that.

I nod encouragingly. 'Lovely name.'

'Gary likes Daisy or Lola, but I want something traditional.'

'And if it's a boy?'

'Gary likes Gary Junior,' she says, frowning at this prospect. I'm amazed. Usually she's scarily loyal and won't allow even a gentle piss-take of her spouse. 'But I like the name Billy.'

'Gorgeous,' I say. 'Well, Billy or Sarah, hello in there,' I add in the direction of her tummy.

Anyway, I suppose you'd better tell me what Ray said to you,' she says, taking the conversation by the scruff of the neck and shoving it back in its original direction. This is how chats with Hayley tend to go. They can leave you feeling quite seasick.

'It's not good Hayley. He went to prison for manslaughter. He killed someone by mistake when he committed arson.'

Hayley's scornful face says it all.

'I know. It is unreal. Awful. I was so freaked out when I found out. But I'm afraid it gets even more complicated. You see, he's come back to find us now because, actually I really don't know how to tell you this, but he's not well.'

'And?'

'No seriously, he's really not well. He's got cancer.'

'Good.'

I'm shocked to hear Mum's harsh sentiments echoed. It upsets me. 'Don't be like that. He's got it really bad. In fact, he's been told he's only got six months.' I pause in order to let her digest this, but although her eyes are glistening slightly, her expression doesn't really change.

'He wants to know when he can see you,' I continue. 'I said I would sort it out. I know what he's done in the past is horrendous and I'm angry too but he doesn't want to die without getting to know his daughters first,' I add, rubbing in the urgency of his plight, in case it hasn't registered already.

'Well he should have thought of that before,' Hayley says and then I know I'm in for a fight.

'How can you be so callous?' I ask. It amazes me how the minute Hayley shows a bit of humanity she always has to ruin it the next by being so cold. 'If you don't see him, you'll regret it one day and then how will you live with yourself?'

'How will I live with *myself*?' rages Hayley, and her pupils dilate into tiny specks in her blue eyes. 'How can he live with *himself* is more like it? Look Marianne, if you want to be a fucking mug your whole life, that's fine, go ahead, but I am not going to waste my time seeing a low-life scumbag just because science says he's my dad. I don't have a dad,' she says, and I feel a chill run up my spine. I'm unnerved by her words. Maybe I am a mug? I don't know, I'm just going on my instincts at the moment.

'Fine,' I say in a low voice. I don't want to antagonise her any more than is necessary given her state.

I get up and go to see myself out.

'I'll see you next Wednesday,' she says, an instruction not a request.

'Fine,' I repeat. 'What time?'

'Scan's at ten-thirty so we need to leave at nine-forty-five. I want to get there early.'

I nod, slip my shoes on and leave.

CHAPTER TEN

The next few days settle down into a version of normal. I go to work and, when I'm not at work, I practise the violin as much as is possible. Normally, when I'm not travelling, I try to have weekly lessons, but my teacher's on holiday at the moment. She's given me plenty of homework though, which mainly consists of studying Bach's solo Sonata and a couple of other pieces. Practising is the one thing always guaranteed to level me out and calm me down, or at least it is when Mum's not yelling at me to 'Put a bloody sock in it'. Meanwhile, Mum tries to make things up with Hayley by going round to her place with the Next directory, so they can look at baby clothes together and investigate cots and prams and so on. By managing not to mention *Sing for Britain* Hayley slowly starts to forgive her.

What isn't normal by any means is the fact that if I want to speak to my dad, all I have to do is pick up the phone and dial a number. My feelings continue to oscillate between being livid with him one minute and desperate to see him the next. Strictly speaking I know I should be as furious with him as Hayley is but for many, many reasons, my anger is superseded by wanting to enjoy the fact that I actually have a father to get to know. Being totally honest with myself, I don't care what the wrongs or the rights of the situation are and so it is that slowly but surely I start making contact with him more and more frequently. He understands the situation and lets me take things at my own pace. He also knows how to handle it when the anger takes over once again and I start being horrible to him. When this happens he just backs off until I've got it out of my system and am prepared to be civil again.

I feel quite reckless and still haven't got round to telling Mum anything about my secret rendezvous or my conversations with him. I know what her reaction will be when I do though, which I do appreciate. I still think she should have been honest with us but at the end of the day she's the one who bothered sticking around in order to raise us. But for now I'm taking a leaf out of her book and taking the easy option because I don't want anyone shattering the bubble I'm in.

The only thing I'm not relishing is what to say every time Ray enquires about Hayley. He keeps asking when she'll be ready to see him, though I think without me having to say too much he appreciates what the situation really is.

*

Then, on the Wednesday morning I'm due to pick Hayley up for her scan, I get yet another bolt out of the blue.

Since Ray's reappeared in my life I've forgotten about Andy, so typically, now I'm not thinking about him constantly, he phones.

'Hello stranger,' I say, once I realise it's him. This is such a corny thing to say I immediately want to rewind time and say something less ridiculous but thankfully he doesn't pick me up on it.

'Hey,' he says, his familiar laid-back drawl instantly reminding me of happy times and incredible nights. 'What have you been up to?'

'Oh you know, this and that,' I reply, not wanting to elaborate on the phone. *Catching up with my long-lost father who I thought was in Australia but has actually been in prison for manslaughter, but is now dying of cancer,* just doesn't seem like telephone conversation material somehow. 'It's so nice to hear your voice. Where are you? What have you been up to?'

'I'm in Rome, having a blast,' he says. 'But listen, I'm nearly done here so I reckon next on my list of places to see has to be London. I guess I've been saving the best till last because I want to see you Marianne, I've missed you.'

'Oh, me too,' I say, my voice catching. I'm so excited.

'So I'm going to book my flight for Friday.'

Friday? Jesus, talk about short notice, though thinking about it, compared to how spontaneous we were when travelling round the islands, this is major forward planning. However there's so much going on at the moment, I worry that I might not be quite ready to see him in a mere couple of days' time.

'Oh fantastic,' I rally; not wanting to pour cold water on the news I've been waiting for for ages. I can hardly believe he's finally coming. 'That's great, though just to warn you, we're having the crappest April ever. It's rained nearly every day this month.'

'Bit of rain doesn't bother me. It's not been much better here to tell you the truth.'

'So where are you going to stay?'

'Well, that's the bit I was getting to. I was wondering if I might be able to crash at yours for a bit? You know, just till I get myself sorted.'

'Oh.' I hadn't expected that. 'Well I'll have to check with my mum. You remember that I live with her, right?'

'Yeah, but hey, that's all right, I'm good at charming mothers.'

I grin, thinking of his brown, strong body. I bet he is, but I still have my reservations. Somehow it's hard to picture him sitting in Mum's house on the royal blue sofa watching TV, a plate of one of Mum's dinners on his lap. It'll change the dynamic of our relationship completely.

'But you know we live in Chigwell, which is outside the centre of London? So you wouldn't be anywhere near all the tourist spots or sights, so I wouldn't be insulted at all if you wanted to stay somewhere a bit more interesting.'

'The only sight I want to see is you,' he says.

My heart melts. 'Really?'

'Yeah, I've missed you heaps Marianne, and I think about you all the time.'

'You do?'

'Course.'

I grin daftly down the phone.

'Do you think about me?'

'Oh yes, I do,' I say with a start. I'm happy and yet for some reason this whole chat is feeling surreal, though I don't know why. After all, this is exactly what I've longed for. 'Look,' I say eventually, 'I'll have to talk to my mum but I'll email you straight away and let you know what she says.'

'You're the best,' he says.

Five minutes later, I put down the phone feeling a mixture of things. I'm flattered and pleased by how much he's obviously missing me, but a bit fluttery with nerves too about the whole 'him coming to stay with us' situation. Still, I shove these doubts away. After all, this is Andy, who I spent every minute of every day with for months, during which time we didn't row even once. So what could go wrong? It'll be so great to see him and what else had I expected? He's a traveller who'd never be able to afford London hotel prices. I was being inhospitable. Besides, who knows? If things go well between us, maybe I'll even end up going back to Australia with him eventually. Briefly I wonder what Ray would make of him, but it's a thought too far, so I focus my attention back to what today holds.

For today is the day Hayley gets to see her baby for the

first time and I, Aunty Marianne, am going to be there too, due to an amazing lack of interest from the father.

In fact, Gary's absence from today's scan is bothering me so much, that this is one of the first things I say to Hayley after I've picked her up in Tina.

'So how come Gary doesn't want to be at the scan again?'

'He does want to be there,' says Hayley, sounding very defensive. 'But he's got a meeting he can't get out of. He was gutted when he realised there was a clash.'

'But he's his own boss,' I state.

Hayley glares at me.

'What?' I ask innocently.

'Nothing,' she scowls.

'No, go on, what?' I persist. 'I can tell there's something you're annoyed about so you might as well just tell me.'

'Seriously, it's nothing,' Hayley replies before finally letting out a huge defeated sigh. 'It's just… I don't know. Gary's very… traditional and I think he thinks it's a bit weird for men to be at these things. Like he wants to be there for the birth, but he said he's probably going to wait outside if it gets really hardcore.'

'You what?' I laugh, flabbergasted by this new insight into how shallow my brother-in-law is. 'You are joking aren't you? Aren't they supposed to be there for you *because* it might get hardcore and you might want them to be around to comfort you?'

Hayley shrugs, refusing to look at me. 'I don't know. It is a bit weird… but maybe he's right. Loads of people say it ruins their sex life once their man has seen them in that state.'

I despair. 'Well he should stay up your end then.'

'That's what I said,' agrees Hayley, but then she checks herself. 'Anyway, it doesn't matter, I don't know why I'm even thinking about all that now. Need to make sure the baby's all right first.'

'Course it will be,' I reply. Then, to change the subject I add, 'Hey you'll never guess who's coming to London in a couple of days?'

Hayley stares blankly out of the window, not looking remotely interested.

'Andy from Thailand.'

'Oh. That'll be weird, won't it?'

'No,' I say, feeling annoyed. By this point we're approaching the hospital so I drop Hayley off and go to park, which takes about forty minutes – Hayley's insistence on leaving so early was wise. By the time I find Hayley again, sitting in the waiting room of the antenatal department, flicking distractedly through a seven-year-old copy of *Take a Break* magazine, it's already time for her appointment, but they're running late.

I can tell Hayley's nervous, which is probably entirely natural. I am too in an excited sort of way and am dying for them to call her name so we can get on with it. I feel quite envious of the couples we see coming out, clutching scraps of curly paper that have pictures of their babies on.

Couples who have already had that first glimpse of their little ones.

'Hayley Evans,' calls someone finally.

Hayley and I leap to our feet. 'Thank god for that,' giggles Hayley. 'I'm bloody desperate for the loo.' As she's been instructed to, she's been dutifully glugging back water to make her bladder full, which will apparently help see the baby more easily. I imagine it floating around, doing backstroke on a sea of Evian.

Inside the small scanning room the nurse is blasé and calm, having done this a thousand times or more. We, on the other hand, are positively jittery and at one point Hayley even turns to me and whispers, 'Glad you're here.' I squeeze her hand, too sentimental to reply. My sister can be such an old bag but I love her dearly really.

'This is your first baby, Mrs Evans?' asks the nurse, as she checks Hayley's notes.

'Yeah,' confirms Hayley.

'Well, just hop on the bed if you would, then if you can undo your jeans a bit and pull your top up that would be great.'

Hayley does as she's told and I notice her hands are shaking as she fiddles with her belt.

I smile at her in as reassuring a way as possible and give her a little wink.

'There we are then,' says the nurse in a soothing voice. 'So, I'm just going to put some gel on your tummy, which will feel a bit cold.'

'OK,' says Hayley and my heart goes out to her. She looks so vulnerable and for once there's no hiding how she really feels. This baby means the absolute world to her and it's been so long in coming she'll probably end up spoiling it rotten. It's so exciting I think as a new wave of emotion hits me. I reach for her hand, half-expecting her to bat me away but she has no qualms whatsoever about taking it in hers and gripping it hard.

The nurse finishes squirting gel onto Hayley's tummy and then picks up the device that will see into her belly. She places it on her skin and immediately a shape of some sort can be seen on the screen next to us and a sort of thumping whooshing sound is picked up.

'Oh my god,' cries Hayley 'Did you hear that, Marianne?'

'Yeah,' I nod, grinning.

'That's the heartbeat isn't it?' said Hayley, tears pouring down her face. 'That's my baby. Is it all right? Does it look OK?'

'There it is,' says the nurse, reaching over for some of the hospital tissue that's usually used for wiping gel off stomachs, but handing it to Hayley so she can wipe her face. She's obviously entirely used to dealing with overwhelmed mums.

'Now, just let me have a proper look for a minute and then I'll turn the screen around again.'

'OK,' says Hayley full of sentiment. By now she's squeezing my hand so hard it's starting to hurt, but I don't mind at all. 'Did you see it?' she gushes. 'Did you see it Marianne?'

'I certainly did,' I smile back at her. Then my heart sort of lurches in my chest because suddenly I'm not so sure I like the expression on the nurse's face. I could be wrong but it seems to me that she's looking concerned.

'What?' says Hayley, and I realise that in turn she's scrutinising *my* face, at which point I immediately try to cover up any sign of worry.

'Nothing,' I say brightly, rearranging my expression.

'Why were you looking like that? You looked worried.' To my horror Hayley swivels herself around on the bed so she can stare at the nurse who's still busily moving the camera around Hayley's belly with one hand, while using the other one to tap buttons on the keyboard in front of her. Her face is very concentrated and unfortunately Hayley also seems to pick up on whatever it was that I had, for now I can hear panic in her voice, 'What is it? Tell me, is something wrong?'

The nurse looks at us both but her face is studiously impassive and she seems determined not to give anything away at all. 'I won't be a minute,' she says lightly, turning the screen further towards her so we can no longer see it at all. 'I just want to get the doctor and ask him to check something for me.'

'But what is it?' says Hayley, who is starting to sound a bit hysterical. Not that I'm feeling particularly calm myself.

What the hell was going on? I'm suddenly overcome by a terrifying sensation that I think is probably dread.

'Don't worry,' says the nurse. 'I'll be right back.'

As she heads out the door, Hayley turns to me, looking desperate, 'Please Marianne, make her tell us what's going on. Go and ask her for me.'

So I let go of my sister's hand and rush into the corridor feeling a bit sick and wishing Gary was there. He's an idiot but he's also her husband and should be here supporting her. She needs him, and his absence, given that he'd had the choice, seems so wrong. Especially now it seems things might not be entirely straightforward.

'Excuse me, my sister's just a bit worried. Is everything OK?' I call after the nurse who's already halfway down the corridor.

She turns but merely smiles and nods in a way that tells me precisely nothing before carrying on. It's so frustrating.

'Try not to worry, I'll be back in a minute,' is all she'll say.

The next seven minutes feel like years. Hayley just lies there weeping and I don't know what to say, apart from to try and comfort her with platitudes, which deep down I feel probably aren't true. 'It could all be fine,' I keep saying. 'Maybe she's new and just isn't sure about something? Maybe it's twins?'

This is the one thing I suggest that makes Hayley briefly look quite hopeful to the point where I almost feel sorry

I said it, for of course there are probably so many other reasons the nurse could have gone to get a doctor.

Finally she comes back, with a reassuringly professional looking, middle-aged doctor in tow. I'm glad he isn't really young. Somehow the situation seems to require his age and experience. Still, I tell myself, it could still all be OK. Maybe it *is* twins?

'What is it, doctor?' begs Hayley, who by this stage has got herself into a complete state.

'Let's just have a look and then I'll be able to tell you a bit more,' he says calmly.

His unruffled, kind manner seems to do the trick. Hayley stops crying for the first time since the nurse left the room and as he squirts yet more gel on her belly and starts having a good look at the contents of her tummy for himself, she stays very, very still. He seems to be concentrating on the area almost at the top of her bikini line and at one point is pressing in so hard I can tell Hayley's finding it quite uncomfortable.

'Sorry,' he says but Hayley doesn't reply, clearly too numb with fear. I feel sick and wish there was a chair I could sink onto. I stare hard at the doctor, willing him to look up with a reassuring smile, to tell us everything's OK.

During this whole process however his eyes never leave the screen and only after a good five whole minutes of looking at whatever he's looking at, by which point he's sure of what that is, does he turn to Hayley. Looking directly at her he says softly, 'I'm very sorry to have to tell you this

Mrs Evans, but I'm afraid your baby isn't developing as it should be at this stage.'

I can't bear it. It's just too awful.

Hayley lets out a low moan of distress. Then, looking panicked and utterly broken at the same time she says, 'But… what do you mean? We heard the heartbeat. Didn't we Marianne? So it's alive isn't it? And isn't that what you want at this scan, to hear the heartbeat?'

'It is,' agrees the doctor. 'But unfortunately there are many other things to look at too and I'm afraid it looks like your baby is missing a chromosome.'

'Well can you do something about that?' she says, her voice a broken whisper. 'I don't mind if the baby's disabled or something. I don't care,' she says and dissolves into sobs that rack her whole body. 'I'll love it anyway.'

I can't bear to see my sister in so much pain and by now I'm crying too, silently wishing I could make it all go away. This is beyond a nightmare and so unfair. Why her baby?

The doctor shakes his head and grabs some tissue so he can wipe the gel off her belly. 'I'm afraid, Mrs Evans, that your baby hasn't formed properly at all. In fact, the likelihood of your baby making it to full term is extremely unlikely,' he says gently, yet in a way that offers no window of hope for her to latch on to. 'Even if it did survive the full nine months, which I don't believe it would, it wouldn't live for very long after it had been born. It has a very rare condition. However, what I can tell you is that there's absolutely no reason it should ever happen again in subsequent pregnancies. Though for this baby I can only stress that there really is no hope.'

'So, what are you suggesting?' wails Hayley. 'I don't understand.'

'Well,' says the doctor, 'I would strongly recommend that we book you in for a procedure within the next few days.'

'You mean an abortion?' Hayley whispers, as the total horror of the situation starts to sink in.

My heart drops to my boots.

'Yes,' he confirms.

Hayley starts crying again, but for a long time no sound comes out of her mouth. When it does, it's the most wretched noise I think I've ever heard. 'Hayley I'm so sorry,' I say, wrapping my arms around her and stroking her hair, wishing I could make it all better but knowing I can't.

*

We leave the hospital utterly shell-shocked. Unlike the happy couples we saw earlier, we leave that room looking and feeling devastated, which can't help the nerves of the poor couples waiting to go in. Hayley can't stop crying and I don't know how I get us home in one piece, but I do.

'Stay with me,' she pleads as we walk into her house.

'Of course,' I say, immediately. I notice Hayley hasn't taken her shoes off. Not that I'll be pointing that out but it shows how upset she is. 'I'm not going anywhere.'

'How am I going to tell Gary?' she says suddenly, a fresh set of tears streaming down her face.

'I don't know babe, but why don't you do it soon. Get it out of the way. Apart from anything else he'll want to look after you.'

She nods and I fetch the phone for her. She dials the number but then bottles it. 'I can't do it,' she says, handing me the phone. 'I can't say it.'

I shake my head, not feeling it's my place to break such dreadful news, but she looks so pitiful that in the end I take it from her. It's already ringing.

'Babe,' Gary says, thinking it's Hayley. 'Hello darlin', how did it go? Has he got a big schlong like his dad?'

'Gary it's me, Marianne. I'm afraid I've got some bad news.'

To his credit Gary's home in twenty minutes. We hear him speeding into the cul-de-sac like a deranged boy racer, and when he charges into the house I feel really sad for him too. It's only just occurred to me that of course today, he's lost a baby too.

The minute he sees Hayley he scoops her up into a big hug and she sobs into his shoulder.

'I'm so sorry Gary,' she keeps saying.

'Don't be silly babes,' he says, stroking her blonde hair off her puffy, devastated face. 'You've got nothing to be sorry about.'

Relieved to hear him saying the right thing and happy that she's with the person she's supposed to be with, I leave the sad couple to it and make my way back home wondering why life can be such a complete and utter bitch sometimes.

CHAPTER ELEVEN

Hayley is naturally shattered and grief stricken by the loss of her baby. Though somehow having to face an abortion seems the cruellest part of it all and I lose count of how many times she asks me whether she should ignore the doctors and try and keep it, no matter how severe the baby's disabilities. Later that afternoon she'd phoned the hospital and got the news that she was scheduled in for a termination on the following Monday morning, meaning she had another four whole days to get through before it would all be over. It's all so horrific.

Try as she might, Hayley simply can't wrap her head round the idea that, in a few days' time, she'll be required to sign a form, effectively agreeing to kill her beloved, much wanted child. Logic's no replacement for feelings and although Gary and I have tried to make her see, in the gentlest way possible, that she has no choice, she's still torturing herself about it.

Of course Mum was horrified to hear what had happened, but because she made the mistake of not being wholly enthusiastic from the very beginning about this poor little mite who'll never be making it into the world, Hayley's refusing to see her. In fact, she's refusing to see anyone other than Gary and me. Hayley doesn't have many friends and the ones she does have aren't the kind she feels comfortable seeing in such a vulnerable, raw state. So she's locked herself at home, refusing to eat or do anything except lie listlessly on the sofa. When I turned up unannounced the day after the scan I was shocked by her appearance. Hayley's usually so groomed and immaculate, but right now she was a mess. Her hair was lank and greasy, her face was bloated from crying, and she was wearing her pyjamas in the middle of the afternoon.

I agreed to take *another* Monday off work so that I could take her to the hospital, despite the fact I'd bunked off last Monday and that I'm also taking Friday afternoon off so I can pick Andy up when he arrives. At this rate I'll be lucky if Roberto doesn't fire me, but I don't really care. If the worst comes to the worst I'm sure I can probably find a job in another salon. This time I also decide not to question why the hell Gary isn't going to be there to support his wife when she goes in for the procedure. Pointing out that he's a spineless twat isn't what Hayley needs right now, though when he took me to one side and asked whether I would go instead of him, at the time I could have cheerfully throttled him. His flimsy excuse was that girls were better in 'these sorts of situations', which is pathetic.

Gary's the worst kind of coward as far as I'm concerned but I'm not going to cause any fuss. All Hayley needs right now is for us all to be there for her and for histrionics to be kept to a bare minimum.

I don't tell Ray what's been going on until Friday morning. He's been off the radar a bit, which I discover is because he's had a 'bad few days', although he refuses to elaborate on what this actually means. Still, although he may not be particularly forthcoming about his own situation, I am impressed by what a good listener he is. He doesn't shy away from the details, like Gary has, and isn't squeamish. Instead he's philosophical, wise and… kind actually. As we talk I find myself wishing that Hayley would give him a chance. He also tells me that Mum had a miscarriage after I was born.

'You what?' I say, stunned to find this out.

'Yeah, it was after you. Your mum fell pregnant straight away but lost it at about two months I think it was. She was devastated. All I could think was that we already had two beautiful girls and should be thankful, but I think for a woman it don't matter how many children you've got, losing one is always just as painful. Poor Hayley. It's got to be hard when you ain't got any little ones to help ease that pain. I want to see her Marianne.'

'I know you do,' I reply slightly impatiently. It's been such a stressful time and I'm feeling at the end of my tether. 'But it's not as easy as that, is it?'

'I know,' he agrees. 'And don't think I don't know that. The fact that you're even talking to me is something I appreciate so much but I just wish I could…' At this point his voice cracks slightly but then I hear him clearing his throat, pulling himself together. I'm glad. I'm not feeling tolerant or strong enough for him to start going over the 'what ifs' of the situation right now. They hardly need spelling out.

'Anyway, what you got planned today then?'

'Um… well you remember I told you about Andy, the guy I met in Thailand?'

'Yeah.'

'His plane's landing at twelve, so I said if he got the Heathrow Express that I'd pick him up from Paddington station. I've taken the afternoon off work because I'll have to be there for about two.'

'Do you want me to come with you?'

'No,' I answer incredulously, wondering how he could possibly imagine that I would want that.

'Where's he staying, then?'

'With me. At Mum's.'

'Is he now?'

'Yeah.'

'And your mum's all right with that, is she?'

'Yeah, she is actually. In fact, she's quite excited about meeting him.'

'Ain't she worried about hanky panky going on in her house?'

I take a deep breath. He's doing that thing again where he's straying into real dad territory, which jars because he simply hasn't put in the hours to have earned the right to be that protective or paternal. Sad but true. It's also a bit ridiculous given that I'm not fourteen.

'I'm thirty-one,' is all I say. I don't add that I'm planning on moving into Hayley's old bedroom with him because she has a double bed and that I am thoroughly looking forward to having sex for the first time in ages.

'True. Sorry.'

'It's fine.'

'OK, well call me later to tell me how Hayley's doing will you?'

At two o'clock I'm at Paddington station standing outside Accessorise in the middle of the main concourse, which is where I'd texted Andy to say I'd be waiting. I'm nervous. I keep thinking I need the toilet, my mouth's dry and my palms are clammy. It wasn't his fault, but Andy was choosing to turn up during one of the most complicated patches in my family's history, to the point where, over the last couple of days, I've almost been tempted to put him off coming altogether. Having to keep him entertained and make sure he's all right feels like an imminent burden if I'm being completely honest. Still, I'm sure it'll all pan out.

By now it's two-fifteen and I'm just wondering whether I should ring him when suddenly Andy rounds the corner and I get my first glimpse of him in four months. A feeling of cold dismay seeps through me and for so many reasons I suddenly, and sincerely, wish I'd listened to my instinct and made that call to put him off. He doesn't seem to have the same reaction.

'Marianne, how you doing baby?' he says, rushing towards me and sweeping me into his arms.

I must remain completely rigid though, because when he puts me down again he says, 'Aren't you pleased to see me?'

'Um, yes,' I lie, though the truth is, my heart's just fallen through my boots and I've realised I've made a terrible mistake. It's the most awful feeling ever and possibly the worse thing is, I know I'm being desperately shallow, a quality I've always loathed in Gary. Yet the fact remains that the minute I clapped eyes on Andy, the way he now looks has put me off him completely.

So here it is, for I'm going to have to be straight about this. I can't see any way of avoiding it. The last time I saw Andy he was really brown and looked like he truly belonged on the beach. Every hair on his gorgeous, muscular arms had been bleached a silvery blonde by the sun and his limbs were toned, tanned and sinewy. Prior to today I've also only ever seen Andy wearing shorts, t-shirts and flip-flops, and his hair has always been unkempt and full of salt from the sea. Now, however, I hardly recognise this person in front of me. His tan has faded completely, which has transformed his entire face somehow. Not only that but he's looking quite jowly and, now that they're no longer standing out from a tanned complexion, his blue eyes look watery and insipid. His hair has clearly been brushed, and cut into a deeply square side parting, which makes him look about twenty years older than he actually is. His clothes, oh my god his clothes, I hardly know where to begin. He's wearing the worst jeans known to man. Let's just say that they're high-waisted, baggy and topped off with an awful jumper, like the sort your Nan might give you for Christmas. If she really hated you. On his feet he's wearing trainers, only they're the kind of trainers old people wear for comfort or because they have bunions. The type of trainers fat tourists wear. It's like seeing someone and not being able to put them into context. But maybe I'm being hasty. Poor guy will after all be tired after a long journey. Maybe once I've got used to his new appearance the spark that got us together will reignite? Or am I scraping the hope barrel?

I smile weakly at him and then I notice, underneath the jumper, a hint of a paunch, which along with the new chins he's sporting is the most mysterious thing of all because when I last saw Andy his stomach had been washboard and his face had been chiselled. As I stare at him aghast, taking all of this in, I notice the size of his backpack. It's the size of a house. This immediately reminds me that we haven't met here for a casual cup of coffee, but that he's supposed to be coming home with me… to stay. What have I done?

A loud announcement is being made over the tannoy, *The train on platform five is the two twenty-three to Exeter, stopping at…*

As the list of stations starts, I panic, and for a strange second contemplate legging it to platform five myself.

Exeter sounds nice and far away from here, far away from him and this desperately awkward situation.

'Are you OK? You look so freaked out. Oh sweetie you're all emotional aren't you? Oh, come here and let me give you a cuddle.' Limply I let him draw me into his woolly armpit, which at least allows me to grimace in the way I want to without him seeing.

'So, how long do you see yourself staying?' I ask tentatively, not sure I'm ready for the answer.

'As long as it takes to persuade you to come back to Oz with me,' he says, staring at me in a disturbingly soppy way.

It's the worst answer he could have possibly given, for if he's serious, that means he'll be here for eternity, which is how long it would take him to persuade me to emigrate anywhere with him and that jumper. This was terrible. I scan his pasty face, searching for the beach bum he'd been before a European winter had turned him into a deeply average, square, unfit-looking bloke, devoid of any style whatsoever.

Oh my god.

It was only a holiday romance...

I hate myself. Why could I not have realised that a little earlier than this particular moment? Still, I must give him a chance. You never know. Maybe I'm jumping the gun?

'Shall we get going?' he says in his broad Aussie accent. 'I've got to tell you I'm feeling a bit wrecked. Might need a bit of a lie down when we get back to yours, eh?' he says, and then he winks.

I don't know whether to laugh or cry.

It takes hours to get back to Chigwell. Practically every road we need to take is being dug up for no apparent reason so progress is painfully slow. Thankfully Andy doesn't pick up on how tense I'm feeling and is happy to natter away about what he's been up to since I last saw him. Meanwhile, I'm busy quietly hatching a plan. It would be far too cruel to tell Andy what treacherous thoughts I'm having straight away, so I decide to stick things out – while avoiding any physical contact whatsoever – in the hope that my feelings might change again. In the meantime I'll tell him he has to stay in Hayley's room alone because Mum doesn't feel comfortable us sharing a bed under her roof. Then, if I still feel like this, after a while, I'll let him down gently, explaining that I still really want to be friends but that any romantic aspect to our relationship is finished, kaput, over.

While thinking all this I smile glibly away while Andy tells me stories about all the amazing pasta dishes he sampled in Rome, which at least explains the paunch. The way he says pasta, as in 'parsta', is excruciatingly irritating so I'm pleased when my mobile rings. It's Hayley and, given everything that's going on at the moment, I feel compelled to apologise to Andy – something I can see myself doing a lot of in the near future – and to swerve into the kerb so I can phone her back.

'Hayls?' I say when she picks up. I can tell she's there

but not saying anything. Then I realise this is because she's crying.

'I'm having a miscarriage,' she eventually manages to blurt out between sobs.

'Oh Hayley, I'm so sorry,' I say, immediately drenched in panic. 'OK well sit tight and I'll be straight over. Where's Gary?'

'Here,' she says faintly. 'But Marianne, I need you.'

It's odd, I've spent years yearning for a closer relationship with my sister. Now, due to these tragically horrible circumstances, it feels like one has been forged. Over the last couple of days she hasn't so much as expressed, but has demonstrated how much I mean to her. However, as lovely as this new sense of closeness is I would gladly swap it for her old spiteful self, if it meant she was happy again and she wasn't suffering this terrible ordeal. It's all rather confusing from an emotional point of view.

'I'm on my way,' I tell her immediately before turning to Andy. 'I'm so sorry to do this to you. I know you've only just got here, but I'm going to have to drop you at mine,' I say, indicating to rejoin the traffic. Mercifully we're quite near home by now. It's four-thirty so the only person in danger of being in is Mum. Can I really strand him with her? Can I really strand her with *him*?

'What's up?' he says.

'It's my sister. She's pregnant but I think she's having a miscarriage so I really need to get round to her place I'm afraid.'

'Jeez,' he says, looking genuinely concerned. 'I'm sorry to hear that. Of course, just drop me wherever. I'll be fine till you get back. Hey, I've got myself halfway round the world so…'

In that instant I'm unbelievably grateful that despite his dire dress sense, he has at least retained the same laid-back demeanor he had in Thailand. He'd be fine.

*

Ten minutes later I roar into our road, screech to a halt and race up the path to the house leaving Andy to manhandle his rucksack out of the boot. I open the door, which isn't double locked, so I know Mum must be in.

'Muuuuum,' I yell. 'Muuuuuuuuuum.'

'What is it Marianne?' she says, rushing out of the kitchen. 'What's happened? Why are you yelling like that?' Did he stand you up?'

'No, but you need to say that I can't stay in his room with him.'

'What?' she says, looking bewildered.

'Andy's here, right here in fact,' I say, giving her a look as he strolls up the path behind me.

'G'day,' he greets her.

'Oh, hello,' says Mum, immediately on full charm offensive, though I can see from her expression he isn't quite what she'd expected. I'm overcome with an urge to take her to one side and explain that he isn't what I'd expected either and that I have photographic evidence to prove it.

'Come on in then love, don't be shy. We don't do shy around here, do we Marianne?' Mum says, nudging me and winking.

'It's great to meet you, Mrs Baker,' says Andy, striding into the hallway, slinging his rucksack off his shoulder.

'It's Mrs Baxter actually. I was a Baker and now I'm a Baxter, but you can call me Alison anyway. Any friend of Marianne's and all that. Ooh look at your big bag. That looks heavy. Martin can help you with that later. You probably want to get that big jumper off too love, you must be boiling.'

'Mum,' I say, desperate to interrupt and hopping from one foot to the other so frantic am I to get to Hayley.

'Thanks Mrs Baxter and can I just say I never would have guessed you were Marianne's mum. You look more like her sister. She didn't tell me you were such a stunner.'

'Oh, Andy,' Mum says, slapping him lightly on the arm while I look on dumbfounded, wondering how this scene ever came to be played out in my hall. 'Aren't you naughty, though I suppose I do have my moments,' she adds, running a few paces towards the banisters, which she leans against so that she can fling herself back into a pose.

'Mum,' I snap impatiently.

'Though I have to work at it these days.'

'Mum,' I try again wearily.

'What Marianne?'

'I've got to go. Hayley phoned. She's having a miscarriage.'

'What? Oh no. My poor baby!' gasps Mum, looking totally shocked.

'I know, but don't worry, I'll make sure she's all right. Can you just look after Andy for me till I get back?'

'Shouldn't I come with you?'

'I think it's better if I go on my own,' I say tactfully, knowing full well that Mum's the last person Hayley will want to see right now. Andy winks at me solemnly. I shiver before smiling weakly back at him. Can this really be the same person I was so crazy about just a short time ago?

Anyway, Mum seems to get the message and although she still looks really worried, she nods her head and, without further comment, leads Andy through to the kitchen, leaving me free to charge back to Tina. I'm grateful for her complicity.

*

When I arrive at Hayley's twenty minutes later, Gary opens the door looking pale.

'Am I glad to see you,' he says, looking quite faint.

'Where is she?'

'Upstairs,' he says, gesturing with his head. 'She just had a bath but she's in our bedroom now.'

'Right,' I say, taking off my shoes and wondering what on earth I should be doing now I'm here. 'Are you sure she shouldn't be at the hospital?'

'Nah, I did ring 'em, but they said it was a natural process the body would do by itself and to come in tomorrow, once it was all over so that they can check it's all… come out.'

He grimaces. I sense more from disgust than anything else.

'So she's definitely losing the baby then?' I enquire gently.

'Yeah… I mean… she has already,' he says, still looking uncomfortable. 'I don't think there's any question about that.'

'I'm really sorry,' I say.

'Me too, Marianne,' he says, clearly out of his depth and desperate to 'hand over' to me. Sure enough, he turns and heads for the kitchen as though now that I've arrived he's free to go. I'm livid with him for being so useless and not at all sure I'm really equipped to deal with any of this myself. Still, I head up the stairs, albeit with a sense of impending doom and trepidation.

'Hayley,' I say, knocking on the bedroom door. 'Hayley it's me, I'm here.'

She doesn't reply so I try the door, which isn't locked, and walk in. Hayley's lying in bed, pristine in clean py-jamas. Her face is very pale and her hair is damp and straggly, fanned out on the pillow behind her.

'Oh Hayley, I'm so sorry.'

'Me too,' she says.

'Are you… is it?'

She nods hard, blinking away tears.

'Oh babe, I'm so, so sorry,' I repeat, feeling helpless.

'S'okay,' she wails suddenly. 'I just feel so empty.'

My heart contracts in sympathy for my poor sister.

'Still,' she says, staring fixedly ahead. 'Least I don't have to go into hospital and have it killed.'

Her choice of language makes it hard to know what to say but I stop hovering at the doorway and come to sit tentatively on the edge of her bed.

'When did it happen?'

'I had tummy ache all day yesterday and some bleeding, so I knew I was probably going to have a miscarriage. Then it got a bit worse and I thought that was it but then about an hour and a half ago, it really kicked off…' She gazes at me slightly glassily. A bitter, watery smile hovering on her lips. She turns away, keen to hide the fact her eyes are welling up with tears again. 'The hospital told Gary to give me an aspirin, which was a fucking laugh. It was agony. Sorry to get you over here by the way. Probably a bit pointless now it's over,' she adds matter-of-factly, and I can tell she's embarrassed about having reached out to me during her time of need. The shutters have gone down again, but I don't want her burying this one. I don't want things to revert back to how they always are between us.

'Hayley? Turn round Hayley,' I beg her. 'Please? I'm your sister and I'm glad you called. I want to be here for you and I want you to be able to talk to me about how you're feeling.'

Hayley turns around slowly, only to shoot me a look that's laced with contempt. 'Don't get all fucking hippy dippy on me Marianne. I don't want to talk about things for hours on end. What's the point? My baby's been flushed down the toilet so that's that.'

'Hayley,' I say, hurt and shocked by her brusqueness. 'Don't say things like that. I know you don't mean it.'

She shrugs but it seems that today, being so angry is too draining even for her to manage and her face crumples as she gives in to how she's really feeling once again.

'It's all right,' I say gently. 'It's all right Hayls. You're allowed to be upset you know. It would be weird if you weren't. I know you're hurting and I understand because it's so, so unfair.'

'I'm sorry,' she whispers and her bottom lip trembles with the effort of keeping it together. We're both in very alien territory here. 'Because...' she trails off.

'What?'

'Well... my friends are all a bit crap and Gary's... well Gary's Gary but actually you've been really, you know...'

'What?' Despite the fact she's on the verge of tears I'm going to force her to say it.

'You've been really... nice to me through all this,' she says almost warily, as though being nice to someone in their hour of need is downright suspect.

'You're my sister,' I state simply. 'I'll always be here for you.'

'Wasn't your boyfriend supposed to be coming today?' she enquires, wiping her hand across her face, determined not to cry any more.

'He's here already,' I reply, wishing she hadn't reminded me.

'You don't look that happy about it,' she remarks flatly.

'I'm not,' I mutter, not keen to elaborate. It doesn't feel appropriate talking about anything other than what's just happened really.

However, Hayley seems to sense this because she says, 'Look, you might as well tell me. Apart from anything else it might take my mind off things for a second. And that would be good.'

She has a point and, besides, laughing at my misfortune is something she's always enjoyed so I give in and tell her what's going on, 'Oh god Hayley, he's awful.'

She looks confused.

'Andy's awful. I know it's mean but I've gone right off him. The minute I saw him I realised what we had was just a holiday romance, to the point where I don't think we're going to have anything in common here. Plus, and I know this is bad, but I didn't fancy him even remotely.'

'He can't be *that* different,' she muses, looking as I'd suspected she would be, quite pleasantly distracted for a second by the awkwardness of the situation I'm in.

'He is. He's white and fat and is wearing high-waisted jeans and a woolly jumper. Like a really big fisherman's jumper with a pattern on it. I've only ever seen him in shorts and t-shirt before.'

'Oh my god,' says Hayley chuckling for a second, though the poor thing stops as soon as she started, as from nowhere she's suddenly overwhelmed by another wave of grief for what she's lost today. It seems to have ambushed her completely, for this time she gives in to it, covers her face with both her hands and sobs. I'm relieved in a way and before I've had time to analyse what I'm doing, acting purely on instinct I get up and go to the other side of the bed, where I climb in next to her and hug her tight. For a while we stay like that, her venting some of the pain, misery, grief and disappointment that she's feeling and me rocking her back and forth but making no attempt to stop what she so obviously needs to do.

Later, once she's started to recover a little she starts laughing self-consciously as it occurs to her that we're locked in an embrace, 'What are we doing?' she says, pulling away from me and sitting up in bed, wiping her by now very puffy face with the back of her hand.

I shrug and sit up too. 'I don't know, but we're sisters aren't we? So not a massive deal really. Besides, we used to get into each other's beds all the time when we were little.'

Hayley sniffs hard and nods. 'I suppose,' she says reaching for a tissue from the box next to the bed.

We stay silent for a while until Hayley says flatly, 'Put the telly on then.'

A re-run of an ancient episode of *Dallas* provides a perfect hour of mind-numbing entertainment as we remain sitting in bed, solemnly leaning against her big pillows like *The Two Ronnies*.

During the ad break I glance at Hayley and notice that she has a strange look on her face.

'What?'

As she replies she determinedly avoids catching my eye. 'I think I will see Ray.'

My heart leaps and instinctively I know I have to tread carefully with what I say or she'll change her mind. But I'm pleased. I would hate her to regret not seeing him and it be too late. I think this is the right thing for her to do.

'O-K,' I say cautiously, fighting back the temptation to ask what made her change her mind.

'Will you arrange it?'

'Course.'

'Good.'

We don't say any more on the subject. I can tell she doesn't want to discuss it and besides, she's got other things on her mind.

By the time I head home an hour or so later I'm drained, exhausted and horrified too as it occurs to me that when I get home, on top of everything else, I have an amorous Antipodean to deal with.

CHAPTER TWELVE

For a split second after I've put the key in the door, I pause. I want to gather my thoughts before seeing everyone. A long deep breath does the trick. Head held high I finally turn the key and push the door open. 'Hi, I'm back.'

Mum comes scuttling out of the kitchen. 'How is she? How's my poor Hayls?'

'She's OK. I mean she's not OK, she's devastated and it's been traumatic and everything but she'll *be* OK… eventually.'

Mum deserves and needs to be filled in, but I'm so wiped out I can hardly speak.

'I'll pop over and see her tomorrow. What do you think? I could go now but do you think she might be a bit tired?'

'I think you're right Mum. She needs to sleep. Go tomorrow. She'd appreciate that.' I hang my jacket up on the coat hooks. 'How's, er, Andy doing?'

'Lovely,' says Mum, visibly brightening. 'Him and Mar are getting on like a house on fire.'

'Really?' I can't imagine what they can possibly have to

say to one another. Mind you, I can't imagine what I have to say to him either so…

'Oh yeah, in fact we're going to have a little barby tonight. First of the year. It was Andy's idea so you can imagine how ecstatic Martin is.' She rolls her eyes in mock disapproval. 'They're at B&Q now buying a gas canister.'

'But it's cold.'

'Cold?' she says, wrinkling her nose up. 'Don't be silly, it's the end of April. I didn't even have to have the heating on this afternoon.'

'Right,' I say faintly, just as my phone starts ringing. It's Ray.

'Er, I'm just going to take this call Mum. I won't be a minute,' I say, heading into the kitchen.

'Don't mind me love,' she says, following me in. 'I'm just defrosting some burgers in the microwave, but when you're finished maybe you could set the patio table? I asked Pete but he's busy.'

'Er yeah sure,' I say, darting into the utility room that's directly off the kitchen and shutting the door behind me so she can't hear. 'Hello,' I whisper into my phone, slipping right to the back of the small room and wedging myself in next to the fridge-freezer and Martin's golf clubs.

'Marianne, I was worried. I've been trying you all afternoon.'

'Were you? Sorry. It's been a… it's been a pretty full-on day actually. As you know I had to pick up Andy from Paddington and then um… well, Hayley lost the baby.'

'Oh no,' says Ray. 'Poor girl. Is she OK?'

'Well… you know.'

'I can imagine. That's dreadful. Still, I bet she's glad she don't have to go through with the operation next week yeah?'

'Yeah,' I agree. 'Also, I'm not going to promise she won't change her mind, but she said today that she will meet up with you.'

'You're joking,' says Ray, sounding gobsmacked. 'Wow, well that's t'rrific news. I don't believe it.'

'Who are you talking to?' says a voice behind me. I jump out of my skin and spin round, no doubt looking guilty as sin. I hadn't heard Mum come in. She's bearing down on me, packet of burger baps in one hand, pot of coleslaw in the other.

'No one,' I say. 'Just Jason.'

'Marianne, you should tell her it's me,' Dad huffs down the phone. 'You've got every right to be talking to me.'

'That doesn't sound like Jason,' says Mum looking furious and depositing the baps and coleslaw on top of the tumble drier. 'Is that Ray?'

Startled, I nod.

'Give that here,' she says, lunging for my phone. I'm far too slow to react and the next thing I know she's wrestled it away from me.

'Now, you listen to me,' she squawks into it. 'You stay away from my daughters, do you hear Raymond? You've got no right swanning back into their lives like this. You made me a promise and we don't want you anywhere near us.'

I can't hear what Ray says back, but it doesn't sound good, though I'm with him quite frankly. I don't appreciate my mum's use of the royal 'we' at all and also don't like her talking on my behalf, when she has no idea what I actually think about anything. Largely due to the fact she's never thought to ask.

'Why would I want to talk?' Mum's screaming now, looking utterly incensed. 'I ain't got nuffink to say to you that I haven't said a million times already.'

Her rage has brought back her old, less-refined voice with a vengeance.

'No, don't *you* dare,' she yells, sounding more and more like an old fishwife. 'Do you hear me? Don't you…'

She pulls the phone away from her ear and stares at it. 'He's hung up,' she exclaims, outraged beyond belief.

'What did he say?' I ask timidly, backing away from her.

'That he's coming round,' she says, looking frantic.

'What did you mean when you said "things I've said a million times already"?'

Something about the level of panic in her face moves me to ask my next question before she's answered. 'And how much does Martin really know about Ray?'

Her expression tells me everything I need to know.

'Mum, you have to tell him.'

'Don't tell me what I *have* to do young lady. This is all

your fault. I told you not to speak to him, but what do you go and do behind my back?'

At this point the stress of the last few days catches up with me. I can literally feel blood racing to my head and end up screaming back at her.

'I've done nothing wrong,' I yell.

It's her turn to look startled.

'Look, I know him reappearing is really tricky for you Mum. I get that and that's why I haven't said anything. But at the same time you can't dictate what I do, because he's my dad, so surely I have every right to talk to him if I want to.'

'But he's a criminal Marianne.'

'Yes. I know. Or rather he *was* a criminal who has served his time as it goes and of course I'm struggling massively with the fact he did terrible things in the past but I don't care.'

'What do you mean you don't care?'

'I mean that although I haven't forgiven him for everything I just want to see whether I can. Before it's too late. Because what nobody else seems to be realising is that we don't have a lot of time left so there's no point wasting it by sulking in order to prove a point. And besides, if you must know, I don't completely hate him.'

Mum blinks rapidly.

'And he seems to like me. He's not some ogre. He shows an interest.'

'And what's that supposed to mean?' splutters Mum, the veins in her throat protruding unattractively.

'It means that I've spoken more to him in the past week about stuff to do with me than I have with anybody…' I trail off because just then we hear the front door opening. Martin and Andy, it seems, have returned from their quest to B&Q and are laughing and chatting as they come into the house, blissfully unaware of what old harpies lie in wait for them.

In direct contrast to the state Mum and I are in, they sound ridiculously happy and jovial. In fact, by the sound of it, Mum probably hadn't been exaggerating about how famously they're getting on.

I sigh loudly, despairing of everything. 'Come on,' I huff impatiently to Mum who seems to have frozen to the spot. 'I'm sure Ray won't turn up. He was probably just winding you up.'

'Do you think?' she says, her eyes, which are plastered in blue shimmery eye shadow, wide with anxiety.

I nod and indicate to her to move out of the way so I can get past. Still pent up with stress I shove open the utility room door and march through to the hall.

'Hi,' I say dolefully, forcing myself to get a grip of my emotions and manfully raising a smile, albeit a fairly weak one, for Andy, the man who feels like a random stranger.

'Hey,' he beams back happily, immediately making me feel like the world's biggest bitch, which in turn makes me feel even more resentful of him. I'm pretty sure I'm not a massive bitch, so being made to feel like one because I don't fancy him is horrid and annoying. I wonder briefly what he and Martin can have been buying at B&Q that Martin doesn't already have. Between them they've got about eight plastic bags.

'Oh my god, how's your sis, sweetie? Is she OK? Are you OK?' Andy asks, his face falling as he remembers where I've been.

'She's fine, thanks for asking.'

'Oh good,' says Martin, grave for a second. My stepdad's wearing beige canvas trousers, which I believe, in outlets like Millets, are described as utility trousers. On top he's sporting a blue and pink pastel golf jumper and the whole ensemble is topped off with hush puppies. As he stands with his hands on his hips, looking quite the 'Man at C&A', he says, 'Terrible business. Poor Hayley, the lord works in mysterious ways sometimes that's for sure. Still, I'm sure one day she'll be blessed with a little one, eh?'

I nod.

'Anyway, you never told me Andy here was almost as much of a barbecue nut as I am, Marianne. We've had a riot down at B&Q, haven't we son?'

'Too right,' says Andy, who has at least shed his awful jumper, though surprisingly I almost wish he still had it on because underneath the offensive knitwear, he's been hiding not only a pale pink polo shirt, which clings to his huge belly, but also a bum bag. The revelations just keep on coming because at that moment it dawns upon me; Andy is Martin's sartorial twin.

'That place is awesome, so many great products on offer. Though I said to Martin here, you can't have a gas barby mate. It's simply not right.'

'So you'll never guess what we've gone and done, love,' chuckles Martin gleefully as Mum appears, absent-mindedly clutching the packet of baps again. From nowhere Andy bursts out laughing. Then, to my further surprise, he proceeds to high five Martin who for no discernible reason is suddenly also completely beside himself.

I can't believe how excited the two of them are and am starting to think that maybe they have done something truly incredible. Robbed the store perhaps? Fashioned a tree house out of wicker baskets? Arranged a protest march to Trafalgar Square against gas barbecues? Martin's face in particular is lit up, like a small boy on Christmas Day.

'What have you done?' says Mum flatly.

'Oh I've gone a bit mad I'm afraid, but if you don't like it you can blame Andy here,' says Martin, nudging his new barbecuing partner in crime.

'Now hang on there a minute, mate,' gushes Andy, grinning madly. 'That's just not fair. I'm not taking all the responsibility.'

Mum and I look at each other bemused, wishing they'd just hurry up and spit out whatever it is they're trying to tell us, which let's face it, we both know probably isn't going to live up to the build-up it's getting.

'Oh dear,' says Martin, wiping away a tear of satisfied mirth. 'You know what, you're just going to have to come and see love,' he says, grabbing Mum by the arm and ushering her out the front door. I follow at an unenthusiastic pace. Andy keeps winking at me, which is really getting on my nerves.

'Look at this monster,' says Martin, practically shitting himself with excitement.

'It's a beaut, come and see, baby,' adds Andy.

Baby? For a second I wonder who he's talking to. All the stress is taking its toll a bit. I feel terribly distracted and my eyes keep being drawn to his bum bag like a magnet. I'm feeling quite deranged really.

'There,' says Martin proudly and I look up to see that strapped on top of his Volvo estate is the biggest god damn barbecue known to man. In fact it's so big it hardly even qualifies as a barbecue. It's more of a monstrous oven, complete with hot plates and three separate grills.

'Hee hee,' says Martin rubbing his hands together.

'It's enormous,' says Mum, flatly.

'I know my darling, but you're not cross are you? I hope not, because I think we're going to have such fun with it and you'll never guess what else?'

'What?' says Mum, looking stunned to find out there's more.

'Andy says he knows how to barbecue… are you ready for this? This is so mad,' he chuckles. 'In fact I still think you might be having me on,' he says to Andy, in a matey aside. 'Anyway, he *says* he can barbecue… fish! I mean, I thought we were being a bit adventurous with those lamb steaks last year. Do you remember those Al? They were gorgeous weren't they, with a bit of that nice rub from Asda, t'riffic, but fish I tell you…'

As Martin prattles on Andy saunters over to where I'm standing. Sliding one pale, chubby arm around my waist he says softly, 'Your old man's a genius, babe. I should have known I'd fit right in with your family.'

There are so many things wrong with this sentence I hardly know where to begin but am too busy wondering why Mum's staring over Martin's shoulder with her mouth open to worry about it. As I follow her gaze, it occurs to me that Andy might want to reserve judgement on that last statement anyway. For walking purposefully down the road, towards our house, with a look of conviction on his face, is Ray and he doesn't look best pleased.

'In the house,' says Mum suddenly, shoving Martin in the chest in a desperate bid to shut him up.

'In a minute love,' he says, mistaking her urgency completely. 'I know you're hungry. So am I, but give us a second to get it off the roof and get the charcoal inside. We don't want to drop it do we? Now, Andy, give us a hand will you?'

'Sure thing, mate.'

At this point the men still haven't noticed Ray striding up the path, making his way purposefully towards his ex-wife. By the time he finally comes to a stop in front of Mum, she looks like she's seen a ghost. It's all very weird. This, of course, will be the first time they've come face to face in many, many years. I look on nervously.

'Alison,' he says, in his unmistakable growl.

'You shouldn't have come here,' she says, clutching her chest.

It's only now that Andy and Martin, who are busy grappling with the roof-rack straps, finally notice the menacing looking stranger in the black leather jacket who's in our midst.

'Can I help you?' says Martin, looking quizzically at Ray.

'I doubt it,' says Ray. 'But your missus can.'

Martin turns to look questioningly at Mum, who is seemingly frozen to the spot.

'Alli?'

'Leave it Martin.'

'Yeah, leave it Martin,' repeats Ray.

'Who's that?' says Andy, wondering back over to me while looking anxiously at the tableau that's playing out in front of us.

'That,' I whisper, 'Is my dad.'

'Who are you?' Martin's saying, seemingly irritated, more than anything, that his big barbecue moment is being spoiled.

'Tell him Alison,' says Dad. 'Tell 'im, because I ain't here to play games and we need to sort one or two things out. I want to see my daughters. I know I should have done this years ago, and I can't tell you how much I regret the fact that I didn't, but I've come to my senses. I know what it is I want and I can't let you have things all your own way any more.'

'Now I'm sorry,' says Martin who, despite being six foot, looks comparatively weedy next to Ray. His voice is so mild too, totally unthreatening. I suspect Ray could have him for breakfast in many ways, but hope he respects Martin enough not to take advantage. How my dad's about to conduct himself matters to me greatly, I realise. I don't want him to resort to aggression. Martin's probably about to give him plenty of ammunition, but doesn't deserve to be bullied.

'I don't know who you think you are, but I will not have you talking to my wife like that. Alison's ex-husband is in Australia, so you are talking nonsense, plus you are on my property.'

'Australia? Seriously?' Ray laughs. 'I can see why a little girl might fall for that one, but a grown man?' He throws his head back and lets out a belly laugh, his face creased in contempt at Martin's stupidity. I cringe.

'Alison?' says Martin, wrong-footed.

We all stare at Mum, but when she fails to say anything Martin ends up turning to me for answers.

'He is my dad,' I confirm reluctantly, knowing that no matter what Mum thinks, it all has to come out in the open at some point. 'Australia was a load of bollocks. He's been in prison and now he's really ill. But Mum never wanted to hurt you, Martin. She loves you.'

'Yeah, it weren't anything to do with you. It was all about how ashamed of me she was. Ain't that right?' Ray says icily.

At this point I glare at Ray. It's not fair for this scene to be playing out in front of Martin.

Mum brings her hand to her mouth and, looking like she might throw up, runs back inside the house. In the meantime Martin draws himself up to his full height, and squares up to dad. Andy hovers nervously behind me.

'If Marianne's saying it then it must be true, but that still doesn't give you any excuse for upsetting my wife on my property, on my driveway.'

You have to hand it to Martin. His loyalty to my mum is unwavering, remarkable. Not even a hint of the betrayal he must be feeling is evident on his face. For a second Ray looks so angry I honestly think he's going to lamp Martin one on the chin but then he seems to talk himself down, though you can see it's a battle to do so.

'You're right,' he says eventually.

I feel flooded with relief. I don't want Ray to be a thug. And I certainly don't want Martin to be thumped when he's the only one around here who hasn't done anything wrong. Ray said he learned a thing or two in prison about how to handle things and this is a chance to prove that both to himself and to me. I need to know he can control himself.

'Which is why I'm asking you, man to man, if I can

come inside and discuss a few things? With both of you, like grown adults.'

Martin considers this for a moment, staring hard at Ray and then at me, taking in my miserable expression.

'I suppose you'd better then,' he says resignedly, the twitch in his cheek the only sign of how churned up he must be feeling.

'Thank you, Martin,' I say. 'I think it probably is for the best if we all get everything out in the open now.'

The two men trudge inside at which point I turn to Andy and say, 'Sorry about all of this.'

It's only just dawned upon me how much drama he's already experienced during his first afternoon 'chez Baxter'. If I were him I'd probably be feeling pretty apprehensive about staying with us.

'No worries,' he says, surprisingly unperturbed. 'I just can't believe you told me life here was boring. So far it seems anything but. Shall we go and see what's happening?'

I don't appreciate him viewing my family's dramas as a soap opera put on for his own personal entertainment but perhaps it's better than him being completely freaked out. Feeling weary I follow him inside.

*

Outside, on the patio in the back garden, among the swing chairs, tables and many other pieces of patio furniture, a heated discussion is taking place between Mum, Martin and Ray, who are standing in a triangle configuration. I linger nervously at the sliding doors, chewing skin around the cuticle of my thumb, something I always do when I'm freaking out. Andy – rather boldly I think – barges past me in order to go outside too, but then seems to prevaricate, changes his mind and reverses back until he's stood directly behind me. I take a deep breath and try to pretend I haven't just noticed how big his arse has got. Did he do anything *but* eat 'parsta' in Rome? Without warning he wraps a flaccid arm around my waist, at which point I feel my shoulders rise to an unnaturally high level. Then he leans right into me from behind, which feels totally wrong and alarmingly unnatural. I'm so tense and, at this moment in time, would gladly give away my violin and entire wardrobe for a massage. Any more stress and there's a chance my spine might actually snap.

'You don't have the right,' Martin's saying, as Mum stares at the ground looking sheepish, her arms folded in a way that shoves her cleavage right up. She looks guilty and ashamed, like she knows she'll have a lot of explaining to do later.

'But that's where you're wrong,' Ray insists, collapsing heavily onto a chair and rubbing his face with his hands. He looks exhausted. 'I'm their dad and nothing you say can change that.'

'I'll have you know I'm the one who's raised your daughters!' exclaims Martin who, in his v-neck sweater, looks very suburban compared to Ray. There'd never need to be any guessing as to which capital city my dad was born and bred in. He's a Londoner through and through. Chalk and cheese, my mum's two husbands.

'You say you're their dad, but where were you? Where were you when it was their birthday, or when they needed picking up from school, or there was a parents evening to go to?'

'I was in prison!' yells Dad frustratedly, sounding really hacked off now. 'So not massively convenient for doing things like the school run, funnily enough. Gordon Bennett man! Do you think I wanted to spend the best part of my life locked up? Do you really think I didn't think about my girls and what they might be up to every single day of my pathetic fucking existence? 'Cos I did.'

'There's no need to swear,' says Mum tentatively. Dad shoots her a filthy look, which silences her once again. I contemplate escaping upstairs but feel like I need to remain nearby in case I'm required to wade in, so stay where I am.

'Well you say that,' splutters Martin, who is understandably struggling to absorb so much information. 'And I agree, prison is hardly the best environment for kids to be, but you just told me you got out years ago! Where were you then?'

Ray sighs heavily and shoots my mum a look that is loaded with meaning. Catching his drift Martin turns to his wife.

'Well?'

Mum chews her lip as she works out what to say. 'Ray did contact me a few times,' she offers eventually. 'When he was inside and then also when he got out, but I told him I didn't want anything to do with him and that the girls were happy and doing better without him in their lives.'

I feel like I've been punched in the solar plexus and for the umpteenth time wonder how she could have done that. Andy, who I've wriggled free from by now, purposefully catches my eye, making a sort of 'Oh dear' type face. I suddenly wish fervently that he wasn't here. This has nothing to do with him and I certainly don't want him making stupid faces at me. In fact it seems weirdly insensitive to me that he's standing here spectating at all. After all, he has about as little emotional investment as your average rubbernecker. Frankly, I wish he'd piss off.

Avoiding eye contact with him, I look instead at Martin who I feel really quite sorry for. He swallows as he tries to compose himself, obviously bewildered at how all of this could have gone on without him knowing anything about it.

Sensing that he's at a loss, Ray, who my sympathies also lie with, interjects. 'Listen Martin, it ain't all Alison's fault. I was nothing but trouble back in those days and she just wanted an easy life. Besides, I didn't have to listen to her. I could have forced the issue but I went along with what she said because it was easier than questioning it I suppose. Did I really think they were better off without me? Maybe. Was I better off without them? Definitely not, but I took the road of least hassle, which I will never forgive myself for. But, you should know that I'm very grateful to you for looking after them so well. I mean, you've obviously done well for yourself,' he says, making a sweeping gesture around our cluttered patio. He looks quite drained suddenly and my heart lurches with concern.

'And it's wonderful that they've been cared and pro-vided for, but I'm afraid that still don't change the fact that actually I *do* have rights, and so do they. I ain't seen Hayley yet, but me and Marianne here have been getting to know each other and it's the best thing that's ever hap-pened to me.'

I feel instantly choked.

'I mean, for me to discover I've got this bright, beautiful, clever daughter who's seen the world and who plays the violin like a dream is the most astonishing thing.'

Mum looks astonished herself at this last bit. Her brow furrows in surprise. That was probably the last thing she was expecting Ray to come out with. Plus, I don't think it's ever occurred to her that I play the violin well. As far as she's concerned it's just a din. More a vile din than a violin. A din that gives her a headache.

'Of course I get that credit has to go to both of you and I'm not saying her turning out so well has anything to do with my genes, but that don't mean I don't want to know her now. I'm not well Alison,' he says, looking directly at Mum, who visibly blanches, so affected is she by finally being forced to look into his eyes. 'I've got cancer and it's terminal, so it ain't as if I'm going to be around bothering you all the time anyway.'

This plain truth is too much for me to deal with.

I burst into tears at which point everyone turns to stare at me, as if they'd forgotten I was even there. It's the first time I've let the immense sadness of my dad's situation overwhelm me completely. I don't want him to die. I've spent enough time with him already to know that I want him to be around. It seems so senseless hearing him fight for permission to see me. It's ridiculous because it simply isn't up to Mum, or Martin, whether I see him or not. It's up to me. Meeting him has opened up wounds I didn't know even existed and the only way to heal them is to find out what makes my father tick. In other words, I need to find out about half of the puzzle pieces that made me. I already feel a certain sense of peace that I was missing before. I feel like he gets me. I also suspect that if only he'd been around I might have made more of my life so far.

However, as much as I want to articulate all of this I can't. I'm too upset so end up stuffing my fist into my mouth, and fleeing to my bedroom.

The last thing I see as I race inside is Andy's perplexed, pasty face gawping at me. For some reason he's now clutching the burger buns, that by now have seen better days, and it briefly dawns upon me that he probably hasn't eaten anything since his flight all those hours ago. Still, won't do any harm.

As I lie on my bed weeping, I know someone will knock at my door but don't know who to expect.

As it turns out it's Mum.

'What do you want?' I sniff.

'To talk Marianne, let me in please.'

I get up and let her in. She comes in and perches on the side of the bed.

'I can't believe he turned up like that,' she says nervously.

'Can't you?' I rage. 'Is it really so hard for you to get your head round? You've kept him apart from us for decades but did you really think he'd never want to see me and Hayley ever again?'

'I'm sorry,' she says and hearing her apologise is an immense relief. I wouldn't have put it past her to try and sweep the whole situation underneath the carpet. She is the ultimate ostrich and despite the fact that years of secrets, lies and deception have just been uncovered, she'd be more than capable of pretending it's all been a bit of a silly fuss, which would have driven me mad.

'For what? What are you sorry for?' I say, wanting her to spell it out.

'For making you feel bad about wanting to see your dad,' she admits. 'I see now that it was wrong. Only… well I suppose I've seen Martin as your dad for so long now. He's been so good to us and loves you like his own.'

I know he does,' I say. 'And the last thing I want is for him to be hurt by all of this. You know I care about him a lot too. But I want this opportunity to get to know my real dad again. I know he's done bad things, but I can't help it. It's all I've ever wanted.'

'I know.'

We both sit in thoughtful silence for a while.

'Sorry,' I mumble eventually.

'It's OK. I think you needed to get that off your chest.'

'I do know it can't be easy for you.'

'I know, I know,' she soothes.

'What's happening downstairs now?' I enquire, wiping my tear-stained face.

'Well, Ray's sitting in the garden, waiting to see whether you'll see him. Martin's trying to pretend everything's normal, although I think deep down he's very cross with me.' She pulls a guilty face. The sort of face a small girl might pull when caught with her hand in the sweet jar. Martin's a push-over, we both know that, but personally this time I'm not so sure he'll let her get away with what she's done without at least a bit of a fight. She's been lying to him for years.

'Anyway, Mar's still insisting on starting up the barbe-cue even though it looks like it might rain and Andy's just getting on with it really. Oh, and Pete's having a burger in his room. I microwaved it because he was too hungry to wait for Martin. I made one for Andy too, like a little starter.'

'Andy must wonder what sort of a nuthouse he's come to,' I say dolefully.

'Yes,' says Mum. 'But I must say he's lovely Marianne. Though not quite the "surf dude" I imagined.' 'Yeah,' she continues, giving my knee a little tap. 'And not so keen on that jumper he was wearing, but that's all right, we don't love our men for their fashion sense, do we? I've been trying to get Mar into leather trousers for years.' Now it's her turn to give me a searching look. 'You don't look so sure though love?'

'I'm not really. I think men over a certain age who aren't rock stars probably shouldn't wear leather.'

'Eh? No, not about that, about Andy.'

'Oh… right, well I'm not, about that either.'

'Oh dear, that's a shame.'

'So are you going to be all right now if I want to see dad? Given that there's nothing to hide from Martin any more,' I say, unable to stop a fresh batch of tears freefalling down my face. 'And given that time is not on my side.'

'Yes,' she says, looking pretty sad herself. 'I don't know that I'll ever be able to forgive him Marianne and I'd rather not have him shoved in my face so to speak, but it's not as if he's going to be around for very long anyway… I suppose… and I really am sorry about that. You know… that he's ill. When you said it before I thought he might be exaggerating but I can see he's telling the truth. I feel terrible about it really.'

'Me too,' I sniff.

'Now, are you going to come downstairs and actually spend some time with this chappie of yours, or are me and Mar going to have to entertain him the entire time he's here. Not that Martin would mind. He's taken a right fancy to him.'

This produces a watery, faintly despairing smile from me.

'Come here you,' says Mum, pulling me in for a self-conscious hug. 'You know you girls mean the world to me, and Pete of course.'

Feeling a bit better and relieved that at least things are finally out in the open, I blow my nose into a tissue. 'Why don't you go back down Mum? I'm fine and I'll be down in a minute too. I just need to sort my face out.'

'Good idea lovey,' she agrees, just a little too enthusiastically for my liking.

CHAPTER THIRTEEN

When I reappear downstairs it's an awkward scene that greets me. Mum's trying to act as if Ray isn't even there, and like everything is perfectly normal by putting on a display of loud talking about nothing in particular, which she accompanies with lots of irritating, false laughter. Meanwhile, Martin's bristling with humiliation and unease, which somehow makes Mum's efforts all the more strained. It's obvious Martin's dying to be on his own with Mum so he can confront her about her lies. However, with Ray still there, he has to make do with diverting all his energy towards the barbecue, which Mum's already referring to as 'Barry the barbecue'. And of course, amidst all this tension and strangeness is Andy, who must have the hide of a bloody rhino.

I watch him trying to ingratiate himself with whoever's listening – so that's no one – by telling stories about what the two of us got up to in Thailand, which is tiresome and strangely inappropriate given how fragile we're all feeling.

The only person who seems totally unselfconscious is Ray who's still sitting on the same garden chair I left him on, obviously determined to stay until there's some sort of conclusion.

'All right?' he calls over, having spotted me lurking by the patio doors.

'Yeah,' I say.

'So, now it's all out in the open, we don't have to tiptoe around any more. All right? Your mum might not like it, and that's her business, but from now on I don't want you worrying or having to make up excuses to see me,' he says, and not just for my benefit.

I nod. 'OK.'

'But anyway, seeing as you seem all right, I'll make tracks now. Let you lot get on with having your barbecue,' he says wryly, making a point of looking up at the clouds, which are looking ominously rainy. Then he pulls his jacket tighter round him before looking across at Martin and pulling a face. I look away because I want to giggle and don't think it would go down well if anyone saw me doing so.

Ray gets up, comes over and touches me on the elbow. 'I'm sorry that my coming back has caused so much upset by the way.'

I shrug and shake my head dismissively. 'Don't be silly, it's fine. Well, you know, not fine, but just one of those things.'

'So anyway, what are you up to tomorrow? Or are you hanging out with lover-boy?' he says, jerking his head in Andy's direction, who looks delighted by this reference to himself and rewards me with a creepy wink.

I turn my back to him and give Ray a dirty look, fully aware that he's taking the piss. It must be obvious to him what a disaster that whole issue is.

'I mean, I'm sure you'll want to spend a bit of time together discussing grilling techniques,' he adds in a sly whisper.

'I'm working tomorrow actually,' I reply, narrowing my eyes, while my brow knits into a warning frown.

'Oh, by the way Marianne, speaking of work,' interrupts Mum, who's been busying herself round the barbecue, in a blatant attempt to suck up to Martin and get back in his good books. She looks thankful for a reason to stop. She's being so cloying she's probably making herself feel sick. 'You got a call earlier. Someone needs you to do a party on Sunday, if you're free. Their fairy's ill, or something like that. Someone recommended you.'

'Oh,' I say, head swirling. Once again it's incredibly inconvenient that Andy's here because actually doing a party on Sunday would be great. I don't have any more party bookings for a few weeks, so could do with the money. Apart from anything else I want to pay for some violin lessons. My teacher's back from her holidays soon and I'm desperate for a session.

'Um, well it kind of depends on Andy,' I say loudly, hoping he'll get the hint. He too is busy fiddling with the new barbecue, filling it with charcoal.

'Fine by me, sweets. You just carry on,' he says, grinning at me drippily, and I notice he's managed to get ketchup down his front already from his 'pre-dinner' burger.

'OK,' I reply, relieved but also wondering what on earth he's going to do with himself during all the time I won't be here. If only he'd get the hint.

'Let's speak soon then,' says Ray. 'Although, I'd love to see you in your clown costume on Sunday. Sounds bleedin' hilarious.'

'Feel free,' I say, suddenly wondering hopefully whether the sight of me dressed in my clown clothes might put Andy off. If so I'd happily put them on now. I'd happily do a number of things that ordinarily I'd shy away from. Stick my hand in the toaster, eat a jar of peanut butter on a hot day with nothing to drink, pierce my labia, share a sleeping bag with a scorpion. You get the picture.

Ray and I say goodbye and as soon as he's left, Mum and Martin disappear into the house to 'discuss' a few things, leaving Andy and I alone for the first time since he arrived at the house. He comes over to where I'm slumped despondently in a chair and pulls up a lounger.

'It's so good to see you baby,' he says lovingly.

'It's… really nice to see you too,' I say, though I'm distracted by the sound of Martin's raised voice floating through the window. It isn't a sound you hear often.

'So good to see you,' he repeats somewhat unnecessarily.

'Yeah…' I agree faintly. 'Bit weird somehow, you know, not being on a beach in the sun, and you being here for the first time my mum and dad have seen each other in years and when my sister's lost her baby but… great… though I'm a bit worried about what you're going to do now you're here. You see I've got to go to work tomorrow and it looks like I'll have to work on Sunday now too and…'

'Don't worry,' he says, reaching over to stroke my face, which makes me want to heave. I feel like such a bitch but I can't help it.

'You just do what you have to do and don't worry about me. I'll go into town tomorrow and see some sights probably. You can just point me in the direction of the station and I'll be fine.'

'OK,' I say, grateful at least for how capable and independent he is.

'Besides, Martin has already said he's around tomorrow and that he might take some days off work so that he can take me to the driving range and to somewhere called Homebase I think it was, which would be awesome.'

'Right,' I say faintly.

*

Six days later and I'm wriggling into my Custard the Clown outfit. I'm a bit late because I got distracted listening to Bach's concerto for two violins and lost track of the time. It's hard to describe what happens to me when I listen to the classical music I love, but it's a form of escape for sure. It relaxes me and has the ability to transform my outlook, my energy and mindset. It's the equivalent to taking my brain out and running it under a cold tap.

For some people exercise achieves the same thing, for
others reading or other types of music. For me it's the
synchronicity of an orchestra, the way the instruments
weave together and the haunting sound of my favourite
instrument taking centre stage.

Anyway, it's worked its magic this morning and I feel
ready for the day ahead.

Just then my phone goes. It's Ray.

'You still "clowning around" this morning?'

'Yep.'

'Lover-boy going with you?'

'No, he's out with Martin, and please don't call him that.'

'Out with Martin, eh? Blimey, think of the fun those two
musketeers must be having.'

I suppress a grin, refusing to give Dad the satisfaction of
knowing he's making me laugh. Truthfully, I'm so relieved
I'm able to offload Andy on to Martin and have been doing
so all week. He's been trying to persuade me to sneak into
his room at night, but I've also been telling him I've got
headaches and that I need to sleep alone until they're better.
Last night however, he ended up trying to sneak into my
room and indeed bed, three times in total. In the end, out
of desperation, I told him I was on my period, which did
the trick. However, my avoidance of all physical contact
seems to be increasing his ardour, so sooner or later I'm
going to have to sit him down and have the inevitable 'we
need to talk' talk.

'I'm in your neck of the woods as it goes.'

'Are you?' I say, heaving up my braces, while balancing the phone between my ear and my shoulder. Damn, now there's pan-stick make-up all over my phone.

'Yeah, so feel free to say no but I was serious about wanting to come with you today, and not just to take the piss. If you're up for it I could be with you in ten. I'd really like to see you in action.'

I shrug, before adjusting my wig in the mirror. 'Come then, though they might think it's a bit weird that I've bought you along,' I add, secretly worrying that Ray will stick out like a sore thumb at a kid's party.

'I'll keep out the way I promise, and if they ask, I'll say I'm your glamorous assistant.'

'Fine,' I say, loathe to refuse a request to spend time together. Besides, things I ordinarily would fret about, no longer seem worth the effort.

*

When Dad turns up and I answer the door, his reaction to my costume is the usual – surprise followed by deep amusement.

I wouldn't really mind – seeing him laugh is actually very gratifying – only he's not alone. Standing next to him on the front step is Matthew. At least I assume it's Matthew, only because I've heard a fair bit about my dad's nurse and this person is wearing a white male nurse's uniform. He's quite tall, probably in his early thirties, has a slim build and light brown, curly hair – not curly as in my clown wig curly, curly in a good way – wavy and a bit unkempt. He has a really pleasant, open face. Very friendly, with brown eyes that crinkle up at the sides as he smiles. His congenial appearance is offset though, in a ruggedly masculine way, by what's probably about a three-day growth. Basically, he's what my mum would call 'a right Bobby Dazzler', or to put it a less cruise-ship way, he's fit. Gorgeous in fact.

So it's obviously completely fantastic that I'm dressed as a clown.

'Matthew, meet Marianne. My youngest daughter.'

'Ah right, very pleased to meet you, Marianne,' he says, extending a hand and smiling at me.

'Hi,' I say, desperately trying to sort out my wonky wig with one hand while shaking his with the other.

'I'm your father's support nurse.'

'Oh, of course,' I reply. 'Great to meet you. Just to say I don't usually dress like this.'

'That's a shame,' Matthew smiles warmly. 'It suits you!'

I laugh weakly and then the three of us stand there in awkward silence until Dad finally pipes up, 'Right, well thanks for the lift Matt, and for everything else as usual. I'll see you soon and perhaps you two will meet again under slightly more normal circumstances another time?'

'That would be great,' says Matthew politely, while I quietly die inside.

Once Matthew has finally headed off, no doubt laughing to himself about what an utter freak I am, Dad and I squash into Tina and sit in companiable silence, which is only interrupted sporadically by him spluttering as a new wave of laughter at my outfit overtakes him. His laugh is a deep, throaty, belly laugh; an unfamiliar sound and therefore another reminder of our estrangement over the years.

'You're out of order,' I say eventually. 'That was so embarrassing. He must think I'm a right freak.'

'I had no idea you'd already be suited and booted. But don't worry about it, Matt's a good boy. He'll think you're brilliant.

I give him a look that says that I very much doubt that.

'So, when's your next music lesson?' he manages to say eventually with a straight face, finally aware that if he carries on laughing I'm going to start getting properly annoyed.

I glance across. 'Why all this interest in my days and how I fill them?'

He stares fixedly out of the window. 'Got to pack it all in, ain't I?'

'Oh,' I say, regretting what was a pretty stupid question in retrospect. I gulp. 'Well, Mrs Demetrius has been on holiday, but she gets back next week so I'll probably have a lesson next Thursday evening. That's when I usually go.'

'Can I come?'

'Course, yeah,' I reply, scanning the house numbers as we drive by. 'If you want to.'

'We here then?' asks Dad, as we pull up to a semi-detached, well cared for house that has balloons tied to the gate.

We look a right pair as I struggle up the path in my clown shoes. As I ring the bell I hear a squeal from the other side of the door. I turn and signal to Dad to join me, thankful that due to the spring-like nature of the day at least he isn't wearing his leather coat.

An attractive blonde mum answers the door. 'Hiya, thanks so much for coming at such short notice. Look at you, you look brilliant! I'm Julie by the way.'

'Nice to meet you, and glad I could help.'

'I was totally desperate. I think I explained to your mum I had a fairy booked but she phoned to say she was going on a hen weekend instead.'

'Oh, well that's charming,' I say.

'I know, I wasn't particularly impressed I can tell you,' says Julie, rolling her eyes. 'Still, come in and I'll get my daughter to come and say hi. I think she's pretending to be shy right now. Lexie the clown's here,' she calls.

Small feet appear at the top of the stairs.

'Come on,' encourages her mother. 'Come down and say hello to Custard and... sorry, are you together?' she asks, finally registering Dad who's standing behind me.

'Yes, sorry,' I say. 'This is Ray, my... assistant for the day.'

She doesn't look terribly sure about this and I can see her wondering what to say. Ray flashes her his most ingratiating smile though, and eventually I think she realises that we've come as a package and that therefore she doesn't have much choice other than to be cool with it while cross-ing her fingers we aren't about to raid her house.

'OK, well come on in, ah Lexie, there you are.'

'Hi Lexie,' I say enthusiastically. I can instantly tell she's the shy type and that she'll be difficult to get much out of.

'All right Lexie,' says Dad, in his rasping voice. I was amazed when I found out he hasn't smoked for years. Sometimes it sounds like he's on thirty a day.

'Hello,' the little girl says shyly, winding herself round her mum's legs, like a cat.

'Come on in and get set up then,' says Julie. 'And I'll get the kettle on.'

*

Forty minutes later and the party's underway. Dad proves to be surprisingly helpful setting up but what's even more astounding is how much Lexie takes to him. She still isn't one hundred percent about me, the weirdo in the blue curly wig – who can blame her. Ray however, the ageing felon, she loves.

As I watch him chasing her round the room, whipping her up into a state of hyper excitement I feel a stabbing pain of regret for all the years of fathering I missed out on as a kid. Now is not the time to start wallowing or getting maudlin however so I force myself to focus back on the task in hand. A handful of kids have arrived by now and more are on their way in.

Ten minutes later, a small crowd is gathered round me

cross-legged on the floor. 'So, has anyone seen my friend, Harry the hedgehog?' I say.

'He's behind you,' they chorus frantically, and they're right. However, a children's entertainer is required to pretend to be not only blind, but deaf and unbelievably dense too. Of course, the truth of the matter is that my hand's wedged up Harry's backside, so not knowing where he is, probably pushes the realms of feasibility. However, small children never seem to question my horrific powers of observation and these are no exception. And I know they aren't just being polite and thinking, 'Poor old dear. Doesn't even know where the puppet is when it's wedged on her own hand,' because small children don't suffer from such social constraints and always say what they're really thinking. Which is why when one little boy asks Ray if he's a grumpy pirate, it's so funny. To be fair I can completely see where he's coming from.

Fortunately Dad takes it in good humour and replies that that's exactly what he is, for which I'm very grateful. Things could have got awkward if he'd said, 'No you little shit, I am not a bleedin' grumpy pirate.'

I glance across to Ray. He's sitting astride a kitchen chair, seemingly tickled pink to see me in action and laughing his head off. Mostly *at* me I'm sure, but actually having him here is really nice. Nobody's seen me 'doing my stuff' before and it makes a nice change. Then a late arrival changes my mood.

For entering the room in patent party shoes and an outfit

that screams, 'I dressed myself and my parents went with it,' is none other than Maisie. As in Simon's daughter. Nightmare!

Thankfully, however, Simon is nowhere to be seen, for attached to Maisie's hand is a woman I can only presume to be 'mummy'. Mummy's predictably gorgeous though. I feel a pang of pity for her for being married to an unfaithful shitbag.

A little girl interrupts my reverie. 'Why aren't you saying anything? You said you were going to do magic.'

With a start I realise lots of small indignant faces are staring at me so I get back to the trick in hand though inevitably brat fink sees to it that it isn't long before our previous history comes to light.

'I don't like that clown,' I hear Maisie lisping evilly from the other side of the room, pointing her stubby finger in my direction. 'That clown sucks.'

'Maisie,' implores her mother indulgently. I wait for her to admonish her but she doesn't. Hence, why one should always blame the parents. Still, soon enough Mummy leaves, probably looking forward to a Maisie-free few hours – I know I would be – at which point I relax. I'm not worried. I can handle four-year-old Maisie who simply isn't a worthy adversary.

At tea-time Dad and I sneak into the garden for a breather from all the chaos and noise inside.

'You're a natural at this,' Ray says, grinning. 'Seriously,

I'm well proud of you, there's not many who could be so patient.'

I shrug but inside feel lit up by his praise.

'That Maisie kid's a handful though, ain't she? Right little brat. I don't remember you or Hayley ever being that annoying. Probably needs a good hiding,' he adds, somewhat controversially. 'Someone needs to teach her some manners.'

'Her dad could do with a lesson in those too.'

'What d'you mean?' asks Ray, gulping back the tea Julie's made him.

'Oh, it's silly really,' I explain. 'I was out one night and got chatted up by this bloke. Anyway, thankfully I didn't fall for his bullshit because the next day I was doing another party and he turned up. He was only there to pick his daughter up who happened to be none other than the delightful Maisie.'

'You're joking,' says Dad, looking stunned. 'So he's divorced or summink is he?'

'No, most definitely married,' I add. 'Because when he recognised me he looked like he'd seen a ghost.'

'Did he now.'

'Yeah,' I say, shaking my head at my own naiveté. 'I confronted him and he made it very clear his wife wouldn't be particularly impressed if she knew what he'd been up to.'

Ray's visibly angry. His jaw's clenched and his cheek starts to twitch somewhat alarmingly.

'But it's no big deal,' I say quickly. 'Seriously, I mean it's not like I care or anything, and no one got hurt.'

'That's hardly the point now, is it Custard?' asks Ray and in that instant I wish whole-heartedly I hadn't said anything.

'Are you guys OK to come back in now, we're about to cut the cake and er, Lexie wants her picture taken with you Ray, if that's OK?' interrupts Julie, doing her best to conceal how odd she thinks it is that her daughter has taken such a shine to my father.

Glad of a natural conclusion to the conversation that's taken such an uncomfortable turn for the worse, I dash back into the fray.

*

Ten minutes later and mums and dads are starting to show up. I pray hard that Simon doesn't show his face. I wouldn't put it past Ray to say something. Another example of how naturally paternal and protective he is, and yet that still jars a bit. Having spent a bit of time with him now, I have to admit that I'm starting to feel worryingly attached. I feel... fond of him. Plus, although it makes me feel disloyal to admit it, I seem to have more of a connection with him than I do with certain other members of my family. Yet despite all this, there's no getting away from the fact that he's still a relative stranger – excuse the pun – one who has gate-crashed my life and turned it upside down in the most brutal way. I really like being with him but at times the whole situation, that is to say, know-ing he's dying, is so bittersweet I feel like I can hardly breathe. It's all a bit of a head-fuck to tell you the truth.

Naturally Simon *does* turn up to collect devil child. I sigh when I see him appear, though thankfully this time I barely care about the fact I'm dressed as a clown and am therefore looking about as sexually attractive as a hairy wart. I mean, I care a bit, but not in the same heart-stopping way I did last time. Not in the way I did when Matthew turned up at my front door either, at which point I cared a lot. He was lovely. Anyway, I have bigger concerns in my life, like a long-lost, ill dad. Not to mention a lovesick Andy who's skulking around my house, waiting and plotting to have his wicked way with me.

Simon catches my eye for about a millisecond and im-mediately ushers Maisie, who I suspect may be banned from all future parties from this day forth, away. Not caring one iota I turn round and start concentrating on the other children, doling out their party bags. As I do though, I notice out of the corner of my eye that Ray's looking in Simon's direction, and that his eyes are screwed up in consternation.

I shake my head at him, warning him to leave it, but to my dismay he ignores me and heads towards the hall.

My heart plummets. Oh Christ, what's he up to? I dread to think and find myself praying that he's unselfish enough to leave it alone.

By now I'm practically hurling bags at children.

'There you go, that's yours, thanks for coming,' I gush.

'Why have I got a girl's bag, I don't want a girl's bag,' whines one boy.

'Oh gosh, have you got a girl's bag? I didn't mean to give you that but if you wouldn't mind, perhaps you could just… deal with it?' I ask, looking frantically in the direction of the hallway.

The boy's answer is to open his mouth and give me an incredible view of his tonsils.

'OK, OK,' I placate, desperate to stave the wail that's clearly about to be issued from his open mouth. 'Of course you can't have a girl's bag. I don't know what silly old Custard was thinking,' I say, reaching for my bag and producing a comedy hammer made out of foam and beating myself on the head with it.

'Silly, silly Custard,' I say and the boy's tears turn to laughter, the hysterical type, a result of changing emotional gear so quickly.

I rummage desperately around and finally find a gender-appropriate party bag, all the while thinking 'Please Dad, don't be outside wrapping Simon round a lamp post'.

Finally all the children are sorted out, leaving me free to squeeze past chatting parents into the hallway – not an easy task when you've got boats on your feet. Some of them laugh openly at the sight of me in my blue wig and normally I'd take full advantage of their amusement by handing out my business cards left, right and centre. Right now though, I have too much on my mind to bother. I'm a very flustered clown.

There's no sign of Ray in the hall so I head for the front door. As soon as I've opened it Maisie appears, at waist level, a truculent apparition who barges rudely past me.

'What are you doing?' I ask lightly, hoping she isn't on her way back in to call an ambulance, having just witnessed a grumpy pirate assaulting her father.

'Daddy said I could get another piece of cake,' she lisps before sticking her tongue out at me and marching into the house. She really is a delightful little thing.

Placing one enormous shoe tentatively out of the front door, I pluck up the courage to follow it outside. The first person I see is a completely unharmed Simon. He's chatting into his mobile phone in the front garden, to the left of the house.

'All right Custard?' growls a familiar voice behind me.

I jump out of my skin and turn around.

Ray's leaning against the wall, arms crossed. I look from him back to Simon, who for now is entirely unaware of our presence.

'What are you doing out here? You weren't going to do anything were you? Please don't. I'll be livid if you do.'

'Calm down,' Ray says, looking faintly aggrieved. 'I ain't done nuffink and I'm not going to either. I wouldn't do that to you. Specially not at a kids' party. What do you take me for?'

I feel ashamed and defensive. 'Well what are you doing out here then?'

'Keeping an eye on Mister. That's all.'

Just then Simon gets off the phone at which point he notices me. As soon as he does, a mean grin spreads across his face and instantly I feel wary of what he might say. I try my hardest to appear righteous and a bit haughty but it's futile given that there's a huge grin painted on my face.

'Ah, Marianne, the glamorous actress,' he says. 'What's the matter? Can't keep away?'

Keenly aware that Ray's watching our every move, I pick my way tentatively down the gravel path towards him.

Once I've reached him, annoyingly I can feel a ticklish piece of wig in my eye. I blow upwards in order to get rid of it before saying, 'I think you owe me an apology.'

He regards me with a look of contempt and edges towards me until his face is only inches from mine. 'I have got something to say to you as it goes,' he says.

Feeling pleased and relieved that he's finally come to his senses I say more cockily, 'Spit it out then.'

'OK,' says Simon, clearing his throat. 'I just want to say, that if you know what's good for you, you'll stop doing parties for anyone who goes to the Rainbow nursery, or for any child who's going to Chigwell Primary next year.'

'Pardon?' I say, not convinced I've heard right.

'In fact,' he continues in the same deathly calm, low voice, 'I don't ever want to see your stupid painted face anywhere near my daughter or her friends again, and if I do I shall be telling the parents around here precisely what sort of a little slut you are.'

I gasp. 'How dare you?' I say, as hot tears spring into my eyes. I can't believe he's being such a bastard. At this point we're kind of circling one another and I glance briefly back towards Ray, who although is still leaning against the wall has his gaze fixed in our direction. He's looking vaguely concerned so I give him a weak thumbs-up to put him off the scent. I can't be totally sure he wouldn't smash Simon's face in if he knew what he was really saying.

'Oh I dare,' Simon says coolly, really invading my personal space now, his face uncomfortably close to mine.

'And let me tell you,' he continues, 'That around here, I'm pretty damn popular with the mums. Especially one or two of them,' he sneers unnecessarily. 'So, if you say anything, it'll be my word against yours, Coco. Not that what you'd say would count for anything anyway. You're pathetic.'

A lone tear courses down my face, but I know from past experience not to rub while wearing pan-stick so watch forlornly as it splashes onto my shoe. My bloody wig is still getting in my eyes. I shove it up slightly. Simon smirks.

I know there are so many things I should be saying back, only my mind's gone completely blank. Still, thankfully it seems that Simon has finished his piece. He turns to go, presumably to retrieve devil child from the house.

'You all right Marianne?' calls Ray, his face full of

anxious concern. He's purposefully kept his distance out of respect to me but now I half-wished he hadn't.

'I'm fine Dad,' I reply shakily.

Having heard, Simon turns back for a second, a contemptuous expression on his face. 'Dad?' he repeats, as if this is one of the funniest things he's ever heard.

My heart sinks. 'What's so funny about that?' I say grimly.

'Nothing, now if it's all right with you and your charming father I think I'll get back to my child thanks.'

'Go for it,' I say lamely.

And if he'd just left it there, everything would have been fine. But he doesn't. Instead he has to leave us with a parting shot.

'Should have known,' he smirks, voice full of contempt. 'After all, the apple never falls far from the tree.'

That's it. I've had it and, at the same time, recover the power of speech. 'How dare you judge us? At least respect the fact that you're the one in the wrong and that therefore you owe me an apology.'

Then Simon does another thing he shouldn't. He laughs, which to a small degree is understandable because of course I'm still dressed as a clown. So therefore, me trying to convey fury probably *is* a funny and pitiful sight, but that still doesn't make it OK. And then I do something pretty low, which thinking about it, probably does rather betray my roots. Shaking like a leaf, I find myself turning towards Ray, meeting his gaze and nodding my head, in a small yet decisive gesture, one that's probably imperceptible to Simon and yet gives Dad all the encouragement he needs.

'Thank bleedin' gawd for that,' he mutters.

Then, avoiding a couple of surprised-looking parents who are emerging from the house, offspring in tow, Ray unfolds his arms and strides purposefully up to Simon. Unfortunately, Simon's still so busy laughing at me like some idiotic pantomime villain – mmwwaaahhahah – that he isn't remotely aware of what's happening. Though he soon shuts up when, from nowhere, Ray grabs him by the scruff of the neck and hauls him towards the side of the house. Horrified by what I've instigated I make my way over to the parents who are standing at the door, mouths open.

'Ha ha,' I laugh inanely. Then, when that doesn't satisfy them, I add mysteriously, 'No need to be worried. We're just showing that guy some material from our new act.'

Which means as much to me as it does to them.

They seem to accept this strange explanation though so, future clients placated, I leave them and leg it as fast as I am able – *fucking shoes* – to the side of the house. By now Ray's manhandled Simon right down the side alley and despite having made it happen, I feel sickened as I watch him being shoved around. I can't believe Ray's strength. Simon's feet are barely dragging along the ground and I watch in amazement as with one arm Ray then picks Simon up and slams him against the wall, at which point he – shitbag – looks absolutely terrified. He's the colour of putty, and for a fleeting second it's all quite satisfying, until that is, good sense prevails and I realise I have to end things before they get truly out of hand.

'Put him down,' I order.

'What?' says Ray, looking terribly disappointed by my change of heart.

I nod, adamant that I only wanted to scare him. Not kill him.

Ray snarls menacingly but, thankfully, does as he's told. Simon collapses to the ground like a crumpled puppet, at which point I realise Ray had been holding him at least a foot off the ground. For a sick man he's certainly very strong.

'Now, unless you want me to kick you into the beginning of next week, apologise to my daughter,' he growls.

Simon remains splayed on the ground, clearly too nervous to make even the smallest movement. Spineless twat.

'Oh get up, will you,' I snap.

Wordlessly he does as he's told before edging silently past Ray, avoiding his glacial stare. When he gets to me he stops and, looking somewhere over my right shoulder, murmurs, 'Sorry about the other night.'

'It's fine,' I mumble back.

'I didn't quite catch that,' says Ray.

'I said,' repeats Simon, his voice catching, 'I'm really sorry about the other night.'

'Now fuck off,' adds Ray. 'And if you so much as look in my daughter's direction again, or cause any shit for her whatsoever, I will come round your house in the middle of the night and you will wake up wearing your nuts as earrings. Do I make myself clear?'

Simon nods and does as he's told. He fucks off, leaving Ray and I eyeballing each other in the side passage. He's the first to break the silence.

'Now don't tell me you didn't get just the smallest kick out of that, Custard?'

I stare back at him as disapprovingly as I can, but finally the image of Simon's previously smug face looking so petrified is too much and my face ends up breaking into a reluctant grin. I still don't wholly approve but have to admit that getting revenge is pretty satisfying. It's also good to have someone looking out for me and fighting my corner. Actually that's not quite accurate. What I really mean is it's good to have my dad looking out for me.

CHAPTER FOURTEEN

'He's a teddy bear,' I say on the phone to Hayley that night. 'Honestly, wouldn't hurt a fly.'

'Yeah,' she says stonily. 'Well I'll be the judge of that.'

'How are you anyway?' I add, worried that in retrospect I might be laying it on a bit thick, given what I witnessed the previous afternoon. The haunted look in Simon's eye is something I won't forget for a long time.

'Fine,' she replies and I feel a deep sadness that since losing the baby, my sister has chosen to revert back to her stand-offish ways. She let me in, briefly, but now it seems I've been shoved unceremoniously back out again.

'Good, well I'm really pleased you've decided to see Ray, though I can't think why you want to do it at Mum's. Why don't we go somewhere different, the three of us, somewhere that's neutral territory?'

'Because,' says Hayley crossly, 'Mum may be an annoying cow sometimes but at least she's always had my best interests at heart. And besides, I'll feel safer meeting him somewhere I don't think he'll cause a scene.'

'You're making him out to be some kind of nutter,' I protest. 'But he's really not like that and…'

'I don't want to argue about it,' she says. 'Just because he's got you wrapped round his finger doesn't mean I'm going to roll over like some little puppy and if you keep bugging me about it, I won't see him at all. Besides, I need to talk to Mum about stuff so by coming over I can kill two birds with one stone.'

'OK,' I say, knowing her threats aren't idle. 'That's fine. Hayley are you OK? I know you must be so sad and just want you to know that I am here for you. Even if it's three in the morning, if you need to talk, just pick up the phone.'

'Weirdo. I'm hardly likely to do that, am I?'

At least I've said it. 'Right, so do you want to do it Tuesday night then? Is Gary coming?'

'Course, he's my husband isn't he?'

'Yeah, funnily enough I do know that,' I say impatiently. I thought it was a fair enough question. As far as I can make out Gary shies away from anything that is remotely delicate to handle.

'And I'll get to meet your Andy,' she says meanly.

'Mm,' I say, refusing to rise to the bait. Right now 'my' Andy is downstairs sharing a cosy TV supper of chicken Kiev, smiley face potatoes and carrots with Mum and Martin as they play along with *Who Wants to be a Millionaire*. Not quite the scene most intrepid travellers dream of but he seems happy enough. In fact he seems disturbingly bedded in and content.

I'd fully intended to have 'the chat' with him tonight, but once again have been defeated by the day and now feel too shattered to cope with it. I'll have to have it soon though. The 'I've got my period' excuse has just about run its course. In fact earlier, when he asked me whether I still had it and I said yes, he suggested I see a gynaecologist.

As soon as I've got off the phone from Hayley I phone Ray to impart the good news that his eldest daughter has agreed to see him in a mere two days' time. The bad news is that she wants to do it here. She might as well have suggested we all meet for a casual drink in a pressure cooker as far as I'm concerned.

*

On Monday I experience the novel feeling of being glad to get into work. Apart from anything else it's nice to see Jason.

'All right,' he says, looking pleased to see me. 'How are you, stranger? What's going on in the weird and wonderful world of Marianne Baker then?'

'You don't want to know,' I say, slipping off my jacket.

'Er, why would I ask if I didn't want to know? You're the one who's gone all quiet and mysterious on me lately.'

'OK,' I say, sighing and signalling to him to follow me into the staff room. Once we're both in, I shut the door behind us.

'Are you all right?' Jason says, taking in my serious

expression. 'Seriously, I feel like for ages now you've been avoiding me and I want to know why.'

'I'm fine,' I sigh. 'It's just… I know you think I've been mucking you around and being a bad friend but I really have genuinely had a lot on my plate. Basically, in the last few weeks, I've discovered that my dad is here, in England, but that he's dying and only has months to live. Hayley's been pregnant but has lost the baby and Andy, the guy I've mentioned to you before, the one from Thailand, has turned up on my doorstep. Only I don't like him any more and of course all this is going on under Mum's roof, and living there is not only humiliating at my age but incredibly hard work and stifling too. Apart from that it's been quiet,' I say, mustering up a weak smile. 'Just your average few weeks really.'

Jason's facial expressions are struggling to keep up. I register a lot of genuine pity and sympathy for me, along with a huge dollop of shock, all of which threatens to unhinge me completely.

'But I don't really want to talk about it all today, if that's OK. I will at some point bore you with all of it, in detail, I promise, but today I just want to try and forget about it…' I will myself to keep it together, not wanting to go to pieces just as the first customers are starting to arrive.

Despite having a head full of questions, Jason immediately touches me lightly on the arm in a gesture that's both comforting and understanding. 'Don't you worry,' he says. 'It can all wait, and full marks for having the most unbelievable answer ever to the question "what have you been up to". Don't ever let anyone tell you you're not full of surprises.'

I smile back gratefully, not convinced I'll be able to hold it together if he's nice to me any more. With that in mind I take a deep breath, turn round and open the door. The salon's already a noisy hubbub of hairdryers, music and chattering so I decide to set to work cleaning brushes, which turns out to be surprisingly therapeutic. Frankly I have to take these mundane moments where I can because at the moment they're few and far between. The next set of relationship Olympics are only a day away, for tomorrow evening our dad is meeting Hayley for the first time in years.

*

The next day, after another mind-numbing yet strangely soothing day at work, I can't work out who's more nervous about Ray's summons to our house. Ray, me, Hayley, or Mum. When I get home she's already there with Gary, sat round the breakfast bar with Mum. It doesn't take long for me to notice that they're surrounded by *Sing for Britain* paperwork.

'What are you doing?' I ask.

'Oh Marianne, fabulous news,' gushes Mum. 'Hayley's reconsidered. She's going to enter *Sing for Britain*.'

'Why?' I ask aghast.

'Why not?' Hayley counters stroppily. 'Just 'cos you

don't think I'm up to it, doesn't mean they won't. I'm thinking of doing a power ballad.'

My heart sinks even deeper into my boots. Meanwhile Gary stands behind her, a silent lump of masculinity. He's eating a banana, which certainly doesn't help him appear less like the missing link.

'Look,' I say patiently, 'It's been a long day and I don't want to argue. Do whatever you want. It's your life and I hope you do well.'

'I can hear you don't mean that,' says Hayley who's back to her groomed self again. Her hair hangs down her back, shiny, blonde and glossy in a way that can only have been achieved at the hairdressers.

Just then the doorbell rings. We all look at each other, panicked.

'Where's Martin?' I ask.

'Out,' says Mum. 'He's taken Andy and Pete out for a meal at the pub. I thought it was probably best they weren't here.'

I nod in agreement as the door rings again.

'Is anyone actually going to get that then?' asks Gary, looking mildly amused by the situation, which is pretty mean considering there isn't anything funny about it as far as we're all concerned.

'I'll get it,' I say, wanting the first face my father sees to be a friendly one.

'Oh my god,' I hear Hayley gasp as I wander through

to the hallway. 'I'm about to meet my dad. How fucking weird is that?'

'Language Hayls,' I hear Mum say followed by, 'But you're right, it is weird.'

I open the door.

'All right,' says Ray, hands thrust deep into their pockets.

I can't help myself, I find myself looking over his shoulder, checking to see whether he's brought Matthew with him. Not that there's any rational reason why he would. Still, I'm almost a bit disappointed when I realise he's definitely not there. I made sure I look half-decent tonight, just in case I got the chance to rectify Matthew's opinion of me after the clown debacle. Silly really.

'All right, you OK?'

'Yeah, yeah, just you know… bit…'

I nod, demonstrating that I know exactly what he means, trying to ignore the butterflies that are in my own belly at this precise moment. 'Come in then.'

As Ray follows me through to the kitchen I feel rigid with nerves and hardly dare turn around to see whether he's OK.

'Hello,' I hear him say to everyone.

Mum sort of melts into the background, her face hardening a bit as soon as she sees him. Gary finishes off his banana, and Hayley remains rooted to the spot on her bar stool, two high, pink patches colouring her cheeks.

'It's good to see you,' says Dad, tentatively looking

directly at his eldest daughter. 'Thanks for agreeing to see me.'

I will Hayley to give him something to work with. Hello would be a start, but she just stares at him, her expression impassive. Clearly he's going to have to do all the running and when I really stop to think about it, that's probably fair enough. He did abandon us. And yet I have progressed so much from the place my sister's in now, that being so brittle and cold seems like a waste of time really. I want to speed things up to the bit where she stops trying to punish him for what he's done and accepts the fact that she can't change the past but can improve the future.

'Do you want us to leave the room?' I ask over-brightly, turning to both Hayley and Dad. 'You know, if you want a bit of privacy.'

'Anything he's got to say he can say in front of every-one,' says Hayley, and her voice is scathing.

'Well, what do you want to know?' tries Dad. 'I mean, I'm sure Marianne's filled you in on what's been happening, and it goes without saying that I'm so sorry for not being around. I wish things had been different. With hindsight I wish you girls had always known the truth, though the fact you didn't was partly your mum's decision.'

At this Mum looks utterly indignant. Eyes narrowed, she exclaims, 'Don't you dare go pinning this on me Raymond. How dare you? I wasn't the one who went to prison.'

'All right, all right,' says Ray, holding his hands up in defence. 'I'm not saying you were. I'm just trying to point out that things aren't always as black and white as they seem.'

I cringe. This approach isn't going to work well with Hayley. I know my sister and a bit of begging for forgiveness is probably more the kind of thing she's after, and yet Ray's coming across as prickly, probably due to nerves. Even I can see he could do with being a bit more contrite.

He falls silent and looks at Hayley expectantly. Once again I find myself staring at her, willing her to say something, anything, even if it's a burst of angry vitriol, which would at least demonstrate she cares. The silence becomes awkward. I frown at her but she pretends not to see and folds her arms across her chest. I don't know what she's expecting him to do.

Ray clears his throat and turns his attentions to Gary. 'So, you must be Hayley's husband then? Good to meet you. When did the pair of you get hitched?'

'Nearly three years ago now,' says Gary pleasantly enough, and Hayley shoots him an evil.

'Fantastic. I wish I could have been there. Bet you looked a picture, Hayley.'

'She did,' agrees Mum frostily, refusing to look in Ray's direction. 'Stunning she was. Martin was proud to give her away.'

It's a cheap shot. I glare at Mum but she glares back.

'There's a photo somewhere,' pipes up Gary, mouth full of his last bit of banana. 'Do you want to see it?'

'Oh yeah,' says Dad affably, pointedly ignoring Mum's dig. 'That would be great. I'd love to if that's OK.'

'Oh for fuck's sake,' shrieks Hayley suddenly, giving us all a heart attack. 'What is this shit? Why are you talking to him like everything's normal? You killed someone,' she shouts. 'You killed someone and then disappeared out of our lives completely.'

'I know,' says Dad quietly.

'So don't expect me to sit here making chit-chat with you about my wedding,' she snarls. 'Which obviously you would have been at had you bothered to have anything to do with us our entire lives. As it is I couldn't give a shit about what you have to say and I only agreed to see you so you'd get that into your thick head.'

I gasp, shocked by my sister's aggression. Gary, who's shifting from foot to foot, looks mildly embarrassed and even Mum looks uncomfortable, which seems to win out because next she says, 'Hayley, maybe cool it a bit sweetheart.'

Dad shoots her a surprised but grateful look, as do I.

Maybe what Hayley said is warranted? Maybe even deserved? Yet surely, taking into account the exceptional circumstances we're all aware of, she could water things down a little? Only Hayley could manage to make Ray be the one everyone feels sorry for in this situation.

'Look, I know I've made massive mistakes in my life,' begins Ray calmly. 'And I'm not expecting things to be like the bleedin' Brady Bunch within minutes of meeting each other, but shouting like that ain't going to solve anything.'

'Are you OK?' I ask suddenly. I notice he's sweating a little and he looks ever so unsteady on his feet.

'Yeah,' he says, not wholly convincingly. 'Any chance of a glass of water?'

'Yeah course,' I say, rushing to get him one.

Ray walks forward and sits at the table.

'Are you really OK?' says Mum, who I know wouldn't be enquiring after his health to be sociable. I can't be imagining things then. He must look a bit dodgy.

'Yeah,' says Ray, looking distinctly pale now and wan. 'Just give us a minute.' He bends forward and puts his head between his legs. I assume he must be feeling faint.

I glare at Hayley who's looking mildly discomforted, but only mildly. I realise in that moment that him feeling ill probably contributed to his slightly odd manner earlier.

'See what you've done,' I accuse.

'Oh fuck off,' she snaps back. 'Don't go laying this shit on me. He's probably only pretending, to make himself look better, anyway.'

At this Dad looks up momentarily but is clearly in too much of a state to respond to what she just said. He's looking really ill now and my heart begins to race with stress.

'Dad, what can I do?' I say, handing him the water and helping the glass to his mouth. He must be feeling too weak or too lousy to cope with it though because feebly he flaps my hand away. I feel totally helpless. 'Shall I phone someone, an ambulance or something?'

'Nah. There's no need,' he manages to say, but he's taking deep breaths and looks like he's feeling really dizzy.

'OK, just take a deep breath Dad.' Bizarrely, I'm very conscious that I'm calling him Dad, not Ray like I usually do.

'I think maybe call one anyway,' pipes up Mum in a quiet voice.

'Really?' I say, searching her face for clues, trying to surmise what her take on the situation really is. She looks deadly serious.

'OK, I'm going to call 999,' I say tearfully.

'Since when did you give a shit about him?' Hayley yells at Mum, who sighs and refuses to answer. So I do instead.

'Since she can see that in this case she should rise above her personal feelings and be humane!' I cry, feeling really emotional now as my fingers stab wildly at the numbers on the phone.

'Oh don't be such a drama queen,' snaps Hayley. 'You're always…' She doesn't get much further though, because seconds later Ray slides to the floor in a crumpled heap.

Mum screams. I don't know what to do and feel like I'm about to have a heart attack but am jolted back to the here and now when a voice on the other end of the phone says, 'Which service do you require?'

'Ambulance,' I reply and as I rattle off details of what's happening, our address and so on, I look straight at Hayley, who to be fair is looking pretty stricken with guilt right now, especially when I say the words, 'It's my dad. He's got terminal cancer and he's just collapsed.'

*

The next few hours are intense and stressful. The ambulance staff are amazing though. They arrive within minutes and as two people check my dad over and stretcher him out to the ambulance, a third crew member fires questions at me about his medication and all sorts of other things I don't have a clue about. I feel ashamed that I can't be of more help and petrified in case this is it. You see I'm counting on having a few months with him and I *need* every single one of those and I know he does too. To have anything less would feel like we'd been swindled. After hearing the news in March that he was going to die it took him two weeks to come and find us at the beginning of April. Now we're nearly at the end of the month already, but there should still be five months to go. Maybe more. You often read about people who manage to keep going for years, against all the odds, but right this second I'd settle for a few more months. Anything less is too awful to contemplate.

Of course there isn't time to voice any of these thoughts but as I clamber into the ambulance I vow that if he comes through this, I will find out everything I can about what the next few months are to entail, about his treatment, everything. If I'm going to be of any use to him at all I need to know and, on a selfish level, want to prepare myself psychologically.

The last thing I see before they close the doors is Mum waving sadly at me from the pavement. Her expression is something I'll never forget. She looks so freaked out. I can tell she's worried about me of course, but more than that I know that seeing Ray, the man she once loved, going through this, has been really frightening and has played havoc with her emotions. Curiously I feel glad. I've been feeling really annoyed with her recently. Mostly for having played her part in keeping Ray away for all these years but also for being so bloody nice to Andy when she can see I can't stand him. But her reaction now is a needed reminder that despite her faults she's a kind person, unlike Hayley, who I'm livid with. Why couldn't she have been a bit calmer? As the ambulance whips through Chigwell at high speed, blue lights flashing, sirens blaring, for the first time in my life I find myself praying hard. Ray has to make it. I'm not ready to say goodbye. Plus, if he did die tonight, Hayley would never forgive herself and I wouldn't wish that on anyone.

As soon as we arrive at the hospital Ray is taken off for a battery of tests, but thankfully we don't have to wait long for some answers. I say 'we' because half an hour after I arrive, Mum and Hayley turn up. I'm grateful for the support.

'Hi, you must be Mr Baker's family,' says an approaching doctor.

'Yes,' I say, though the irony of that statement isn't lost on any of us.

'OK,' he says, taking a seat next to us. 'Well firstly, let me say that Mr Baker is in a stable condition and that he's going to be all right.'

I burst into quiet tears.

'Why did he collapse, Doctor?' asks Mum.

'We ran some tests and found that his blood count was exceptionally low. In fact so low that we're giving him a blood transfusion right now. He's too weak to answer many questions, but with cancer of the colon there's always a chance he's been bleeding a lot rectally, which would explain the severe drop in his haemoglobin levels. Has he seemed particularly tired to you?'

The three of us look at each other helplessly but eventually I recover enough to say something. 'He was fine on Sunday. I mean, if anything he seemed well, but I thought he looked really tired earlier. Sort of weak and shaky.'

The doctor nods. 'He would have felt very weak indeed and he's been a bit vague about what he was doing exactly at the time of collapse but anything unusually stressful, either emotionally or physically, may have proved too much.'

Hayley's cheeks flame red with shame.

'Are you going to keep him in?' I ask tearfully.

'Yes, for a couple of nights. He'll need the rest, but hopefully after that, having had a transfusion he should feel much better again.'

'Are you his main doctor?' I ask.

'No. His oncologist is Mr Clarkson, though if you have any questions I'll be happy to answer them.'

'Thanks,' I say, quiet tears sliding down my face.

The doctor turns to go but as he does Hayley suddenly pipes up, 'So, er… is there definitely nothing you can do Doctor. You know, to cure him,' she says, and though her tone is brusque, her anxious face betrays her, telling us all she cares very much indeed about the answer.

'I'm afraid not at this stage,' the doctor replies gently. 'There is however plenty we can do to help the quality of life he has left and to manage his pain. We're slowly introducing him to our palliative team who are brilliant at what they do, and of course Matt is still in regular contact with Mr Baker at this stage. You have met Matthew I take it?'

'Yes,' I say at once. Mum and Hayley look surprised and I know our faces must give him some indication that ours is not a normal family set up and that we don't have much of a clue about anything. I find myself desperate to explain myself to the doctor. Somehow it matters to me that this man doesn't think we're all completely heartless.

'I met him really briefly,' I continue. 'Matthew is dad's support nurse,' I explain to Mum and Hayley.

'Right,' nods Mum, squeezing my hand. 'Course he is.'

That night, because my dad's been put in a private room, the hospital allow me to sleep the night on the small camp bed next to him. Not that I sleep much. Instead I while away the hours staring at Ray's face, full of so many conflicting emotions and checking all the time the rise and fall of his chest. Mum and Hayley went home a while back but I couldn't contemplate leaving, so stayed and watched as the nurses set up a drip, which contained a cocktail of drugs to ensure Dad had a pain-free, restful night.

I cry silently for a long, long time, until finally I slip into a dreamless sleep.

The next morning I'm woken up by a brisk knock on the door. My heart misses a beat and my eyes spring open as I try to remember where I am. I'm horribly groggy and it takes a while but eventually I figure out my location because I spot Ray staring down at me from his bed, already wide awake.

'Morning you, we've got a visitor,' he says. 'All right Matthew?'

Still lying down, I pull my blanket up, embarrassed. I'm still half-asleep and almost wish I was wearing my clown outfit again. At least that way Matthew wouldn't be able to see how thoroughly undelightful I look first thing in the morning after a traumatic crying session.

'Hi Ray, morning Marianne. How are you guys today?'

Urgh. Why me? I have no choice other than to sit up and be friendly or he'll think I'm incredibly rude.

'I'm not too bad mate. Not too bad,' says Dad. 'Marianne's been a little angel keeping me company.'

'Ah excellent. Nice to see you again by the way. How did the party go?' he says, smiling down at me.

'Yeah, great,' I say, desperately trying to sort out my

flattened hair with one hand while deciding to omit the bit about Dad nearly beating someone to a pulp.

'Cool, well it's nice to meet you properly. It was a bit hard to see what you looked like before.'

'Hmm,' I mutter, smiling like a pathetic idiot. Only because I'm just not sure what else to say. Conducting a conversation with someone you don't know while essentially lying in bed simply doesn't feel right. Especially not when they're towering above you, shower fresh and ready for the day while by contrast you've just woken up and your eyes feel like they've been bread-crumbed.

'I was telling Matthew the other day how you play the violin like a pro,' interjected Dad.

'Er... I don't really,' I mutter, blushing and wishing he'd leave now so I could get out of the camp bed and make myself look human.

'Sounds great,' says Matthew at which point I feel about five years old. Dad could be so embarrassing. And then all at once that negative suddenly feels like a real positive, and I end up rather enjoying the fact that I have a dad to embarrass me. I guess it's kind of a normal thing.

Thankfully Matthew turns his attention back to the patient now. 'Well, I just popped in to see how you were doing Ray but I've had a chat with Jane who you met the other day, from palliative, and I think they're going to suggest a cycle of chemo soon so, if you want to have a chat about that before making a decision, then let's do that.'

My heart lurches with hope. 'Well that must be a good

sign, if they're still going to keep treating you with chemo,' I can't prevent myself from saying.

Ray looks at me and is about to say something but then pauses and glances at Matthew who looks a bit surprised. It's then I understand that I'm clutching at straws.

'It's palliative care only now, Marianne,' says Ray gently. 'But you never know, might give me a bit longer, eh?' he adds, over-brightly.

I still have no idea what palliative means but get the general idea. I swallow. Now I really want this Matthew character to leave. I'm embarrassed and feel terrible for having showed my hand. If Ray can be brave and stoic about his fate then what right do I have to be anything but?

When Matthew leaves a short while later, Ray, who seems to be in a much better state today, says, 'He's a good bloke, Matt.'

'He seems nice,' I agree, finally clambering out of the torturously uncomfortable bed.

'He was the one who encouraged me to find you girls.'

'Oh, it wasn't your idea then?' I enquire, smoothing down my rumpled clothes. I try to sound blasé but in fact feel quite hurt. I want finding us to have been his idea. Not someone else's.

'Course it was, but it was Matthew who I talked things through with. It was a big decision coming back into your lives but he nudged me towards doing it sooner rather than later, if you know what I mean. You know, after I'd been told… Anyway he's been a good friend. He's well chuffed about the fact we're back in contact as it goes.'

I blink, not wanting to think about the day Ray was told there was nothing more they could do. I can't begin to imagine how terrifying a moment that must have been. I'm terrified of dying and don't know how I'd cope with the fear. It dawns on me then that Matthew isn't just a nurse but a counsellor and friend rolled into one. Thank god for Matthew I suddenly think, for Ray certainly hasn't displayed much fear or rage in front of me, which has been puzzling me a bit I suppose. I know he doesn't have many friends he can talk to. As far as I can glean all his old muckers are of the old-fashioned, emotionally retarded variety, who aren't in touch with their feelings, or anyone else's for that matter. They certainly wouldn't express them to one another anyway. But if he's able to have those moments with a professional like Matthew, I suppose it leaves him free to try and enjoy the time he has left with people like me for instance.

During the next couple of hours Ray and I have a bit of breakfast and watch some TV. I feel shattered, having been through the ringer emotionally and physically, though it goes without saying I don't moan about feeling shit to Dad. The irony that I look in worse shape than him today doesn't pass me by though.

Later, I'm really pleased when at visiting time Hayley appears with some grapes and a very different attitude. Once I've had a word with her outside the room, just to fill her in on things the nurses have told me, she comes back in and says sheepishly to Ray, 'You gave us a bit of a fright there.'

I give her a small, stern smile of encouragement. I know how difficult this is for her, but it's also what she needs to do and I want her to remain this calm for all our sakes.

'Yeah, I'm sorry about that,' Ray says, doing his best to sit up and smiling through the pain he's apparently feeling in his liver today. I hate this insight into quite how terribly ill he is. I've had my head in the sand I guess. Still, the reality of his situation has certainly sunk in now.

'Hayley's got something to say,' I prompt, determined to make sure my sister goes through with what we just discussed in the corridor.

'Don't worry about it,' Ray says. 'I can understand why you don't want anything to do with me. One daughter out of two is a result given my past and you're totally within your rights to want nothing to do with me. And I'm really sorry if I came across as an arsehole at the house. Being honest I was just so nervous and I hadn't slept the night before for thinking about it all. By the time I arrived I was in a bit of a weird state. I'm sorry.'

Hayley looks away. 'I'm sorry too,' she mutters. 'I've had a really hard time lately and I suppose I was… lashing out… a bit. I mean, I do think you've been crap but I get that you're not well, so probably don't need a load of earache from me.'

'It's all right,' he says, but I can tell he's beginning to feel tired again.

'We should go,' I say. 'But we'll come back tomorrow during visiting hours again. Do you want me to bring anything?'

'Nah, you're all right,' he says. 'And Hayley, thanks. What you said means a lot and, Marianne thanks for everything. I'm sorry both of you had to see me collapse.'

'Don't be stupid,' I admonish.

We turn to go, Hayley slightly hesitantly as if she's trying to decide whether or not to say anything else. However, I'm keen for Ray to get some rest so I guide her towards the door.

Outside I'm surprised and very touched to find Mum waiting for us.

'Everything OK?' she asks sadly.

I nod, trying to be brave but it's suddenly all too much and I end up bursting into tears. 'Oh Mum, he really is going to die,' I say.

Drawing me and Hayley both in for a hug she replies, 'I know angel, I know. I can hardly believe it myself.'

CHAPTER FIFTEEN

The rest of the week is a write off. When I get home from the hospital I climb into bed but get a heart attack when two minutes later Andy pokes his chubby head round the door and asks whether I'd like him to join me.

My reply is 'bugger off', which is just unsubtle enough for him to get the hint so he huffs off with Martin for a grand tour of his offices instead, muttering all the way about how moody I am.

The next day Hayley and I go to visit Ray as soon as I get out of work and are told that he's definitely going to be given a three-week cycle of chemotherapy. Apparently it will make him feel like shit for a while but might help prolong things. So it's worth a go.

I tell him that I want to keep visiting for the duration of the treatment but he's adamant that he doesn't want me to see him when he's sick and worn out. He does reassure me however that Matthew will be keeping a close eye on things and that the hospital have also decided to keep him in for the whole three weeks rather than send him home for the recovery periods in between. I leave feeling – and

I know it's irrational – jealous of Matthew for getting to spend more time with him than I will, but know I have to respect Ray's wishes.

I'm left with no choice other than to get on with things and get back to work. And work I do. Roberto is delighted at my change in attitude and I make it into the salon on Friday, Saturday, Monday and Tuesday.

By the following Wednesday I'm in dire need of my day off again. Though without work to hide behind, or Martin at home to take advantage of, it means I have no other choice but to finally spend a whole day with Andy. Alone. We've been like passing ships in the night, which has been fine by me, though admittedly, when I stop to think about the whole situation it's incredibly bizarre. At a certain point he's simply going to have to accept that he can't stay lurking in my house like some kind of lodger, eating everything in the fridge and hanging out with Martin when we aren't even making an attempt to be together. Pawing at me occasionally doesn't constitute a relationship after all. So, determined to at least give him a look at London before I urge him to naff off back to the other side of the world, I come up with a packed day of sightseeing that would surely leave even the fittest athlete too tired for sex.

*

'Come on,' I say, dashing off the London Eye, as it comes to its slow stop. 'We've only got half an hour to get to the Tower of London if we're going to fit in Madame Tussauds before we go home.'

'Jeez,' says Andy, looking done in. It's May by now and the weather has finally turned a spring-like corner, so the jumper has come off, although it's still wrapped around his sturdy waist, which if anything has got even sturdier since Mum introduced him to Findus crispy pancakes. 'This is great and everything, but being honest I wouldn't mind calling it a day and heading back to Chigwell. I feel done in, and besides I just want to get you on your own. We haven't had any alone time since I got here,' he adds sulkily.

'I know,' I say, staring guiltily at my toes. 'But if I'm honest Andy, it's such a complicated time right now, it's hard for me to feel romantic.' This is me edging my way towards the truth.

'You have got heaps going on,' says Andy, looking thoughtful. Then, 'Look, I'm going to come right out and say this because I don't believe in beating round the bush or being dishonest.'

They're running repeats of Neighbours on UK Gold at the moment and in that moment he reminds me more than a little of Joe Mangle.

'Go on.'

'You've changed, Marianne. I mean you're still super fit and everything and I fancy you just as much as I ever did, but your personality has changed. You're not the same girl I fell for in Thailand.'

'I'm not…?' I say, wondering who I am then.

'No,' says Andy regretfully. 'You were so bubbly out there, so carefree and a great laugh, but here you're so constrained. You always look so grumpy and I'm starting to wonder whether the girl I got to know in Asia only comes out when she's on holiday?'

This last bit he says in an unbelievably patronising way, like he's talking to a small child.

'Right…' My gaze wanders momentarily as someone whizzes past on rollerblades. The South Bank's full of people enjoying the sunny weather. Workers are spread out on the grass, eating their sandwiches, getting their hour's fix of fresh air, no doubt wondering why the weather always improves after the weekend has finished.

'Look, I don't want to hurt you Marianne. I know how much you're into the whole idea of "us" and who knows, maybe things will pick up again. But for now I think we should take our foot off the pedal and see how things pan out. Or we could just be friends with benefits since we're so hot for each other?'

I gulp and frown at the same time, hardly able to believe what I'm hearing. I think rapidly, desperate not to mess up this situation that suddenly seems to have swung in my favour by making me the victim.

'I think that might hurt too much,' I say solemnly, suppressing an urge to grin. 'I think the best thing is to take things day by day, or if you want to just call it a day now,

I suppose we could. Maybe that would be easier? You know, like a clean break. Maybe you could move out?'

'No, I couldn't do that to you,' he says earnestly, chin quivering with pudgy self-righteousness. 'I want to give us another chance.'

'Right,' I say weakly, staring into the crowds of people walking down the South Bank, feeling quite insulted and also frustrated that essentially nothing has been resolved.

*

Later, back at home, I decide it's time to stop mucking about and to nip the whole situation in the bud, and fast. Letting him call the shots is pathetic and cowardly of me. I simply have too much stuff on my plate at the moment to continue this ridiculous charade of pretending there's even a small chance we can be together. There's simply no reason why he should stay with us any more. We have nothing in common. I don't fancy him or even like him, so him living with me and my family when we have so much stuff to deal with is ridiculous. He has to go, so I decide to make myself crystal clear.

'Andy,' I say, watching him stuff his face. Mum's made him a toasted cheese sandwich and there's cheesy grease dribbling down his chin. At moments like these I catch myself staring at him, as I try to remember why I liked him so much in Thailand, where mysteriously he seemed so much more appealing. I suppose we didn't eat much apart from fish and the odd banana pancake whereas here he eats like a horse, though that's probably a bit unkind to horses.

'Can I have a quick word? In my room,' I say.

'Yeah,' he agrees at once, looking excited. My heart sinks as I realise he actually thinks I'm going to jump his meaty bones. I despair. Still, his ardour only reinforces my decision to rectify this absurd situation.

'So,' I say, closing my bedroom door behind me. 'I wanted to start by saying…'

I don't get any further however, for to my total horror Andy pulls me round and drags me into an embrace. He sticks his revolting tongue enthusiastically down my throat. I can taste cheese.

I squeal like a pig and bash him on the back with my fists until finally he twigs that I'm not happy at all.

'For fuck's sake,' I bluster, having finally wriggled my way out of his grip. 'What are you doing? Stop mauling me all the bloody time. I didn't get you up here for a love-in. I need to talk to you.'

'Oh,' says Andy, looking deeply put out. He's panting slightly and wipes his hand across his mouth, a gesture that makes me want to pull my own hair out.

'This isn't working,' I state. 'I'm sorry and everything, but it hasn't been since you arrived; only I've been far too worried about hurting your feelings to tell you the truth. But now I've got so much on my plate and I just can't handle worrying about you too. I'm really sorry,' I say, trying not to cry. Wanting to cry has nothing to do with the fact we're breaking up but because I really do have a lot on my plate and whether he's there or not it is still all terribly hard.

'I see,' he says eventually.

'Great,' I say, fully expecting him to show some initiative now by packing his bag immediately. I assume he'll be embarrassed and want to make amends for being so slow on the uptake. Like any normal person, now he understands the situation, I'm sure he'll want to leave as soon as is humanly possible, which is why I'm so surprised when he asks, 'So what do we do now?'

'What do you mean what do we do now?' I ask, bewildered. Why did he even have to ask? *We* didn't have to do anything. *He* had to vacate my house as soon as possible and give me some much-needed space.

'Well I get the message, but Martin and I have got so many plans coming up.'

'Such as?' I enquire, starting to sound like Basil Fawlty at his most frustrated and deranged.

'Well, we were going to build a rockery in the garden next weekend for starters and then he wants to take me to DFS because we still haven't got round to going yet. Plus we were going to get together with his mate Derek and see about renovating his caravan and…'

'Look, Andy,' I interrupt, rubbing my face with my hands, feeling drenched in stress. 'I'm sorry and everything. I know you've had a great time with Martin, but this is my house, where I live, so I just don't think you staying here any more is going to work out.'

At this point Andy looks like this is such an outlandish statement I almost begin to question my own judgement.

'Well I guess we need to talk to Martin then. See what he thinks,' says Andy gravely.

I feel like screaming.

'OK, you're just not getting it,' I say steadily, his reaction making me question now whether I can cope with even one more night under the same roof as him. Where was a bouncer when you needed one? He was being so unreasonable.

'Oh I'm getting it all right Marianne,' he says petulantly. 'But maybe it's time you realised that it's not all about you.'

'…right,' I say, beyond frustrated, unable to grasp what it was he wasn't able to get. He was acting like I'd been talking Swahili and frankly, given the circumstances, is being unbelievably selfish. My dad is dying.

'Andy, can you give me a second?' I ask, desperate not to be looking at his pudgy face for even a moment longer. If he's going to be difficult about leaving my house, he can at least get out of my room.

'Sure thing,' he says, strolling out of my room, but unfortunately not out of my life.

*

That night I barely sleep. Andy's refusal to budge is playing heavily on my mind so endless hours pass miserably with me tossing and turning as I wonder how on earth I'm going to get rid of dough boy. Holiday romance turned squatter from hell.

In the morning it's no surprise that as I head for work I'm feeling exhausted to the point where the only thing that gets me through the day is the knowledge that I have a music lesson to look to forward to that evening.

I'm really excited about this. It's been far too long. My teacher has been away on the trip of a lifetime to South America and is finally back. I'm hoping I won't be too rusty as I've been practising for at least an hour a day. I feel really sad that Ray isn't able to come with me like he wanted to. There's no question of this for the time being however. The chemo is underway and apparently taking its toll. When I phoned the hospital for an update earlier, he was too weak even to chat.

I miss him.

I miss my dad. This is an alien thought. Until a month or so ago I didn't even have him in my life to miss. Suddenly there's a big bubble of grief rearing its head in my belly, for with that last thought comes the knowledge that soon, missing him will be all I can do.

Walking through Mrs Demetrius' door is like applying balm to my weary soul. Her house is one place where I can stop thinking, stop worrying about my life and how everything is going to unfold. I can practically feel my skeleton relaxing as I enter the hall and find myself engulfed in my teacher's ample bosom.

'I've missed you!' she exclaims, the bangles on her arms jangling.

'Me too,' I say sincerely. 'I want to hear all about your trip.'

'Plenty of time for that,' she replies. 'Promise I'll bore you about it later, but right now I'm dying to hear you play.'

My lesson is supposed to last an hour, I'm there for three. Maybe it's because of everything that's going on at the moment but I play with more passion, more feeling than I ever have before. When I finish the concerto that I've been rehearsing, Mrs Demetrius is moved to tears and later, after she's shown me the photographs from her trip, she is unable to resist mentioning her favourite topic of conversation.

'You have to apply this year, Marianne. I've spoken to them about the process and look, I've got some stuff for you to read.'

Reluctantly I take the Royal College of Music prospectus from her.

'You've missed this year's open day but the woman in admissions said I can phone and book a private tour. They do them regularly. It would only be for an hour and South Kensington is hardly far away. Will you at least consider that? I'll come with you.'

It's easier just to pretend that I'll give it some thought, otherwise I know she'll only keep on at me. I flick idly through the brochure and have to admit it does look amazing. It's full of photographs of students playing in orchestras, or in music lessons. The buildings are majestic and it all feels like a world away from my own life. I can't even imagine how incredible it would be to be somewhere where all you were supposed to be thinking about was music. I wonder whether the people whose faces are peering out at me know how lucky they are. It's all ridiculously unattainable for someone like me though. Besides, even if I were to apply this year, which I'd have to do before October, I wouldn't be able to start until the September after. By which point I'd be far too old to be a student. I'd look ridiculous. No, that ship has sailed, I decide stubbornly. Thinking ahead to the autumn causes a sudden almost physical ache in my stomach as my brain contemplates what may or may not have happened by then. I'd managed to banish my worries from my head for the duration of my lesson but obviously they were all just waiting round the corner.

'Time will fly, Marianne,' nags Mrs Demetrius, which only deepens my anxiety. 'And I know you can't picture it now but believe you me, October will be here before you know it, so you have to think about it. It's still not too late for you. You've got your A grade in A level Music and you play like a dream.'

'What about the fees?' I mutter, sounding miserable.

Mrs Demetrius sighs heavily. 'You know as well as I do that on that front there would be a way. We'd have to find a way.'

I can only imagine she's referring to Martin and I feel a

jolt of irritation. Surely it's not really up to her to decide whether my family could afford for me to go – which I don't think they could – though deep down I know it's her comment about October being here before we know it that's really responsible for the darkening of my mood. If my dad lasts six months from the time of diagnosis that means he's only got until then so I don't want time to whizz by. I don't want it to be October. Instead I need time to pass in the same way it did when I was a little girl at school. Back then the six-week summer holidays seemed endless. Now, six weeks goes in a flash.

'What's wrong, Marianne?' she asks, having figured out that there must be more on my mind than just my future. 'You look so sad. Tell me?'

So I do. I sit and tell my lovely teacher, who's also a great friend, everything that's happened since that fateful night in April. The night my life changed for ever. And she listens and for now that's all I need.

CHAPTER SIXTEEN

Over the next few weeks it feels like whichever way I turn there's something tricky to confront. Andy refusing to budge from my house is becoming a major issue as I'm feeling increasingly uncomfortable in my own home. At one point I ask Martin and Mum to back me up by asking him to get the hell out, at which point they sheepishly admit that they've had a little chat with Andy and have agreed he can stay on as a lodger.

'It's just, he's so helpful around the house,' Mum says, as if that makes everything OK.

'And he deserves a break,' adds Martin. 'He's a good lad and just because things haven't worked out with the pair of you, doesn't mean we can't show him some good old-fashioned British hospitality. And besides,' he continues stoically, 'We'll miss him when he's gone. Australia's a long way from here.'

I stare at him aghast as his eyes start to glisten suspiciously. Frustrated beyond belief I leave him blinking and head for my room – where I seem to be permanently hiding out these days. It dawns on me then that rationalising anything with that pair of lunatics is going to be an uphill struggle so I give up. After all, why would anyone care what I think?

I try giving Andy the cold shoulder hoping he'll be the one to take the initiative and evict himself, but that doesn't work either. Desperate to get rid of him somehow, at one point I resort to asking him bluntly when he might be thinking of heading back to the other side of the planet but his answer is irritatingly mysterious. 'When the time is right,' he says, like he's Mary frigging Poppins, waiting for the wind to change. Not that there's an umbrella on the planet big enough to carry his bulk skyward.

So life continues in a strange state of limbo. I certainly won't be heading off on my travels any time soon so instead I continue to save as much as I can. By now I've got over two thousand pounds in my savings account. And for now, like me, it can just stay put.

As for my dad, and that *still* feels a strange thing to say, he's got through his chemo cycle and miraculously it seems to have given him a bit of a boost, although that may be down to the steroids he's also been prescribed. Either way, Ray himself says he's having a good patch so, determined to make the most of it, we see each other a lot. Our time together is intense and permanently laced with sadness and a yearning for things to be different. We quiz one another on all aspects of our lives. He wants to know everything about my life growing up and even the smallest detail seems to fascinate him. I too feel an urgent need to squeeze as much as possible out of our time together but am also mindful of how ill he is and how exhausted he can get.

It's the end of May when I finally make it round to the flat he's been living in since he got out of prison. I turn up with my violin, which he begged me to bring.

'Here we are then,' he says, opening the door and gesturing to me to go in first.

'This is nice,' I say, my eyes devouring their surroundings, and it is, it's fine. It's small, but spotlessly clean and in his manor of Hackney. However, walking into the living room through from the tiny hallway, it's the lack of anything personal that gets to me and which feels a bit depressing. There aren't any pictures in frames, no clutter of any description, although he does have loads of CDs on a shelf, which for want of something better to do I go over to examine.

'Blimey, you've got such a wide range of music.'

'That surprise you, does it?' Dad says, hanging his coat on the back of one of the three chairs that surround the small table in the corner, which is where he obviously eats his meals. The kitchen is miniscule.

I shrug and carry on looking at the CDs. They vary from Johnny Cash and Elvis, to Elgar and Elaine Paige singing show tunes.

'Fancy a cuppa?' asks Dad.

'Yeah please, thanks,' I say, experiencing a pang of something that might be fear, or sorrow, when I notice that among the few books that are on the shelves is a copy of

Lance Armstrong's book and one called *Chicken Soup for the Soul*, a help book for cancer sufferers. I am immediately struck by a renewed sense of admiration at how well Ray is dealing with what's happening to him.

We don't talk about 'it' much. Somehow I can just tell he doesn't want to, so that's fine by me, and yet of course his illness, his situation, encroaches upon everything.

This is proved yet again half an hour later, by Dad's reaction when I mention how I bumped into Teresa at the club some weeks ago now.

'You've gotta get in touch with her,' Dad insists. 'Do it. You don't seem to have a huge number of friends, so the ones you do have you must look after.'

I sigh, knowing he's right. Only sometimes it's so draining having to consider everything on a 'life's too short' basis. Obviously when someone knows they're going to die imminently, it makes a huge difference to their outlook. If I were in his position I would also want to try and live each day fully, to let the people close to me know how much they mean to me, and yet is that really how one is supposed to exist on a day-to-day basis? The reality is that the vast majority of us have no idea when our days will be numbered, which allows us to get bogged down with our day-to-day worries, to moan about stuff that doesn't even matter in the grand scheme of things. And when it comes to people, although it might not necessarily be right, isn't it sometimes downright easier to take them for granted, just a little, on occasion? Recently I've come to see that although putting things off that you could do today isn't necessarily the best thing, it's also a luxury that most of us never really appreciate.

'I will call her,' I say, not wanting to upset Ray.

'Do it now,' he says firmly. 'That way you won't forget.'

I feel backed into a corner. Firstly I can't think of a reason not to and secondly I already recognise that look. I may only have known him a month and a half but have managed to deduce that my dad is stubborn. As stubborn as me.

'All right,' I say, getting my mobile out of my pocket. 'I'll ring her, but just for the record, I've made hundreds of friends. They just don't live in England.'

Dad rolls his eyes, humouring me. 'Bloody lot of use they are then,' he mutters.

'Teresa,' I say for she picks up almost instantly. I've got butterflies in my stomach. 'How you doing? It's Marianne. I was just wondering if you fancied going out sometime?'

Thankfully she agrees. In fact she sounds genuinely pleased that I've rung and we arrange to go back to the club where we bumped into each other in a couple of Saturday's time. That day will, in fact, be the day of Hayley's *Sing for Britain* audition, so I figure I'll probably feel like having a drink after that anyway.

'Well done you,' Dad says, looking really chuffed. His evident pride in having helped fills me with affection.

'Now let's listen to some music together and then,

perhaps if I ask nicely, maybe you'll even play some for your old dad.'

And so it is that time marches on and May has come and gone.

CHAPTER SEVENTEEN

The big day dawns grey and slightly dreary considering it's the middle of June. What big day am I talking about? Hayley's big day. Actually, correct that, Mum's big day. The weather may be deeply average but nothing's going to dampen Mum's downright scary enthusiasm. Not even the fact that Dad's coming with us.

Since their initial disastrous meeting and Dad's collapse, Hayley has met up with Ray a few times, always alone, which suits me fine. It feels right that the two of them should try and forge their own relationship.

It also leaves me free to enjoy *my* time with him in peace. My sister's pretty much reverted to her old ways, refusing to discuss anything with me that might be remotely difficult such as how she's feeling or whether or not she's going to try for another baby. Every time I see her I am overwhelmed with sadness about it. I know she's hurting and just wish there was more I could do to make her feel better. As it is I just pop round as much as I can and, if she's in one of her odd moods, I tolerate it more than I normally would. At least I know her meetings with Dad must have gone relatively well because if they hadn't I would definitely have heard about it.

From Ray's point of view he's just grateful she's letting him in. I am too and have to admit, when I discovered that Hayley had asked him to come along to the *Sing for Britain* auditions, I had a job at keeping my amazement concealed. Though let's be honest, Hayley's going to need all the support she can get once she's unleashed that voice of hers on to the public.

And so it's a motley bunch making their way up to an arena in South East London by tube. There's me – I don't want to be here to witness my sister's demise, but am the only one who realises how badly she's going to get torn to shreds by the judging panel so need to be. There's Hayley, obviously, Pete, who Mum insisted should come along to show support, Mum – you can imagine what sort of state she's in – Martin, Ray – who's in a wheelchair, which we're all trying not to look shocked by – Matthew, his far better than average looking support nurse, who has kindly agreed to come along to help out – yes! – Gary... and... wait for it...

Who could clearly not be missing from such a big Baker/ Baxter family day out? Why, of course, the idiot I had a holiday romance with nine hundred years ago... Andy.

Well, obviously he has to come doesn't he? Why, it's only right and natural he should be here, despite the fact his mere presence brings out murderous thoughts in me and that he has NOTHING WHATSOEVER TO DO WITH US.

Sorry.

It's just he's still lingering like a bad dose of food poisoning and has ingratiated himself so far up Mum and Martin's arses I'm beginning to think he'll be here for ever.

His stubborn refusal to leave is *really* starting to grate now. It's just plain odd frankly and him not budging and being all 'pally' with Martin means I'm growing to hate him in a way that practically brings me out in a rash every time I stop to think about it. He's got his feet firmly under the table and because I don't have the time or energy required to uproot them, it looks like he's here to stay indefinitely. It's so typical of my ridiculous life.

Right now I'm sitting on the tube opposite Hayley. We all have seats, apart from Matthew who's standing with Ray, making sure his wheelchair doesn't roll off anywhere. As we rattle around in the tube carriage, making our way towards Hayley's certain showbiz death I can't prevent myself from questioning her about her musical choice.

'So, are you still set on doing Céline Dion?'

'No,' says Hayley. 'You pissed me off at the time but having thought about it, Mum and I think you may have a point. Loads of people have done it in the past and actually it might feel a bit dated now.'

A *bit* dated. I force myself not to look incredulous.

'Plus, I'd only be compared, like when people try and do a "Mariah", so I've chosen something else.'

'Thank god,' I say with feeling, imagining those soaring notes in her squawky voice. 'I mean, thank god you're now going to stand out from the crowd.'

Hayley shoots me a murderous look.

'I can't stand Céline Dion,' pipes up Matthew cheerfully, earning himself respect from me and a frown from Hayley. Unperturbed, he grins back at her. He looks so disarmingly handsome Hayley quickly changes her tune, lowering her heavily made-up eyes in a coquettish fashion.

I feel a stab of something that feels horribly like jealousy in my stomach. Despite the fact she's married and in the presence of her husband, she still can't help but flirt with every male that comes her way. Having pulled out all the stops today she's looking gorgeous too, so I wouldn't blame Matthew if he fell for her very obvious charms. Everyone else does.

Honestly I can't tell you how soul-destroying it is at times, knowing I share Hayley's DNA, yet having come off at such a genetic disadvantage. I mean, if I really pick them apart, our features probably aren't that dissimilar. Yet the way hers are arranged on her face simply make for a far superior end product. It's sickening. My sympathies lie deeply with Beyoncé's sister. It can't be easy.

Today Hayley's wearing a navy rain mac, and she's tied the belt round her waist. I dread to think what she might, or might not, have on underneath. She's had her long blonde hair blow-dried into a 1940s wave. She's got red lipstick on, high heels and false eyelashes.

'What are you going to sing then?' asks Dad, who's lost a bit of weight recently but is looking pretty well on the whole. I hate seeing him in a wheelchair, though he did say it was only because it's bound to be a long day.

'Well,' says Hayley, 'I still need to do a power ballad obviously…'

I despair.

'So I've picked *Bleeding Love* by Leona Lewis.'

'Oh, fantastic choice,' enthuses Martin gravely.

'Nooo,' I wail.

'Oh for fuck's sake Marianne, what now?' snaps Hayley.

'It's too low for your voice and you've gone from the sublime to the ridiculous. *My heart will go on* is all up and down the scales whereas *Bleeding love* is all one level so if you're even remotely off key you'll sound like a dirge. Besides, it's not a good tune to do acoustically and they always say they're looking for the next big thing, some-one relevant and fresh. Not someone who's churning out karaoke versions of singers from years gone by. It just won't sound relevant.'

Gary's sitting next to Hayley, munching crisps. Today he's wearing long, baggy shorts, Adidas flip-flops and a sequined ACDC t-shirt – though I doubt he could name even one ACDC track. 'Who do you think you are all of a sudden?' he says, giving me a creepy wink, 'Simon Cowell?'

I give him a withering look.

'Well I think *Bleeding Love*'s a great choice,' says

Martin, who's wearing brand new sandals today. Surely a man wearing sandals isn't entitled to a musical opinion.

'Look,' interjects Ray, fighting to be heard as the tube whizzes through the tunnel. 'If Hayley's anything like as musical as Marianne, whatever she sings will knock their socks off. So why don't we just let her go with what she's comfortable with?'

I feel as though I've been told off and had, of course, forgotten that Dad has no idea how bad Hayley is. Because of this he must have jumped to the logical conclusion that if she's auditioning for a huge network show, she must be talented. I've done nothing to persuade him otherwise because I don't tend to enjoy slagging off my sister for no reason and of course, according to Mum, she's Chigwell's answer to Judy Garland. Still, I feel stupid now and like I've been made to look as though I'm being mean and bitchy, when in fact I've genuinely only got my sister's best interests at heart. From now on I'm keeping my mouth shut. Arms folded, I gaze out the window.

'What would you do, my angel?' Mum asks Pete. 'If you were auditioning.'

Pete shrugs. He looks thoroughly unimpressed at having been dragged along today.

'Go on, what would you do?' I repeat, curious to know.

'I wouldn't. *Sing for Britain*'s a pile of exploitative crap,' he mumbles.

'But if you *had* to,' I insist. 'If someone was going to kill your entire family if you didn't.'

Pete considers this long enough for us to know that given the choice he'd far prefer us all to be massacred than appear on the show.

'OK, if your entire Elvis collection was going to be destroyed.'

'*In the Ghetto*,' he responds instantly.

'That would be OK,' I say. 'I bet the judges would be glad of something so original. Though I still think anyone trying to emulate someone so famous is risking comparison.'

'Well I agree with Martin,' interjects Andy, who's wearing his awful bum bag today, short shorts, which frankly are obscene, topped off with his tight, pale pink polo shirt. I can tell that the woman sitting next to him is trying her best not to make contact with the hairy flesh of his fat, white thighs. I shudder involuntarily.

'*Bleeding Love* is a great choice. I've come to really love Leona since I met you guys. She's a total classic,' Andy adds, like anyone gives a shit what he thinks.

I can't help it. I turn and give him what can only be described as a death stare, which satisfyingly he recoils under.

'What would you sing Marianne?' asks Matthew, in a friendly enough way, though I'm not convinced he isn't laughing at us all, just a little. It's hard to tell. His face seems to naturally always be verging on a smile.

'Don't know,' I shrug, feeling a bit embarrassed and unable to get myself out of my awful mood. 'Can't sing.'

'OK, what would you play?'

'*Bitter Sweet Symphony* by The Verve perhaps?' I mutter eventually. 'It's a pop show so I guess that might go down all right. You know the string section at the start? Or perhaps a Queen number? Or *Toxic* by Britney Spears? The strings are great in that.'

'Now that I'd like to see,' he replies, nodding approvingly. His brown eyes are so warm and friendly. I can't help but compare him to Andy who looks peevish and unhealthy next to him. Matthew clearly does a lot more moving than my ex-paramour too.

'*Bitter Sweet Symphony*'s pretty much one of my all-time favourite tracks.'

I'm surprised. I look at him and smile. Matthew smiles back and I look away feeling pleased yet unsettled as I experience a wave of totally inappropriate lust. Probably partly triggered by meeting a vaguely kindred, musical spirit. Not something I'm particularly used to.

'I don't think someone standing there playing the fiddle would exactly capture the imagination of the public though somehow, Matthew,' laughs Mum raucously. 'And besides, I had a vision last night and in it, the judges definitely told Hayley they were looking for a powerhouse like her.'

I glance at my dad who I can tell is trying not to laugh. When he catches my eye he gives me a little wink. I might be imagining it but I swear Pete notices our facial exchanges and smiles to himself too.

It's strange but good to have Dad with us and something I never would have believed could happen a year ago.

I think Martin finding out about the past has helped Mum immensely. It must have been hard keeping so much a secret and now that the truth is out there and Martin hasn't left her, she's found it relatively easy to allow Ray into our lives. She hasn't spent much time with him of course, but they've shared exchanges on the doorstep and each time it's got a little easier and less frosty. Essentially they're both being adults about the situation, and as a result are able to cope being altogether today.

*

When we finally arrive at the arena Hayley starts getting quite nervous. I'm not bloody surprised. By the time we reach our stop it's obvious that most people on the, by now, stuffed full carriage are also heading for the auditions. As we approach the stadium thousands upon thousands of people are all moving in the same direction. As a result it takes our group a while to get there but once we have, the first thing we do is get Hayley registered. She's given number 33980. It's going to be a long day all right, and Mum's already acting as if she's on drugs, squealing and squeaking with excitement. The words 'peak too early' spring to mind just as she takes off her jacket, revealing a t-shirt that has '*Hayley's your winner*' plastered across her expansive bosom. I roll my eyes but can't deny experiencing a frisson of excitement about the fact we're all actually here. It's pretty surreal. Of course, given that I often escape England in the winter, I've not been around to watch every series, but when I am here I love the show. Though I have no idea how anyone could put themselves through the ordeal of trying out for it, unless they were absolutely sure as sure can be that they were supremely talented.

We stand amidst a sea of people. People who all genuinely believe they have a shot at topping the charts. Camera crews are roaming about, getting sections of the crowd to cheer on cue. This is all mildly entertaining for a short while though it isn't long before my initial excitement wears off and I start feeling a bit claustrophobic. Then Mum sinks to a new low.

'Here, Matthew lovey, push Ray out a bit further so they can see the wheelchair next time they come round.'

'Pardon?' I say, sounding as stunned as Matthew looks.

'You know,' she says, nudging me. 'You don't mind do you Ray, it's just they're bound to let us go to the front if they see we've got a disabled in the group.'

Matthew, who's too polite to say anything, waits to see what I'm going to say next and I'm all set to protest when Dad winks at me.

'I honestly don't care love and, to be honest, your mother probably has got a point. Besides, I don't know how much more of this flaming screaming I can take.'

There isn't much I can say to this so I shrug helplessly at Matthew, though refuse to take part in working out the mechanics of getting Ray's chair out. I don't approve of exploiting his illness, even if he doesn't appear to mind. I also don't like being in a crowd very much and am starting to feel a bit anxious and tense about the entire situation. In the end we're so hemmed in that it takes not just Matthew, but also Gary and Martin, to manoeuvre his wheelchair through the crowd to a side position at which point Mum's evil plan only goes and works when an eagle-eyed researcher spots us and immediately insists we go to the top of the queue. Though admittedly, she's a little taken aback when she sees the size of our party. Pretty soon, however, we're all inside the building in the vast, hangar-like waiting area.

It's a change of scene, but still bedlam. All around us people are tuning up, while proud friends and relatives gaze admiringly at them. The sound of everyone warbling away to themselves as they practise is a muddle of noise. Still, thankfully we do at least manage to find a spot where there are a couple of spare seats.

'Are you all right?' I ask Dad.

'Yeah babe, t'rrific,' he replies, though in all honesty he doesn't look that great. He already looks shattered. Silently I question the wisdom of him having come along.

'Right, shall I get our little picnic out?' says Mum, who by contrast is literally having the best day of her life. She's so upbeat and chirpy I'm almost tempted to ask Matthew whether he's got any spare valium he can sort her out with. She's doing my head in.

Feeling irritated, I watch as she bends down from the knees so that she can lay out a blanket on the floor, as if we're at a posh garden party, as opposed to waiting in a packed, concrete room with no windows. Struggling to get up again in her tight pink pedal-pushers, she goes to open up the rucksack that Martin's been carrying for her.

'Right, I've made some little sandwiches, we've got some pork pies, sausage rolls, nice ones from Greggs, Scotch eggs, crisps, cold sausages and then I've got some naughty things for afters. Any takers?'

'I couldn't eat,' says Hayley, as the reality of how many people she's competing against slowly dawns on her. She looks distinctly worried.

I take no satisfaction from this. I'm too busy wondering what Dad's saying to Matthew. They're a few feet away from us and Matthew, who's bending down so that Ray can say something to him, is listening intently. I wonder whether something's wrong. Maybe he feels faint like he did the other week? Feeling positively twitchy at this point, and totally unable to be cool about anything, I cross over to them to find out what's up.

'Everything all right?'

'Yeah, yeah,' says Ray. 'T'rrific thanks. It's a day out innit?'

'What are you two planning then?' I ask, sounding even to my own ears rather shrill and neurotic. *What's wrong with me today?*

'Nothing,' says Matthew. 'Ray's got a bit of back pain so I'm going to give him some codeine.'

'Is it bad? Only if it is, maybe you shouldn't stick around here all day? How much pain are you in exactly?' I say, fighting with the fluttery panic that I'm suddenly experiencing.

'It's not that bad babe,' replies Ray calmly.

'Well that's what you said that day you came to the house to meet Hayley and look what happened then. And how do I know you're telling me the whole story? I mean, you said the chemo and the transfusion and the steroids were all making you feel better, and yet today you're in a wheelchair.'

I know I'm sounding almost accusatory and I don't mean to, but what I'm saying is true. I can't keep up with the rapid changes and declines in his health.

'Listen, do you fancy a quick walk to get a drink?' asks Matthew.

'Er no, I think Mum's bought loads of drinks if you're thirsty,' I reply vaguely before continuing my rant. 'I'm not being horrid, Dad. It's just that you coming here is crazy and it worries me if it's going to make you feel like shit. If you're feeling bad then you need to rest, and I'm not sure that this is the place to…'

'I fancy a drink from one of the machines though. Come with me, Marianne?'

I look at Matthew, confused. Why was he interrupting? Then I realise. He doesn't want a drink, just the opportunity to talk to me out of earshot.

'Oh… well maybe actually, yes, let's get one.'

We walk a little way away from the group.

'Are you OK?' asks Matthew.

'Um… yeah, fine,' I lie. The truth is I think I'm on the verge of a really badly timed panic attack and am almost finding it hard to breathe. 'It's just there's a lot to think about at the moment and I'm not so sure this is the best environment for Ray and…' I'm all set to gabble away for the foreseeable future but Matthew isn't having any of it.

'Hey, take a deep breath,' he says, gently but firmly. I'm about to protest but then realise that actually someone taking charge of my panic is a good thing. It needs reining in, so I do as I'm told. I take a deep breath. Then I take another and another and slowly the extra oxygen seems to have an effect and I feel myself returning to something approaching normal.

I don't know what's wrong with me, or why I've chosen to feel so strung out about everything at this precise second. I think perhaps it's the combination of the wheelchair, coupled with seeing how reliant Ray is on Matthew. I feel so helpless knowing that I can't do anything to *make things better*. The truth is I also don't want Matthew to be the one Dad relies on. It should be me, his daughter. I'm the one who cares about him the most. I wish he didn't have to go through this nightmare. I wish it wasn't him. I wish it wasn't *my* dad. I don't say any of this out loud but it must be written all over my face and I can feel the panic rising again.

'I know how hard this is for you,' says Matthew, who by contrast is the definition of calm and composed, his eyes full of warmth and empathy.

No wonder Dad likes hanging out with him so much. How can I compete? Why do I even want to compete? He's Dad's nurse for goodness sake and yet I can't shake this feeling that Ray spending time with anyone else means less time for me. And time is something we don't have much of. I feel my eyes welling up ominously. Oh Christ, don't do this now. It so isn't the time or the place.

'Look,' says Matthew, gently holding my arms so I'm forced to look at him and have to listen to what he's saying. Muddled in with all the other things I'm feeling I'm now aware of a definite thrill in response to this physical contact.

'I hope you don't think I'm speaking out of turn here, but I want you to know that your father is an amazing guy and very strong. He's coping extremely well on an emotional level.'

'Is he though?' I say, needing to know the absolute truth. 'Is he really, because I don't get how he can be. It's so… so awful and shit and… sad.'

'He is,' says Matthew firmly. 'I mean, it's all relative and sure he's had his moments and will continue to have good days and bad. He wouldn't be human if he didn't. But generally speaking, he's fairly resigned to his fate compared to many I've seen. He's resilient and philosophical, which helps.'

'He's so brave about it,' I say, biting my lip and looking somewhere over Matthew's left shoulder. 'Only the trouble is…' I say, concentrating very hard on not crying. 'The trouble is, Matthew that… I'm not sure I am… you know… coping very well on an emotional level.' My voice cracks and I have to blink very hard but just about manage to hold it together, although it's touch and go because Matthew's looking at me with such kindness I hardly know where to put myself. He gives me a moment to compose myself.

'I'm sorry,' I manage eventually, clearing my throat. 'It's not exactly part of your job description, dealing with unhinged relatives.'

'It kind of is, actually,' he says cheerfully.

'Oh. Well I really didn't want to be doing this here today.'

'I know,' says Matthew. 'Which is why I bought you over here. I could tell a few emotions were brewing.'

'I guess you're used to reading these sorts of situations,' I say, flooded with newfound respect for what he does and relief that I seem to have got my feelings back under control, which is when the embarrassment hits me and I can't look him in the eye any more.

'I wouldn't quite say that,' Matthew replies. 'After med school I specialised in oncology because I want to help fix people, and very often we do. I still find cases such as Ray's tough but it's my job to make things easier for the patient. And today I'm here as a friend more than anything. He's a cool guy, your dad.'

'Thanks,' I say, flashing him a watery but grateful smile. What he did every day was humbling.

'Shall we go back?' Matthew asks suddenly. 'I think your boyfriend's trying to get your attention.'

'Boyfriend?' I say, feeling baffled. I wasn't aware I had one of those. I glance over at everyone, trying to ascertain who Matthew's referring to and am horrified to see Andy waving a chubby arm at me, signalling to me that I'm missing out on Mum's picnic, which she's just finished spreading out. I'm furious and flap at him to try and get him to stop waving at me. Why does the fat pig have to assume everyone else has a rampant appetite like him?

'Oh, he's not my boyfriend,' I protest, but it's too late, Matthew's already making his way back over to the group. I follow him, feeling mortified. I don't want *anyone* mistaking Billy Bunter for my boyfriend but it feels especially important that he doesn't. He's so nice and so attractive. I can't help but think I wish I'd met him under different circumstances.

CHAPTER EIGHTEEN

'Do you want a little drinkie?' asks Mum as I approach.

I shake my head.

'How about you my angel?' she says to Hayley. 'Can I get you something to lubricate your throat?'

'Oi, what do you think she's going to be doing in there?' quips Gary, guffawing heartily at his own wit.

Mum laughs weakly but looks grossed out. Pete frowns and my brow furrows so deeply it won't be long before Botox becomes something to seriously consider. Martin grins inanely but checks himself when he sees Mum's disapproving face. Andy, however, has the nerve to high five Gary.

'Good one mate.'

'I meant do you want a drinkie Hayls?' tries Mum again.

'No,' Hayley snaps. 'I'm not hungry and I'm not thirsty either. If I want something I'll ask.'

'Fair enough,' says Mum, making a face at Martin as if to say '*Ooh! somebody's grumpy*'.

'To be fair, I know how Hayley feels,' says Martin, ever the peacemaker. 'It's a nervy business.'

'Do you know what?' says Mum, taking a break for a

second from opening packets of stuff no one really wants. 'I'm actually not nervous. Can you believe that?'

'Well yeah,' growls Ray good-humouredly. 'Given that you ain't the one about to do the bleedin' singing.'

'Don't be such a bastardo you,' says Mum wryly and for a second I think she might actually be flirting. 'No, what I mean is, that I'm not nervous because Hayls is gonna knock 'em dead. I know she is. It's her destiny.'

I despair.

'Give her a chance Mum,' I feel compelled to say. 'Don't you think comments like that put the pressure on?'

Hayley gives me an uncertain smile.

'Here here,' agrees Dad. 'Leave the poor girl be and let her do her thing.'

I wait for Mum to rebuff him as she most certainly would if Martin had dared to say such a thing, but she doesn't. She tuts loudly, but it's not very convincing. I almost burst out laughing when I clock Martin's face. He looks genuinely amazed that his wife hasn't put her ex in his place.

'Well,' interjects Andy, in his Australian drawl. 'If none of you are going to get started on Alli's amazing picnic, I'm going to have to do the honours. Be rude not to,' he adds, reaching out a paw for a sausage roll.

Inside I scream.

'I'll join you mate,' says Gary, looking up from his iPhone for the first time since we arrived.

I look at Pete. He's the only other person in the group – apart from myself – who obviously gets that this entire farce is madness. He's also, and bizarrely this seems to include Ray, probably the only other person who'd rather be anywhere else right now. Afghanistan, a Turkish prison, anywhere.

We sit for hours and hours with nothing much happening. At this rate I'm starting to wonder whether I'll be late for my date with Teresa this evening, so I text her to let her know what I'm doing. She texts back telling me to keep her posted.

It grows increasingly obvious that not everyone who has turned up today is going to be honoured with an appearance in front of the judges. There are simply too many thousands of people for that to be possible. However, after a lot of time spent scrutinising the people who *do* seem to be getting picked out by the researchers, I quickly figure out that they are looking for one of three things: the talented, the untalented, and the quirky – the freaks of nature. Anyone who's simply average isn't cutting it.

By four o'clock Mum's snacks are running low, largely thanks to Andy and Gary, although severe boredom means we've all tucked in a bit. Then finally, just as I'm starting to think the whole day might have been a complete and utter waste of time, a researcher who is looking for people to film with here in the holding room spots our group and suddenly looks like all his Christmases have come at once.

'Wow, so which one of you guys is here to audition?'

'I am,' says Hayley coyly, deciding it might be time to slip off the light raincoat she's been wearing all day. The researcher's eyes nearly pop out of his head. I don't blame him. Her outfit is extraordinary and in an entirely reflex action I spin round to see whether Matthew's noticed. He has. Of course he bloody has.

Underneath her mac, Hayley's wearing a minuscule, navy, polka dot playsuit, which is very figure hugging and shows off her long legs. Often, Hayley has the tendency to look a bit tarty, but actually this outfit has quite a 1940s look about it and shows off a tantalising amount of boob as opposed to a scary amount. She looks a knockout and, now that I can see what she's wearing, her make-up and hair suddenly make sense.

I glance at Dad, who looks like he'd like her to put her coat back on. Gary's drooling, Andy's jaw is dragging on the floor and Matthew is trying not to look but failing. Personally, I'm with Dad. I'd like her to cover herself up immediately. Meanwhile, Mum has her hands clasped together at her chest, looking so proud she might explode. Once again I momentarily experience something that feels a lot like jealousy. Still, I should be used to it by now. Just when you think Hayley can't look any better she pulls something like this out of the bag.

'And this is your family?' asks the researcher.

'Yeah,' says Hayley. 'They're all here to support me. This is my Mum, Alison.'

'Hello darlin',' she says bounding forward, her set and curled hair bouncing with her. 'I can tell you now you'll be glad you've spotted my Hayls. She's a star in the making.

In fact, you're probably looking at the Christmas number one right now.'

'Brilliant,' says the researcher, looking decidedly unmoved by her proclamation and far more interested in Hayley's cleavage. 'So, who's everyone else?'

'This is my sister,' says Hayley, turning on the charm so much I hardly recognise her. 'This is my husband…'

The researcher looks noticeably disappointed.

'…this is my stepdad Martin, and this is my Dad…'

'Your Dad?' he says and I swear his eyes light up as he detects a fantastic sob story unfolding before his eyes, which are very unsubtly taking in Dad's wheelchair. 'Wow, well hi guys. Listen, if you don't mind I'd love to take Hayley off for a second and have a quick chat, and in the meantime perhaps our crew could do a bit of filming with you guys?'

'That sounds brilliant,' squeals Mum. 'Ooh Martin, you ready for your close up babes? Oh my god, what is Sheena going to say about this, eh? Finally I won't have to hear her going on about being on *Deal or No Deal* any more.'

'OK…' says the researcher.

'She didn't win much anyway. Silly moo got greedy.'

'Right… well I'm James and ah, perfect timing. This is Rick, one of our cameramen. Rick if you could film all these guys please.'

'I don't want to be filmed,' I announce, suddenly feeling panicky again. If I was here with an incredible singer I might be keener, but I can feel a car crash coming on and quite frankly I want no part of it.

'OK,' says James, not remotely bothered that I won't be featuring. 'And of course anyone who *is* up for being filmed must sign one of these release forms.'

Mum practically wrenches them out of his hands. 'Oh don't listen to old misery guts there,' she says frowning at me. 'We'll sign whatever you like, won't we Mar?'

'Absolutely,' he agrees.

'Totally,' says Andy, who's wiping clean the inside of a crisp packet with his finger. To my disgust he sucks the crumbs off his finger then starts poking around in the picnic debris, to see whether there's anything left to demolish.

'I'm not going on,' states Pete.

'Fine,' says the researcher and I feel an unusual pang of empathy for my brother. Good for him.

'If you don't mind, I'll step out too,' says Matthew.

'Right, stop mucking about you lot and let's get on with it,' says Mum.

I can't watch, so as Rick and a soundman prepare to film Mum, Martin, Andy, Dad and Gary's televisual debuts, I wander off to find a bathroom.

By the time I come back it's all over – I took my time – and Hayley, who has rejoined us, isn't looking nervous any more but dangerously puffed up and cocky.

'Oh my god Marianne, James said he's never heard a voice like it and that I'm definitely going to be seen by the judges. He slipped me his phone number as well,' she adds in a whisper, so Gary can't hear. 'Not that I'd ever do anything obviously, but if he fancies me it might be useful, don't you reckon?'

'Er… yeah. Brilliant,' I say lightly. Have I been naïve all this time? Maybe Hayley will get through purely on the strength of how outstandingly gorgeous she looks. I do want her to do well, I'm not that mean, but musically speaking it's enough to trigger depression, it really is.

Still, I meant what I said. I want my sister to do well, so when a few minutes later they come to fetch us to take us through to yet another holding area I find myself crossing my fingers.

Mum's beside herself. 'Oh my god I might wet myself.'

'Nice,' remarks Ray and she actually giggles.

'Shut up Raymondo.'

I exchange gobsmacked looks, first with Hayley and then with Martin, who clears his throat loudly in order to get his wife's attention and to make it clear he doesn't approve of her flirting.

'Oh stop it you, love of my life,' she says dismissively. 'I just don't see why we shouldn't all try and get on that's all. Make an effort for the girls.'

'S'pose you're right,' says Martin bravely, refusing to look in Ray's direction.

'Thanks Alli,' says Ray before giving her a cheeky wink.

Mum's face immediately drops into a frown of pointed disapproval but as she looks away I can see that she's blushing madly. It's bizarre and makes for uncomfortable viewing and yet in that moment I know that things between my parents will be amicable enough from now on. For that I'm pleased.

Glad to be out of the grim holding area we troop down the passages of the arena, Hayley marching ahead, a woman on a mission, Gary beside her like a bouncer. Mum and Martin are scuttling along behind them, then Matthew's pushing Ray along and finally bringing up the rear is Andy, then me and then Pete. At one point, Andy, who's panting from the exertion of walking, turns and grins, but I just look back at him as if to say '*What do you want? Who are you? Why are you here?*' He gets the hint and looks away again, his face a bit shifty.

'OK, here we are then,' says James the researcher, fiddling around with his headset. By now we've reached another room, not dissimilar to the first one and yet our excitement levels go up a notch because this is clearly where stuff is actually happening. The people in here are definitely going to be seen by the judges and there's a large telly showing us exactly what's going on in that inner sanctum. More interestingly than that, standing by the screen being filmed is the presenter of the show, Sy Lovejoy.

I look at Hayley, trying to catch her eye, but she's retreated into a world of her own. I don't blame her. What she's about to do is simply terrifying and the reality far removed from the experience of watching it all unfold from your living room. Still, I have to hand it to her, she looks impressively focused and poised.

Unlike Mum.

'Bloody hell Martin, we're only here lovey,' she shrieks,

looking demented and gripping his arm so tight it makes his eyes water. 'I can't believe it. It's like a dream come true. I'm so excited I could do a little whoopsie truth be known. Oh get me, what am I like, eh? AaaaEEh!'

This last noise is precisely that, just a noise. Proper reasoning has deserted her. She seriously needs to calm down.

'Right,' says James, smiling faintly at my strange mother. 'So, Hayley's going to go on next if that's all right, and what we'll do is have you guys round here, watching on a monitor. Ah, here's someone I'd like to introduce you to who I think you might be familiar with. This is Sy Lovejoy, our presenter.'

'Aaaaah,' screams Mum again, like a teenage groupie. 'Oh my days. It's Sy. Hello my darling, I'm Alli. Oh aren't you handsome,' she says clutching her chest. 'And tiny too, like a little diddy man. Honestly, I could gobble you up.'

'Mum,' snaps Hayley incredulously.

Gary sniggers at the word gobble.

Thankfully Sy Lovejoy, who's more handsome in the flesh than he is on TV, takes Mum's hysteria completely in his stride. 'Thanks for that, Alli was it? It's lovely to meet you all. Is this all your family then?'

'Yes, they're all my little chickens,' she says ludicrously. 'Well except him,' she says, gesturing behind her towards Ray, rolling her eyes to the heavens. 'He's my ex. Oh, and that lovely young man with him is his nurse. And this is Andy, who isn't mine either, but is like part of the family really, aren't you babes?'

'Oh yeah,' confirms Andy confidently.

'And this,' says Mum, sweeping her arms out as if announcing royalty, 'Is my Hayley, who, between you and me Sy, is probably going to win.'

'Oh wow,' says Sy cheerfully. 'Well let me be the first to congratulate you then.'

'She's my wife,' states Gary territorially, apropos of nothing. It's a strange thing to suddenly come out with and doesn't exactly invite any more chit-chat.

There follows an awkward silence during which I look around at my family wondering what the hell Sy must be thinking. As it is, luckily for us all, someone's started talking to him in his earpiece anyway. He puts a polite hand up in order to excuse himself so he can listen to his instructions from whoever's talking to him.

'Well that was embarrassing,' I say to Mum.

'Why? Because you didn't say anything?' she replies in all seriousness.

The next thing I know, whoever's on before Hayley is about to start. We watch on the screen as the man introduces himself to the judges. It's really odd seeing them all on the screen as we have done hundreds of times before, yet knowing they're only metres away.

The contestant is a man in his mid-forties called John, who turns out to be a pretty amazing singer. He works in telesales but sings in clubs at the weekend. He's got a deep, soulful baritone and the judges' only real criticism is that he sounds like a club singer – funny that. Still, everyone with the exception of Julian Hayes gives him a yes, which is enough to put him through to the next round. As John leaves the room he punches the air, and the next thing I know he's walking past us and being leapt on by his proud waiting family.

'Why did they put him through? He was rubbish,' Mum keeps mouthing at us all, which isn't true and is also very rude. I glare at her and at one point catch Matthew's eye. I roll my eyes at him, trying to convey '*I honestly don't know how I came to be related to such a nutbag*' but he remains politely diplomatic. I'm terribly conscious of what he must think of us all but realise I should probably stop staring at him every five seconds or he might decide I'm the oddest one of the bunch.

And so it is that I drag my eyes away and glance over towards Dad and the others instead. It's weird. I keep fully expecting Dad to be irritated by Mum, but instead he seems to view her antics as highly entertaining, and even now is quietly chuckling away to himself while she leaps about in front of him. In a moment of clarity I realise Mum amuses him, probably always did.

James, the researcher, approaches us again. 'OK, if anyone who hasn't signed a release form wouldn't mind waiting somewhere else because Hayley's on next and we're going to film you guys and your reactions while you watch her performance.'

'Oh my god, oh my god, oh my god…' Mum squeals ad infinitum as Pete, Matthew and I are shunted out of shot. Fortunately, we're allowed to remain only feet away. I'm relieved. I would hate to miss the action.

'He seemed pretty nice,' says Matthew as the three of us wait nervously for Hayley's turn.

'Who? Sy?'

'Yeah.'

'Yeah he did,' I agree. 'Sorry about Mum by the way. She can be a bit much sometimes but she means well.'

'Don't be silly,' he grins. 'She's cool.'

'Mm, cool,' I muse drily. 'If you say so, although I'm not necessarily sure that's the first adjective that springs to mind. Not that I have the right to say absolutely anything obviously, given that from time to time I dress as a clown.'

'But that really is cool,' says Matthew. 'It's brilliant, and I bet you're fantastic at entertaining the kids.'

He's so nice. Even if his definition of what's 'cool' and 'brilliant' are a bit warped.

Now Matthew follows my gaze over to where Mum's doing a little dance round Hayley.

'What are you doing Mum?' I shout over to her, hoping if I frown hard enough she might stop.

'Bit of Reiki, lovey. Get her energies up.'

'Right,' I say before turning to my brother. 'As a matter of interest, do you find her bloody embarrassing too, Pete? Or is it just me?'

Pete stares balefully back at me but doesn't commit either way.

'Aren't all mum's a bit embarrassing?' asks Matthew. 'Aren't they supposed to be?'

'I don't know,' I answer truthfully. 'Are they? Is yours?'

'Er… yeah I guess, sometimes.'

'OK, so I can tell by the way you said that, that yours is infinitely more sane and far less embarrassing than mine.'

'She's just excited,' says Matthew, though admittedly with less conviction. Mum's really upped the ante now. If she doesn't stop leaping about, there's a strong chance Hayley will belt her one.

'I mean if Hayley's as good as Alison reckons she is,' says Matthew, 'Then maybe she does have a chance of winning? Which let's face it, would be pretty life changing.'

'Mm,' I say, hating myself for being so miserably negative when everyone else is so excited.

'I guess we're about to find out either way,' says Pete flatly to Matthew.

The judges are ready. They've had a quick break during which we could see them onscreen being powdered by the make-up ladies and given drinks. My stomach lurches with excitement when the camera hones in on their faces and momentarily I feel quite star-struck. It's all so bizarre. After that, everything happens quite quickly. As soon as the cameras are rolling again we see the floor manager signalling to Hayley. She disappears from the room, but within seconds we see her appearing on screen. She pretty much struts out from the wings towards the X that's marked on the middle of the floor, which is where she's been instructed to stand. She looks born to be on camera and for a minute even has me convinced. Maybe we *were* looking at a winner?

CHAPTER NINETEEN

It's amazing how much a silence can communicate sometimes. The one that hung heavily in the air of our tube carriage on the journey home managed to be not only tense, but mortified. I'm too weary and traumatised to go into details now but let's just say that Hayley's furious about how her audition went. She's also, understandably, horrified because none of us have any doubt that she *will* be featuring on *Sing for Britain* all right, only for all the wrong reasons. We don't know this for sure of course, but if I had to bet either way I'd say she'll definitely be making an appearance.

'If *you* hadn't got involved, I would have got away with it,' Hayley fumes in Mum's direction.

The rest of us gaze about the carriage, screwing up our faces, either scrutinising the advertising or studying the tube map with over the top levels of interest. Anything that means we don't have to look at Mum or Hayley.

'As it is, they're bound to show it because you made such a fucking tit of yourself,' Hayley continues.

'Hayley,' says my Dad wearily. 'I know you're upset, but don't speak to your mother like that.'

'Absolutely,' agrees Martin, trying to sound authoritative, which doesn't suit him at all.

'And you can both fuck off an' all,' my livid sister splutters, looking less beautiful than usual. Rage has contorted her face into an unattractive snarl, plus one of her false eyelashes is flapping off at the side. It's not a good look. All her 'get up and go' has got up and gone, though to be honest her awful experience has rubbed off on us all. As far as I'm concerned we all look, and feel, like a big deflated bunch of losers.

'And besides, what right do either of you have to tell me what to do?' she adds despairingly, having switched the focus of her vitriol from Mum, to Martin and Dad. Though it's obvious she's only lashing out due to her own sheer mortification.

By now Dad's quite ashen with tiredness and he doesn't answer. He looks disappointed by Hayley's behaviour though, as does Matthew – a vague silver lining I suppose, looking like a supermodel isn't everything in life etc.

Still, I guess it must have come as quite a shock to Ray to discover how badly deluded Hayley and Mum have been with regard to my sister's 'talent'. He's definitely smiled at me in a vaguely apologetic way a couple of times too, so I think he now gets that earlier I was only trying to help, not hinder. I wasn't jealous, I was worried.

'I think we should all calm down,' interjects Martin

mildly. 'Then, when we get home we'll have a nice cup of tea and say no more about it. For what it's worth, I'm very proud of our Hayley. It took a lot of guts to get up there in front of all those people.'

Mum, who's been terribly sheepish ever since 'the incident' nods gravely.

'Well said, Martin,' pipes up Andy. 'And can I just add that, personally, I'm with Alli. I think you sounded awesome up there Hayls and if you ask me, the judges got it totally wrong. Plus, when you got in there Alison, you reminded me of a lioness protecting her young. It was like, totally amazing.'

'Thank you Andy,' says Mum gratefully, staring at Andy as if what he just said was a fine and awe-inspiring piece of rhetoric as opposed to utter bullshit. If she chooses to listen to him, before long she'll be convincing herself she was right all along. What a horrifying thought.

I'm busy groaning inwardly when, for a fleeting moment, Matthew catches my eye. There's a hint of a question there and I'm pretty sure he's wondering what I'm doing going out with such a dickhead. I have no idea how to convey that I wouldn't touch said dickhead with a barge pole, so can't bear to face him. I turn away.

'They probably won't end up using our bits anyway,' Mum adds hesitantly. 'They have so much to choose from I'm sure.'

Again, our silence is deafening.

'And if they did,' she continues, clearly trying to

convince herself more than anyone else, 'I reckon it would come across fine, no matter what you mouldy old lot think.'

*

That night it's unbelievably fantastic to escape my stupid family and to get out of the house. A sort of 'don't mention the war' style pact has been made about what took place today, which is fine by me. Of course, the whole world will be finding out what happened sooner or later, but for now I'm as happy as them to block it out. It would have been all too easy to cancel Teresa claiming tiredness and post-traumatic stress disorder but I don't, and as soon as I see her standing outside the club waiting for me I'm really glad.

'Tell me then,' she says at once. 'How bad was it on a scale of one to ten?'

'Eleven,' I reply immediately, marvelling at how natural it feels to be meeting up with her after all this time. There's no awkwardness between us whatsoever, despite having missed out on so many months and months of friendship.

'Let's get inside, get a drink and you can relive every excruciating second of it for me,' she says, and suddenly the prospect of talking to someone who has precisely no vested interest in how Hayley did is a wonderful one.

'Thanks Teresa,' I say, feeling quite overcome.

'You're very welcome,' she says, flashing me a wide, sincere grin in the sort of heart-warming way only Teresa is capable of. In that moment I know that not only have we totally forgiven each other for drifting apart but also that I won't ever take her for granted again.

'Sorry,' I say, because suddenly I'm welling up. 'I'm being a right soppy prat, it's just it's so nice to see you. I've missed you so much. It really hit me when I bumped into you that time.'

'Me too, you silly cow,' says Teresa, hooking her arm through mine and leading us both towards the entrance of the club.

'There's a lot going on with me right now,' I add, suddenly desperate to offload. 'I don't know if you've heard about any of it…'

'I have,' says Teresa, stopping to drag hard on the last bit of her cigarette before stubbing it out with her shoe. 'Darren heard from Steve, you know, Steve who works with Gary. Your dad's back isn't he? And he's not all that well?'

'No. In fact, that's a bit of an understatement…' I trail off.

Teresa looks at me thoughtfully, weighing up the situation.

'Well,' she says eventually. 'In that case, I reckon what we need is not just a drink but several so come on you, let's get in there and then, after we've let off a bit of steam, we'll have a proper talk about it all yeah?'

'Yeah,' I say, grateful beyond words for her talent at knowing exactly how to handle things, and feeling something akin to relief to be with her. We enter the cavernous club at which point we're swallowed up by the booming thud of bass.

The next day, I wake up feeling a smidge hung-over, yet calmer than I have in ages. Hanging out with Teresa was like medicine. The conversation was horribly one-sided but I know she didn't mind. It was such a relief to talk honestly about my dad and how I feel about everything that's happening. I also reneged a bit on my family's pact by telling her a bit about our disastrous trip to *Sing for Britain*, though once I'd said it all out loud, I could see how funny it really was. Obviously I'm going to have to leave the country when it comes on telly, but Teresa found the whole tale so amusing it got things into perspective I suppose. Halfway through the evening I gave silent thanks to Dad for forcing me out of my inertia and into arranging to see my friend. He was right of course. Good mates are hard to come by and worth holding on to. And let's face it, over the next few months I was going to need all the friends I could get.

*

For days after the event, at home there's a definite vein of embarrassment in the air, coupled with an obstinate refusal to admit out loud what a truly humiliating debacle the whole episode really was. Personally I keep my mouth shut and carry on as normal.

I go to work, keep my head down, try to stop thinking about Matthew, who seems to have wormed his way into my psyche, and vent all my frustration towards Andy instead. Frustration that turns into pure hatred the next Sunday when, back from a children's party and desperate to get into the shower – the weather's finally starting to get hot so wearing a heavy clown costume is a little… shall we say clammy? – I catch him clipping his toenails in the bathroom.

'Can't you at least lock the door when you do that?' I berate him angrily.

By way of reply he stares at me balefully, an expression I suspect is supposed to incite sympathy when in fact it makes me want to slam the toilet seat down hard onto his fat hobbit foot.

'What?' I snap. 'Don't look at me like that.'

Andy sighs and lowers his foot before saying solemnly, 'You and I need to talk.'

'OK,' I agree, wondering whether finally he might have got the message that I just want him to disappear.

'I'm getting the distinct impression that you're not finding it easy living with me.'

'You could be right there,' I say, nodding my head furiously.

'So…'

'Yes?'

'So, I wanted to recommend a really good self-help book called *Battling with your inner demons*. Apparently it's really good for people with anger issues.'

'No Andy, no,' I disagree. 'You see, that's not what I need at all.'

He stares blankly at me.

'Don't you get it?'

Looking baffled he shakes his head.

'Right,' I continue slowly, trying to keep a lid on the anger that I do indeed have within me. 'What it is, is that I just think… I think that it's a bit… weird… you… being here still. And I know you like it here,' I rush on, raising both hands up to prevent him from interrupting. 'And I know you love hanging out with Mum and Martin but at the end of the day this is my home and it has been weeks and weeks now since you arrived.'

'I see,' says Andy solemnly. 'In which case I do get it,' he adds, tapping the side of his nose conspiratorially. 'You don't need to say anything else.'

'So you'll move out?' I ask, feeling like I might weep with happiness.

He looks shocked to the core. 'Oh, no. I mean, I thought that's what you meant you were going to do. After all, at the end of the day, you're the one with the problem, so if you want to move out I fully understand. You have my blessing and I won't stand in your way at all.'

'Aaaeurgh,' I rage, slamming the door behind me.

'Aaah,' yells Andy back. I stare at the door wondering what he has to yell about.

'For crissakes Marianne, what's wrong with ya? That got me on the toe.'

Oh.

'Well… good,' I scream, wanting to rush back in and hurl him bodily out of the window. Although what I do in reality is what I've been doing for months now. I retreat pathetically to my room where I plug into my iPod and one of my favourite violinists, Hilary Hahn, playing Tchaikovsky's violin concerto.

A few hours, one soothing concerto and some therapeutic violin practise later, I've managed to calm down. I'm hungry, so I skulk out in search of food.

'Oh darling, I still think he got it so wrong,' I hear Mum saying for the zillionth time as I enter the living room. As I come round the corner I find Andy sitting at one end of the kitchen table, stuffing his face with a toastie, which my mother has clearly 'rustled up' for him, while Hayley is at the other, looking po-faced.

'I don't want to talk about it any more. He didn't get it wrong,' she retorts furiously. 'And how come until now you've always agreed with everything the judges have ever said?'

She has a point.

Mum looks up and stares blankly at me for a second. 'Thank god you've finished playing that ruddy instrument. What a flipping racket.'

Andy half-chokes as he laughs uproariously at her dig. I glare daggers at him.

Sometimes I simply hate my life. What the hell am I doing living in this house at my age? I've got to get out.

Though how I'll do this I'll never know. It will require
some thought but I think I've reached a point where it has
to be a priority.

*

A few days later I get a call from Dad. He sounds pretty
down.

'What you doing?' he says.

'Not a lot,' I reply. 'Just got back from another scintil-
lating day at Roberto's.'

'Right, so what are your plans? Are you off on one of
your jaunts soon or summink?'

'No,' I answer, probably a little too promptly. How can
he think I'd go anywhere now, when he's so ill.

'Why not? That's what you do innit?' he says, sounding
grouchy.

'Are you in a mood with me or something?' I ask tentatively.

'Nah, I just wish you'd give me a straight answer sometimes. Truthfully, it frustrates me that you don't seem to
have any idea what you want to do. And if you're waiting
around for me to pop me clogs then don't. I want you to
live your life, not spend it sitting around waiting for stuff
to happen.'

'Well thanks,' I say, feeling hurt. 'S'cuse me for thinking you might actually want to spend some time with me
before…'

'I do,' Dad interrupts at once. 'I do and I'm sorry, I

don't mean to be out of order it's just your apathy really concerns me Marianne.'

I don't like where this conversation is headed so decide to change the subject.

'I've got a music lesson booked in next Thursday. Do you want to come? I mean, don't feel you have to but you did say you'd like to hear me play.'

This seems to do the trick. His mood transforms.

'What time? I've got check-ups in the morning.'

'It's not till six-thirty.'

'In that case I'll be there,' he says far more brightly. 'Only I might need a lift.'

'Done, and I'm pleased you're coming. Apart from anything else it might stop my teacher from banging on about applying to music college. She's booked an appointment to have a tour round it next week.'

'Has she?' he says with such joy in his voice I regret not having finished my sentence quicker.

'Yeah she has… though I was about to say I doubt I'll bother going.'

Dad sighs heavily and an awkward silence ensues while I try and work out what to say next. I can tell he's in a strange old mood. He breaks it first.

'Today, for once, I don't have to be at the hospital so can I come round later? Hayley's gonna be there ain't she?'

'Course you can come round, and yeah, Hayley will be here. In fact she seems to be spending most of her time here lately. I reckon her and Gary must be having a bad patch or something.'

*

When he turns up Dad looks exhausted, although that seems to be pretty much par for the course these days. He's also come by mini-cab, so obviously feels too weak for the bus.

'Are you OK?' I ask after I've let him in and followed him into the sitting room.

'Not too bad,' he says. 'Not too bad... not that great either but...'

To my horror as he sits gingerly down onto the settee I notice him wince with pain. Hayley, who's flicking disdainfully through Mum's copy of *Bella* magazine, has obviously noticed too because looking wary she puts it down.

'You all right?' she demands to know in her usual tactful way. She always sounds so angry.

'No, it's nuffink. I'm fine,' he insists, screwing up his face as he forces back down whatever pain he's undoubtedly feeling. The next second he's back in control once more.

'So,' I say brightly. 'I've told Mrs Demetrius you'll be at my lesson next Thursday if you still...'

Just then, Mum interrupts by poking her head round the door. 'Oh, I didn't realise you were here Raymond. You all right, lovey?'

'Fine thanks,' replies Dad, avoiding her eye completely.

'I'm going upstairs for a workout in a minute,' Mum

says, slithering round the door coquettishly. 'I've got a new DVD. It's Coleen Nolan's. Got to give these things a go haven't you? Keep the old figure. Especially after an extra little éclair at tea-time,' she adds. Dad still doesn't take any notice and I can tell Mum's peeved because she wants him to look. Wants him to take in her shiny black leotard, pink leggings and black legwarmers.

'You should wear trainers though Mum. Wear those wedges and you'll turn your ankle,' says Hayley.

'Oh whatever,' says Mum rolling her eyes, standing with her hands on her hips, having given up on Dad. 'Anyways, I'm gonna take a cup of tea up with me while I do it, so I don't get dehydrated. So, if you want a cuppa, speak now or for ever hold your peace.'

'Great, thanks,' Ray answers off-handedly and Mum leaves the room looking disappointed not to have had more attention.

As soon as she's gone I start again, determined to talk away the strange atmosphere. 'Anyway, don't worry if you don't want to come because I've played loads for you recently, but if you do, like I said before, Thursday might be a good day.'

'I'll be there,' says Dad. 'And what about you Hayley? What are you going to do with yourself now all that *Sing for Britain* business is over?'

'Dunno,' she replies sulkily, shrugging her shoulders and gazing at her fingernails.

'And you, Marianne?'

'What?' I say.

'What are you doing with yourself?'

'What do you mean what am I doing?' I say, sounding immediately defensive even to my own ear. 'I'm working and I'm saving and I'm hanging out with you aren't I? How many times are you going to ask me?'

Ray shakes his head and looks so sad and so serious, I start dreading what he might be about to say. I've never seen him like this before.

'Shall I put the telly on?' I say, hell-bent on lightening his mood. 'Let's find some mindless rubbish to goggle at.'

'Did you see *Britain's Next Top Model* the other day?' says Hayley, staring at her feet, which have clearly been pedicured recently. Usually stunningly gorgeous people are at least dealt ugly feet as a reminder that they're still human, but not our Hayley. Even her feet are pretty with perfectly even toes.

'If I was younger I'd try and get on that show I reckon,' she says flicking her blonde mane over her shoulder.

'Christ,' I say. 'Can't we at least get over your last attempt to get on telly first please?'

'There's no need to be a total bitch,' spits Hayley.

'Stop it,' Dad interrupts and his voice is ragged.

I stop in my tracks, halfway towards the TV, remote in hand. 'What?'

'Don't talk that way with each other. I can't stand it. It's so disrespectful,' he says, and a flash of something crosses his face. 'Look, I've come round today because I've real-ised that I need to tell you girls a few things.'

'Well, go on then,' says Hayley calmly. 'Spit it out. There's obviously been something you want to get off your chest ever since you got here so get on with it will ya?'

'It's just,' Ray wavers for a second but then seems to make up his mind once and for all and ploughs on. 'I notice things that are so bleedin' obvious, only not to you and I think maybe they have to be said.'

My heart lurches with unhappiness. He looks in such turmoil.

'Dad, are you OK?' I ask tearfully. 'Do you feel ill?'

'Yes Marianne. Of course I feel ill. I've got cancer. So I feel very ill and very sick but then that was always going to be the way.'

I'm taken aback by his frankness. He's never spoken so harshly to me before either. I'm terrified I might be about to cry. I clear my throat and dig my nails into my palms.

'Here's the tea then,' says Mum, barrelling in with a tray of tea and biscuits. 'It needs another minute or two to mash nicely but... oh, everything all right in here?' she trails off, having taken in our stricken faces and the strange atmosphere.

'Sit down Alison,' orders Dad.

'I can't. I'm busy,' says Mum. 'I've got to do this workout before Martin gets back from the pub so I can reheat his tea.'

'Please?'

'Oh all right then I will,' she says, giving us a 'look' and kicking off her wedges as she sinks into the settee. 'But there's no need to look so serious Raymondo. No one's died.'

Hayley tuts. I despair.

'What?' says Mum obtusely. 'Are you gonna pour Hayls? Or shall I be mum?' she cackles at this but then *finally* shuts up.

'What is it, Dad?' I ask, trying to sound as calm as I am capable. 'Tell us.'

'Firstly, I know I've probably got no right to sit here and say anything to any of you. I haven't earned the right. I get that and I also can't tell you how much I appreciate you all letting me into your lives. But the thing is, as you all know time ain't on my side so I can't take ages building bridges.'

'Just say what you've got to say, Ray,' orders Mum.

'Right,' he says. 'OK, well the thing is that I look at you all and I worry. And if things were different I'm sure I'd keep shtum but… I need to know that you're all gonna be OK.'

'Course we are Dad,' I insist, nodding my head manically. 'Aren't we Hayls?' I say, wanting back-up.

'Yeah,' she nods emphatically.

'Well, I'm not so sure about that,' Dad says. 'You see, I look at you Marianne and I wonder what it is that's stopping you from trying anything. You don't have any direction, any confidence. No self-belief and I don't know why, 'cos you're a diamond. A top, top girl, but the only person that don't seem able to see that, is you. Then Hayley, I look at you and I can tell you're not happy. You can't be. Not judging by the way you go around treating people. You're 'orrible to your sister. You don't show her no respect and it don't show you in a very good light. I think you take your unhappiness out on other people but it don't do you any good whatsoever. I know you want to be a mum and you'll be a great one, but before a kid comes along you need to do a bit of work on yourself. You can't expect a baby to be the answer to everything.'

Shocked, I look at Hayley, wondering how she's going to react to this. I don't know how Dad dares say this. She'll kill him. However, Hayley looks more stunned than anything else. Her mouth forming a perfect O.

'And Alison,' Dad continues, clearly now on a roll, 'You're a great mum. I'm not saying you ain't and I am so grateful to you for taking care of them for all these years when I've been out the picture and totally useless. It's obvious you love the girls.'

'But?' she says, one eyebrow arched.

Dad sighs. 'But you need to wake up and smell the coffee. Hayley ain't ever gonna be a star. She can't sing. Seriously,' he continues, ignoring the fact that Mum's jaw has just hit the deck. 'Them judges were right. Her audition was one of the worst sounds I've ever heard. In my life.'

Mum looks livid and opens her mouth to protest. 'I'll have you know Raymond…'

'No,' he says sternly. 'I don't wanna hear it. She can't sing and yet you're in her ear'ole every day telling her she can because you're living some kind of dream through her. But it's wrong Al, completely and utterly wrong and bleedin' unfair. Isn't it time Hayley got to tell you what she wants to do with her life? Give her some space to find out what that is because I don't think she's ever been asked. Then you've got Marianne here who is unbelievably talented, who has a gift as far as I can make out, and yet you've failed to even recognise that fact. And if someone doesn't, soon it will be too late. She's thirty-one and what's she doing?'

'What do you mean she's got a gift?' she asks indignantly.

'There you go,' blusters Dad and I gesture at him to calm down. I don't want a repeat of the last time he got himself all wound up. 'What do *you* mean what gift?' he says steadily, having taken a deep breath. 'She's musical Alison. Really musical and she should not be fannying around the world doing f' all when she could be here studying and making something of herself. Otherwise she'll end up doing naff all with her life like we have. Did you even know that her teacher reckons she should be applying to the Royal College of Music? As a mature student? Bloody mature student if you ask me but there you go. It could be done and that's the *Royal College of Music* Alison. Do you know what a big deal that would be?'

Mum looks utterly flummoxed.

'I'll take that as a no then,' Dad says, running one hand through his hair.

I stare at the floor, battling with all kinds of conflicting emotions. On the one hand I'm not so sure he's right. How would he know how talented I am or not? On the other I'm so, so touched by his faith in me.

'Well, that's charming that is,' says Hayley. 'Why don't you come out and say what you really mean eh Dad? I'm shit and Marianne isn't.'

Dad looks despairingly towards his ex-wife as if silently beseeching her to help him out. She doesn't though. Her arms are folded and she looks downright huffy. She also looks ridiculous sitting there in her leotard. She's got major VPL going on too.

'Look,' he tries again. 'Hayley, the last thing you are is shit. I ain't saying you're not a beautiful, lovely girl but as far as I can see you ain't a very happy one. Like a lot of people who have been treated differently all their lives 'cos of the way they look, you need to do some major work on your personality. You're horrible to people at times and don't seem interested in what anyone else is thinking or feeling. I know that's partly because you're hurting about certain things but that still don't make it all right love. Although it don't help when you've got people putting pressure on you to be something you ain't. I feel sorry for you. I do. And like I said, you need time to work out who you are. But you've got to realise that no one's gonna do it for you. And as for you, Marianne.'

I jump out of my skin.

'It's all very well you floating along and I know you ain't had much encouragement, but so what? You need to wake up. Your head's buried in the sand and I don't get it. When I die I need to know that you've all woken up and figured out what is going to make you happy. All three of you. You have to, because without sounding clichéd, this isn't a dress rehearsal. And I should know.'

As the three of us sit in stunned silence, desperately trying to digest everything Ray's just said, the door suddenly swings open and Andy puts his fat, nosey face around it.

'Hey guys, so sorry to interrupt...' he says, sounding anything but sorry. '... I was just wondering if those mini pizzas were for now or later, Alli?'

'Oh...' says Mum quietly. 'Um, they're for later, but go ahead and have them now if you're hungry lovey.'

'Cheers Alli,' he says, giving us all a thumbs-up before disappearing again.

Once the door's firmly shut again Dad quietly adds, for good measure, 'And seeing as I'm speaking frankly, I might as well also ask, what the hell is Chubby bleeding Checker still doing living here?'

CHAPTER TWENTY

Everything Ray said that afternoon stays with me for ages. I simply can't get his words out of my head. Being honest I suppose I can see why he feels so frustrated with me. I don't know what holds me back sometimes either, but am starting to wonder whether it's got anything to do with the fact that Mum and Hayley have never really understood me or acknowledged my passion for music. They haven't meant to but years of comments have whittled away at my confidence. Whereas Dad on the other hand seems hell-bent on telling me I can do anything I want, achieve anything if I put my mind to it and it's refreshing. It makes me feel vaguely capable. Makes me feel that perhaps I *should* at least go and have a look at the College? What harm would it do? Precisely what have I got to lose?

*

The next day, on Wednesday, out of the blue, Matthew calls. I presume to talk about Ray.

'I hope you don't mind me ringing. Your dad gave me your number because I just wanted to check you were OK.'

'No, I don't mind,' I reply honestly. Truthfully I feel a bit relieved as if subconsciously I've been waiting for him to ring all along. I also feel jittery and awkward. I obviously fancy him.

'So you're OK?'

'Yeah, thanks.'

'Good, it's just I know you've got a lot to deal with at the moment.'

'Mm, are you referring to Dad? Or to the fact Hayley embarrassed our entire family and Mum disgraced herself?' I continue, trying to sound light and humorous as opposed to neurotic and unhinged. 'Or, maybe you're more worried about the fact that come September at least fifteen million people will be witnessing the downfall of my relatives?'

'All of the above, I guess,' he says, but I can tell he's smiling. 'Anyway, I'm glad to hear you can see the funny side.'

'How come you're ringing though?' I say, suddenly anxious. 'Is Dad OK?'

'Um, yeah,' says Matthew, sounding doubtful. 'Have you seen him recently?'

'Yes.'

'OK, well, like I said, I just wanted to see whether you were OK, but maybe I shouldn't have?'

'No it's fine,' I reply, blushing madly. I'm still pretty embarrassed about the vulnerable state he saw me in that day. A part of me wonders whether he's ringing because he likes me, but a bigger part thinks he might feel sorry for me because I acted like such a freak.

'So… er what are you up to later?' Matthew says eventually, once it's become obvious he's not going to get anything more out of me.

'Going to see Hayley,' I reply. 'I'm going round to make sure she's OK. After all, she's the one who's going to take all the flack for this when the show comes out and she's had a hard time lately.'

'Right,' he says and then pauses as if debating whether to say something else or not.

'Was there anything else?' I enquire, hating myself for hoping there is. *What's wrong with me?* It's so inappropriate to start lusting after my dad's nurse, even if he is fit. It's hardly the time to be thinking about romance at the moment either, not when I have no idea how long Ray's got left.

'Er, no, good luck with your sister,' he says. 'And I guess I'll see you around.'

'Sure, see you around,' I say, wondering what on the earth the point of that was.

*

Driving to Hayley's I feel irrationally bothered by Matthew's phone call. It's just confused me because I had wondered whether he was going to ask me out but ultimately it all felt a bit pointless in the end. It's a shame. The man is gorgeous and under any normal circumstances I'd be allowing myself to fancy him rotten, even if he is out of my league. However, the circumstances are completely abnormal so it's ridiculous that I should even remotely care. He's my dad's nurse, so even thinking about him is one big enormous waste of time and deeply wrong. Maybe it's even illegal to like him? I'm not sure. I'll Google that one later.

Turning into my sister's cul-de-sac I take a deep breath. Right, I need to go in there feeling Zen-like. She sounded almost suspicious when I rang yesterday to tell her I was coming round but all I want is to try and have a chat, and to regain some of the closeness we shared when she was pregnant. To make my dad happy by improving our disastrous relationship. I'm doing this for him.

I ring on the bell.

Gary opens the door. Bloody hell.

'To what do I owe this pleasure?' he says smarmily.

I recoil as his eyes pan up and down my body.

'Is Hayley in?'

'No. You seem to be making a habit of this. Turning up when I'm in and she ain't. Anyone would think you were trying to get me on my own or something.'

'Hardly,' I snort. 'It's just you're never at work.'

'Being your own boss has its benefits,' he says lightly.

'So, where is my sister anyway? She said she'd be here. We made an arrangement,' I say, unable to hide my frustration at Hayley's rudeness. The last thing I was expecting was to have to deal with my muscle-bound brother-in-law on my own, yet again.

'We had a row as it goes,' says Gary.

'Oh.'

Damn. This is none of my business and I know better than to get involved with Hayley's stuff. Still, it must have been a pretty bad one for her not to have even bothered calling me.

As if on cue my phone beeps, telling me I have a text. I quickly have a look.

NOT AT HOME. LAST MINUTE CASTING CAME UP FOR MODELLING JOB. SORRY.

'Oh,' I repeat dumbly, feeling really crestfallen. Why does she always feel the need to lie to me? I'm her sister. She shouldn't feel it necessary to make stuff up. Why couldn't she just say they'd had a row.

'OK,' I say to Gary. 'Well, tell her I came to see her. She's obviously busy so we can do it another time.'

'No,' says Gary. 'She'll feel bad she missed you and she'll be back soon I'm sure. She ain't busy. She's just sulking somewhere. Why don't you come in and wait? Truth be known, I could do with a chat.'

My heart plummets. The last thing I feel like is counselling Gary, but what can I say?

And so it is that with a huge sense of déjà vu I find myself bending down to take my shoes off, while my brother-in-law stares down at me.

Minutes later we're sat next to each other on the white sofa. I'm not sure who feels more awkward. Actually, yes I do. Definitely me.

'So, what is it Gary?' I prompt, having realised he's not going to make life easy by starting off proceedings.

'Well, it's Hayley and all this business about wanting a baby.'

'Y-es,' I say doubtfully, not sure I'd refer to her maternal yearnings as 'all this business,' but there you go.

'She's talking about adoption.'

I can't conceal my surprise.

'I know. That's what I thought. I mean, what do we want to go and get some mong kid we know nothing about when we can have our own? Loads of people have… you know… them… miscarriages,' he says, wrinkling his nose. 'So I don't know why she's panicking so much. It ain't like I haven't got lead in my pencil and I certainly do not want some foreign kid, ta very much. Not in my house.'

I hate him.

'Well, have you asked her why she's considering adoption so early on?' I attempt. 'I mean she must be feeling pretty desperate to have leaped to that stage so quickly though, by the way, I think people who adopt are to be applauded. And I don't think using the word mong is acceptable.'

Though what I really want to say is '*you're a despicable pathetic excuse for a man*'.

'I can't get no sense out of her,' says Gary dolefully. 'She keeps going on about doing something useful with her life when I'm like, what about being my Mrs? And she got that job, modelling them moon boots.'

'Moon boots?'

'Yeah, you know the sports shop on the high street? They wanna photograph Hayley, in their ski boot thingies, for the shop window.'

'Right…'

'I'm not sure she even loves me any more to be totally honest,' he says, sounding outraged at the mere thought.

'Really?' I say faintly, feeling incredibly uncomfortable. Of course truthfully I can't understand why she ever *has* loved him, but she married him so she must see something in him. She's always so scarily loyal about 'her Gary'.

'And I ain't so sure I love her no more, either,' he adds, more unexpectedly.

Suddenly my heckles are up. 'Don't say that, Gary,' I say immediately. 'I don't want to hear it. She's my sister and she's had… no… she *is* having a really difficult time at the moment.'

'Yeah,' he says, shifting further towards me and looking at me strangely.

'What?' I say crossly. He's annoying me now.

'Nuffink,' he says licking his lips and looking round the room furtively for a second in a way that makes me feel nervous.

'What is it? What are you doing?' I demand to know as he slides even further towards me until he's only inches away.

'Don't be like that,' he says and by now he's really

invading my personal space. He's also staring at me in a dopey, off-putting way that's frankly repellent.

'Don't be like what?' I say primly.

'You know, all grumpy,' he replies in a husky voice and to my horror, he sounds a bit turned on. 'Come on. Don't play games with me, Marianne. I know you want it as much as I do. You're a right little flirt, you are.'

'What the hell are you talking about Gary?' I yell, and at this point I leap about five foot off the sofa so eager am I to be on the other side of the room where self-consciously I stand, smoothing my skirt down as far as it will go.

'All right, keep your knickers on,' he placates. 'Calm down love, I'm only having a laugh. Thought you might be up for a bit of Gary lovin', that's all. Nothing wrong with a bit of a kiss and a cuddle is there?'

There is so much I could say to this, so much I *should* say to this but, to what I know will be my eternal regret, all I manage to do is laugh, because the fact he thinks I'd be even remotely interested in kissing or cuddling him strikes me as too comical to do anything else. There's a strong possibility of course that I'm also suffering from shock.

While I piss myself laughing, at first Gary joins in, as if he's in on the joke and laughing with me. Eventually however, when I don't stop, he begins to look unsure and then insulted at which point the smile drops slowly from his face.

'Sorry,' I manage to say eventually, at which point the humour of the situation vanishes and is replaced by sheer outrage and disgust. 'Seriously though Gary what the hell are you thinking? You're married to my sister in case you'd forgotten, so "Gary lovin'",' I say, as sarcastically as I am able while using my fingers to make mocking inverted commas in the air, 'Is unacceptable with anyone but her. Are you unfaithful to my sister?'

'No,' he answers sulkily, though he doesn't sound completely convinced and won't look me in the eye.

I know I'm not going to get anything else out of him though so sighing hard and shaking my head in despair, I leave, wondering what on earth I'm supposed to do now.

CHAPTER TWENTY-ONE

I'm not entirely sure how I make it home in one piece. I'm so distracted I can barely drive in a straight line. The second I get home I call Teresa, desperate to talk things over.

'All right babe?' I say when she picks up. 'You got a minute?'

'Yeah, yeah fire away. I'm glad you've called actually. I've got something to ask you?'

'Oh right, what is it?'

'I was wondering if you'd consider being my maid of honour when I get married. I mean, it won't be for another year or so still, 'cos we've got so much saving to do, but it would mean so much to us if you said yes.'

'Oh my god!' I say, really delighted and touched to have been asked. 'I'd love to. Are you sure?'

'Yeah,' she says vehemently. 'Course. I know we've had our ups and downs and that lately we've let things slide but you've always been my best mate and I don't want to lose touch again. Hopefully this will mean we won't.'

'Absolutely,' I agree. 'I feel the same way and I'm really chuffed. Thank you so much. I feel honoured!'

'Pleasure,' she says and I can practically hear her grinning. 'Anyway, what did you want?'

'Oh god,' I say, brought back to earth with a bump. 'It's about my moron of a brother-in-law Gary, actually. He really crossed a line today. He was all gross and flirty with me and it made me wonder whether he's ever been like that with anyone else. Given that you know everyone in Chingford and Ilford I figured you might have heard whether he's ever been a er... naughty boy with anyone?'

'It isn't really for me to say,' she replies instantly.

'Oh, so that means yes then,' I say, heart plummeting.

'Look, I don't know for sure but according to Stacey he slept with her cousin, you know Kimberley who works at the leisure centre?'

'No, I don't think so.' I reply. Oh god. This was just dreadful.

'Well anyway her, though if I had to stand up in court I wouldn't swear on it. Having said that I have heard rumours about other girls too,' she adds, sounding understandably uncomfortable. 'So I don't think he exactly keeps it in his trousers.'

'Right,' I say mournfully. 'Well thanks for letting me know. Oh god, what am I going to do? Do I tell Hayley? She'll freak.'

'I don't know,' says Teresa gravely. 'I mean, is it really such a good idea? You know what she's like, she'll kill

you. And besides, she might know anyway and just choose
to turn a blind eye.'

That hadn't occurred to me, but I thought it was doubtful.
'I'll think about it,' I say. We chat for a further ten minutes or so, mainly about what Teresa wants to do when it
comes to her hen night, but while discussing the merits of
Ibiza versus Benidorm my head is swimming. When we
ring off I know that unfortunately it probably will be until
I've decided what to do about Gary. I wish I didn't know.

If I tell my sister that her husband is an untrustworthy
rat it will devastate her and lead to an almighty row. Plus,
let's not forget he was up for playing around with *me*, his
own sister-in-law for god's sake. For the first time I even
find myself wondering whether losing the baby might have
been a very tragic blessing in disguise. Gary was an utter
twat, but at least there wasn't a child tying them together.
At the moment.

'Marianne,' Mum hollers up the stairs. 'Pete and Andy
are having a bit of din dins with me and Mar. Do you want
some?'

'What is it?'

'Tuna pasta bake.'

I haven't eaten anything for ages, partly because I'm
nauseous with worry over this Gary issue. However, as is
the way with the human instinct to survive, my stomach
suddenly decides it doesn't care that much, it's starving.

'Down in a sec.'

*

'Marianne,' says Andy cheerfully, once I'm sat at the table, trying to force down my pasta. 'I feel like I haven't seen you properly in ages.'

Why is he still here? At this rate I'll be moving out of home before he does.

'So, how are ya?'

'Oh… er, all right,' I mumble.

'You look pale, love,' says Mum, who's been making a real effort ever since Ray's speech, which I think left us all with a lot to think about. 'You sure you're not sickening for anything.'

'I'm fine,' I say, not wanting to talk. I just want to eat enough to keep me going then slip away again. Until I've talked to Hayley I can't think of anything else.

Just then the doorbell goes.

'I'll get it,' says Mum, springing up from her chair. 'Ooh look at me, I've only gone and got pasta down my cleavage.'

'Lucky pasta, eh?' quips Martin immediately.

'Ah yeah,' agrees Andy. 'Alli's got a great pair of breasts on her. You're a lucky man mate.'

Unbelievable.

Pete glares at him.

'Look who's here, everyone,' says Mum coming back into the room with a big delighted grin on her face. 'It's only our Hayls and Gaz. You should have said you were coming. You could have had your tea with us.'

I'm so taken aback I drop my fork, which clatters onto

my plate. Shit. I can't face him, but I don't have any choice of course, and all too fast he's standing there, one thick arm draped around my sister.

'All right?' he greets everyone, before giving me a weird sidelong look, which I translate as a desperate plea not to say anything about him coming on to me.

'Hiya guys,' says Andy. 'Pull up a seat mate,' he suggests, as if it's his house.

I don't know what to do. I can't create a scene in front of everyone but neither can I bear to be in the same room as Gary, so I push my food away. 'Thanks for that Mum. It was lovely.'

'You not eating any more lovey?' she says.

'Here I'll help you out with that,' says Andy, reaching out a chubby hand for my plate. From nowhere I'm filled with the urge to stab it with a fork. Apart from anything else I'd be interested to see if he whizzed around the room like a balloon that had been blown up and then let go.

'Well, that's charming that is,' says Hayley cattily. 'We arrive and you bugger off. Aren't you even going to ask me how my modelling casting was?'

Given that her casting is totally fictitious I don't dignify this with a response. Instead I leave Mum cooing excitedly at the mention of the word casting, push past her and thunder up the stairs as fast as possible to my room where I grab my keys and phone, race back down and leave the house.

*

While I'm pacing the streets trying to figure out what to do, Dad rings.

'All right,' he says.

'Hey Dad,' I reply, striding into the local park. It's a beautiful summer's evening, which doesn't match my turbulent mood at all. There's a delicious breeze and the expanse of green before me is bathed in clear, golden light.

'Everything OK? You spoken to Matthew recently?'

'Er, yeah,' I say, wanting to get him off the phone. My mind is consumed with how to tell Hayley what's happened in the kindest way because I've more or less decided that I have no choice but to tell her. 'He rang the other day. Not sure why really.'

'Reckon I could take a guess,' says Dad.

'What do you mean?' I say, jumping on this loaded statement.

'Well, you know, I think he might have taken a bit of a shine to you, that's all. Once I told him old "chunky but funky" weren't your boyfriend he was well pleased.' He chuckles for a second. 'It was probably my fault he thought you were attached in the first place, because ages ago when Matthew asked me who Andy was, I just said he was your fella from Thailand. Anyway, I tell you what, you could do a lot worse than Matthew.'

'Are you trying to set me up?' I say, sinking onto a bench and turning my face up to the warm sun, which has an instantly calming effect.

'Would it be the worst thing in the world if I was?'

'It would be the most embarrassing,' I say. 'And besides, there's no way anything could happen between Matthew and a member of your family. It would be unethical.'

'That's what he said.'

'You've talked about it?' I screech, wondering precisely how much Dad has been trying to match-make. Poor Matthew. How excruciating for him, and for me.

'Like I said the other day, Marianne. I see things. I may be ill but I ain't blind and that boy likes you,' says Dad, and despite everything that's going on, I can't help it, I feel my heart lift with hope and go for a little joyful tap dance around my ribcage.

'Well, it's impossible anyway,' I say, staring down at my flip-flops.

'Maybe not. After all, he won't be looking after me for ever will he? At some point, in the probably not too distant future, my care will be fully handed over to the palliative team, at which point Matthew will sign me off as one of his patients so…'

'Don't say that Dad,' I protest, knowing full well that once he's fully signed over by his oncologist to palliative, it will mark the beginning of the end. He'll be officially dying. 'You are nowhere near ready for that yet,' I say firmly. 'You're doing great.'

'Mm,' Dad muttered. 'I don't know Marianne. I'm not feeling that great truth be known. I've been feeling quite… well, I ain't been feeling so good lately.'

'Don't be silly,' I say, tears rolling down my face. A lady

walking her dog gives me a strange look as she walks past, but I don't care who sees me.

'Marianne, I need you to accept what's happening.'

'I can't,' I reply hoarsely.

'Look, these last few months have been magic. Getting to know you and Hayley has been the best thing to ever happen to me so…we're lucky really.'

I do not feel lucky. Not in any way, shape or form.

'You should have come earlier,' I cry, saying out loud what I've been thinking for ages. 'You should have come to find me before.'

'I know,' he agrees sadly. 'I know and we should talk about that before I go.'

'Don't talk like that,' I say. 'It's only June. You've got ages left.'

Dad sighs heavily. 'It don't work like that Marianne. When they say six months, they're just preparing you for the end, not making any guarantees. It don't mean you've got exactly six months from now. I'm doing well to be here really. With some poor buggers they say six months but they end up lasting only a few weeks.'

'Please Dad, please. I can't do this right now. Just promise me you'll hang in there a bit longer will you?' I say tearfully.

'OK,' he says simply, though without much conviction.

'Thank you,' I reply, and numb with misery I hang up.

*

When I get back to the house, an hour later, after much soul-searching, everyone's out and the house is quiet. I decide to get the inevitable over and done with and to phone Hayley. No matter what kind of a mood she's in, I'm going to ask whether we can meet up so that I can tell her gently what kind of a philandering bastard she's living with. She deserves to know and she deserves better. It'll be awful and no doubt she'll be shocked, angry and want to strangle the messenger but I don't have any other choice. Only once I've dealt with this horrendous task will I allow myself to examine further what my dad said earlier about himself, about Matthew, about everything. I simply can't put Hayley off any longer though. She's my sister and if the tables were turned I'd want to know.

As it turns out however, I don't have to wait even a second more for as I push open my bedroom door I get my second heart attack of the day.

'You gave me a shock,' I gasp.

Equally surprised, Hayley spins round, a half-guilty expression on her face.

She quickly rearranges it into a frown. 'What are you doing sneaking around like that?'

'Er, excuse me,' I splutter. 'I'm not sneaking anywhere. More to the point, why are you in my room?'

Hayley shrugs and as she does so, her long blonde hair falls prettily over one shoulder. She tucks it behind her ear. 'I can't believe you're still living here, with Mum, in your old bedroom,' she says, managing to make it sound as pathetic as it probably is.

'Yes, but what are you doing here?' I insist, trying to stay calm. If the roles were reversed she'd be screaming blue murder at me.

'You had the hump and I wondered why. Gary said I should ask you.'

A wave of nausea washes over me. Right, there can be no more pussyfooting around. What kind of a sick game was Gary playing anyway?

'Hayley,' I begin, as calmly as possible, when in truth I'm terrified of the words I'm about to say. The words that will change Hayley's life for ever and hurt her irrevocably. The words that will undoubtedly destroy her marriage.

'Hayley, I don't know what he's said but I have to tell you something.'

'Fine, although I still think it's a bit mean you haven't even asked how my casting went,' she interrupts, for no reason I can figure out other than she feels like being catty. She can never resist an opportunity to have a go at me.

'It's like you're jealous or something.'

'But you weren't even at a casting,' I say, flabbergasted by her attitude. 'But even if you were, then to be honest with you, I've got more important things on my mind as it happens. But since you've gone there, don't lie to me Hayley. You don't need to. I know you weren't at an audition, and I know you had a row with Gary, which is the real reason you weren't there. I know because I went round to see you. I did get your text, only by then Gary had already told me that you two had had a row.'

'And what gives you the right to go gossiping behind my back with my husband?' she snarls spitefully.

I can't take any more of her nastiness. 'Please don't be like this with me,' I say, getting tearful. 'Don't be so bitchy all the time. Something's happened and I've been so upset about it I can barely bring myself to even tell you but I have to because if the shoe were on the other foot I would want to know.'

'What is it?' she says, looking nervous, mainly of me I think. She's not good with people being upset around her. She tends not to do sympathy.

'When I was at yours… Gary… he… oh Hayley I'm so, so, unbelievably sorry to have to tell you this but… he sort of tried it on with me.'

Hayley's face drains of all its colour and her stare seems to pierce my soul.

'I'm so, so sorry but I had to tell you obviously. You need to know what kind of a man he is. I mean, I don't think he would have gone as far as to sleep with me but he was definitely up for a bit of playing around and… to be completely honest, I'm not totally sure he hasn't done it with other people too.'

Still she says nothing, but I understand. It's a shock. I move towards her expecting to have to comfort her any second now, once she's absorbed what's happened. She'll feel dreadful for me too no doubt, once she's realised what her vile husband's put me through.

'Oh Hayley it was so awful. It was so embarrassing and all I could think was how upset you'd be and what an idiot he was being and…'

'How dare you?' she says, only she says it so quietly and so icily, at first I'm not convinced I've heard right.

'You what?'

'How fucking dare you speak a word against my husband? He said you'd try this but I wouldn't believe it. I said you may be fucked in the head but that you weren't an evil bitch. Turns out I was wrong.'

'Hayley, what do you mean?' I say, beyond distraught. 'How can you even say those things?'

'You're a lying little slut and just because I've got everything you would like to have for yourself you think you can try and ruin it for me. Well you're not going to get away with it.'

'Hayley, think about what you're saying. Do you really honestly think I would make something like this up? He came on to me I'm telling you. I know it's hard to hear but please believe me, this is the last conversation I ever wanted to be having.'

'Bitch,' she yells, edging ever nearer towards me. 'Gary told me how you came on to him and how you've been trying to get him into bed for years. Only I'm so stupid I told him he was talking bollocks. Told him you weren't a disgusting little slag, except I was wrong.'

'You weren't,' I wail, but don't get any further because from nowhere, suddenly Hayley slaps me hard round the face.

The sound reverberates around the room and in that second everything changes.

That's it.

She hasn't just crossed a line she's flung herself bodily over it and years of her selfishness, her shit, have finally caught up with me.

Clutching my face and trembling, now I'm the one advancing towards her. 'I never want to see you again,' I find myself saying, in a voice so full of white fury even Hayley recoils. She puts her hands out. 'Look, just chill out OK? I shouldn't have hit you…'

But I have no interest in listening to what she has to say any more. 'From this day forward you are no longer my sister and I don't want to have anything to do with you or your disgusting pig of a husband.'

'Don't you dare try and…'

'No, don't you dare,' I scream at the top of my lungs and I'm so angry I hardly recognise myself.

She stares at me, her mouth set into a strip of misery, her eyes cold, yet satisfyingly frightened.

'I've spent my life tip-toeing around your feelings,' I yell. 'Always aware that as far as everyone around here was concerned, for some strange reason your life was more important than mine. I have learnt over the years how to blend into the background. How to keep most of my opinions, my thoughts and my feelings to myself because when I do speak up no one cares what I think anyway. This entire house has always revolved around you. Mum's pride in your looks, your wedding, your modelling, your life. Only I don't know why, because although you may happen to look a lot like some supermodel, other than that you're just an arsehole. And you know what Hayley?'

During the stunned, possibly petrified and very frosty silence that ensues I notice I'm actually trembling with rage. 'You know what? I don't care any more. I don't care and I'm not going to live my life worrying about what I can and can't say because you're so "sensitive", because inside you're not a very nice person so, frankly, you don't deserve it.'

'Well that's rich coming from the whore who tried to cop off with my husband,' Hayley replies, her hands in tight fists by her side, but I know that for once she's listening because although her eyes are blazing her tone is more defensive than anything.

'You've always been jealous of me Marianne, but that doesn't give you the right to make shit up about Gary,' she adds, though again, in less of an assured way.

I can tell she's spooked. I'm glad.

'Jealous? Of you? Are you completely stupid? Can't you hear what I'm saying? I pity you. I pity you for being so pathetic that you can't see how much of an unfaithful prick your husband is. I feel sorry for you for being so deluded and for being so insecure that you've never been able to go without male attention for more than five minutes without panicking. And I despise you for robbing me of a sister by choosing to be such a disgusting cow to me all the time.'

'Robbing you of a sister? Oh as if,' Hayley retorts, her voice dripping with contempt.

'You have. We were close when we were kids. You used to look out for me. Hard to imagine now but you even used to give me a cuddle when I was sad or if I was missing Dad. Don't you remember? Only as soon as boys started being interested in you, you couldn't give a shit. Suddenly I became nothing more than irritation.'

'Not true.'

'Oh it is,' I say, refusing to let her pretend otherwise. 'I have tried over the years to show you that I care, to be there for you, to talk to you but you are as cold as ice to me half the time and I've got no idea why.'

'Haven't you?' she whispers.

'No,' I say. 'But if there is a reason then I'd love to know what it is.'

Hayley stares back at me for ages.

'Maybe I didn't want to be responsible for you all the time,' she says eventually, albeit reluctantly.

'What do you mean?'

'Oh, forget it,' snaps Hayley, 'I can't be bothered with this.'

'Er, I don't think so,' I retort immediately. 'No, if there really is something you've got to say, and I'm not sure there even really is, then you need to say it right now. Or forget about ever having any kind of relationship with me ever again.'

'Fine,' yells Hayley.

'Fine,' I echo. 'Well, go on then. Get on with it.'

'Well, why did I have to be the one to pick up the pieces after Dad left?'

'What do you mean?' I reply. I wasn't expecting that.

'What I mean is that I was only six myself, for crying out loud, but I always had to be the "big girl".'

I'm still not entirely sure where she's going with this but, for the first time ever, it dawns on me that there might be more to Hayley's aloofness than I have ever truly understood.

'Go on,' I say with a heavy heart.

'He broke my heart too when he left, you know. But you Marianne, you were so devastated, such a daddy's girl. And Mum was so depressed for ages that I had to look after you in a way. I became the mother for a while. And I tried to make it all better. I did. I felt so sorry and almost... guilty that I couldn't make things different, that when I was older I suppose I just couldn't handle it any more. I didn't see why I had to be the one making everything all right all the time. Seeing you in pain just made me feel worse about the fact he'd fucked off so I hardened up a bit. Just made things easier.'

'Oh Hayley, I am so so sorry,' I say, instantly ready to forgive and desperate to make amends for the pain she'd felt as my older sister, worrying on my behalf.

But Hayley hasn't finished. 'Don't bother being sorry. It's pathetic. And besides, I'm glad I changed because why would I want to be close to a cheating bitch like you?'

'Hayley,' I begin. 'Why do you do this?'

'Do what?'

'You open up and I just begin to understand but then you can't help yourself. You have to start with the name calling and the venom.'

'Oh get over yourself. I couldn't give a flying shit what you think about anything. I think you're tragic and a husband stealer, lowest of the low.'

I'm shaking with anger now. 'You are aware of what you're saying aren't you?'

'Yeah,' she says, petulant but unsure again. She does this every time. Speaks without thinking, without considering the damage she's causing.

Well I'm not going to put up with it any more.

'Fine, well if that's all you can say then I don't want to see you any more, so please get the fuck out of my room.'

And with that, looking more shaken than I've ever seen her before, Hayley finally leaves. And only once I've heard her run down the stairs and slam the front door behind her, do I allow myself to sink onto the bed and sob like I've never sobbed before.

As I do, I make a decision. I am done with this family. I am done with my sister and from now on am going to start looking after number one so that I don't end up stuck here for the rest of my life. Dad was right. I've wasted enough time believing that I'm not good enough while feeling like second best. I need to explore what potential I might have. Nobody else is going to do it for me.

The next day I put a call in to my teacher and ask her if it's too late for a tour of the Royal College of Music.

CHAPTER TWENTY-TWO

When the doorbell goes Mrs Demetrius gives me a little nudge and a wink, and it's hard to tell which one of us is more excited about Dad being at my lesson today. Well, I say lesson, it's more an opportunity to play them the pieces I've picked for my audition. When you apply to the Royal College of Music, provided you've visited the place and got an A grade in A level Music, you are automatically given an audition. For this potentially life-changing event they require that you play the first movement from a concerto plus one contrasting piece.

I did offer to go and pick Dad up from his flat today but he wasn't interested and was adamant instead that he'd meet me here. As soon as I open the door I realise why.

'Dad hi, oh… and Matthew, hello, I didn't know you were coming,' I say, frowning pointedly at Dad.

'I asked him to,' he says grinning. 'I needed a lift and thought he might enjoy hearing you play.'

I flush red from the tips of my shoes while wishing I'd worn something different. I've got baggy boyfriend jeans on, a scruffy old cardi with a camisole underneath, and my roots need doing.

'Hi,' says Matthew, looking as awkward as I feel. I can't help but wonder whether Dad is only imagining that he likes me. Poor guy probably feels too terrified to tell him that actually he couldn't be less interested in his weird, violin-playing daughter.

'Well come in, come in,' says a voice behind me, and Mrs Demetrius comes bustling up the hallway to save the day.

'This is my dad, Ray,' I say to my beloved teacher.

'Well,' says Mrs Demetrius, giving him a little wink. 'How about that? You're back from Australia then?'

God love her for that opening gambit.

'Something like that,' Ray replies cheerfully as we all stand in what is a fairly confined space, grinning idiotically at each other. His spirits seem high today. They have been ever since I announced my decision to do everything in my power to try and get into music college. Having pro-crastinated for years and years, suddenly I seem to have transformed into the most determined person in the world and Dad can tell. He can tell that I really want to do this, mainly for myself, but also for him, and for Mrs Demetrius. The two people who believe in me.

'It's good to meet you,' he's saying now. 'This is Matthew, my nurse, who also happens to be a very good friend of mine.'

'Wonderful to meet you too, and do call me Nina,' she says, giving Matthew a proper once-over. 'I've been telling

Marianne to do so for years but she prefers the formality I think!'

'Nina it is then,' says Dad. 'I'm excited to be here truth be told. I want to see for myself that you think Marianne's as good as I think she is. She's too modest for her own good.'

'Couldn't agree more,' says Mrs Demetrius, waving everyone inside and wafting purposefully back through her hall, towards the dining room where her piano is, and where her music stand is set up. Her big grey cat follows her.

'So, here we are then, this is where it all happens,' she says, once we're all gathered in the room and Dad and Matthew have sat themselves down on the dark red velvet sofa. 'And can I just say before Marianne starts, that your daughter does indeed have a rare and wonderful gift. A gift I believe she'd be crazy not to do something with.'

Ray's face breaks into a wide grin, so big it looks like it might crack his thin face. 'See,' he says, grinning firstly at me and then Matthew.

'Yeah er, listen, Matthew,' I pipe up, deciding to throw him a lifeline. 'It's really kind of you to bring Dad and everything but I'm sure you'd rather not be stuck here listening to me play on such a lovely day so do feel free to go and grab yourself a coffee somewhere.'

'No way,' he says, looking slightly bashful. 'As long as *you* don't mind I'd love to stay and listen, though I did tell your dad I was worried you might think I was gate-crashing.'

At this point both Dad and Mrs Demetrius give me such ridiculously unsubtle looks it's unbelievable. Dad's is a '*See, what did I tell you?*' kind of look, my teacher's is a '*Ooh, check out what a lovely bit of crumpet he is. On pain of death don't mess this one up girl,*' type of look.

It's all horrendously embarrassing and I decide there and then that the best thing to do is probably just to get on and start playing.

'Well, in that case, um what I've been thinking is that I might attempt the Mendelssohn…'

This warrants a loud intake of breath from my teacher for she knows this is about as advanced a concerto as I could possibly have chosen.

'And for my contrasting piece a solo Bach sonata.'

'Perfect,' says Mrs Demetrius, clapping her hands together before taking a seat at the piano.

We're there for two hours in the end. Once I've played the two pieces I've selected, with Mrs Demetrius accompanying me, there is much discussion about why they should be the ones for my audition, and then Mrs Demetrius gets me to try playing a few other things, just to be sure. My dad seems spellbound throughout and to be fair, so does Matthew. I know I sound surprised, but then so few of my contemporaries show any interest at all in classical music so when someone does enjoy it, it's a rare novelty.

'That,' says Dad, wiping away a tear, 'Was beautiful. It moved me.'

'I second that,' says Matthew, and my heart leaps with the praise because I can tell he means it and even better *he's not laughing at me...*

'So, we're all agreed on the pieces then,' says Mrs Demetrius. 'Though I'm going to have to seriously brush up on the Mendelssohn myself because I'm not all that familiar with it.'

In that moment I realise that I don't just love my teacher because she's a brilliant and passionate teacher, but because she's only ever seen the best in me. She hasn't made any snap judgements about my dad. She's the most accepting person I know and I experience a huge pang of affection for her. I also realise in that moment how much I must have frustrated her over the years by not trying.

'If she *don't* do them it would be criminal,' says Dad, his voice gruff. He gets really affected by music, just like I do, and then it dawns on me that of course in actual fact it's the other way around. I get really affected by music just like *him* and have obviously inherited my passion for it from my father.

'OK, I'm just going to come out and say what we're probably all thinking,' says Mrs Demetrius. 'I am so re-lieved Marianne that you are *finally* going to give things a shot and try to pursue music in a serious way. She's good enough guys, I'm telling you.'

'We don't know that for sure,' I say, slightly sulkily, as

nerves threaten to unhinge my new-found confidence for a minute. 'Do you know that about two and a half thousand people audition for the college every year, but that there are only two hundred and forty spaces available?'

'That is tough,' says Matthew, looking quite taken aback by these grim statistics.

At last, someone with a vague sense of reality.

'What is it?' says Dad.

'What's what?'

'Look, of course you might not get in, and I hope we haven't made you feel like if you don't, you will have failed, 'cos that isn't how I see it. If you don't get in, it just means you can explore other options. On the other hand, you might just do it, so what is it that holds you back from wanting to give things a shot?'

I swallow and although I've tried hard never to confront the answer to this question, find myself replying to it completely truthfully, at which point it dawns on me that I've known the answer all along.

'I don't want to fail at my music, because if I do, then it's over. I don't care about doing anything else, so don't want to hear that I'm not good enough.'

'But now that you've admitted that you want your future to involve music, if you don't get in to the College we can work out another plan,' promises Mrs Demetrius. 'Look how much pleasure I've got out of teaching over the years, for example.'

'And isn't it better to at least know either way, rather

than being in permanent limbo?' says Dad, who's looking a bit exhausted by this point.

'Shall we go soon, Ray?' says Matthew.

'Yeah,' he agrees.

Head whirring away, I go to see them out.

'Thanks so much for bringing him,' I say to Matthew at the door, once Dad's unsubtly barged past us, turned to give me a wink and then shuffled up the path, in order to provide us with a chance to speak to one another. Honestly, he's acting like Mrs Bennett – minus the bonnet –, so hell-bent does he seem on offloading one of his daughters.

'Not at all,' says Matthew, flashing me that heart-stopping smile. He really does have a gorgeous face and standing here, looking up at him, I think how much I'd love him to kiss me. Not right now with my dad and teacher watching – that would be weird – but at some point.

'If I'm honest, as much as it was nice to see your dad it was you I wanted to see really.'

He stares at me, trying to gauge my reaction to what he's just said. It's the first time either one of us has said anything direct about liking one another.

'Right,' I reply, at a loss to know what to say. It's a very strange situation. I mean, it's not going to be easy to segue from him being my dad's nurse to us casually going out on a date, like a normal couple who have met at a party. It wouldn't feel right somehow. After all, the thing that has brought us together is my dad's illness. The saddest and most harrowing thing I've ever had to deal with.

'I know it's a really weird time for you at the moment, but perhaps at some point you and I could meet up for a coffee?' he says, looking as conflicted as I feel.

'Um, yeah, but is that… you know, allowed?'

Matthew wrinkles up his face at this and looks rather doubtful. 'That's the thing, probably not really, but if it is just coffee, then I don't think we'd be doing any harm?'

'Right… well maybe then… anyway, Dad seems to be in good spirits,' I say cheerily, reverting back to what I know we can talk about.

'He does, in fact he's doing very well at the moment. More well than one would expect.'

'Really?'

'Yeah, it can happen sometimes. It's like he's taken on a new lease of life.'

As we contemplate this fact, we both find ourselves glancing over at the subject of our conversation, at which point he calls over, 'You coming, Matt?'

'I'll see you,' he says, flashing me a grin, and I feel a wave of something so intense I hardly know where to put myself.

'And by the way, you were absolutely amazing today. Thanks for letting me hear you play. Your dad really wasn't exaggerating.'

'Thanks,' I say, frantically trying to think of a more humorous riposte. I can't though and as Matthew turns around and makes his way up the path I just stand there gormlessly. He's too bloody good to be true, frankly.

'Don't take too long making your mind up about that one, my darling,' says a voice in my ear. I turn to find that Mrs Demetrius has sneaked up on me.

'What do you mean?' I say suspiciously, my eyes still on Matthew's very attractive rear view.

'What I mean is, he is bloody gorgeous, clearly crazy about you, and you don't want to lose out.'

'Who knows?' I say. 'My judgement's not that great when it comes to men. You only need to see who's staying at my house right now to see that.'

'True, but there's nothing wrong with my judgement and I can tell he's a keeper. Seriously, if I were half my age I'd be after him, I can tell you. And as for that face and oh, that bum.'

'Mrs Demetrius!' I exclaim, though to be fair, she has a point.

*

Three days later, during which I studiously avoid Hayley and do nothing much but practise in my room, Mrs Demetrius and I are on our way to South Kensington for my visit to the Royal College of Music. As we emerge from the bowels of the London Underground into one of the smartest parts of London, my phone rings. It's Dad.

'You on your way?'

'Yeah, yeah,' I say, rolling my eyes at my teacher, who's stopped at a kiosk to buy some mints. He's so excited it's ridiculous, but also very sweet. 'How are you Dad, anyway? You sound good.'

'Honestly? I feel great at the moment. I don't know what it is Marianne but even my blood counts are good. It's almost like… I'm improving… or something.'

'Really?'

'Yeah, I mean obviously I ain't, so don't let me kid you about that but… maybe I will have a bit longer than I thought. To be honest I've got them all a bit stumped back at the hospital. Though personally I put it down to wanting to see whether you get into this place or not. Though no pressure obviously,' he adds instantly.

Despite being swamped with immediate anxiety as, once again, the weight of my father's expectation lands squarely on my shoulders, I find myself laughing. 'Bloody hell. You're as bad as Mum was with Hayley about *Sing for Britain*.'

'Hardly,' he protests, managing to sound indignant and slightly doubtful at the same time as he considers this as a possibility. 'I did mean what I said you know. I really don't want to put no pressure on you. Apart from anything else, you're right. If I were a betting man, I probably wouldn't put money on you getting in. The odds are totally stacked against you but that don't stop me from being so bleeding proud of you for trying. And it's really important that you know that…'

He trails off and as he does so my heart contracts for I can hear he's become a bit choked. Having bought her mints, Mrs Demetrius puts a hand on my arm, a gesture to let me know that we should get going, but then spots that

I'm starting to fill up myself. She mouths, '*Are you OK?*' I nod back and try to reassure her by smiling.

On the other end of the line I can hear Dad desperately trying to compose himself. When he finally continues, his voice is determinedly chirpy again. 'Anyway,' he says, 'I'll be proud of you either way and if you don't get in, like I keep saying, there are plenty of other colleges that'll have you in a heartbeat.'

Even I know this is probably true, but rightly or wrongly, to me it feels like an all or nothing situation.

However there's not much point admitting this to him so instead I reply simply and sincerely, 'Thanks Dad.'

*

I must have needed to hear what he just said though, because as Mrs Demetrius and I continue our journey, arms linked, my nerves start to slowly dissipate and I feel more together and far calmer than I did before. I also find myself wishing that I could take more pleasure from the fact that Dad's doing so much better health-wise, but instead feel weirdly suspicious about it. It seems a bit too good to be true somehow.

*

Needless to say it takes precisely 0.5 seconds for me to fall head over heels in love with the College. Quite simply it's an incredible place, a temple of music, where music lovers from all over the world come together under one roof to worship the subject. The College is internationally renowned for being the best, which I knew before but seeing so many foreign students about the place, especially ones of Chinese origin, only heightens the feeling that the College is world class. Admittedly I look and am older than most of them, but don't think I'd stick out too much and certainly wouldn't be the only 'mature' student. Here I would be able to immerse myself in studying while not feeling remotely self-conscious or apologetic about what some of my own peers view as my strange or geeky penchant for classical music, because everyone else would be feeling exactly the same way as me. Plus, it soon becomes clear from what our guide is telling us, that the students benefit from the knowledge of some of the most amazing teachers in the world. It's like heaven on earth and the thought of being able to play within an orchestra is thrilling and such an incentive. I was in the school orchestra but the string section was pretty small and I never used to find it much of a challenge. The Royal College of Music is better and more wondrous and inspiring than I ever could have imagined. Of course, this is precisely what I wanted to avoid, because now how am I going to feel if I don't get in?

*

Now that I've seen the College and my dreams and ambition have become a reality, which I desperately want to fulfill, I dedicate most of my waking hours to what feels like one long permanent practise session. Spending so much time in my room suits me down to the ground anyway, as I'm desperate to avoid Hayley and her beefy lech of a husband at all costs.

I haven't heard from Hayley since the row, which is fine by me. I won't ever let anyone speak to me like that ever again.

I do take a break to meet up with Teresa now and again however. Having our friendship back on track is the best thing to happen to me in a long time. Sometimes we talk about what's going on with me, at other times she gets to do most of the talking for a change. She tells me about how she's thinking of doing an evening course in something, and about her wedding plans, all of which is a welcome break and distraction. She's the only person I confide in about applying to Music College. I don't tell anyone else because if I don't get in, which I have to keep reminding myself is the most likely outcome, I won't have to disappoint anyone or torture myself by having to keep on explaining.

Meanwhile, since Dad had a go at all of us, Mum's become far more patient about me playing when she's in the house. There have been noticeably fewer barbed comments from her and she's hardly yelled at me to 'pack it in' at all. On one occasion she even poked her head round the door and had a little listen for a while. Wonders will never cease, although I'm not sure I'd want her doing it on a regular basis. Sitting on the edge of my bed, she insisted on nodding her head while tapping her wedge-sandalled foot along, like she was listening to soft rock instead of Mozart, plus she was completely out of time, like a metronome gone berserk. It was very off-putting.

She's asked me a couple of times what's going on between Hayley and me but I'm keeping silent on the matter. What am I supposed to say? Of course, the truth is what's happened pains me but she's the one who needs to figure things out. Not me. If she can do that and wants to make amends then of course I'll talk but until then it's up to her.

*

Then, one day, as I'm returning to the salon from my lunch break, I notice Jason waving at me through the glass to get my attention. Wondering what can possibly be so important that it can't wait till I've walked through the door, I hurry in.

'What?' I enquire, as he drags me over to a quiet corner.

'Hayley's been in to see you.'

'Right,' I reply.

'No, hang on a minute Marianne. I don't know what's happened between the two of you but she was different to normal. She kept saying she was really sorry and that she needed to talk to you.'

His concern feels over the top.

'And I swear she wasn't being stuck-up or annoying like she usually is,' he continues. 'She hadn't even bothered drying her hair, which you and I both know is a big thing in her world.'

'Oh, don't you start falling for her "little Miss Manipulative" act. You don't know the half of it.'

At this Jason looks really quite hurt.

'Look, I'm sorry OK,' I add, checking to make sure no one's listening. There's a lady waiting to have her highlight foils taken out, who's pretending to read a magazine, only I can tell she's ear-wigging. 'It's just that my sister doesn't care one iota about anyone except herself. If she did she wouldn't turn up at my workplace making a scene. She'd ring me or something.'

'I think on this occasion you've got it wrong,' he says firmly. 'Judging by what a state she was in this morning I think she does care.'

I'm amazed by his treachery. 'So, based on Hayley popping in here for five minutes and batting her baby blues you've managed to deduce that she's had a total personality transplant when you don't even know what we're rowing about.'

'Oh stop pretending you don't care and just give it some thought,' says Jason going off, scissors in hand, to see to his next client.

I can't help but feel a bit annoyed with him. It feels like he's taking her side.

*

The next day, I'm just getting the booster seat out for a little girl to sit on for her haircut when Jason approaches me again, this time saying, 'You've got a visitor.'

I roll my eyes, not needing to ask who it is. Deep down of course part of me is glad she finally wants to talk but I don't think this is the right place or time. She knows that by coming here she's got me cornered though.

'Come on, I've put her in here. My next client's not in for ten minutes so I'll mediate if you like,' he says, herding me reluctantly towards the staff room. I follow him in, expecting to find my sister at her most fired up and ferocious, which is why I'm wrong-footed when instead I discover a crumpled mess of a person sitting on a chair, looking as though the weight of the world is on her shoulders. She's wearing a sun-top and leggings, which more than display her killer body, and yet her demeanor is decidedly un-Hayley like. It's as if she's shrunk, she looks so deflated and the way she's hugging her huge fake Miu Miu bag, it's as if she's shielding herself.

'Hiya,' she says mournfully, looking up properly for the first time.

I almost fall over with shock. I've never seen Hayley look so bad. I've never seen Hayley look bad full stop but clearly with her there's no such thing as half-measures because today she looks absolutely terrible. Her face is puffy and swollen, indicating that she must have been crying for hours. Normally she'd rather die than let anyone see her in such a state.

'What is it?' I ask immediately. 'What's he done?'

She shakes her head sorrowfully.

'What hasn't he done? Or should I say *who* hasn't he done?'

Ah. Teresa was right then.

It's very disconcerting to see Hayley looking so unusually vulnerable and so… rough. Obviously I feel sorry that she's had to find out that her husband's betrayed her and yet I'm still so cross about the way she spoke to me and the fact she hit me that it doesn't seem natural to approach her in the same way I normally would, or to reach out in any way.

'What happened then?' I ask dispassionately, sounding more like Hayley than Hayley.

'He said it was all my fault,' she sniffs and Jason, who is still with us, shakes his head.

'Here, do you want a tissue?' he says gently, leaning in to offer her one.

'Thanks,' she says, smiling weakly at him.

'And you must tell Marianne what's happened.'

'Hang on, how do *you* know what's happened?' I demand to know.

'I told you,' Jason replies, looking all defensive. 'Hayley came in yesterday while you were on your lunch break and she was so upset I ended up popping out for a coffee with her. Didn't I?'

Hayley nods.

I despair.

'Right,' I huff, disappointed that Hayley has managed to wrap the last remaining male, who hadn't previously been under her spell, firmly around her little finger. 'So what was your fault anyway?' I ask, determined not to let her tears fool me into feeling sorry for her until I've heard what she has to say. Knowing her, they're probably only for effect anyway.

'I told Gary that I didn't believe that you would have tried it on with him,' she whispers.

'And?'

'And eventually he admitted that he might have been… a bit flirty with you.'

'Well it's very good of you to finally believe me.'

Jason gives me a warning look to keep calm.

He's right of course. I shouldn't lose the upper hand by losing control of my emotions. Apart from anything else it's not dignified.

Hayley meets my gaze fully for the first time. 'I'm so sorry,' she says, only so faintly I have to strain to hear her.

'Right,' I say, hating the fact that despite my best efforts, I can already feel her getting to me. She looks so pitiful that despite myself, I start to feel sorry for her, as usual. 'Well what did you say when he admitted that it was him and not me who was out of order? What was his excuse?'

Hayley shrugs and then gulps. 'He said…' a tear runs down her face. I have literally never seen her like this and I'm slowly starting to think it might not be an act after all.

I look at Jason. He's such a softie at the best of times and right now he looks positively devastated to see my sister in such a mess. She does look wrecked and knowing

Hayley as I do, if she *was* putting it on, she probably would have applied her mascara first. It's funny, I never knew she had such fair eyelashes. What with the puffiness of her face, the straggly hair and lack of make-up, today she's looking – and I can hardly believe I'm saying this – quite ordinary. It's disconcerting.

'He said,' she stammers and her hands are trembling, 'That it was my fault that he was so sexually frustrated because all I ever talk about is wanting to be a mother, which apparently is a turn off.'

'What?' I gasp, wondering how Gary dare even utter such bullshit.

'What a prick,' interjects Jason. 'Sorry.'

'That's OK,' shrugs Hayley, flashing him a watery smile while scrunching up her tissue. 'He also said,' she continues in a low voice, 'That when I made such a tit of myself at *Sing for Britain*, that he was ashamed to be my husband.'

'Well, embarrassed might be more of an appropriate word. Ashamed is a bit harsh,' I reply honestly. It's not that I want to give Gary even an inch, but truthfully, having heard the audition with my own ears, I might have to concede his point a bit on that one. If I'd been married to her I would have considered emigrating.

'But the worst thing he said,' she wails. The tears are back in force and at this point I'm no longer doubting their verity in any way at all. There's no way she's faking and, hearing the vile comments Gary's made, I'm not surprised she's so upset. And that's not taking into account he tried to snog her sister. Horrible bastard.

'The worst thing he said…' she weeps, struggling to spit it out.

'What babe?' I ask softly, finally admitting total defeat by going to sit next to her and stroking her back. 'Come on, it can't be any worse than what he's already said or done.'

'He said that it was my fault I lost the baby because… I'm such a stress case.'

I gasp and at this point words completely escape me. Angry tears spring into my own eyes. 'He actually said that?' I manage eventually.

'Shit,' says Jason angrily, punching one hand into his open palm. 'You didn't tell me that yesterday. What a complete and utter wanker.'

'I know,' she howls. 'And I married him, so what does that say about me as a person?'

'It doesn't say anything. We all make mistakes. As I know only too well. But more importantly,' I say, 'What are you going to do about it? You can't let him get away with this. He's the lowest of the low.'

'He is,' she agrees vehemently. 'And you know what? I do want a baby more than anything. More than words can describe in fact and I really miss the one I had… you know, so, so much. I mean I really loved it…'

I nod hard, to demonstrate that I really do understand that, and that it's totally understandable that she's still grieving.

'… and yet… in a way, in a really horrible way, I'm glad I didn't have it, but only because I would hate my precious baby to have that fucker as its dad. He even shagged Kimberley Meadows you know? And she is such a skank with her ratty hair extensions.'

'Oh Hayley,' I say wrapping her in my arms and hugging her tight. I'm overwhelmed with sadness for her and have forgiven her completely for everything. I feel so sorry for her. She's so weird and it must be such hard work and so draining being her, but underneath all her neuroses and cold exterior is just a girl who wants to be a mum and is devastated because she lost a baby. A girl who hasn't had a dad to show her the way, so probably as a direct result, has clung to any male who's shown her the slightest bit of interest.

While we're hugging and Hayley's sobbing noisily into my shoulder, Roberto pokes his head round the door looking a bit narked, probably wondering what the hell Jason and I are doing when there are customers waiting. Still, once he's surveyed our little scene he just gives us a concerned look and leaves us to it. Jason nods at him gratefully. Hayley doesn't even notice him come or go.

'I'm sorry I was such a bitch to you,' she mutters into my shoulder at one point.

'It's fine.'

'It's not. But I'll make it up to you,' she says and I know how incredibly hard it is for her to say this. It means a huge amount.

I go back to my original question though and say gently, once she's calmed down a bit, 'What are you going to do?'

'Oh, I've done it,' she says, and Jason and I exchange glances wondering for one awful second whether she might have actually killed him.

'What have you done…?' Jason asks nervously on behalf of both of us.

Hayley looks up. That last bout of crying certainly hasn't helped her look any better. Her eyes are so piggy now, they're barely visible.

'I told him in no uncertain terms that he was a horrible, ugly, thick, pig-headed wanker with a tiny knob.'

For a fleeting second, despite the gravity of the whole scene I find myself wishing that Gary's dad, Derek, could be here too, to hear Hayley's incredibly colourful, but terribly apt description of his hideous son. To be fair, I couldn't have put it better myself.

'Good,' said Jason approvingly, practically applauding. It occurs to me that he looks particularly pleased to hear Gary's willy being described so disparagingly and know in that instant he's fallen for her. They always do, though admittedly not usually while she's looking like this.

'Then I kneed him in the balls, packed a bag, left the house and told him I'd be in touch via a lawyer.'

For a second, even through her tears, she looks incredibly proud. Not as proud as I feel though.

'You actually did that?' I say.

'Yeah,' she says, biting her lip, tears threatening to overcome her again. 'Yeah I did.'

'Good on you girl,' says Jason wholeheartedly, at which point he crosses the small room so he can share in what has become a rather snotty, very emotional group hug.

CHAPTER TWENTY-THREE

During August the weather suddenly becomes about as hot as it ever can be in England. Martin's in his element of course, for this means he can justify bringing home hose attachments, barbecue accessories, flowerpots… the list is endless. In short, his mission in life at the moment is to fill up the garden with as much stuff as he is physically able. Of course, he has his assistant, Andy, to aid and abet him in this task. Andy who has taken to wearing only his trunks around the house, which is pretty offensive. Even Mum and Martin have finally grown a bit fed up with his lack of financial contribution to the household so, as of very recently, he has at last got a job. Unfortunately he'll be working at TGI Friday's burger joint in Enfield so I can't see his weight situation improving any time soon.

Of course this also means he'll probably never leave, but by now he's been here so long anyway, it's got to the point it almost doesn't feel strange him being around. I've got used to feeling permanently irritated by him and it's only when I stop to think about it for a second that I am reminded how odd it is that the random Australian I had a fleeting holiday romance with, in Thailand, now lives with us. I deal with this by not stopping to think about it very often. It's just easier that way.

Meanwhile Hayley's moved back home and has started divorce proceedings against Gary. That sentence has its good points and bad points. On a good note it means Andy has been forced to move out of her old room and is now on the sofa – hee hee – which hopefully might help encourage him to depart one day. On the downside, Hayley's moved back home, meaning I have to put up with her on a day-to-day basis, which actually isn't half as bad as this once would have been.

The fact that she's following through with her plans to divorce dick-splash is brilliant and I'm proud of her for being so strong about it. Having said that, she's also taken to spending quite a bit of time with Jason, which is fine, except I can't help feel like she's transferring her baggage from one man to the next without sorting anything out for herself first. Continuing the baggage analogy – the suitcase being her life, its contents being her emotional state – if only she were to unpack all her soiled clothes herself, before putting them through a hot wash, giving them a nice iron, then re-packing them neatly away again, I can't help but think it would be far healthier, more healing and would make her a stronger person. As it is, she's finding someone else to deal with her dirty washing for her, while she lies on the bed, which is easier in the short run, but means she'll never know what's been re-packed.

OK, I'm confusing myself now. In short it annoys me that she can't be without the security blanket of male company for even five seconds at a time. I'm pretty sure Jason is harbouring a huge crush on her and on a selfish, slightly childish, level I also feel like she's hijacked my friendship. I'm trying to be grown up about it though because what I can't deny is that hanging out with a nice, normal person, is having a really good effect on her. My sister is definitely easier to be around than she is normally. She still has an opinion on everything I should be doing/wearing etc but is learning to curb her constant desire to express it and equally I am finally learning to stick up for myself.

The rest of my time is spent either with Dad, Teresa, or day-dreaming about Matthew. With regard to this, from time to time I wish he'd man up, flout the rules altogether, throw caution to the wind and come round and ravage me. As it is there's been a deafening silence from that end.

So nothing much has changed. I practise, I work, I keep my head down and everything's fine and yet, underpinning everything, is the rather grim feeling that what's really going on is one long torturous waiting game. Dad's still doing really well but as much as I hate to admit it, I am fully aware that this is only going to be the pre-cursor to him getting worse again.

One day, as these and other terrifying thoughts swirl

around my head, I'm suddenly overwhelmed by a spontaneous desire to act on impulse for once. I blame the
music. I've been playing along to a concerto on my iPod
and get so inspired I find myself abandoning my practising, throwing my violin down on the bed and dialling
Matthew's number. My fingers are shaking so badly it's
a bit of a job but I get there in the end.

'Hi,' I say when he picks up, worried that if I pause
even for a second I'll change my mind and hang up.
'It's me, Marianne... Baker. Anyway, would you like to
meet up for that coffee you once mentioned? Although I
actually hate coffee, but I could always have something
else. And don't worry if I've got totally the wrong end
of the stick...'

'You haven't,' says Matthew and I can almost hear that
gorgeous grin of his beaming down the phone. 'In fact,
I'm glad you've called. Only, seeing as you have, if you
don't mind, I'd prefer to meet up one evening for a drink.'

'Really?'

Oh god. Now that's changed everything. Meeting for
a drink, in the evening, puts things on a braver, but more
frightening, date-type footing. That'll teach me for being
spontaneous.

'Yeah, if that's OK? We wouldn't be doing anything
wrong. We'd be meeting as friends. And besides, we can
go somewhere like The White Horse in Epping Forest.
Do you know it? It's slightly out of the way I know but
no one from the hospital goes there.'

'Fine by me,' I say cheerily, though inside I'm panicking a bit now. He's obviously thought about this and is only half-convinced it's a good idea.

'OK, so how about tonight then, at eight? They do really nice food too, so we could always have something to eat.'

'See you there,' I say, wondering what the hell I've done.

'See you there,' Matthew agrees and we ring off.

*

I spend hours getting ready and choosing what to wear. Eventually I settle on a tea dress with bare legs and biker boots and then finally I'm ready.

As soon as I get to the pub I spot Matthew. He's at the bar talking to the barman and I know that if I didn't know him already I would have noticed him straight away, as I think half the females in here have already.

'Hi,' I say shyly.

'Hi,' he says, spinning around. 'Wow, you look gorgeous.'

'Thanks,' I say 'I don't scrub up as well as my sister but I do my best.'

Even as the words come tumbling out of my mouth I know that this is just about the worst, most needy sign of mental issues thing I could have said. *What's wrong with me?*

Matthew gives me a quizzical look. 'Your sister is

really pretty, but she's not my type at all. Far too high maintenance, if you don't mind me saying. She's got that sort of ice queen thing going on.'

'Really?' I say, disproportionately pleased and unable to disguise it. I'm pathetic.

'Put it this way, Claudia Schiffer was never my favourite of the supermodels,' he says, leaning back against the bar, looking fit as anything in jeans and a plain shirt, which is rolled up at the arms.

'Who did you like then?' I enquire lightly.

'Um, probably Kate Moss,' he says. 'I like girls to look a bit intriguing, like they'd be a laugh to hang out with. Anyway, you shouldn't be so down on yourself. You're the sister that turns heads, I reckon.'

My jaw is literally on the ground. And all this before we've even had a drink.

'Gosh,' I say, blushing madly. 'Well, thanks.'

'Right,' says Matthew, who's gone almost as red as me and is now doing everything in his power to avoid looking at me directly. 'Anyway, I'm going to have a pint, what do you want?'

'Oh, um, a vodka and tonic please.'

Half an hour later, sitting in the pub garden, I am trying to accept the fact that I really like Matthew. There's no getting away from it. He's amazing. He's funny, clever, interesting and every time I look at his face I'm filled with an urge to grab it with two hands and snog it clean off. I simply cannot stress how downright sexy he is. Plus, to top it all, I now know, given what he said earlier, that he likes me back. I'm also fairly convinced that because we're on home turf and I've seen him in a variety of situations now that he's not going to suddenly change before my very eyes like Andy did. I am not being *holiday romanced*. I'm not falling for him because I'm in paradise and have been conned by the sunshine, the freedom, the strong Thai whiskey and illegal substances. I am being romanced by him because I enjoy being around him and like hearing what he has to say.

However, there is of course, as ever with things that are so wonderful, a problem. He's my dad's nurse, so I'm still not convinced I should even be here. However, once we've chit-chatted for a pleasant thirty minutes or so, chemistry zinging all around us as we do so, literally screaming into our ears and other orifices – '*Go to bed with one another*' – he is the first to summon the elephant from the corner of the room.

'I really hope you don't think badly of me for asking you out today, Marianne?' he begins. 'It's just that… and this isn't an easy thing to say… It's just that there was no doubt in my mind that I wanted to ask you out at some stage, so my plan was to wait. But then when you rang earlier, I figured that if I waited for Ray to… well anyway, at a certain point it might have seemed a bit maudlin to ask you then. Inappropriate somehow.'

'I know what you mean,' I say quietly, my stomach lurching with fear as it always does at the mere thought of the day he's subtly referring to. 'And I'm glad you did because I'd rather get to know you a bit now, no matter what the medical ethics might be, because as you say, when that time does come, I suspect I'll be in a bit of a state for a while.'

Matthew nods. 'I know.'

'And I don't want the thing that defines us getting to know one another to be so sad,' I add, blinking hard as tears threaten. Christ I've done more crying these last few months than I have my whole life put together.

Matthew nods again. 'We've got your dad to thank for introducing us to one another so for that I'm very grateful.' He looks thoughtfully at me. 'I just really hope that no matter what happens, you'll allow me to be around for you as a friend, when things get difficult.'

Now I'm confused. What's he saying?

'What I mean is,' he says, obviously having picked up on my stricken face. 'Is that I don't want to be just friends with you Marianne, I mean, I think you know that.'

Oh my god when he looks at me like that I feel so turned on I hardly know what to do with myself. Now I'm turned on and crying at the same time. Weird combination.

'But what I'm trying to say is that I'm happy to be pragmatic. We haven't met under normal circumstances, so I suppose normal rules don't apply. I get that there might well be a period soon when you don't feel like embarking on anything "romantic". Not that I'm making any assumptions here, I just think it's probably better to say these things now. Oh god this is hard. I'm making a right dick of myself aren't I?'

'No, you're not,' I say adamantly. 'I'm just grateful that you're brave enough to say the things that need saying out loud.'

'OK good,' he says, supping his pint.

'And I appreciate it,' I add.

'Good, so anyway, enough of all that heavy stuff,' he says, smiling again. 'As long as you know that when you need me to back off and just be a friend for a while, that's what I'll do. I'm happy to wait as long as it takes.'

'OK,' I say. 'Sounds good to me.'

'Great.'

'Great.'

'Though that time hasn't come yet,' I say unsubtly, worried that he's going to go all restrained on me.

Now he turns and gives me a full-blown grin. 'Good,' he says.

A moment passes where we stare at one another, right into each other's eyes, but it's not remotely uncomfortable.

'In that case,' he says eventually, leaning in towards me. 'Would you mind if I kissed you, because I've been dying to for ages?'

I shake my head, just as his hand starts travelling lightly up my leg. I'm shivering with lust when the next thing I know his gorgeous face is finally advancing towards me and I'm being kissed like I've never been kissed before. It's a tender, passionate kiss and when he finally moves away, he fixes me with his brown eyes but for once he isn't smiling. 'OK we need to get out of here right now,' he says hoarsely.

I can't speak so nod instead and the next thing we know we're literally running through the pub.

CHAPTER TWENTY-FOUR

The next day I'm happily prancing round the house like Julie Andrews in *The Sound Of Music* when Mum asks, 'Flipping 'eck what's got into you Marianne?'

'Nothing, I'm just in a good mood,' I beam back at her.

Hayley, who's filing her nails on the sofa, gives me a look and arches one eyebrow magnificently. I've always wished I could do that.

'I reckon it's not *what's* got into her, it's *who*?' she says drily.

'Oh you are filthy,' cackles Mum delightedly, enthralled by Hayley's gross innuendo. 'Go on then, tell me, fill me in, as the actress said to the bishop,' she quips, getting up to get the biscuit tin.

I mouth 'thanks a lot' at Hayley who sticks her tongue out at me.

Mum has a good old rummage in the tin before selecting a Penguin. 'You know I love a bit of goss Marianne and, besides, I'm glad you're getting a bit of action. It's about time someone put a smile on your face lovey. I wish our

Pete would hook up with someone. I reckon he could do with a bit of "*how's your father*" an' all.'

'Certainly puts a smile on our face, doesn't it my princess?' says Martin, coming in from the garden, obviously having caught the tail-end of our conversation.

He's wearing socks, sandals, short shorts and nothing on top. What is it with him and Andy? Why can't they be horrendously body-shy like Pete, which is far easier to live with.

'Hello my darling,' says Mum, mouth full of Penguin but attempting to pout none the less. 'Look at you, you hunk of love.'

Hayley and I exchange frowns.

'Oh don't look like that,' says Mum. 'I had you girls so young I'm only just in my prime now, and anyway, you should be happy your mother's in such a loving and intimate relationship.'

'Oh god,' I moan, no longer feeling skittish like Maria, but more like one of the despairing nuns at the Abbey.

'Anyway, you can hardly talk,' she says to me before winking conspiratorially at Martin who, having wiped his sandals on the mat, is now striding in towards the sink to wash his hands.

'Oh please shut up Mum,' I whine, like a surly fourteen-year-old.

Suddenly Andy appears, wearing his TGI uniform, about to head off for a shift. No doubt psyching himself up to devour three cheeseburgers upon immediate arrival. 'Hey, what's happening guys?'

'Marianne here's got herself a lover,' says Mum, still winking away. Hayley collapses forward, giggling into the sofa.

It's amazing how quickly a good mood can evaporate.

'Oh yeah,' says Andy a bit testily. 'Well I just hope whoever the poor bloke is can cope with mood swings.'

'Ouch,' says Martin, though in a very jolly way.

'Only joking,' Andy adds quickly, when he sees me glowering at him, realising he may have over-stepped the mark.

'Fuck off Andy,' I bark viciously.

'Marianne!' reproaches Mum.

By now Hayley's properly cracking up, and has abandoned all her nail paraphernalia so she can concentrate fully on the Andy and Marianne sideshow.

'And I don't know why you're laughing,' I end up saying. 'Have you seen who's on the front of the *Radio Times* this week?'

'No,' says Hayley, less cocky now. Her eyes looking around for Martin's magazine.

'Julian Hayes. *Sing for Britain* kicks off in a fortnight.'

Below the belt I know, but it shuts her and the rest of them up, which means I can go back to feeling ridiculously happy and pleased with the world. For today, I simply refuse to let anyone burst my Matthew bubble. We had such an incredible night together. After the pub we ended up back at his flat, and I won't go into details other than to say that the earth moved. It was everything I hoped it might be and that, given half a chance, I could fall for him completely.

*

Three weeks later, however and my bubble has already burst, nothing has gone to plan with Matthew and I'm not feeling quite so cheerful. Before I go into that though I should let you know that so far Hayley has managed to escape public humiliation. The first episode of *Sing for Britain* only featured auditions from Glasgow and Manchester. However, this might well be her big embarrassing week because on tonight's show they're definitely going to be in London. The presenter, Sy, said so at the end of last week's programme. And he should know.

More worrying than all of that though is the fact that Dad's not looking great at the moment. There's also a definite tinge of autumn in the air, which is terrifying. Dad's initial six-month prognosis runs out in a matter of weeks. I feel like we're living on borrowed time, and keep trying to find positive articles on the internet about people who have defied all medical expectation by living far longer than expected. These cases do exist and yet for every positive tale, there's always another that simply reinforces the view that once you're riddled with the horrible poison that is cancer, you will die because of it. Put simply, it's not a case of if, but when, and there's no getting away from the fact that Dad is looking more obviously ill than he has done before. His face has become quite gaunt and as a result of the weight loss, his teeth are starting to look a bit big for his mouth. Like bad veneers. He refuses to discuss what the hospital are saying in any detail but I can tell that the burst of hope he experienced around the time I went to visit the Royal College of Music has pretty much evaporated.

One vague silver lining – and this is probably desperation as opposed to positivity at work here – is that my concern for Dad means at least I haven't been fretting as much about the Matthew situation as I normally would be.

I feel so stupid. One minute I was on top of the world and felt like I'd met the man of my dreams, the next I could sense something had changed, and Matthew reverted to acting like a polite stranger. This was unbelievably disappointing given the night we shared. In fact I'm still not convinced you can fake that sort of strength of feeling. Yet nothing changes the fact that with a growing sense of horror and alarm, the first time we spoke after we'd 'got it together', I realised he was making civil small-talk to the point where it honestly felt like I was on the phone to a friend of my mum's or something. He even commented on the weather.

'So, it's not so warm today is it?' I think was what he said. 'Might even need to wear a jacket?'

I was so disturbed by this complete change of attitude and apparent cooling off towards me, that at the time I merely replied with a very lame, 'Yes, though the weather man did say it would be nice again tomorrow.'

I know. Not exactly a conversation to inspire passion in anyone. Still, I let it go, but put the phone down feeling freaked out and worried, a feeling that grew over the next couple of days, during which time I heard nothing from him. I spent these painfully long days battling with panic while wondering what I'd done wrong, leaping on my phone every time it made a noise only to be confronted with an email from somewhere like Tesco or a text from Mum. Then finally he phoned again, only it went even worse than before and felt like he was merely going through the motions of a phone call, like when you're phoning a relative you barely know to thank them for a Christmas present. This time I confronted him though.

'Matthew, this is all very nice and everything, hearing about your day,' I said. 'But are you sure you're all right?'

'Yeah,' he'd answered vaguely.

'Right,' I'd said, not convinced. 'So, when am I seeing you? Do you fancy doing something on Thursday night?'

'Thursday?' he'd repeated. 'Um, that would have been great Marianne, but you know I think I have to work late on Thursday. We could meet at the weekend maybe?'

'Oh, OK,' I'd said perkily, trying not to betray the fact that my mind was racing. Why did he sound so doubtful? 'Well, I can't do Saturday during the day because I'll be at the salon, and Sunday afternoon I'm booked for a party, but my Saturday night is totally free.'

'Ah,' he'd sighed, and my heart had sunk. 'Saturday night's not great for me. I said I'd meet a mate for a few pints.'

'Oh,' I'd said, and so it continued in this lacklustre vein, with him sounding utterly half-hearted while dodging any opportunity to meet up, and me quietly suffering.

*

Later on, when I could stand it no more, I grew some balls – metaphorically speaking obviously – picked up the phone and called him again.

'Why are you doing this?' I said, going straight for the jugular.

'Doing what?' he said, sounding surprised.

'Being like this. Answering anything I ask you with one-word answers and enquiring after my health and how my family is. You've been doing it for ages now and I want to know why you're mucking me around like this when I had thought we'd had a great time together the other night. Didn't we?'

'We did, and I'm not,' he sighed.

'You are,' I insisted, determined not to cave in, which went pretty much entirely against my very nature. 'One minute we're in bed and you're saying lovely things to me and the next you're being all weird and cold and polite on the phone and I can't stand it.'

Matthew paused. I could tell he was debating what to say and in that second I regretted confronting him because suddenly I wasn't so sure I wanted to hear the truth. Maybe I'd been absolutely crap in bed? Maybe he'd met someone else, or remembered he was married? Maybe, if I'd kept up the pretence that everything was OK I could have lived under the happy 'ish' delusion that we were a couple for a bit longer?

'OK,' he said eventually and his voice sounded heavy, weighed down with worry. Not the greatest indication that everything was going to be all right.

'I'm sorry, and you're right. I should have been more honest about what's been going on in my head.'

'Oh god,' I muttered.

'That night in the pub, the night we… you know. Well, as terrible luck would have it, someone from the hospital was there. So unlucky, but there you go. Anyway, a colleague of mine called Jill saw us and asked me about you the next day at work. I didn't want to lie so ended up telling her about you, and also about how I knew you. She was pretty shocked.'

'Right,' I muttered.

'And I guess she gave me a bit of a reality check,' he said, warming to his theme, 'Which has left me a bit freaked out.'

'Why?' I demanded to know.

'Look Marianne, I promise I'm not mucking you around,' he said. 'Or at least I don't want to anyway. I really, really like you, more than I've liked anyone in a long time if you really want to know and god, going to bed with you was so amazing... but...'

I knew there was a 'but' coming. It had been brewing quietly for days.

'I love my job and I worked bloody hard to get through medical school so can't risk being struck off. Jill made me see that this could happen. It *does* happen to people who get involved with patients, or with relatives of patients, and it seems crazy to risk my entire career.'

Bloody Jill, I thought petulantly, though deep down I knew what he was saying was true, even if it did feel over-dramatic. I mean, who the hell were we harming?

'Marianne, are you there?'

'Yeah, I'm here,' I replied softly, biting my lip.

'I need to wait until your dad isn't in my care any more,' Matthew said steadily and at this point I could tell he had it all worked out and that this wasn't up for debate. I'd wondered why he couldn't have just told me what had happened days ago, rather than leaving me alone with only my over-active imagination for company, to figure out what he might be thinking?

'Your dad is still my patient, but...'

'He won't be for ever,' I whispered, helping him express what we both know he's getting at.

'Yes,' Matthew replied hesitantly, and I could hear the turmoil he was in, trying not to upset me any more than was necessary. 'So, what I'm hoping is that, if you feel the same way as me, you won't give up on me.'

'Fine,' I'd said, sounding anything but. 'Only maybe it would have been nice if you could have manned up and told me that without me having to drag it out of you.'

'Ouch,' replied Matthew. 'But I'll let you have that. I'm sorry and you're right of course but probably the only reason I haven't broached the subject is because really I don't want to have to put things off. Apart from anything else, who knows who might snap you up in the meantime?'

'Flattery will get you everywhere,' I said flatly, unable to resist a watery smile.

'So,' said Matthew, sounding nervous. 'Will you wait?'

'I don't know,' I replied, surprising myself with my answer.

'Oh,' Matthew had said and he'd sounded so fed up that my heart positively ached with mixed emotions.

'I'm not trying to be mean, or to get you back for having spent the last few days half-torturing myself, but if you'd just told me what was going on then of course I would have waited. After all, what you're saying is perfectly reasonable.'

'But?'

Ah, now he knew how that bit felt.

I swallowed. '*But* what's upset me is that I have spent my whole life putting things off and sticking my head in the sand about everything, and I can't do it any more. I'm also not sure I can be with someone who's like that themselves. Life's just too bloody short and too precious.'

This speech comes as a surprise even to me, but I realise

then that I really mean it. What's happening with Dad has affected my whole outlook. I like Matthew so much but just can't afford to be anything but more dynamic and more decisive with every aspect of my life going forward. I've been sleep-walking for too long.

'Right,' said Matthew, sounding pretty dejected at this point.

'I'm sorry,' I'd said sincerely, feeling monumentally disappointed and a bit stupid to tell you the truth. I felt like such a fool for having spent the last week pining for him and fretting, when in his head we'd been over before we'd even properly begun.

'Don't go like this,' said Matthew. 'Let me do what I should have done in the first place, which is to take you somewhere and explain.'

'No, there's no point,' I said. 'I totally get what you're saying and I'm not saying I don't ever want to see you again. I do. But maybe we should have a bit of a break and just see what unfolds with no pressure on either of us?' I said, and that was that.

*

I've been analysing it all ever since of course, wondering whether I played it right, but the truth is he really hurt me by not being honest from the outset. It pissed me off. Though deep down I also suspect I may have been lashing out just the tiniest bit. You know, railing against the world because of what's happening with Dad. However, I can't do much about that. It's all very confusing.

Anyway, here we are, it's Saturday, I'm at work, and am looking forward to/dreading an evening of *Sing for Britain.*

'So, are you coming round or what?' I said to Dad on the phone during my break.

'I don't know. Is Hayley's downfall something I really want to witness?'

'Probably not, but we don't even know for sure whether she'll be on, and if she is we can cheer Hayley up after. She's saying she's not going to watch but you know she will. I'll pick you up after I've finished work. Roberto said I can finish early.'

'All right,' Dad says. 'Obviously it means I'll have to cancel all the hot dates I had lined up for tonight, and I'll have to inform the nightclubs I won't need to be on the guest list any more, but for you, I'll do it.'

I laugh but only half-heartedly because my head is busy spinning, trying to work out whether or not to ask the next question. I know I shouldn't but I can't resist. I have to know.

'Dad?'

'Yes babe?'

'Have you heard from Matthew at all?'

'No, why? Ain't you?'

I haven't told Dad much about what's gone on between Matthew and me, so I think *he* thinks we're seeing each other.

'Course I've heard from him,' I manage eventually. 'It's just I wondered if *you'd* seen him. That's all…'

'I saw him… when was it? Er, the day before yesterday when I went in for a check-up and blood tests and stuff. He was quite busy with other patients so we didn't chat much. I'll be seeing him on Monday at the hospital again though. Why? He ain't giving you the run around, is he?' he asks, his voice weaker than usual, the timbre less gruff.

'No, no. It's all cool,' I say hastily, not wanting to burden him with my angst. 'Well, see you later then.'

As I put down the phone I sincerely wish I wasn't at work so that I could do some thinking in peace. Home's always full of people and it's difficult enough finding the time to practise my violin let alone do any proper fretting. So of course all of that ends up happening when I'm lying in bed at night. At three o'clock in the morning it always seems crystal clear that of course what I should do is ring Matthew and tell him I've been a total fool. That of course I'll be waiting for him, for the rest of my pathetic life. When morning comes however, the situation always seems a bit less straightforward again.

'Oi, daydreamer, when you've got a sec, would you mind shampooing my lady's hair please?' interrupts Jason.

The next few hours pass in a haze of dullness and before I know it, it's time for me to sweep up and leave.

'Will you be watching tonight then?' I ask Jason, as I manoeuvre my broom around his second to last customer of the day, knowing he'll know what I'm referring to –

even if there wasn't the possibility that Hayley was to be appearing on it tonight, *Sing for Britain* fever has already gripped the majority of the population.

'Yeah,' he says, looking sheepish for a second. 'In fact, I'm coming to yours as it goes. Hayley asked me to come over, to give her a bit of moral support in case she's on. I can't wait. She's being all modest about it but I reckon she'll be brilliant'

'Oh right,' I say, feeling rather left out of the Jason and Hayley gang. Neither of them have said anything to me, but I think they've been hanging out with each other quite a bit.

'Actually, hang on one sec Marianne.' 'So, is that all OK then?' he says to his lady, producing a mirror with a flourish in order to show her the back of her newly coiffed hairstyle.

'Ooh yeah, that's lovely thanks,' she says.

Jason helps her out of her gown and once she's picked up her handbag and gone to pay, he takes the broom out of my hand, thus forcing me to look at him and says, 'Listen, I've been meaning to say this for weeks now.'

I think I know what's coming. He's about to officially tell me he's fallen for Hayley. It's predictable and I would be happy only I worry Hayley will dump him as soon as her ego has mended itself.

'I just wanted to say that I wasn't bullshitting when we used to slag off Hayley. I genuinely thought she was a knob.'

'Bit harsh?'

'At the time, not really, no,' he grins.

'Can you stop gassing in the middle of the shop-floor please?' says Mark, one of the senior stylists and Jason's cousin.

'Come outside,' says Jason, and obediently I follow. He pushes open the fire exit and once outside lights up a cigarette.

'What was I saying?'

'You were insulting my sister,' I remind him.

'Oh yeah, Hayley. I was saying I used to think she was a total knob, only recently I've got to know her a bit and what I've realised is that underneath all that make-up is a surprisingly lovely girl. Anyway…' he hurries on, sensing that now I'm eager for him to get on with it and to get to the punchline.

'What I'm trying to say is that I'm kind of into Hayley and that I hope you're all right with that. Not just because you're her sister but because I also count you as a good mate.'

As I stare at his earnest face, my heart contracts with real affection for my friend Jason. He's solid as a rock, and if Hayley could only fall for him too I honestly don't think she'd ever find anyone better. I'm pleased for him, worried and anxious too because it all feels far too soon, but hey, Hayley was never going to be single for long it seemed, so I'm mainly pleased.

My reply to his rant is a big hug.

'Love you,' I say, as he squeezes me back. 'Hayley's

a bloody lucky girl but, be careful. She's been through a lot of shit with Gary and while I'm sure she thinks you're the best thing since sliced bread, well, you know how she can be.'

Jason nods ruefully. 'I do, and believe me I'm not rushing anything. I haven't really said anything to her about how I feel. If anything she's the one who's been making noises about wanting to take things further.'

Blimey, I hadn't realised quite how much had been going on between them while I've been busy worrying about my own crappy, non-existent love life.

*

At seven-thirty that night, as the familiar *Sing for Britain* music booms around our living room I survey the bunch of weirdos I'm gathered with. Mum and Martin are snuggled up on the sofa sporting matching slankets. In case you aren't sure what a slanket is – and I promise it doesn't reflect badly on you if you don't – it's a blanket with sleeves. Slankets are made out of polyester, are exceedingly static and despite the fact it's a relatively mild, if a little damp, September day Mum and Martin have deemed it chilly enough to get theirs out of the cupboard where they've been festering over the summer. Hers is bright pink, his is lime green and in them they look as though they're part of some strange cult. They look bloody ridiculous.

Andy's perched on the arm of the sofa like a big fat

parrot, looking far less worried than everyone else about what might be about to appear on prime time TV. He's bunked off work tonight for this big event and is currently plowing his way through a value pack of crisps, which are supposed to be for everyone.

Of course essentially we are all sitting in what has become Andy's bedroom, so in among us all, strewn around and about are his clothes, his toiletries, his stuff. Even Mum looked vaguely irritated when she had to move a pile of his dirty laundry before sitting down. I can't even say he's overstayed his welcome because, as far as I was concerned, he wasn't welcome in the first place. Anyway, moving on…

Jason is sat on the royal blue leather pouffe and Hayley is sat at his feet, her head leaning on his knee from time to time. It's very odd seeing them together, and not just for me, there have been a few raised eyebrows around the room. Then again, she is still married to Gary, and they did only split up a few weeks ago, so it's not surprising it feels a bit weird to see her with another.

To be fair to Hayley though, she's being remarkably nice to Jason. She seems to have softened somehow and is being more civil to us all, which is something that's also taking a bit of getting used to, and when they look at each other it's all quite tender and sweet. I still maintain it's a shame she's not going to have any time on her own to work out who the hell she is but if she has to be attached, I'd far rather she was attached to someone nice.

Looking at the two of them makes me feel sad that Matthew's not around.

My dad's been given the most comfortable armchair to sit in. He's got his Graseby syringe driver with him, which enables him to self-medicate as and when he needs a bit of pain relief. Obviously it's not a brilliant sign that he has it with him, and I know he's been suffering from quite a few aches and pains lately. Pete's hovering, silent as ever and no doubt desperate to escape to his room.

Just then I'm pulled sharply from my reverie when there's an almighty scream from Mum, followed by lots of yelling

'Oh my god,' shouts Martin. 'Did you all see that?'

'No, what?' I say.

'Hayley was in a "Coming up next" trailer.'

'Was she?' I gasp, gutted I missed it.

Now Hayley's got her head buried practically into Jason's crotch. 'Oh my god I can't watch,' she shrieks. 'I can't bear it.'

Dad gives me a broad wink and makes a comedy face suggesting that we're in for a right old night of it. As he does, from nowhere, completely and utterly randomly, I'm engulfed once more by the hugest urge to be with Matthew… again. It's all I can do to prevent myself from ringing him and begging him to forget everything that's happened and come round. These floods of regret keep rearing their ugly head during the most inappropriate moments. I have to sort it out because I seem to be spending most of my waking hours staring pathetically at my phone half-hoping he might send me a text.

'Sit down, Pete,' orders Mum suddenly, making me jump. 'You're making me nervous loitering like that. I can't believe this is it. My Hayls is actually going to be on telly tonight!'

Pete does one of the most impressive eye rolls I've ever seen but does as he's told and sits on the floor, next to me.

'Have some crisps everyone,' says Mum, looking pointedly at Andy, who feebly offers the bag around. Pete snatches it off him.

'And then after *Sing for Britain* I thought we might all have a little Chinese, or maybe a cuzza?'

'Great idea my precious. Give you a night off cooking,' says Martin.

Quietly I wonder why he can't give Mum a night off cooking by cooking himself. Still, I should be used to the fact that in this house there are blue jobs and there are pink jobs and never the twain shall meet. God forbid my mum ever took a bin out or Martin ironed a shirt. It would be far too controversial.

'I probably won't have any take-out,' says Andy dolefully. 'I've decided to go on a diet.'

'Have you, darlin'?' says Mum, wide-eyed with concern.

'Yeah,' says Andy looking seriously fed up about it. 'Someone at work was really mean to me the other day.'

'Why? What happened, son?' asks Martin gravely, although how he can look serious about anything while wearing a lime green slanket is beyond me. I notice a definite flicker of something imperceptible on Pete's face when Martin uses the word 'son'.

'Well,' Andy moans. 'I was clearing plates away from table twelve and there were a couple of beautiful looking little onion rings left on someone's plate so I just pinched a couple and ate them on my way back to the kitchen. I hadn't eaten anything since lunch and they were totally untouched,' he adds defensively, having clocked Hayley looking repulsed by his tale of gluttony. 'Anyway, Paula saw me. She's the general manager and if truth be told a bit of a bitch. She gave me a right rocketing in front of everyone and called me greedy.'

'That's a bit off,' says Martin. 'I mean you like your grub all right, but greedy is probably a bit strong, isn't it?'

'Yeah, that's what I reckoned mate. Anyway, truth is, I have put on a couple of pounds recently so I'm going to cut back a bit on portions and that.'

'Well good for you, babes,' coos Mum. 'Though don't go losing all your cuddliness now, will you?'

'The seafood diet would be a good one for you,' chips in Dad.

'Ooh yeah,' perks up Andy enthusiastically. 'I love a bit of calamari.'

'Nah, the one I had in mind was the "see food" diet. See food and you eat it,' hacks Dad, coughing as he laughs his head off.

'Oh, good one,' says Andy, looking deeply offended and scowling in Dad's direction.

Next to me Pete rolls his eyes. Do eyeballs have muscles in them? If so Pete's must be very strong. They get such a good workout every day.

'Oh my god, here we go,' I say nervously. 'Turn it up.'

As Martin fiddles with the remote, all eyes return to the telly where Sy Lovejoy's doing a link to camera. Just behind him, for all to plainly see, are Mum, Martin, Dad and Gary.

'So, earlier on we spoke to Hayley who's thirty-three and from Essex.'

As the screen is filled with Hayley's stunningly beautiful face Mum lets out a huge yelp.

Jason wolf whistles and Hayley blushes and looks all coy. 'Oh stop it, you,' she simpers sweetly, slapping him playfully on the knee.

It's like she's been abducted by aliens who have left her body on earth, an empty vessel that they've filled up with someone pretending to be her.

'I've wanted to sing since I was little, really,' Hayley's saying earnestly on TV. 'It's my dream I suppose and my mum has always encouraged me by taking me to auditions. But I'm thirty-three now so this is my last chance, I reckon.'

'Aeeeeeeh,' screams Mum.

'Ow,' says Pete moving further away from the sofa and rubbing his ear.

'I guess I'd love to follow in the footsteps of the big

divas. I love Christina Aguilera, Mariah, Leona, all the real powerhouses, and I'd love it if this time next year I was living that dream and filling out stadiums like they do.'

Oh Christ.

I glance to my right at Hayley. She's got her hands over her ears and her head is now definitely buried in Jason's crotch, which he doesn't look too unhappy about come to think of it.

You could hear a pin drop in the room until Dad says, 'Yeah, well I don't think that will be happening somehow Hayls. I think you can probably rub "arena tour" off your "to do" list, babe.'

'Shut up,' she says, although it's hard to tell as her head's still nestled into Jason's jean-clad groin so her voice is very muffled.

Now we're back to Sy and my on-screen family.

'So, you must be Hayley's mum.'

'I certainly am,' grins my mother on screen, looking totally manic.

'Oh Alison,' crows Martin in real life, here in the lounge, his head the only thing visible amidst their mountain of polyester. 'You are so unbelievably photogenic. Like a film star, my darling.'

Mum grins but also elbows him to shut up so she can hear what's being said.

'And you're Hayley's husband, Gary, is that right?'

'Yeah,' says Gary, looking like he's been hit with a stun gun.

'Bastard,' yells Hayley, surfacing from the realms of her boyfriend's nether regions for a second.

'Ssssh,' insists Mum.

'Well,' says Sy. 'She's certainly a looker, your wife, and I've got a feeling head judge Julian will agree. In fact if she's as good as she says she is, I think he'll definitely be giving her the thumbs-up.'

'I'm her husband,' states Gary robotically, staring straight down the lens.

Such a weirdo.

'Er right,' says Sy giving us, the audience at home, an inclusive look as if to say '*Yep, he's a bit of a freak isn't he?*'

I agree.

Gary's appearance has caused an icy, awkward silence to descend upon the living room and I notice that at the mere sight of him, Jason is looking downright livid. Still, seconds later, Gary's out of shot again and the focus is all back on Hayley.

'Good luck Hayley,' Sy's saying and then Martin is seen patting her on the back. Meanwhile, Mum's jumping up and down, squealing like a pig and you can just about make out Dad in the background, his head at Mum's waist level due to the wheelchair.

From behind me on the sofa Mum suddenly pipes up, 'Ooh Mar, do you think I'm coming across as a bit OTT lovey?'

Pete and I exchange looks.

'Absolutely not, my princess,' says Martin firmly. 'You look like a loving and supportive mother.'

Pete snorts. It's a snort that sums up more than a thousand words ever could.

It suddenly occurs to me that, so far, there's been no mention of my dad or his illness yet, even though I know they definitely filmed him and talked about it with Hayley. Then I realise that of course they probably won't be exploiting that situation, precisely because Hayley was so awful. I guess, a girl who has a sick dad who turns out to be an amazing singer is one thing, but making a feature of a girl who has a sick dad who can't sing for toffee would amount to nothing less than cruelty. Dad must be thinking along the same lines because just at that moment he says, more to himself than anyone else, 'Think I might be off the hook.'

'Now, Hayley,' Mum pipes up from beneath her fuchsia slanket, 'Just remember lovely that no matter how this goes, you've made it onto prime time telly. No one can take that away from you, my angel.'

Hayley doesn't dignify this with an answer. I don't blame her.

Meanwhile, on screen it's like watching a form of déjà vu unfold. Suddenly there's Hayley striding into the audition room, looking every inch the Hollywood starlet, or at least the Chigwell starlet. She looks beautiful and confident, like someone whose album you'd want to buy. Only we all know that's not how the story's going to end.

'Blimey Hayley, you look amazing,' says Jason, the only one of us who hasn't already been privy to her show-stopping look.

Hayley doesn't reply and is only looking through her fingers.

On screen we witness in close up the judges' reactions to her, and then one of the judges, record producer Georgie Arthur, starts speaking. 'Hello, well I must say sweetheart, you look utterly sensational.'

'Thanks,' Hayley's saying demurely.

'See, that's what I meant by your Princess Diana face,' I shout out, pointing wildly at the screen.

'Oh yeah,' Dad agrees. 'I see that, it's that sort of mysterious look, innit? When you kind of look down but up.'

'Ssssh,' says Mum behind me, flapping at us. She looks nervous, as well she should.

'What's your name?' asks Carisse, the sexy female vocalist who is currently at number one in the charts.

'Hayley Baxter.'

'Well Hayley, I love your outfit. Did you choose it yourself?'

'Yeah I did,' Hayley confirms.

I am suddenly flooded with the memory that this was the point in the proceedings where things started getting a bit cringey. Meanwhile, on screen, Julian Hayes is asking my sister who she came with.

My memory serves me correctly for the next thing that happens is we're all treated to the sound of my Mum screaming backstage, sounding demented, although at this stage everyone in the green room finds the fact she's such a 'character' quite funny.

I wait for Hayley to explain who else she is with but they must have edited it out because next Julian Hayes says, 'So, down to business, what are you going to sing today?'

'They cut my mention out,' says Andy huffily, chubby arms folded, like giant chicken drumsticks.

'And mine,' says Martin, far more affably.

More importantly they've definitely cut out the bits about Dad. I am so relieved.

Meanwhile, back on the TV, Hayley's explaining why she chose to do a Leona Lewis song and her second reference to Mum brings forth another almighty shriek, much to Sy Lovejoy's obvious amusement.

From beneath her slanket Mum's looking rather apprehensive. She turns and looks to Martin for reassurance, which obviously she gets. 'You look wonderful darling,' he says, sounding like he's trying to convince himself as well as her. 'You just look… excited, and look at your gorgeous hair. It's so bouncy and shiny.'

He is a master of diplomacy.

Mum smiles weakly but doesn't look convinced. Out of the corner of my eye I notice Dad's shoulders are shaking as he tries not to laugh.

Back on the telly Georgie Arthur is saying in his Irish lilt, 'OK, well before your mum gets too over-excited out there I think you'd better take it away.'

'Good luck,' says Julian Hayes.

'Turn it off,' screams Hayley from behind me suddenly, like she's only just remembered how bad she was.

'Don't be silly,' says Jason. 'This is hilarious, and besides, I want to hear you sing hon.'

'I said turn it off,' my embarrassed sister demands, sounding far more like the Hayley we all know and love. Springing to her feet she paces the floor in search of the remote, having transformed back into a banshee.

'Hayley calm down,' says Dad.

Meanwhile, on screen she's getting ready. I feel sick. We all seem to have frozen and are suddenly transfixed by what might or might not be shown.

Just as we did on the day, we all watch as Hayley takes a deep breath, looks down and then starts to sing. Except what comes out of her mouth doesn't sound much like singing at first.

What it sounds like is a low moan of pain. I glance over at Jason who's looking puzzled and is staring at the screen wondering whether she's caught her finger in a zip, or stubbed her toe perhaps. What she is in fact doing is trying to emulate the opening of *Bleeding Love* in a dramatic way and suddenly she snaps her head up and stares right down the lens.

Here in our lounge, Hayley appears to give up. Stamping her foot like a sulky teenager she stomps out muttering violently, 'Fucking bastards.' Then we hear her thunder up the stairs and slam her bedroom door behind her.

Rather than go after her, however – which I'm sure would have been what she was angling for – Jason doesn't move a muscle. He's too engrossed by what he's seeing, too perplexed, for on TV Hayley's really upping the ante now as she launches into the first verse. This does at least mean we can finally hear what she's singing, although actually thinking about it, that probably isn't a good thing.

Martin chuckles. 'Ah dear, do you remember at this point we wondered whether she was joking, didn't we Ray?'

Dad nods but mainly looks embarrassed on his daughter's behalf.

'I tried to tell her,' I say to Jason, wishing now I'd done more. She sounds even worse on TV than she did on the day and the audition room looks like the most lonely place on Earth to be. She's completely and painfully out of tune. Sharp to be precise and, as I predicted, the song, which is possibly the most terrible choice for an acoustic version ever, sounds like a weird dirge.

To make matters worse, the camera keeps cutting back to where my mother is bopping away in the next room, doing thumbs-up signs to the camera. It's as if she's listening to something completely different and, egged on by the cameraman, for I suspect all the wrong reasons, she's really getting into it. In fact she's gyrating so much it looks like she's auditioning for a lap-dancing job. *Bleeding Love* is a relatively slow-paced tune, yet Mum's going at it like she's trying to set a record for fastest dancer in the West, proving that she has precisely no rhythm whatsoever.

'OK, stop there please… stop… stop, oh please make her stop,' says Julian Hayes eventually while Hayley determinedly strangles the chorus.

I exhale, relieved that someone is making it end. Apprehensive, I look up. On screen the judges look flabbergasted. To my left Jason looks stunned.

Finally Hayley realises that Julian Hayes is in fact talking to her and stops caterwauling long enough to realise that the judges have fallen completely silent, only not out of respect. The silence is a shocked one and there are lots of close ups of each judge looking staggered that anybody who can look that good can sound that bad.

'What was that?' asks Julian Hayes.

'What do you mean what was that?' retorts my sister on screen, looking confused.

'That,' he says. His face is disappointed. I think he really had wanted her to be fantastic.

'*Bleeding Love*,' mutters Hayley, looking the tiniest bit sulky.

'Bleeding racket more like,' laughs Julian.

'Bleeding ears as well,' giggles Georgie Arthur.

'Look,' Julian Hayes continues. 'I've got to tell you darling that not one note of that was in tune.'

'Ah come on Julian, don't be mean now,' soothes Carisse.

'It wasn't that bad, was it?' asks Hayley, genuinely shocked by his reaction.

'It was worse,' he says gravely.

'Oh my god, poor Hayley,' says Jason, looking horrified on her behalf.

'Mm,' I say. 'Just you wait, it's about to get even worse.'

From the sofa Mum flashes me a filthy look but doesn't respond, for just at that moment a shot of her looking livid backstage appears on screen.

We all watch helplessly as my angry mother barges past two security men and runs down the corridor, on her way to make a complete and utter tit of herself. Now she appears on our telly, in the audition room, having run in looking demented, furious and, if I'm honest, unhinged.

Here at home everyone except Andy is looking very unsure. For some reason I'll never understand, Andy is jigging up and down, rubbing his fat hands with glee, as if what my mother is about to do is a brave and brilliant thing, as opposed to the social equivalent of suicide.

'I don't think I'll be going back to college after this,' says a low voice next to me. I spin round. This is pretty much the most Pete has uttered to me in the last five years.

'Yes,' I agree. 'Still, at least I know where our passports are kept.'

Then it starts.

'How dare you judges?' my mother's shrieking on TV. 'How dare you try and trample on someone's dreams? My Hayley's got more talent in her little finger than you have between the lot of you,' she rages, her chest heaving in righteous indignation. Her eyes are practically popping out of her head and she's panting. Let's just say she's not looking her most attractive.

The director's obviously had a field day, because the camera keeps cutting from Mum to the judges, whose expressions range from gobsmacked, to mildly amused, to nervous. Then it returns to a dismayed, but thankfully silent Hayley.

'Oh my god. Someone make it stop,' Mum wails quietly from the sofa.

Meanwhile, on telly she demands to know, 'How can you just sit there and put someone down like that? My Hayley is a little star, and if you can't see that, you're not the judges I thought you were.'

Meanwhile the 'little star' is glaring murderously at Mum, looking like she'd quite happily kill her.

'Well, I *can't* see it,' says Julian Hayes wryly. 'And unfortunately, I don't think I was the only one who thought your daughter sounded like she was undergoing an operation without an anesthetic. Georgie, what did you think of Hayley's performance?'

'I have to say,' says Georgie Arthur, albeit apologetically. 'It was pretty shocking.'

Mum's nostrils flare. 'Carisse, you always speak sense. What did you think?'

'I'm so sorry. It was bad,' she says. 'And I don't think you're doing your daughter any favours by telling her otherwise.'

On screen, upon hearing this rather harsh home truth,

Hayley bursts into humiliated tears and rushes from the room, tottering on her heels, leaving my mum standing alone in the middle, indignant and ridiculous looking.

People in the green room start to boo.

It literally couldn't get any worse.

Upstairs there's an almighty crash as Hayley throws something, which sounds suspiciously like a television, across the room.

'I have to say, it did sound better when we were actually there,' pipes up Mum tentatively.

'Couldn't have sounded any worse,' says Jason.

Just then we can all hear the ominous sound of my sister thudding back downstairs. She barges back into the room looking mildly deranged.

'If you don't turn off this TV right now I will smash it with my foot,' she threatens, making her point in her own inimitable way. Though to be fair, she is literally dying of embarrassment. 'Who's got the remote?'

Dad and Pete both shrug.

Andy picks up a pair of his jeans off the floor and has a quick look underneath but only finds his hair gel.

I boot his rucksack out of the way, frustrated by how much of his shit is everywhere. 'Maybe you're sitting on it?' I suggest to Mum and Martin, who in a panic try to stand in unison. The static caused by this sudden movement to their slankets means the crackle is audible. Mum's hair is standing on end.

'Ow, did you feel that babe?' moans Martin. 'I think I got a little electric shock off you.'

By now, my sister looks as though she might be about to carry through her threat of kicking the television to death when Pete suddenly pipes up, 'It's here,' and produces the remote from where it's wedged down the side of the sofa.

Hayley grabs it from him and wields it around, stabbing the buttons ferociously; stopping only once her pain is at an end.

Finally there's silence, only in the next second it's shattered by the sound of everybody's mobiles beeping as the texts come flooding in. For once I am utterly glad to be me.

CHAPTER TWENTY-FIVE

A few weeks after Mum and Hayley's social suicide – which actually isn't a laughing matter, they've had so much stick it's unbelievable, some of it even from strangers in the street – I'm with Dad, sitting in the park. It's a blustery October day but the park is full of people trying to make the most of the outdoors before winter arrives. From where we're sat on a bench we've got a good view of the playground on the other side of the common. From here it resembles a noisy cage, full of movement, colour and life. The distant sound of children yelling as they chase each other around carries to us on the breeze.

We've exhausted the subject of Hayley and how we can try and cheer her up, and ever since have both been content just to sit, to enjoy the view and breathe in the fresh air. It's weird, Dad being terminally ill has definitely given me a fresh appreciation of nature, of how very good for the soul it is to be outside revelling in it. He's not well enough to go for walks any more, like we used to only a few months ago, but when I ask him what he wants to do, more often than not he's usually just happy to sit somewhere and watch the world go by. A few weeks ago we had a trip to the coast, to Aldeburgh in Suffolk, a nice drive from Essex, where we sat and gazed at the sea. Medicine in itself. I'm always aware that he's soaking up everything he can. That glimpse of the sea and its steely waves were so appreciated that day, as is every blue sky, the feel of the watery autumnal sunshine on our faces today, and the sight of the huge plane trees that flank the sides of the common swaying in the breeze.

I'm so glad that we can simply sit here together like this, and that he doesn't feel the need to fill every silence with conversation. It's one of the nicest things about him.

'What's happening with you and Matthew, then?'

I spoke too soon.

I sigh and am about to embark on some convoluted explanation when I decide to keep it simple. 'He backed off. I think he does like me but he was very worried about getting into trouble for seeing me.'

Dad doesn't reply at first but having ruminated on this for a while says, 'I thought something was up. Still, you'll be able to get together eventually, won't you?'

I shake my head, more to make him stop than anything. I hate it when he talks like this. As if the end is nigh.

'It's all right,' he says gently. 'I'm all right with it Marianne. You know I was thinking the other day that you shouldn't be so angry about my illness. In a strange way we should be grateful for it, 'cos it's brought us together.'

I know he's trying to be sweet, but actually this last statement just makes me feel quite incensed.

'I wish,' I begin tentatively, aware that I am finally about to voice something I've been struggling with for a while now. I don't want to upset him but at the same time he has to know what I'm feeling, and his illness doesn't excuse everything.

'I wish cancer hadn't been the thing that made you find me,' I say, staring straight ahead. 'I wish you'd just wanted to know us anyway, without needing something so dramatic to make you realise it.'

When Dad doesn't say anything I take it as my cue to carry on. 'I hate the fact it took cancer for you to be interested in your own kids. Why didn't you at least try before? Even if you'd just written us a letter, it would have been better than nothing, surely?'

I daren't look at him as I wait for the answer.

After a while he says flatly, 'Because I'm a stupid person.'

I sigh heavily.

'Look, I wish I could give you a better, more satisfying answer than that but I can't. But it wasn't like I didn't want to know you, I did. I just didn't go out of my way to make it happen because I thought it was easier. Thought it was best for everyone if I didn't "rock the boat".' As he says this he makes weary speech marks with his fingers. Then, burying his hands back deep into the pockets of his jacket he continues sadly, 'Marianne, my life is riddled with regrets. I've spent years of it in prison, a lot of it alone and now look at me. It's not exactly going to go down as the most inspiring existence in the world is it?'

I don't know what to say.

'But there have been good bits. I married your mother, who I loved very much. I mean, I know she's nuts and she don't half talk a lot of shit, but I've always loved her really. She makes me laugh.'

A large gust of wind blows into my eyes making them water. I hug my jacket round me and inhale deeply.

'And, for whatever reason, she feels like home to me.'

He says this so simply, so easily. It's a lovely thing to say and it occurs to me that to have someone in your life feel this way about you, would be a truly incredible thing.

'And the other good things I've achieved in my life are you and Hayley, so why I didn't have more courage, more strength to come and see you earlier I shall never know. I wish I had.'

'So do I,' I agree quietly. 'I just feel like…'

'Go on babe, get it all out,' Dad says.

I swallow hard. 'OK, so I just feel like I would have been so much happier if you'd been in contact. Even if all that that equated to was seeing you for the odd visit in prison it *would* have been better than nothing. You're a good influence on me,' I say wryly, my eyes brimming with tears. 'And sometimes I can't help wondering how things might have turned out if I'd had you to help steer me in the right direction. As it is I've wasted so much time.'

Dad looks up at the clouds that are skidding across the sky and exhales loudly.

'And it just seems so unfair, and cruel, that… just as I've got to know you, I have to lose you.'

'I know, and I'm so sorry,' Dad says simply, reaching out for my hand. I pass it to him and we sit there, side by side, hand in hand for a while, me weeping silently, Dad immersed in his thoughts.

Eventually he says steadily, 'These last few months have been the happiest of my life though, you know.'

'Have they?' I say, wiping my eyes with the back of my hand and sniffing loudly while wondering how the hell that can be true.

'Yeah,' he says, sounding like he really means it. 'I might be ill Marianne, and I might be in pain and all that, but I am so proud of you and so lucky to have had you in my life, even for this short while and I think that's how we have to look at it. It's just better not to focus on the years we've missed out on, but on the months that we have had, because they have been amazing and I want you to… I *need* you to remember that. Will you please?' he asks, and I'm horrified to hear the catch in his voice.

'I promise,' I say firmly, nodding my head, keenly aware of what an important moment this is. 'I promise that I will always remember our time together and all the things that you've told me. And I also promise that I will try not to waste any more time with anything by being… well by being me,' I say and now the tears are rolling down my face.

Dad gestures to me to come in for a hug and I bury my face in his chest and let him stroke my hair while I have a good, healthy cry.

'I love you, Dad,' I manage snottily.

'I love you too babe,' he says, his voice thick with emotion. 'And you know what?'

'What?'

'I didn't know what the word proud even meant till I met you. This pride that I feel now, it's huge, massive. I feel totally full up to the brim with it every time I look at you.'

I wrap my arms round him tighter and am alarmed for a second at how thin his frame feels. 'Thank you,' I say, concentrating hard on remembering every single little thing about this moment. How I feel sitting here with my dad, the feel of his arms around me, the smell of the leather of his jacket, his voice, every little detail. I soak it all up because it's not going to be here for ever. Soon he's going to be gone and I don't think I can bear it but if I can cling on to this moment maybe I'll get through. If I can just lock it away and keep it inside, for I know in that moment that a change is coming, that his body is starting to lose the battle, that it's the beginning of the end.

*

Two weeks later and Dad does indeed take a turn for the worse. Completely out of the blue I get a phone call from Matthew of all people, saying that they were at the hospital and could I come as soon as possible.

I'm there half an hour later, but as I park up my hands are shaking. Let's face it I know I'm probably not about to hear anything very jolly.

Somehow I find my way through the maze of corridors and eventually to the ward where Matthew had told me I could find him. Dad's lying in the last bed on the left-hand side of the ward, looking yellow, gaunt and tired. Clearly no one on this ward is in a particularly great state and there's a smell of illness in the air. Hospitals make me feel pretty queasy at the best of times and today's no different. The fact that Matthew is there helps however and I am filled with emotion as soon as I spot him anxiously looking out for me. Unlike the patients around him, he is brimming with life force and even under the draining strip lighting looks well and vital. I am instantly grateful for his presence but also unbelievably affected by seeing him for the first time in ages. It's all very surreal.

'Hi Dad,' I say as I approach the bed, steeling myself to be brave.

'Hello babe,' he says, though it sounds as if merely speaking is taking all his effort. 'Thanks for coming. I did tell Matthew not to worry about calling you, but he insisted.'

'Well, I'm glad he did,' I reply, in that over-chirpy way one does when talking to a hospital patient. Not once do I look directly towards Matthew during this exchange. 'So, what's up anyway?' I say softly.

'Oh, hang on a minute Marianne,' says Matthew. 'I've

just spotted Mr Clarkson coming. We should probably wait for him.'

'Fine,' I mutter, glancing back down the ward to get a look at the man who is in charge of my dad's health. He's not what I'd expected at all. He's reassuringly hirsute for starters, almost a formidable presence really, and sporting a gold Rolex that seems to scream how successful he is at his job. He reminds me of Tom Selleck back in his Magnum days, which isn't a bad thing by any means. He's dark and swarthy, has a burly build, and walks with the air of a man who knows what he's doing. His face, however, is utterly inscrutable.

Once he's reached Dad's bed, he draws the curtain round us all, giving us privacy from the other patients.

'Hello Ray,' he says, cheerful but business-like. 'How are you feeling today?' he asks, grabbing his notes from the foot of the bed and squinting at them.

'I'm all right, just a bit of muscle pain that's all,' manages Dad, who I'm starting to realise is the master of the understatement. He sounds so weak. 'This is my youngest, Marianne. I don't think the two of you have met yet.'

'Ah no, I don't believe we have, but I've heard a lot about you. Your father tells me you're a very accomplished musician.'

I flame red and feel particularly self-conscious given that Matthew's standing there looking so utterly… himself. It's not that I'm not happy that Dad's proud of me, but me and my music are so irrelevant right this second I can hardly bear it.

I gulp. 'Well you know... I'm OK, so anyway, what's the situation doctor? Why did Matthew think I should get over here?'

'Well,' says his doctor, 'Your father hasn't been feeling too good these last couple of days and has suggested it might be time for us to hand his care over to the palliative team, and we concur with that decision. That department will be better equipped to handle things from here on in.'

'Right,' I say, swallowing hard, determined not to cry. I can't help it, a reflex action I look to Matthew, only to find that he's watching me with such concern it throws me altogether. The whole situation is very overwhelming and of course I'm totally aware that I can't get too visibly upset for Dad's sake. There's a huge lump in my throat though because I'm just not ready to lose him yet. How can it be that although I knew this day was coming, have done from the get go, I feel so horrified and shocked by it?

I perch tentatively on the edge of the bed and take Dad's hand in mine. It feels papery and dry.

'And how do you feel about all of this, Dad?'

'Yeah, I think it's got to that point,' he says. 'And besides, it'll have one or two other benefits I reckon.'

As he says this, he looks firstly at Matthew and then at me. I can hardly believe it. Matthew looks totally alarmed in case Mr Clarkson cottons on to what he's referring to.

'May I have a minute alone with my dad?' I ask every-one.

'Of course, we can wait in the corridor a second,' he says to Matthew, and the two of them shuffle back through the gap in the curtain.

'Dad,' I say gently, once we're on our own. 'If you're agreeing to this for any other reason than because it's the right thing to do for your health, you won't need palliative because I'll kill you myself.'

To his credit Dad laughs but this soon turns into a cough and then I see him reaching for his syringe driver. He presses down on it in order to administer some pain relief.

'I want to be looked after by them now,' he says simply, and I can tell he means it. 'I need the drugs they have, and it's time. It's not a question of giving up or rolling over, or saying you're ready to die, but the palliative team will make what time I have got left far more comfortable.'

'OK,' I say, satisfied that his reasoning is all totally sen-sible but completely petrified about what the near future holds.

'Though it does mean Matthew ain't working with me any more,' he's unable to resist adding, even giving me a small wink as he does so. 'So, if you did want to go on a date with him again, there wouldn't be anything unethical about it whatsoever.'

I roll my eyes and smile and yet my heart is so heavy it's an effort to do so. 'It's complicated,' I say lightly.

If only he knew how unimportant everything except

him felt right now he'd understand that, as much as I do still have so many feelings for Matthew, I am simply not in the right place to explore them.

'By the way,' I say softly, knowing I do at least have one piece of news that will make him happy. 'I've got a date for my audition for the College.'

Dad's eyes instantly perk up a bit and he nods at me to tell him.

'Fourteenth of December.'

'Fourteenth of December,' he repeats 'And how long after that would you find out then?'

'Not long apparently,' I say, feeling sick at the thought. 'Maybe only a few days?'

'Right,' says Dad grimly and I know him well enough by now to know that he has decided in that moment that he's not going anywhere, or at least not until he's discovered my fate, one way or the other.

*

Everybody in the family is extremely affected by Ray's decline. Even Martin, who has been unbelievably sweet and supportive and keeps asking if there's anything he can do, which of course there isn't. No one can. Still, his kindness is gratefully accepted and once again I am reminded of my stepdad's good heart. On a more unexpected note, one night, while I'm huddled up on my bed, staring into space, thinking how I should be practising the violin but unable to get myself into gear, there's a tap at my door.

I'm very surprised to discover it's Pete.

'You all right?' I ask, wondering what emergency can have necessitated such a proactive gesture as actually knocking on my door.

'Yeah,' he says. 'Sorry to hear your dad's not doing great.'

'Thanks Pete,' I say sincerely.

Coming from him this is practically a speech, but amazingly it seems there's more.

'Ray's a top bloke.'

'Thank you,' I say again, vaguely surprised he's noticed. 'He is.'

'You're lucky,' Pete adds, and I have to say at this point I'm a little bemused.

'Really?' I say doubtfully, wondering how the hell he's managed to come to that conclusion.

'Yeah,' he nods seriously. 'You have a really great bond with Ray. Must be nice.'

My heart contracts with unexpected sympathy for my complicated brother.

'Oh Pete. Mum and Martin adore you.'

'Yeah,' he says monosyllabically but having opened up more than he has in a lifetime, that appears to be all I'm getting out of him on the subject. Having clammed up again he slopes off back towards his bedroom.

As he closes the door I feel really sad for him, for of

course I know exactly what he's getting at. I guess he feels a lot like I did for many, many years. Removed somehow from the bosom of the family, and detached, due to not really connecting. The only difference is that there's no chance of another parent turning up on his doorstep one day. No possibility that one of the people responsible for creating him will suddenly turn out to love Elvis, or to hate small talk and socialising with other human beings in general, which would of course provide him with a sense of belonging and of worth. It would make him make sense. Still, as I've been reminded recently, our family is comprised of good people, which is more than can be said of some.

*

Of course Dad himself does have another child, and Hayley is hugely upset by his recent turn for the worse. When she finds out the end may be imminent she does a lot of noisy crying and a lot of shouting, which incorporates many 'It's not fairs'. She's bloody angry and I think it would be fair to say that we're all handling the news in our own way. However, thankfully I've noticed that Jason is amazing at reining Hayley in. Not in a horrible, controlling way like Gary used to, but with love and tenderness and a healthy dose of common sense. I hate seeing my sister so upset and only yesterday we had a good, loud cry together, which turned out to be surprisingly therapeutic.

The last person to amaze me is Mum. On one particularly hideous day in November that I shall never forget, she not only amazes me but dumbfounds and most of all impresses me beyond belief.

Since Dad's been handed over to palliative, I've started accompanying him to many of his hospital visits. Roberto has been completely understanding about what's going on and has said I can have as many days off as I need. This is a godsend, because when I'm at work all I can think is that I should be with Dad. I don't want to regret not making the most of the time I have left with him so, at the moment, I don't want to work much or do any children's parties. Besides, Dad's really weak now so needs help getting out of the car and stuff anyway. As a result of being present at so many of his check-ups, I know exactly how badly he's doing. I have become au fait with all sorts of medical terminology and can now tell you what your blood count should be, how to take blood pressure, and the names of a variety of drugs and what they do. I don't glean an ounce of pleasure from any of this.

On one particular visit, the doctor says that it might be time to visit the hospice.

'I think you'll be pleasantly surprised,' she says. 'It really is a lovely place. Spotlessly clean, well run and full of light.'

Having researched into hospices myself I am completely dumbstruck by her suggestion, given that the average stay at a hospice is around a week to ten days. Surely my dad has longer than this? He's not even bedridden yet.

'He's not ready for a hospice yet,' I state firmly.

'No,' agrees the doctor to my immense relief. 'But he might be in a few weeks,' she continues gently. 'So I thought you might like to have a look at it, so you know what to expect and so you can see what a nice environment it is.'

At this point Dad looks pale, worn out and utterly terrified.

After we've left the hospital, instead of taking him home, I drive him back to ours as I can sense he doesn't want to be alone. As I switch the engine off I notice how dark it is suddenly. Winter is most definitely here. 'Come on,' I say. 'Let's get in the warm.'

To my horror however, instead of getting out, Dad does something he hasn't ever done before. He breaks down and cries. Huge, racking, desperate sobs.

'It's OK,' I say, hugging him tight, determined not to let on how shocking and how heartbreaking it is to see my big bear of a father crying so desperately. 'It's OK, let it out. It's good to have a cry. You need to.'

And we sit like this for a while, me hugging him tight, wishing I could wave a magic wand and make everything all right. Wishing I could tell him it would all be fine.

'Forgive me,' he says minutes later, once he's had a good howl. 'I'm so sorry Marianne. I didn't want you to see me like this, it's not fair.'

'Don't be stupid,' I say, patting his arm. At this precise moment we have switched roles. He needs me to be the adult. He needs looking after and the comfort of someone telling him it will be OK. 'Now, come on' I say, getting out my side and going round to help him out. 'Let's get in and I'll make us a nice cup of tea.'

Once I've got Dad settled in the comfy chair in the lounge, I walk round the corner into the kitchen. The partition wall separates us of course but, aware that he can easily still hear me, I make sure that as my own sadness overwhelms me I don't make a sound.

Seconds later, I hear Mum's voice saying, 'Hello Ray lovey, you all right?'

I open the hatch. Mum's face is full of concern as she takes in Dad's frail appearance. She's carrying lots of shopping bags so she comes round to where I am in the kitchen and dumps them all on the breakfast bar.

'Hello love,' she says, spotting me. 'Is that kettle boiled, I'm desperate for a cuppa. I've done loads of Crimble shopping today. They had some lovely sets at Boots. You know, toiletries and that. Did you know Peter Andre's got a new aftershave out? Tell you what, I'd love to sniff it on him,' she laughs dirtily.

'It's only November,' I say, wiping away the evidence that I've been crying with a tea towel.

'Exactly, only weeks away,' she says. 'Besides, I start with the old Crimble shopping in June, I do. That way the payments are spread out over the year and Martin's none the wiser. Gotta bleed 'em dry while you can, eh? Hey, what is it lovey?'

I look up with a start and shake my head at her, warning her to be quiet. I don't want Dad to know I'm upset.

Mum nods that she gets what I'm saying and looking solemn takes off her coat. She goes back to see Dad again.

'Hello Raymondo,' I hear her say gently. 'Are you really all right, lovey? Can I get you a little biccy or anything? Something sweet might do you the world of good.' Then, 'Oh lovey, don't be sad, what is it? What's happened?'

Abandoning the tea-making I follow after her and find Mum squatting down besides Dad, rubbing his back, looking really concerned for him.

'What is it?' she asks me. 'Will one of you silly buggers please tell me?'

Right.

I take a deep breath. 'Er well, today at the hospital they suggested we go and visit the hospice, and I think it's just freaked us out a bit.'

'Hospice?' she repeats, the colour draining from her cheeks. 'Bit early for that isn't it?'

'Oh yeah,' I agree vehemently 'That's what I said, and it is. But they just thought we might want to go and have a look.'

'And what do you think of that?' whispers Mum to Dad, who looks so defeated today and so desperately sad. Still, ever mindful of everyone else's feelings, I can see him battling to pull himself together and raises his head to meet her gaze.

'It's fine, and I'm sorry,' he manages, still clearly quite overwhelmed by everything. It dawns on me then how brave he's always been, managing to hide his feelings from me and everyone else. He's been so stoic and unbelievably unselfish throughout his illness and yet of course, as a result of that, if the floodgates are opened, as they have been today, everything was always going to come pouring out.

Mum waits patiently for him to gather himself.

'It's fine,' he repeats finally, clearing his throat and sniffing hard. 'I'm just… I'm just a little bit scared of dying alone, but I guess that's the whole point of these places isn't it? And I won't be on my own because the staff will be around all the time.'

'And I will be,' I interject adamantly. 'I won't be going anywhere Dad. I'll be there I promise, making sure you're comfortable and OK and I want you to know that. I won't leave your side.'

Dad nods bravely. 'You're a good girl Marianne, but there's no way I want you to be there the whole time. That would be far too heavy going for you. Nah, don't you worry, I'm being a right old silly. It'll be fine.'

I can see Mum staring at him hard, like she's weighing up what to say next.

'Move in here.'

I turn to her, flabbergasted, and my heart starts pounding so hard it nearly hammers through my chest.

'What?' says Dad who clearly thinks he hasn't heard right.

'Move in here,' she repeats, louder and with more conviction this time. 'There's plenty of space in the front room for a bed, so you wouldn't have to worry about stairs or nothing, and you could use the downstairs loo for wish washing and all that, couldn't you?'

'Don't be silly,' says Dad. 'You're very sweet Alli, but nah. I couldn't let you.'

'No,' says Mum, pulling herself up to standing, her knees cracking noisily as she does so. 'I'm not asking, I'm telling, and I don't know why I didn't think of it before. It's the perfect solution. You'll be here with us, looked after and I'm sure we can get the nurses and that to come here for bits and bobs we can't manage.'

'Alison, I'm gonna need proper medical care babe. And... well, it won't be pretty, if you know what I mean.'

'Well obviously we'll need to look into it all properly,' Mum insists, undeterred. 'You know, we'll talk to the hospital and that but there must be a way to make it work. Marianne would be happy too, wouldn't you lovey? And... so would I. You should be here... you're family. I want to do this.'

There's a silence while Dad and I absorb what she's said during which I will him to agree to what she's offering. I can see him weighing it all up but am surprised by what he says next.

'I love you, Alison,' he says sincerely, not in a dramatic

way, but quietly and meaningfully and looking so devastated it's all I can do not to wail out loud.

'And I care about you very much too,' Mum says back simply, not revealing even a hint of what must be the maelstrom of emotions that are charging through her right now.

'But I can't take you up on your kind offer,' he insists. 'Apart from anything else, what would Martin make of your ex taking up half his ground floor and dying in his living room eh?'

'Martin will understand,' says Mum firmly and I know then that it will happen, for when my mother makes up her mind, that's it, and I can't see Martin changing the habit of a lifetime by disagreeing with her suddenly. Besides, he may be a lot of things but as well we all know he's a generous soul and how could he refuse? We are family. All of us. We're one big, weird, dysfunctional family, not all related by blood. But isn't that most families these days? And doesn't the very word family mean exactly the sort of love and compassion my mum is showing now?

'Oh my god Mum, thank you so much,' I tell her, grabbing her for a heartfelt hug.

'Ooh you daft apeth,' she says, but hugs me back. 'Right, let's not bother waiting around. I'll phone Mar right now. He's in the pub, so bit of luck I'll get him in a good mood,' she jokes, giving Dad a little nudge. 'And then we can work out what needs to be done.'

I look at Dad. He's welling up again, but this time he's also smiling. He looks utterly, utterly relieved and I can tell that Mum's plan has boosted him beyond belief. You see, weirdly – and I have given this a lot of thought – I don't think he's scared of being dead, not like I know I certainly would be, but what he's more scared of is dying, of the actual process and how that will be. Now he knows it will be happening here, with us, I think he feels like whatever happens he'll be able to face it. I have never loved my mother more than I do right now.

'OK?' I ask Dad as Mum flaps out of the room, a woman on a mission.

'Yeah,' he says. 'Though are you sure it's going to be OK, me taking up so much room and everything?'

'You know as well as I do, that you have precisely no say in the matter whatsoever.'

CHAPTER TWENTY-SIX

Ray moving in is the best thing that could have happened. It provides us all with a sense of purpose at a time when ordinarily we'd be feeling very lost.

Of course deep down I'm sure Martin must have fairly mixed feelings about his wife's ex moving in, but if he does he doesn't show it. Instead, true to form, he keeps quiet and treats transforming the front room into a bedroom as one big DIY project to get his teeth into. He could surely be the poster boy for the people who coined the 'Keep Calm and Carry On' saying. When I told him that the hospice would be lending us a proper hospital bed he looked vaguely disappointed. I think he'd been hoping for a bonus trip to Dreams or IKEA. Still, he has been out to purchase a bedside table, which to his enormous delight arrived flat packed, so he's had that to do, and he's also measuring up for a bit of shelving. He's doing it right now in fact, for tomorrow is the big day when Dad moves in. Strictly speaking he's not quite at the stage where he needs to move in yet, he could have waited a while longer, but what would be the point? He'll be far happier and less lonely living here with us. Plus, at the rate his health is deteriorating it's probably safer for him to be surrounded by people.

I sit watching as Martin busies himself about, making what will be my father's final resting place as nice as possible. As I do I experience a huge pang of affection for my stepdad. It must be wonderful to be so mild mannered, to never get your knickers in a twist about anything that doesn't really warrant it. It's so unbelievably unselfish of him to go along with this too without making any objections.

'Thank you, Martin,' I say. 'I really appreciate you letting this happen. People would have understood if you'd said no.'

'Your mother would have had a lot to say about it though,' he says ruefully.

'Oh,' I say, worried suddenly. 'But I hope that's not the only reason you're going along with it, to keep Mum happy.'

'Not at all, I'm doing it because, as Alison pointed out, it's the right thing to do.'

'Oh, good.'

'Your mother's a wonderful woman,' he says, stretching out his back for a minute and gazing into the middle distance.

For once, I'm inclined to agree with him.

'And you're an amazing stepdad,' I add slightly self-consciously, determined to let him know how grateful I am to him, for so many things.

'Well, that job's made far easier by having two such lovely stepdaughters. You're both real crackers.'

'Thanks,' I say.

'And the hospice has definitely got it all under control, have they?' Martin enquires. 'You know, with the bed and that? Because if not, there's still time for me to pop down to…'

'It's fine,' I interject. 'The staff at the hospice have been amazing. The bed's being delivered first thing tomorrow morning and we're being offered loads of support. He'll have a nurse visiting every day and when he's really bad that will increase to twice or even three times a day. I've discussed the LCP with the head of palliative care, a woman called Jane, which was very depressing but necessary and…'

'LC what?'

'Oh sorry, that's the Liverpool Care Pathway,' I explain. 'Basically it's how to help him going forward with his medication and that, and I've signed all the forms of consent and stuff so we're all in order. He'll have all the drugs he'll need and he should be as comfortable as is possible. I suppose from their point of view, him coming here frees up a space at the hospice.'

'I suppose so,' says Martin nodding seriously. 'By the way, I'm going to put the telly from our bedroom in here for him. I'm going to mount it on those brackets I picked up from Homebase yesterday.'

'Thanks,' I say, once again humbled by everything that's

happening. How could I have been so ready to disown all of them all in the past? My family may be 'characters' but they're good people, something they're proving right now. I should be proud to be part of such a family frankly.

As Martin continues moving furniture around to make space for the bed, something else occurs to me

'By the way Martin,' I begin hesitantly. 'I hope you don't think this is none of my business, but I wondered if I could speak to you about Pete?'

'Pete?'

'Yeah, it's just between me and you, I think sometimes he gets a bit jealous of Andy and the fact you're always hanging out together. You know, because you have so much in common with him…'

Martin stops what he's doing and places his hands on his hips to listen properly.

'So, I was wondering whether there was something we could find, some common interest for you and him to do together?'

Martin looks absolutely thunderstruck. 'You really think he gets jealous of me and Andy?' he says.

'A bit, yeah,' I say. 'You do spend a lot of time together.'

'True,' admits Martin 'But then you know as well as I do what a laugh he is.'

Hmm…

'Still,' he continues thoughtfully, 'If it's bothering my son…' he trails off looking pensive. 'Actually, as a matter of fact Marianne, I wanted to have a word with you about that. You see your mother and I were thinking that, what with your dad coming here, it might be time for Andy to move on.'

I can't believe what I'm hearing. Finally! Hallefricking-lujah!

Martin looks pained. 'It's not that we don't love having him around, but there just isn't the space and, between you and me, I'm getting a bit fed up with his stuff always being strewn all over my settee.'

I nod vehemently, before eventually finding the where-withal to say something. 'Oh I don't blame you, and seeing him lying on it in the morning in only his underpants is a little off-putting first thing too isn't it?'

Martin raises his shoulders at first and wrinkles up his face as if he's not really sure but eventually nods his head in agreement. 'Yeah I suppose so, and the other thing Marianne, and more importantly, is that your dad is going to want as much privacy, peace and quiet as is possible in the coming weeks, and we can't help think that he might prefer to keep it to just family members being around.'

'I agree totally,' I say, nodding so violently I almost get a head rush.

'Right, well it's a tough job but someone's got to do it, so I'll have a word with him tonight,' says Martin thought-fully. 'If you're sure you're all right with that?'

For a second I find myself battling with re-emerging feelings of irritation.

'Besides, if Pete's feeling a bit unloved, well that's the

last thing I want,' he says, still clutching his tape measure, hands on hips. 'It's just it's hard sometimes, he never seems to want to come to Homebase or anywhere fun when I suggest it. The other day for example, I was going on a little trip to Comet, with Andy, to buy an HDMI cable and when I asked Pete if he wanted to join us he looked at me like I was mad.'

'It's hard to believe he could turn down such an offer,' I reply wryly. 'But perhaps that kind of thing isn't his cup of tea? Maybe you could go bowling, or get concert tickets, or go to a football match, or something like that? Something that isn't retail based.'

'Right,' says Martin, frowning hard as his mind whirrs, trying frantically no doubt to comprehend how anyone's idea of fun could possibly be different to his.

I've tried.

*

Later on that evening, the house is relatively quiet because Hayley has gone round to Jason's parents' for dinner – yes it has reached that stage already and yes that does mean she's having dinner with my boss – and Pete is out at Josh's. And so it is that, finally, Mum and Martin gather Andy at the table and serve him notice.

I loiter upstairs, torn between not wanting to be involved and being desperate to hear what's said. In the end I compromise by hanging out on the landing, head wedged between the banisters. From what I can hear, Andy doesn't sound quite as devastated as I thought he might be by his eviction. I guess he must have got a bit fed up with sleeping on a fake leather sofa every night which, let's face it, must be quite a sweaty business.

'It's no worries at all,' I can hear him saying. 'You guys have been so wonderful to me and I only hope that one day I can repay the favour. I'd love you to come to Oz so I can show you how a barbecue's really done.'

There's the sound of much back-slapping after this statement then Martin says, 'Oh mate, that would be something wouldn't it? And what do you think you'll do anyway? I mean, we don't want to see you on the streets or anything so do stay till you've got sorted out, won't you?'

At this point I have to bite my hand to stop myself from screaming '*Don't give him an inch. He'll be here for ever!*'

To my surprise though, I hear Andy saying, 'Well, there's a girl at work who's quite keen on me. In fact, we've been seeing a bit of each other recently, so I might see whether I can crash at hers for a while. Besides, my visa runs out soon anyway, so it's nearly time for me to think about booking my ticket back to the homeland.'

I can't hear what Mum and Martin are saying any more, their voices are too muffled, I hope not because they're choking on their own tears. I quickly retreat back to my room. Minutes later however I hear heavy footsteps coming up the stairs and when I look up, a solemn-looking Andy is at my door.

'Hi,' he says.

'Hi,' I say, lowering my violin.

'So, I've been chatting with Alli and Mar and telling them I think it's time I moved on.'

'Right,' I say, wondering whether I can be bothered to pull him up on the blatant lie he's just told.

'And I wanted to say that, although we've had our differences, I know how much you care about me, and you mustn't worry. I'm going to be absolutely fine. In fact, the truth is, I'm in love with someone else.'

'Good,' I say, astounded as ever by his audacity. 'And what's the lucky girl's name?'

'Helen.'

'Right, well I wish you and Helen all the very best,' I say as he lumbers off, presumably to phone Helen and hopefully to pack his bag. I am filled with relief that *finally* I might be seeing the back of the big lummox.

*

Dad moves in the next day. It hardly takes any time for myself, Hayley and Jason to clear out his flat. It would have been an even quicker process had I taken Matthew up on his offer to help, but I politely declined. Seeing him the other day has really thrown me and although he's sent quite a few texts since, I just don't feel like I know what to say back. My only focus right now is Dad.

The hospital bed has arrived, and Mum has put a lovely vase of tulips in his room, bright yellow ones, which look very cheerful. Dad was really touched to see how much effort everyone has gone to. Martin's even let him have the comfy armchair in his room, though went to great pains to say that obviously Dad was still very welcome to hang out in the main living room and that we could just move it to and fro.

'This is very decent of you,' says Dad, looking mildly uncomfortable for a second.

'Don't think anything of it Ray,' replies Martin. 'Mi Casa es Tu Casa.'

And that's all that is said on the subject.

*

That night Mum makes a stir-fry for dinner. Dad hardly touches it, though I don't know why that should come as a surprise. He's been telling me for ages now his sense of taste has altered and he hardly touches his food these days. Despite knowing that a loss of appetite is normal for cancer patients it still worries me how skinny he's getting, and that he's not putting enough fuel into his body. Though to be honest, with regard to Mum's rather flaccid stir-fry, Dad's lack of appetite might almost be a bonus. Still, food aside, it's a great dinner. To all be sat round the table, with Dad a part of the family, is a brilliant feeling and despite the obvious sadness there's almost a celebratory feel to the evening, which is only enhanced by Hayley's announcement that she's been to see a lawyer and has filed for divorce.

'Bravo,' Dad says softly. 'You've done the right thing.

I mean, apart from being a nasty piece of work, Gary was a thick idiot wasn't he?'

Jason looks like he wants to cheer, but Hayley's jaw almost drops onto her plate and despite the fact she hates Gary herself, I know she hasn't taken kindly to Dad pointing out that not only was her ex-husband horrible but also stupid. Suddenly though, I realise that Hayley isn't about to lambast him, but is in fact starting to laugh. Or at least I think she is. It's hard to tell. Her face has sort of creased up and for a worrying second I doubt myself again and revert back to thinking an explosion of outrage is about to occur. Everyone is staring at her warily, waiting for her to speak.

'You're right,' she manages to say eventually, noodles hanging rather unattractively out of her mouth. 'He was *such* a thick idiot.'

I breathe a huge sigh of relief and as I catch Mum's eye she gives me a little wink.

'And a vain one too,' Hayley splutters. 'Do you know he used to get manicures and pedicures?'

'No,' say Dad, Martin and Pete in unison.

'Yes,' roars Hayley, who by now is beginning to lose it so badly she's started thumping the table and has gone quite red in the face. By this point her laughter has become very contagious and pretty soon we're all chuckling. The mere sight of Hayley, who is usually so composed, so out of control with hysteria is hilarious in itself.

'And…' she gasps, mouth open, giving us all an eyeful of her half-masticated food, 'He…'

'What?' we all demand to know, desperate for her to compose herself enough to tell us, and all starting to lose it ourselves. Those of us unlucky enough to have food in our mouths try not to choke.

'He… oh my god he…' It's no good, Hayley's laughing so hard she simply can't get the words out and the anticipation of what this dark secret of Gary's might be is so funny, it'll probably end up being funnier than anything it actually is.

'He… he used to pad his swimming trunks when we went on holiday… you know, to make his package look bigger, but one day…' she splutters, 'The padding came out and it floated across the surface of the pool, only he didn't realise 'cos he was too busy showing off trying to do bloody butterfly across the pool and this little kid went up to him and said, "S'cuse me mate, I think this might be yours".'

'What a woofter,' roars Mum, hysterical tears falling down her cheeks.

By now Martin can't even speak and is bent over double, clutching his sides. Pete is so close to choking he's picked up a napkin and is gobbing half-chewed stir-fry into it, or maybe that's just a clever bit of acting.

'And what about Gary on *Sing for Britain*,' I chime in, and my sides are actually aching from how hard I'm laughing, made even worse as now I recall how odd my ex brother-in-law was on that fateful day. 'The way he was staring down the lens, looking so dense, and what a weirdo he was with Sy.'

'I'm her husband,' imitates Martin, which reduces us all to jibbering wrecks again and has Hayley slipping off her chair and onto the floor leaving her free to thump the carpet with abandon.

A while later, once the hysteria has started to tail off and we're finally all starting to recover, Dad suddenly says, 'All that laughing's worn me out a bit, I might just go and have a little rest, if that's OK?'

'Of course it is,' we all exclaim at once, our moods instantly subdued by concern. I jump to my feet in order to pull his chair out and see him to his room.

'I'm all right, babe,' he says, firmly but gently.

*

Later that night I lie in bed, panicking about the fact that there are only fourteen days to go until my audition for the Royal College of Music. Fourteen days to practise. For many reasons I have never wanted time to stand still so badly and yet in another I can recognise that I am a strung out, tired, drained, emotionally spent mess and that my lifestyle as it is at the moment isn't sustainable. The stress of worrying about Dad is taking its toll. I've become an insomniac, my skin is grey and sallow and my heart feels permanently as if it's racing with anxiety, and yet I don't want there to be a resolve. For there can only be one resolve and it won't be a good one. It's all so surreal.

Lying there I suddenly yearn to speak to Matthew and find myself remembering what he once said about being a friend, when I needed him to be. I think that time has come and, although I know I have Teresa, Mum and Hayley to talk to, right now he's the only person who will do. I look at the clock. It's only eleven o'clock so I figure why the hell not and ring him.

'Hi, it's me,' I say.

'Hello you, how are you?'

'I'm OK. Tired.'

'It's a tiring business,' he replies, knowing exactly what I mean.

'I'm so sorry,' I say dolefully.

'What for?'

I sigh. 'Oh you know… I know you didn't mean to muck me around and I was pretty harsh on you…'

'You had every right to be,' he says.

He sounds sleepy. I wonder whether I woke him up.

'I'm pleased you've called,' he says. 'I've been so cross with myself for blowing it. I keep thinking I should have followed my… you know, my heart instead of my head.'

'No,' I reply. 'You did the right thing and it's all just been so ridiculously complicated…' I trail off, staring into the darkness of my room. 'Some days I don't know if I'm coming or going. I guess with all the things I'm going through with dad it's been hard to think with any sense of perspective, but I would love it, I mean I would really love it, if we could be friends right now. I could really do with that.' I blink hard, almost in irritation. How can there even be any tears left in me?

'I'm here,' says Matthew immediately. 'One friend at your service. When can I come round?'

'Tomorrow?' I suggest hopefully.

'Done.'

*

The next day, I'm just coming in from doing a supermarket shop when I stop outside what has become Dad's bedroom door because I can hear a strange sound. It sounds like chanting.

Abandoning my plastic bags for a second, I open the door a touch and peek in. Dad's lying in bed and there's no sign of any Hare Krishnas, but what I do see is Mum sort of wafting round the room, waving her arms about the place. The curtains are shut and she's plugged in an air freshener, which has made the room smell of pine. It's a strange vignette if I'm honest.

'What are you doing?' I whisper.

Mum almost jumps out of her skin. 'Ooh you gave me a shock. Now ssh, 'cos I'm doing a bit of Reiki lovey, and it's very healing. Can you feel that energy Ray?' she says, turning her attentions back to Dad, waving her hands around over his body. 'It's exceptionally strong.'

'Yeah,' Dad says. 'Yeah I definitely think I can feel something, Al.'

'See,' says Mum, nodding satisfied in my direction. 'Right, well that's probably enough of a treatment for now but I'll give you another one tomorrow lovey, all right?'

'Great,' says Dad. 'Look forward to it.'

'Right,' says Mum, opening the curtains again. 'Well I'm going to get a bit of lunch on now, and I'll bring you a little tray in. Just yell if you think of anything you want specially.'

'I'm fine,' says Dad looking tired and weak. 'I don't want nuffink thanks.'

'Nonsense,' tuts Mum. Happy that her work is done, she leaves the room.

I go to sit next to Dad.

'Did you really feel anything?' I ask curiously.

'Not a sausage,' he answers immediately.

It takes a second or two to digest this but once I have I can't help it. I burst out laughing and although Dad is obviously tired out, for he has shut his eyes again, he grins broadly and squeezes my hand.

*

Later that afternoon Matthew comes round as promised and seeing him again is wonderful. I practically collapse on to him as soon as he's walked in the door. He engulfs me in a huge hug and as we stand in the hall, him holding me tight, I can feel some of the tension in my body seeping out.

'It's so good to see you,' I say into his chest.

'You too,' he says, pulling me away so he can look me in the eye. 'I've really missed you.'

I can't reply, I'm too choked and too happy to see him but I don't have to, I think my face tells the story.

I leave him downstairs so that he can spend a bit of time with Dad and, when he comes up to my room half an hour or so later, I can tell he's quite upset.

'You OK?' I ask, as my door creaks open and Matthew appears round it.

'Yeah, fine,' he says, coming in and sitting next to me on my bed. 'You?' he asks.

'Terrified,' I reply.

He nods.

'Do you think he seems a lot worse?' I can't resist asking, even though I know hearing the answer will be like a form of torture.

'He just seems very, very tired,' Matthew replies diplomatically.

We sit in silence, alone with our thoughts for a while until he says, 'I'm so glad we're talking again.'

'Me too.'

'No, I mean really glad. To be honest I haven't been able to stop thinking about you so I hope you haven't ruled me out altogether.'

I shake my head. 'I haven't,' I say. 'Not at all but I

need to be totally honest with you Matthew, I think when Dad dies I'm going to be a total wreck for a while so I'm probably going to get away for a bit. On my own, so I can grieve and get my head sorted out. Whether I get into the College or not, I need to have one last trip before I start.'

'For how long?' says Matthew, looking a bit anguished.

'Three months perhaps...?' I say, testing the water.

'I could come with you.'

I sigh. 'Matthew I can't tell you how much I would love that, and it would definitely be the easy option, but I feel really strongly that it's not going to be the right time to start a relationship. I already feel half-mad with grief and he's not even gone yet. To be perfectly honest I know I'm full of anger about what's happening but can't really compute any of it at the moment. But that doesn't mean it's not all due to come out soon, and I don't think it would be fair on either of us to burden you with all of it. Don't want to put you off now, do I?' I say, making a feeble attempt to lighten the mood.

Matthew smiles half-heartedly.

'Do you get what I'm saying though? Matthew, I really like you, but my head is permanently swirling and I need to sort myself out or I'll be no good to anyone. Do you know what I mean?'

He nods. 'Yeah,' he says flatly. 'I do.'

I gaze out the window, wondering whether anyone's with Dad. Probably not, so I should go back down in a minute.

'Aren't you going to ask if I'll wait for you?' says Matthew, half-joking.

I turn to face him. He's so gorgeous; I can't ever imagine getting tired of how lovely he looks, but whereas when I first met him my heart would swell with excitement every time I looked at him, now it's too full of sadness to make room for anything else, which is why I know I'm making the right decision. My emotional batteries are totally flat.

I shake my head. 'I'm not going to ask you to wait because it wouldn't be fair. Why should you? Having said that, I really, really hope you do because I know you'll be the first person I'll want to see on my return and I also know I'll be jealous as hell if someone else has snuck in there.'

His reply is to kiss me unbelievably tenderly, but as he does the tears roll silently down my cheeks. It's all too much to handle.

'It's only three months, it'll fly by I'm sure,' he says, pulling away before giving me an enormous bear hug.

I just about manage to whisper, 'Thank you.'

CHAPTER TWENTY-SEVEN

A fortnight later and it's the day of my audition. I hardly even want to go. Dad's sick, and when I say sick, I mean lie in bed all day kind of sick. The kind of sick that doesn't let up, and his rate of deterioration has been frighteningly quick. The last time he sat in his chair was four days ago, and since then he's only managed to sit up in bed a couple of times. He's weak as anything, and hasn't eaten properly for days. In short, my dad is dying. It's horrendous to witness, this decline of his body, mind and spirit; though the spirit is clearly going to be the last thing to go. In many ways his aching, pain-ridden body is becoming a cage.

'Good luck,' he says, his voice reduced to a rasp. Despite what he's going through and how much he's suffering he is only too aware that today is the day.

Fortunately, the nurse appears just at that moment to give him his meds, give him a wash and change his sheets, which galvanises me into action and propels me out of the front door where Mrs Demetrius is waiting in a mini-cab that will take us to the station.

*

The audition goes well. I can't tell you how grateful I am that violinists need accompanying on the piano, because having Mrs Demetrius there is the one thing that prevents me from having a major panic attack and heading for the hills the minute we arrive. As it is, her presence is reassuring; quietly encouraging, plus I know that if I tried to escape she would physically restrain me. So I have no choice but to face the panel of serious, almost dour-looking judges and to play as well as I am able.

I don't have to tell you what I'm thinking about during the first movement of Mendelssohn's incredible concerto, but it's as if all the pain, joy, anger, love and despair that I'm feeling spill into my fingers and travel through the bow, producing so much emotion in the already powerful music. I don't need the sheet music, having practised so much I know my pieces off by heart, so I do most of the audition with my eyes closed, lost in the beauty of what I'm playing and praying quietly to a god I don't know if I even believe in. As the music washes over me, I pray that the immediate future will be as pain free for my dad as is possible, that the end will be as dignified as it can be, and for the strength to see me through it. By the time I've reached the end of my contrasting piece I know that I have never played as well so, if I don't get in, at least I'll be content in the knowledge that I couldn't have done any more.

I think the judges are a little surprised to see my eyes glistening with tears as I come to a finish, but by that point I am beyond caring. I just want to get home. I want to switch on my phone and make sure he hasn't gone anywhere.

I do briefly scan the judges faces to see whether I can glean what they are thinking, but they are silent and impassive, until one of them says, 'Well, we'll be in touch within a couple of days. Thank you so much for coming to see us today Miss Baker, and thanks too Mrs Demetrius.'

'Thank you,' I manage to say, before fleeing the building.

Outside, Mrs Demetrius finds me taking huge gulps of fresh air. She wraps me up in a big bear hug.

'That was magnificent,' she says, her eyes glistening with pride.

'I need to get back,' I say softly, my face conveying my sense of urgency more than my voice. She simply nods. Everybody has stopped trying to make me feel better by pretending that Dad will be fine because no one can say that with any certainty any more. And so it is that we head as fast as we are able back to Chigwell, dropping Mrs Demetrius off on the way, and back to my house where I am beyond relieved to discover that my dad is still alive.

He's fast asleep when I tiptoe into his room. Hayley's sitting by him, staring into space.

'How did it go?' she says.

I shrug. 'OK,' I say. 'How is he? How long's he been asleep for?'

'Ages,' Hayley says, and her voice is a whisper.

*

That night Dad has a particularly bad night. He's restless and in a lot of pain, which is unbelievably distressing to watch. If I'm honest his obvious discomfort makes me feel nauseous. I could never be a nurse. I don't have the stomach for it and I cannot tell you how much I admire those who do have that vocation.

Hayley and I take it in turns to sit with him and even Mum does a stint. So much perspiration is pouring off his brow it's as if he's feverish, and yet to the touch his forehead is quite cold. We do what little we can to make him more comfortable. We mop his brow and try and wet his mouth with water, for he's refusing to drink, and then, at two in the morning, when it all starts feeling a bit scary because he's moaning with pain, panicking I phone the hospice for some advice. They tell me to up his dose of morphine, which I do. More drugs seem to be the only answer at this stage.

By the time the sun is rising in the sky, he's completely doped up but settled and in such a deep stupor of a sleep it's hard to tell whether he's actually conscious.

'Are you OK?' says Hayley, poking her head round the door. I'd insisted that she went to get some rest an hour or so ago but she looks as shredded as I feel and I know she hasn't slept.

I shake my head.

'Come here, babe,' she says.

I do as I'm told and she pulls me in for a hug. I literally cannot remember the last time Hayley hugged me spontaneously, and am still getting used to my sister being in touch with her previously shut-off emotions, yet it feels completely natural.

'I'm glad I've got you,' I mutter tearfully into her shoulder.

'Me too,' she replies with feeling.

I'm filled with intense love for my sister in that moment and am infused with the knowledge that I would not be handling this as well as I am – which is not very well at all – if she wasn't here to go through it with. A sibling is such an important and wonderful thing to be grateful for, even if your relationship isn't exactly perfect. Hayley's the only other person on the planet who truly understands what it feels like to be our parent's child and who, like me, is preparing to lose our father. It occurs to me suddenly that Pete will never have that kindred spirit, that is to say, someone who fully gets what it is to be the spawn of Martin and Alison.

*

Later that day, after a few hours of snatched, fitful sleep, the doctor comes to pay a visit. I ask him how long.

He looks at me thoughtfully.

'It's hard to say, maybe a week, maybe less.'

*

The atmosphere in the house changes altogether. What is happening in the front room now governs everything and, out of respect and sadness, we all go about our day in a muted kind of way. If someone's watching telly, the volume is down quiet. Mum doesn't sing as she goes about her business, though she and Martin do get the Christmas decorations out of the loft.

'It's weird, innit?' says Mum thoughtfully, winding a strand of fairy lights round the banisters. 'There's something about this time of year that's so spiritual, isn't there?'

'Yes Mum, I'd say there probably is something slightly spiritual about the religious occasion that is Christmas, i.e the birth of Christ etc.' I reply.

She narrows her eyes at me. 'Don't be such a sarcy bugger you. What I meant was, that if your dad is going to leave this world soon, then it might as well be at a time when we're all thinking about our blessings and little angels and things.'

I feel bad for teasing for I know Mum well enough to see that she is completely carved up, so now it's my turn to give her a much-needed hug. Besides, I know what she's getting at. Of course in one way, Christmas is pretty much cancelled. I've not had the wherewithal or inclination to even consider braving the crowds to purchase pointless gifts and yet somehow it does feel fitting I suppose, that this process, this ritual of dying is happening at a time so laden with meaning. And it is a process, for what I have come to learn is that Dad isn't just going to die one day, out of the blue. Instead he is dying, right now, but it's a long and drawn-out business. His organs and body are slowly packing up shop and yet his spirit remains intact, so in some subconscious way you can almost see it putting up a fight, only you know that ultimately it's a fight it can't win. It's hideous.

By this point Dad is in and out of consciousness, but later on that day he's not only conscious but also seems to be really aware of what's going on around him and capable of a bit of conversation. Determined to make what lucid moments he has left as pleasant and meaningful as they can be I find a CD of carols by the Kings Choir. I put it on and then sit quietly with him, listening. They're beautiful and uplifting and seem utterly appropriate. At one point he squeezes my hand, just a fraction, but it's enough for me to know he's there and I squeeze it back and tell him how much I love him over and over again and not to be scared.

Two days later I hear from the Royal College of Music. My world changes with the arrival of a single email. I scan it quickly and then take a second to absorb the information for myself. Once I have I head for Dad's room.

The nurse is here, adjusting him in the bed and checking everything. They're coming three times a day now, which is incredibly reassuring as I think we're starting to find the responsibility quite overwhelming as his state worsens. It's a responsibility we're totally dedicated to, but that doesn't mean to say the presence of a medically trained person isn't hugely comforting.

'Do you think he's conscious?' I ask.

'He's in and out,' she says softly. 'But it's great to keep talking because the hearing's the last thing to go.'

I'm not sure whether I find this fact unbelievably terrifying or comforting.

Still, I watch for a while longer as she goes about her business before taking my usual position by the bed.

'Dad,' I tell him steadily. 'I got in to the College. I'm going to the Royal College of Music next September.'

I don't think he can hear me though, and suddenly I'm filled with worry. What if it's too late?

'Dad,' I say again, more urgently. 'I got in, Dad,' but he doesn't respond. Now I get upset, furious in fact. This is the moment he's been waiting for, for all this time. He has to know this before he goes. It feels so utterly important and I can't bear the fact that I may be too late.

'Please Dad,' I try again, tears rolling down my face.

The nurse looks at me for a second.

'He'll hear I'm sure,' she says. 'Maybe not now, but he's only recently had a very strong dose of morphine. I would give it a little while and try again.'

*

I take her advice and leave him to rest. I retreat to my room and fall into a deep, exhausted slumber. When I wake up it's the middle of the night. I've been asleep for hours but as soon as I open my eyes I'm fully alert.

I thunder downstairs, terrified in case I've missed the opportunity to tell him my news. As I push open the door,

I feel horribly nervous, which has become a commonplace reaction every time I enter his room, never sure of what I might find. Hayley's sitting with him though.

'Why didn't you wake me?' I say groggily.

Hayley just shrugs.

I look at my father. He looks tiny. His face has shrunk, caved in on itself almost and his pallor is waxy and grey.

I take a seat next to Hayley.

'I got in to the College,' I tell her.

'Oh my god, that's amazing,' she whispers back.

'Yeah,' I nod.

'Does he know?' she asks.

Now it's my turn to shrug.

'OK, you have to try and tell him,' she insists and of course I agree so I try.

'Dad,' I say in a clear voice, edging closer to him. Hayley gives me a reassuring nod.

'Dad,' I try again and as I do there's a brief flicker of movement in his face. I swallow hard. I hate seeing him like this.

'Go on,' says Hayley.

I focus and manage to say steadily, 'I got in to the Royal College of Music, Dad. I've got a place. I'm going in September and it's all thanks to you.'

For a brief second I think he hasn't heard and that I'll have to try again, but then his eyes suddenly flick open before falling shut once more, as if keeping them open simply requires too much effort, and then he says in a quiet, rasping voice, 'That's my girl.'

'Did you hear that?' I say to Hayley, welling up and when she doesn't reply I turn, only to find my sister has tears streaming down her face too.

'Yes,' she replies, and we are so incredibly thankful for those three small words.

They are the last words my father ever speaks.

*

My dad, my lovely dad who I knew twice during my life, once as a baby and once as an adult, dies at twelve minutes past four that morning.

I wish I could tell you that he died peacefully but it was a fight until the bitter end. A fight for breath, a fight against the pain that was filling up every bone and muscle in his body and a fight to stop his organs shutting down, one that I could hardly bear to watch. The nurses came and Hayley, Mum and I were in and out, staying with him for as long or as little as we could handle until it all became too frightening and horrific to stand. When the end came it was almost a relief that this man who I have come to love so deeply and truly, had finally been put out of his pain and misery, but I am going to miss him so, so much and the pain of that has overwhelmed me and I honestly don't know whether I'll ever get over it.

*

Two days later, Matthew shows up at the house to pay his respects and also to deliver Hayley and I a letter each, which unbeknown to us, Dad had written a few weeks before he died.

It takes me three more days to summon up the courage to be able to read mine. Partly, I think, because I know it will be the last contact I'll ever have with him so want to savour it fully.

When I do finally summon up the courage to open it, I discover that it's not a particularly long letter and that it's written by hand, the slightly spidery writing a reminder of how ill and weak he'd been. It says –

My dearest daughter,

Thank you for everything. Thank you for accepting me back into your life so quickly, without judgement or bitterness. By being so forgiving we made the most of what time I had left. My time spent with you were the best days of my life and I'm so grateful that you had the wisdom to understand something that most people take far longer to realise, and that is that life's too short.

Know that I am truly sorry for all the pain I've caused you in the past. I love you and I leave this world a very proud man. Keep playing, Marianne. You have a talent and it would be criminal for it to go to waste. I hope that, wherever I may be, I will always hear your music for you play like an angel.

Look after your sister, and your mum but, more importantly, look after yourself because you deserve looking after. I've left you and Hayley some money. Please use it to help towards your college fees (if you get in). Either way, put it towards your exciting future, which I know will be golden.

One last favour. At my funeral, please will you play the Adagio from Bach's solo Sonata No. 1? You were playing it the night I came back into your life, so it feels only fitting that you should be playing it as I leave.

Your loving Dad.

P.S Good luck with Matthew!

*

The tears roll down my face and I hold the letter at arm's length, worried that if any splash on the letter it may smudge. His words unleash a wave of pain inside me as I realise how much I am already missing him, yet through my tears he's also managed to elicit a laugh because of his cheeky P.S at the end. It's very poignant of course, because I know that that is exactly what he would have intended and I can picture him smiling to himself as he wrote it, happy that he had the chance to get one more remark in.

The next few days pass in a blur of grief that is so intense, it's all I can do to function and get through them. Hayley is feeling the same way of course and one afternoon when we're sitting in my room together, staring numbly at each other, she asks, 'What now? What are you going to do?'

'I'm going away,' I reply.

She looks completely shocked.

'How can you go away?' she demands to know. 'You can't just piss off now, feeling like this, leaving me like this.'

I silence her with a look.

'All right,' she says. 'That came out wrong, what I meant was, I don't want you to go, Marianne. Not now.'

She's learning, admittedly slowly, but my sister is definitely learning.

I sigh, a long heavy sigh.

'I've got enough money saved in the bank to go away and to help pay for college,' I explain wearily. 'And I'm not running away, it's just that I know I'm going there in nine months so I might as well make the most of this time before I spend the next few years working harder than I ever have before. I'm determined to get to concert standard. Not just because it would have made Dad proud, but because it's what I want. Probably always have wanted, but before that, I need to get away. I need to look out to sea. I need to feel the sun on my bones. I *need* to be away from this house for a while because I'm in so much pain right now I can hardly think straight.'

'But you will still be in pain when you get there,' says Hayley flatly.

'I know,' I say, the inevitable tears rising up in a wave of fresh grief, though by now I'm so used to them I just allow them to pour down my face. 'And I'm not trying to run away from my feelings,' I add. 'Quite the opposite really. I want to take the time to really think about and absorb what's happened. To heal myself a bit…'

I take a second to grab a tissue from the box next to my bed and blow my nose.

'What about Matthew?' she asks more gently.

I look up and smile weakly. 'Hayley, if Matthew cares about me, which I think he does, and if we're meant to be with each other, which I hope we are, then he'll still be here when I get back. Only hopefully I'll be stronger, more sane and ready to think about someone other than myself and what I'm going through.'

'But I'll miss you,' she whispers.

'You'll be fine,' I say. 'And you've got Jason.'

'I know,' she says. 'I know.'

CHAPTER TWENTY-EIGHT

We bury my father just after Christmas on a gloomy, cold day. The service is beautiful, but there aren't huge numbers at the church. There's all of us of course, Matthew and Teresa come, some of the nurses from the hospice and a few of my dad's old cronies whom Mum has contacted. I'm very touched when Mrs Demetrius shows up of her own accord.

The service is lovely. Hayley and I spent a lot of time picking out the readings, which we both manage to get out, albeit with our voices cracking and trembling along the way.

And then, with my dad's coffin before me, I play for him one last time and, as I do, I remember that stormy night back in April and feel thankful for the nine months we ended up having together. It's the first time I've felt an inkling of something other than anger and sadness towards the time I've been cheated of and I hold on to this sliver of positivity with every fibre of my body. After all, Dad was so adamant that he didn't want me to be bitter.

*

After the funeral it's back to ours for tea and sandwiches, laid on by Mum of course, who has been amazing these past few weeks. Matthew comes back to the house too and we nip upstairs together for a private moment.

We lie on the bed together and hug, like two people who've just been told the world's about to end, and he strokes my hair, which is soothing and nice.

'Have you booked your ticket?' he asks, without anything other than genuine interest in his voice.

'Going to do it tomorrow.'

'Well, let me know if you want me to come with you. I've got a day off and I want to see lots of you before you go.'

I nod, wondering whether I'll ever feel more than a few words away from breaking down into tears.

'Right,' I say, sitting up, reluctant to move but determined not to let Mum down by disappearing. 'Come on, we'd better go downstairs and show our faces.'

'OK,' he agrees. 'But first come here a second.'

I turn around to face him, unable to smile, unable to do anything other than stare blankly back at him.

'I just want to say, or rather I want you to know, that I really care about you Marianne,' he says, his brown eyes regarding me with incredible tenderness and warmth.

It's so nice to hear, and any uncertainty I may have been experiencing about running out on him at such a fledgling stage in our relationship is erased altogether. However, I don't feel capable of expressing this, or indeed of saying anything back. I'm too numb, and yet somehow I know he understands, which he demonstrates in the next second.

'Come on you, let's go and see what's happening downstairs,' he says, grabbing my hand and leading me out onto the landing.

*

Downstairs, Dad's friends are getting stuck into a few drinks, as are Mum and Martin, and there's a lot of reminiscing going on. Mum seems transported back in time as she tells tale after tale about Ray and his 'antics' while Martin lets her talk freely without worrying about what he thinks. It's the same selfless quality I appreciate in Matthew. Letting someone be who they need to be without question. Though that's where the similarity between the two men ends. Let's just say that today Martin is wearing a black polo neck sweater with grey slacks.

I go over to where Hayley, Teresa and Jason are chatting with Mrs Demetrius.

'Hiya,' I say. 'Are you all OK?'

'Yes fine,' says my teacher. 'I'll be off in a short while though, I just wanted to come and pay my respects.'

'Me too babe,' says Teresa. 'But I'll give you a call later, yeah? Make sure you're OK.'

'Thank you,' I say to my friend, hugging her tight. 'And thank you, too,' I say, pulling away and reaching out to

Mrs Demetrius and pulling her in for an embrace. 'You're a star for coming.'

When she pulls away she says, 'Right, well I'll be off Marianne, but come and see me for a lesson before you go, won't you. Don't want you getting rusty do we?'

'I'll come I promise,' I say.

I go with them both to the front door, to see the two of them out, and when I've finished waving goodbye, am surprised to find Hayley standing behind me in the hallway looking furtive.

'You all right?'

'Yeah,' she says. 'Sort of, actually there's something I want to ask you.'

'Go on then,' I say.

'I want to come with you.'

'Go on then, Teresa's only halfway down the road and Mrs Demetrius' car hasn't pulled out the drive yet, so if you hurry up you can still wave goodbye,' I say, not catching her drift at all.

'No, when you go away, I want to come with you, if you'll let me?' she repeats.

I'm genuinely not sure I've just heard her right.

'When I go where?'

'Well, come to think of it that's something I should probably make my next question,' says Hayley. 'Since it would be quite nice to know what I'm letting myself in for. If you agree to letting me come that is, of course.'

'I'm going to Australia,' I answer, still in a bit of a daze.

We stare at each other for a second and as we do it dawns upon me what it is my sister is suggesting and that she is absolutely serious. I still don't quite believe she means it though.

'What about Jason?' I say quickly.

'I really like him,' she says. 'I mean *really* like him, but it's like you said I guess, if he likes me then he'll be here when I get back.'

I narrow my eyes. 'But you never go away for more than two weeks at a time and I'm not going to be staying in nice hotels. It'll be backpacks all the way.'

She shrugs.

'And I want to travel around, see the country a bit. Not just stay in Sydney.'

'Look, I can tell you're trying to put me off, so just forget about it,' retorts Hayley, indignant suddenly and blushing madly.

'Wait Hayls,' I say, as she starts to stomp off, back towards the lounge. 'Just wait a second.'

She stops, but her expression is mutinous.

'I'm not trying to put you off,' I say. 'I'm just finding it hard to believe you're totally serious.'

'Well I am,' she says, flicking her hair off her shoulder and out of her eyes. 'If you really want to know the truth, Dad wrote one or two things in my letter that made me think. Plus, I've always been a bit in awe of your travels. I suppose I've always thought you were really brave to go away on your own and to see the world, which I reckon might be just what I need right now. You know, to sort my head out a bit. I also reckon it might be all right going on an adventure with you. But if you're not up for it…'

'Oh my god,' I tell her. 'I am so up for it. I would bloody love you to come with me, but don't go mucking me around. Either you're in or you're not. I don't want you changing your mind on me.'

She shakes her head and a slow triumphant grin starts to spread across her face.

'Are we actually going to do this then?' I say.

'Looks like it.'

'Shit, you'd better tell Jason,' I say, worried suddenly, because for all my speeches about people waiting for you, of course deep down I do worry a bit about Matthew still being free when I get back. I would also hate her to piss off Jason just because of me and…

'I've told him,' she says sheepishly. 'I asked him first how he would feel if I did it.'

'And what did he say?'

'He said he was proud of me and that I should go for it,' she says, her voice full of emotion.

'Well,' I say, desperately trying to keep myself together by taking extra deep breaths. 'In that case, you've got yourself a date.'

'Wicked,' beams Hayley, looking happy for the first time in a long time. Strangely I feel suddenly quite euphoric too. It feels utterly right that after everything we've been through, Hayley and I should head off into the sunset together for a bit of sisterly bonding. I find myself looking up, quietly thanking Dad, praying that somehow he can hear me.

'What are you two looking so suspicious about?' asks Pete, who's meandered through from the living room, looking unusually perky.

'Hayley's coming travelling with me,' I say, unable to wipe the smile from my face. I wish I could tell Dad. I would love to have known what he would have made of it.

'Right,' says Pete, looking chipper.

'Tell us,' I say bemused.

'What?'

'Well, you look pleased about something.'

'Oh well, actually Dad has just asked me if I want to go with him on a bit of a lads' trip.'

'Right…' I say, wondering where they might be off to. IKEA? Slumberland? Asda? The mind boggles.

'To Graceland!' exclaims Pete, cracking a grin so wide it looks like it might be about to split his face in two.

'No way!' exclaims Hayley.

'Yes way,' interjects Mum, barrelling into the hallway to join us in her new, black wedges bought especially for today. 'My precious prince, off to see the home of The King,' she says ruffling Pete's hair, though for once he doesn't look like he minds too much.

'Yeah, it's amazing,' says Pete, literally looking the happiest I've ever seen him.

I'm so pleased for him, envious too of him being able to

go away with his father, but mainly delighted that Martin took my hint and that they might be able to salvage their relationship.

'Ah, come here my bubbas,' says Mum sentimentally, gathering the three of us towards her for a group hug. 'I'm so proud of you. The way you girls read in the church today was really wonderful and Marianne you were brilliant on that fiddle,' she says, a lone tear running down her face. She sniffs hard and blinks it away, refusing to let it get the better of her. 'Your father would have loved it.'

We stay in her embrace, all thinking of Dad.

'And you've put on such a lovely spread for everyone today, too,' says Hayley after a while.

'Oh thank you darlin' I have, haven't I. Those platters of sarnies were very nice, especially the prawn ones.'

The four of us continue to stand there, all huddled together, grateful for each other and aware that we have all gone through so many changes recently.

'I think Ray brought this family closer together,' sniffs Mum.

'He did,' I agree. 'We may only have had him in our lives for nine months, but boy did he change a lot of things in that short space of time.'

'He was a good man,' says Mum. 'And I'm only sorry that…'

'Don't Mum, it's fine,' says Hayley, who has changed possibly more than any of us. She has started to demonstrate that she is a kind person, one who is able to have empathy for others and now it looks like she's going to give standing on her own two feet a try for the first time too.

'Do you know how much I love you all?' Mum asks with feeling.

'A lot?' I suggest.

'Very very much,' she confirms.

'More than *Deal or no Deal*?' asks Hayley.

'Even more than that,' she chuckles.

'*Loose Women*?' says Pete, earning himself a nudge in the ribs.

'Mariah Carey?' I add.

'Don't push it,' she cackles.

* * * * *

ACKNOWLEDGEMENTS

Thank you to Madeleine Milburn, who I respect enormously but also really like. There's always a lot of Twitter love for @agentmilburn from all her clients, because she really is the bee's knees. Thanks too to Cara Lee Simpson for all your hard work.

Huge thanks must go to Sally Williamson and all the team at MIRA for transforming my Word document into a lovely-looking actual book. Being published is my proudest achievement and that's even after I rapped at my sister's wedding.

For obvious reasons this book required careful research and so it was that I had the privilege of spending the day with Jane Hastings. At the time, Jane was head of palliative care at Kingston Hospital and I was completely humbled by what she told me. So thank you, Jane, for your time, your knowledge and for allowing me to ask you endless questions.

Thank you to the gorgeous Jenny Blacklock Allan, who put me in touch with Jane. I think we arranged it during one particularly painful blitz session in the park, proving that exercise can be good for you. Thank you for going the extra mile (good pun there).

Thank you to all the cancer charities that do such important work, in particular Bowel Cancer UK and Clic Sargent, who have both been very supportive of this book. And enormous thanks to the gentleman who bid in a Clic Sargent auction to choose a character name in this book. He asked that Teresa Laphan be a character in the story and so she is!

Lastly, thanks as ever to my family. I don't know what I'd do without you. Mum, Mauro, Sally, Jessica, Jim, Georgie, Isabel (wolf mcsnuff), Paddy, Imogen, Harry and Dr Ned.

Special thanks must go to my dad, Michael, who inspired me to write this story in many ways. I remember so clearly, sitting around for hours one day, talking about what I should write next. 'You should write about death,' he said and so it went from there. You gave me the initial idea and before I knew it we'd also come up with the beginning and the rest is history. Thank you. You have always been so creative and brilliant.

Lastly, thank you to my lovely Lily and Freddie. I couldn't be prouder of the two of you, I can't wait for you to read my books one day and love you both very much.

**save
lives**

Bowel Cancer UK is determined to save lives
and improve the quality of life for people
affected by bowel cancer

The symptoms of bowel cancer include:

- Bleeding from the bottom and/or blood in your poo
- A change in bowel habit lasting three weeks or more
- Unexplained weight loss
- Extreme tiredness for no obvious reason
- A pain or lump in your tummy

www.bowelcanceruk.org.uk
Facebook: /charitybcuk
@Bowel_Cancer_UK

*Have you ever wondered what
your life would have been like if
you'd chosen a different man?*

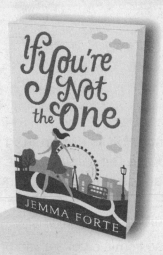

Jennifer Wright is not entirely sure she's happy.
Yes, she's got a husband, two lovely children and a
nice house, but has she really made the right choice
about who to spend the rest of her life with?

When she's knocked down by a car and ends up in a
coma, she has the chance to see where her life would
have taken her had she stayed with her exes. Maybe
looking back will help her to make the biggest
decision of her life…

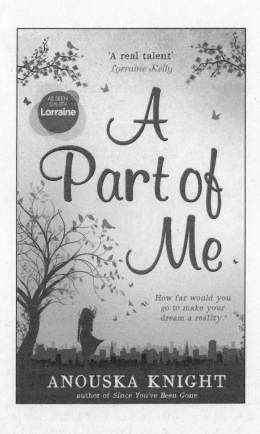

Anouska Knight's first book, *Since You've Been Gone*,
was a smash hit and crowned the winner of Lorraine's
Racy Reads. Anouska returns with *A Part of Me,*
which is one not to be missed!

Get your copy today at:
www.millsandboon.co.uk

A chance to uncover the secrets of her past. A truth that will change her future forever.

Early on the morning of her eleventh birthday, Daria Cato found an unexpected gift—an abandoned baby. Unable to leave the child unclaimed, the Cato family adopt Shelly, but the secrets of her birth continue to haunt Daria.

As closely guarded secrets and sins begin to unravel, piece by piece the mystery of the summer's child is about to be exposed. A mystery no one involved is prepared to face.

www.mirabooks.co.uk

There was a moment when
Ivy Heartley could have told the truth.
But she didn't.

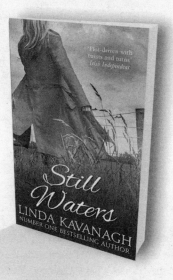

Now she's burdened with a terrible secret—
something so awful that she must constantly live
in fear, since its disclosure could destroy her
marriage, her career as a popular soap-star, and
turn her own son against her.

Will she ever be able to forget what happened?
Or will her past destroy her future?

WHAT DID YOU MISS OUT ON BECAUSE YOU FELL IN LOVE?

Kate Winters might just be 'that' girl. You know the one. The girl who, for no particular reason, doesn't get the guy, doesn't have children, doesn't get the romantic happy-ever-after. So she needs a plan.

What didn't she get to do because she fell in love?

What would she be happy spending the rest of her life doing if love never showed up again?

This is one girl's journey to take back what love stole.

Seven scandalous celebrities
Seven deadly sins...

SEVEN INFAMOUS CELEBRITIES

The supermodel, the thief, the senator, the heiress,
the paparazzo, the pop prince and the playboy

SEVEN DEADLY SINNERS

Someone is watching. Someone has seen through the
shimmer of glamour to the dark secrets lurking
beneath. Someone sees sinners.

ONE PUNISHMENT FITS THEM ALL

The island does not welcome visitors. There is no safe
way to arrive on these shores. Once here you cannot
leave. This is a forbidden paradise. No one escapes.

www.mirabooks.co.uk

Loved this book?
Let us know!

Find us on **Twitter @Mira_BooksUK**
where you can share your thoughts, stay up
to date on all the news about our upcoming
releases and even be in with the chance of
winning copies of our wonderful books!

Bringing you the best voices in fiction

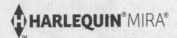